Sole Survivor

The coldness must have gone away since Jonn could no longer feel anything in his chest. That, or it had frostbitten him into numbness. He didn't really care to dwell on it; the blood surrounding his head was the immediate concern.

After the fourth blood-sneeze, he felt the ship settle into its final position. If things were happening like he thought, the *Fury* was now hanging from a salvage hook in one of the *Constantine's* enormous repair bays. He knew it would be a while before the salvage teams got to the bodies, and passed out.

The last time Jonn awoke, two RH crewmen stood over him. He could just make out their voices, but had no idea what they were saying because the drying blood had caked in his ears. Had his head not been tilted at just the right angle, Jonn would have drowned long ago.

He tried to move his arm but felt it still caught up in the wreckage of the near wall. One of the workers pointed at it and said something to the other. The second man was eating some sort of candy bar, and shrugged nonchalantly. Then he reached out of Jonn's sight, and handed the first man something that looked like a …

oh no. oh no. oh no.

… saw.

Look for these other *Shatterzone*™ novels
published by West End Books:

The River of God
by Greg Farshtey

Five adventurers journey into space and brave
the terrors of the "river of God," to find that
madness, murder and riches beyond
imagining await within.

Beyond the 'Zone
by Ed Stark

Written by one of the creators of *Shatterzone*,
this novel takes the reader, for the first time,
through the amazing and lethal shatterzone.
What lies beyond the edge of the universe ...
besides death?

TM

created by Greg Farshtey and Ed Stark

Sole Survivor

by Shane Lacy Hensley

WEST
END
BOOKS.
®

SOLE SURVIVOR
A West End Book/January 1993

First Printing: January, 1993.
Printed in the United States of America.

0 9 8 7 6 5 4 3 2 1

Library of Congress Catalog Card Number: 92-85236
ISBN: 0-87431-226-4

Cover Art by Nick Smith

Shatterzone Logo by John Paul Lona

Cover Design by Stephen Crane and John Paul Lona

Graphic Design by Stephen Crane

Edited by Ed Stark

West End Games
RR 3 Box 2345
Honesdale, PA 18431

To Michelle and Sheila Hensley, for all their support.
With a special thanks to John Hopler.

Prologue

Prologue

T odd Hollings sat and brooded at the end of the universe.

Untold numbers of rocks and debris ranging in size from pebbles to planets spun about the limits of known space, cutting man off from yet another layer of the unknown. The sapient races had been peeling back these layers for centuries now, and Todd knew that it was only a matter of time before the galactic barrier of the shatterzone was cracked and explored.

But not today. For now, the shatterzone remained a spinning maelstrom of death for anyone foolish enough to penetrate its inner depths. The best anyone could do was scratch around the outside, taking offerings of minerals and energy from the very outer layer.

The bridge of the flagship was quiet save for the low mumblings of the technicians below Todd's parapet, and the constant drone of the *Constantine's* engines. This and whirling patterns of the shatterzone danced on Todd's viewscreen and began to lull him into a heavy sleep. But then there was a glint on the screen —

just a tiny flash of silver against the black and brown swirls. Todd raised his heavy lids, fighting off the lullaby of the droning engines. There it was again … a tiny dot amidst the chaos.

Someone finally yelled at him from below and pointed excitedly at the viewscreen. Todd shook off his stupor and saw the port gunners swiveling their chairs to track the incoming target, ready to fire should it prove dangerous.

Suddenly, the silver vessel began to jerk back and forth erratically. Seconds later, it disappeared in a silent flash of light. It had been destroyed, but by whom? The *Constantine* hadn't fired, and no other ships were in the area. So where had the fatal shot come from?

One of the head technicians banged his fingers on a console maniacally, and Todd watched with reverent awe as the man replayed footage of the last few moments on his viewscreen. Green crosshairs tracked the course of the foreign ship as the invisible shot slammed into it, and quickly back-plotted the trajectory to the point of origin. The shot had come from the 'zone.

Reports had come to Hollings' ears of bolter aliens, fleeing through the 'zone, but they always told of single, battered ships, manned by desperate, frightened beings. *This* occurrence was altogether different.

Something else was coming through.

CHAPTER ONE

Ghost Colony

Purplish mist swirled about as the landing craft's humming turbines kicked up the dust on New Akron. The dull gray of the ship blended in perfectly with the lifeless world around it. It was small compared to the corvette it had emerged from, but just large enough to carry the two pilots and eleven anxious armored men.

"Atmosphere check negative, too thin to breathe," came a faint voice from the marine's headsets.

"Pressure check positive, do not adjust," it repeated. "Radio interference moderate, extend whip."

At the pilot's command, the passengers activated their antennae and eleven thin, flexible, rods rose from the back armor of the corporate marines.

"Threat level unknown. Arm weapons on my mark, 3 … 2 … 1 … arm." The men in the rear looked sourly at the two pilots who gave them their orders and whose probing apparatus had lied to them before. With a group sigh, the marines attached the power cables hanging from the backs of their thick armor and screwed them tight against the jack in their rifles.

"Automated defense systems activated." Two compartments opened on either side of the landing craft's thick rear landing struts. From each crawled a spider-like drone armed with a single pulse cannon. Long cables were slowly dragged by the creatures across the dusty land like metallic umbilical cords. The spiders crawled to a position just behind some pock-marked rocks, and extended their telescopic heads. If anything not transmitting the appropriate signal got within five hundred meters, the spiders' cannons would rise into firing position and blast it to pieces.

"Automated defenses in position. Hatch opens in 5 … 4 … 3 … 2 … 1."

Stryker hated the damn spiders. He had never really trusted machines — or the idiots who made them, for that matter.

As usual, he was the first out of the hatch. Corporate policy forbade this, but Stryker came from the old school and still managed to do a few things his way.

The spiders were waiting for him. Their tiny heads spun slowly, always scanning for a possible target. Marine armor was tough, but not tough enough to withstand a pulse cannon hooked directly into the ship's power supply. A blast from a spider's cannon could go through him like a bullet through a tomato, and with the same general effect.

He waved his arm, giving his men the "all clear" signal. Eleven corporate soldiers stepped out onto the lunar colony of New Akron, their heavy metal feet stirring up the thick dust once again.

"Weapons check." Stryker commanded.

Each man clicked on his blaster, thumbed the selector to test, and watched for the signal light that made sure all the circuits were connected and working properly. Stryker saw one man, Duncan, trying to keep his power cable connected.

He clicked on his throat mike, his voice sounding

low and tinny over the closed circuit of the helmet's receiver. "Thought I told you to get that fixed, Dunc." It wasn't a question.

"Took it by the armory, Sarge, but no one was around."

Stryker hooked his own weapon to the forearm clip and grabbed Duncan's rifle and power cord. With a surly look at the marine, he jammed the cord into the stock and tried to screw on the idiot fastener. As he suspected, the grooves had been worn.

"Glove," Stryker subvocalized into his mike. The computer inside recognized the command and activated a strong set of microhydraulics within the gauntlet of his armor. With an incredibly strong pinch, Stryker crimped the fastener down onto the jack. "Glove," he repeated, and the function was automatically switched off.

He shot Duncan another look and glanced out over the small circle of blasted moonscape they had landed in. The ruins of New Akron bordered the horizon with twisted steel architecture reaching into the pale darkness. The dead city was one of the colonies established in the mass exodus from Earth after the invention of the Quantum drive and had prospered for many years before disaster struck.

New Akron was built on a moon of a gas giant on the outer fringe of known space. When another moon elsewhere in the system broke free from its exploding parent, it was quickly sucked into the neighboring gas giant's orbit. Eventually, this new moon had caught up with the smaller one on which New Akron was built, and the colonist's precious oxygen was sucked off in days. The earthquakes and riots that followed all but destroyed the city and the colonists had fled like rats from a sinking ship.

At least, that's what Stryker's briefing said. Now all that was left was a blasted husk of lifeless dust and debris surrounded by a layer of air so thin that a scream would go unnoticed at more than ten paces.

"HUD. Map." Before landing, the *Tyrannosaurus* had flown over the ruins and scanned in a map of the city. The map and what little was known of the colony had been translated by the ship's computers, and then downloaded into the marine's suits. Within each helmet of the 215 kilogram Brodie Mark IV Deep Space and Armored Combat Suit was a small computer that wrapped around the occupant's head from ear to ear. This machine monitored all of the armor's functions, including projecting the Heads Up Display, bio-medical systems, scanner programs, and practically anything else the marine asked it to do.

In response to Stryker's verbal command, the HUD on the interior of his faceplate glowed a pale green with vector-line graphics. "Rally point, *Tyrannosaurus*. Objective, Alpha Lima 1345, 6708."

Eleven black suits studded with metallic cables and venting excess heat in tiny wisps of steam recorded the information as the map and a tiny red dot appeared on the HUDs of each of the marines. The computer imaging showed them exactly where Stryker was headed, and where to return to in case of trouble. This time, it was the landing craft.

Everything was ready. The squad spread out in a standard wedge formation. Simmons and Guibert carried the pulse cannons at the rear of the "v," and Stryker led from the front center.

As he left the crater, he couldn't help but glance at the spiders one last time. One little binary number sent up the wrong wire, or maybe just a programming glitch in the machines' AI, and Stryker his men would be so much flotsam on yet another dead world.

The thought made him angry. And afraid.

It was a full kilometer to the first set of ruined buildings. The team moved quietly through the rocky silt, watching for any signs of privateers or rival corporate forces. In populated cities and courts of the Consortium, corporations played civil and even went out of their way to prove to everyone how nice they were. But in space, in absolute isolation, things were a little different. Stryker and his company had come into violent conflict with other companies and their marines on several separate occasions.

Starlabs had wanted xeno-flora and -fauna rights on Richtus Seven, and had attacked when Stryker's captain ordered them to destroy a particularly vicious rockworm. Jonn had gotten his first recommendation for valor under fire for that battle. He had slain three scientists in exploration suits with a plasma grenade. He didn't see anything particularly brave about that.

The other encounters had been a little less pointless. Randall-Hollings corporate security forces had captured a pirate ship filled with Tiko equipment, arms, and armor. Stryker's boss, Terrin Kelassiter, had told him to get the stuff back, and the two corporations engaged in a three month long war over two or three hundred thousand credits worth of junk.

Nothing was expected today however, so Kelassiter had assigned only one squad to explore New Akron and retrieve any usable equipment. The treaty with RH had been signed weeks ago and Todd Hollings hadn't even been heard from since. There were rumors that they were having a lot of trouble with a particularly nasty gang of shatrats, pirates that roamed the frontiers of the shatterzone in illegal Consortium-banned stealth ships, but no one was really sure and Hollings wasn't talking.

Almost four hundred meters from the drop site, the squad encountered what looked like a blasted out crater full of debris and wreckage. Scaffolding lay like giant skeletons amid the dusty bowl and hundreds, maybe thousands, of silt-covered blocks rested in strange collections throughout the crater.

Stryker paused cautiously at the lip of the depression. He could see clearly to the ruined city beyond, but the strange formations worried him. It wasn't that he was particularly expecting trouble. It was more like something here was just *wrong*.

"Hawkins, Duncan: spread left. Forward fifty. Find out what those mounds are."

Two gray-suited marines bounded down into the crater while the rest of the team squatted beyond the rubble of the lip and covered them with their blaster rifles.

"Use some of that fancy equipment while we're sittin' here, Klein."

"Check. Electro-mag: Off." One of the marines spoke to the computer in his helm and a small indicator lit up inside. A metallic box attached to the leg of his armor fell noiselessly into the dusty soil, its electro-magnets deactivated by the suit's voice-activated servers.

Steve Klein, a veteran of several conflicts and the squad's tech-specialist, opened the box and set up a small, dish-like device. He pulled a thick metallic cable from the rear of the case and stuck the end of it into a special receptacle on his helmet. A few seconds later, the dish began to spin and Klein's HUD was awash with a sensor readout showing two moving and nine stationary forms. "Nuttin', Sarge."

"Check the commo."

The dish stopped for a second, then quickly traversed back towards the drop ship. After a moment or two of self adjustment, it settled into place and Klein was able to radio the pilots. "*Tyrannosaurus*, this is Alpha 287, do you copy?"

"Alpha 287, copy," came a distant voice through the receiver of both Klein and Stryker. "We're picking up two movers about 100m from your position. Is there a problem?"

"Negative, *Tyrannosaurus*, checking safety zone."

Duncan and Hawkins had reached the strange formations and were clearing some of the dust from the nearest group.

"Whatta ya got down there, Dunc?"

There was some interference in the line; a little unusual for a dead planet. "Looks like hover-cars, Sarge. Lots of 'em."

Stryker zoomed in with the Nere-Dorning Sure-Sights installed in his visor. Duncan was wiping the dust from what may have been the front windshield of a hover-car when Stryker heard his stuttering voice over the receiver.

"Oh my G …" his voice trailed off into nothingness. There was a faint swallowing sound, followed by Duncan's heavy breath. It was faster than before. "There's still people in here … but how could …"

Duncan strode to another of the lumps and wiped the dust from yet another windshield. He didn't speak, but immediately ran to another, and another, knocking handfuls of dust into the still atmosphere. "They're all full … people in every damn one. But why would …?"

There was a long silence as the marines digested what their minds were telling them. The crater had been a launch site. The cars were full of thousands of the colonists who had been left behind by the corporate government. Corp officials usually worshiped a merciless god named Profit, and that god often demanded that the impoverished be sacrificed to keep black ink from going red. Such had been the case on New Akron when the gargantuan evacuation shuttles had blasted off the ruined surface of the planet. Hundreds were left behind to suck the last vapors of oxygen from the dying colony.

Stryker could picture the screaming colonists pleading with the corp-sec cops to let them board the evacuation ships as the wealthier elite walked casually up the gangplanks, struggling to hold their luggage in their weak little civilian arms. Some of them might even have looked with sympathy on the struggling, shouting, families below. The company probably even took a few, whomever they had room for that wouldn't inconvenience the paying customers too badly. Life, like the endless space that formed the evening sky of New Akron, had grown somewhat cold in the twenty-fifth century.

The colonists were tools. When the planet failed, the tools were no longer needed. It was a cold reminder to each of the soldiers that they too were mere cogs in the titanic wheels of the corporations.

Some idealistic few thought differently, but they were sadly mistaken.

Stryker decided that his squad was more morose than they needed to be right now and waved them to move on and link up with Duncan and Hawkins in the crater. "Get back in the wedge, people. We got a city to loot."

Stryker turned on the group bio-monitor, a function only the commander's suit possessed. Duncan's heart was beating fast and he was breathing way too hard. Stryker thought about it for a second, and suddenly remembered that the man's family had lived here.

Knock off enough dust and you'll probably find your little sister down there, Dunc, Stryker thought. *But he'll get over it.*

Half a klick later they came across the ruins of an old garage. The inside was empty save for the ever-present dust. The central hub of the city was close by and Stryker took advantage of the available cover by ordering a halt.

"Klein, give me another scan."

"Shit, Sarge! We just did one half a klick back!"

Stryker was usually a soft-spoken but firm individual, but when he gave an order, he expected it to be followed to the letter. That had kept him and his men alive over the years, and the hot-headed Klein wasn't one of his favorite soldiers anyway. Stryker's gravelly voice came over Klein's private channel. "You've got about five seconds to get that dish spinnin'." It wasn't an order. He had given that already.

Klein dropped the commo box into the dust again and made a great show of doing so. His protests weren't lost on the other men, but a few moments later, the dish was spinning.

If anyone could've seen Klein's face beneath the plexiglass face visor, they would've felt a little uneasy at his confused expression. A 3-D map of the nearby lunar landscape was projected against his interior viewscreen, and for just a fleeting second, he thought he saw a point of light streak from the upper left to a point on the horizon just out of sight. But the image was gone in seconds, and it could have been a momentary power surge as the scanning signals uploaded themselves into his suit's computer. Besides, if he told Stryker about it he'd just make them sit here for hours, and Klein had no intention of parking his heavily armored butt on this dusty rock for any longer than it took to earn his paycheck.

Stryker barked, startling Klein out of his confusion, "What's takin' so long?"

"Nothing, Sarge. Just doublechecking everything. I wouldn't want any of these corpses to hop up and scare anyone."

Again, Jonn spoke only to Klein, "You're on report." He switched back to the open channel, "Let's move. Guibert, get in that window and cover us with the cannon. Graves and Shaick take point to the target."

On each of the marine's HUDs, a red dot of light appeared on a ruined building looming massively on the immediate horizon. Graves and Shaick took long but cautious steps past the garage, and started towards the structure.

The point men usually led about seventy-five meters ahead of the formation in open terrain such as this. One of the pulse cannons with its two-kilometer range was left behind to cover them as they crossed the plain. The second was always kept near the squad leader.

Graves was an older man, and one of Stryker's favorites. He should have been a sergeant himself, or maybe even an officer by now. He was more experienced than any of them, but rumor had it that he had crossed Terrin Kelassiter, the administrative head of this sector and Stryker's immediate superior. Getting on the bad side of one's executives was a sure way of remaining a private forever.

Shaick claimed Arabic descent and was Graves' constant companion. They had been in several tight spots together and had always managed to pull each other's ass out of the fire.

Ahead of the two point men sprawled an urban nightmare. It wasn't quite big enough for a city, yet it was much larger than a town. Colonial villages tended to look this way, a central hub of activity without the typical homes and support businesses that usually preceded a settlement of this size back on the home worlds.

Graves could see the streets stretching out before him. Electric and hover-cars were scattered here and there, some overturned, but most just abandoned. Graves zoomed in with the integral Sure-Sights and could see corpses hanging from some of the wrecks. He imagined what it must have been like those last few days as the oxygen soared away like a lost balloon.

That thought made him remember his childhood. He once received a red helium balloon from some occasion or another, and had tied it to the foot of his bed. There had been something simple and beautiful about that balloon, something so profound that he still remembered what it looked like forty-six years later. It floated above the cluttered floor of his room and reflected the scathing moonlight, dancing on a wind that didn't yet smell of smoke and toxic stench. But nothing lasts forever, and four days later there had just been a wrinkled blob of plastic dangling from a frazzled string.

New Akron looked a lot like that.

The veteran was standing on a rise perpendicular to the colony, and could make out a supermarket in the near distance. He spoke softly with the suit's computer, and designated it as the squad's routing point.

"Copy," came Stryker's reply.

The parking lot of the market was covered in the same dust as the rest of the moon, but there were strange lumps here and there. Some were obviously more of the vehicles that Duncan had found at the launch site, but others were much smaller with jutting protrusions. The windows of the building had been boarded over, though the boards were busted in places and scorched in others.

Graves moved slowly into the lot and turned up the heat exhaust of his suit to uncover the strange mound at his feet. The dust was finer than he had guessed and it swirled into a blinding storm of debris and silt.

Shaick saw his partner disappear in the cloud and moved to assist. "Graves?"

There was no reply.

Stryker's voice rung sharply in the squad's ears, "What's goin' on down there? Talk to me, dammit!"

From the cloud came a low voice, it was Graves. "I'm fine. Looks like food was in short supply. In the end."

Shaick appeared beside his companion. In the now settling dust were two human corpses, partially mummified by the dryness of the environment. Their arms were locked together, and one had the hilt of a knife in his brittle hand. The blade was buried deep in the other's ribs. A smaller lump lay beside them. Graves guessed it was probably a pistol. Locked between their free hands was a can of beans.

It was enough to make the veteran sick.

Shaick spoke for them, "Nothin', Sarge. Looks like the settlers had a little war down here over the last couple o' cans of chow."

Shaick left his partner and walked over to the storefront. Someone had boarded themselves inside. Jutting out from one of the holes was the barrel of an antique auto-rifle, a dead hand just visible on the stock. Shaick guessed that some of the other corpses in the parking lot had seen the business end of that antique.

With his armored foot, he kicked in the surrounding boards. Dust flew everywhere but settled quickly. Inside were several overturned shelves and hundreds of emptied cans. In the right-hand wall was a large hole with several bodies piled there. Directly across from the breach sat a man, woman, and two children. Evidently, they had chosen to die by their own hands rather than face the wrath of the angry mob. Shaick knew that the store's owner had probably been on the evacuation shuttle, so whoever this man was had probably taken the store for his family and tried unsuccessfully to keep out his hungry neighbors.

"More of the same inside, Sarge. Nothing useful here."

The rest of the marines walked slowly into the lot and watched as Shaick and Graves finished up the recon. The desperate scene kept them reverently quiet.

"All right. We knew what this place was gonna be like. Now move it," Stryker barked.

Graves walked back out of the store and kicked the interlocked corpses which instantly flew apart into thousands of crumbling segments. The can landed in the dust with a dull thud barely audible through the Brodie suit's amplification system.

A half hour later found the squad gathered around the outside of the building Stryker had designated as their target point. It turned out to be a bank.

Mounted on the outside wall was an automated credit vendor. Most financial transactions were handled by cred-card these days, but hard currency was still occasionally required. The auto teller was one of the few things that hadn't been looted after the exodus. Cash had evidently become relatively pointless as the remaining oxygen wormed its way through the Akronites' respiratory systems and became useless ever after. And it had been too bulky and too exposed a commodity for those going on the shuttles to bother with.

Guibert flipped off the safety on the pulse cannon. "Can I pop it, Sarge?"

Stryker nodded. The men were entitled to a few perks here and there.

The pulse cannon hummed for a few moments before Guibert squeezed the hand-sized trigger that sent hundreds of supercharged particles screaming out of the barrel before slamming into the bank wall. There was a small explosion, and then the faint rattle of hundreds of small aluminum and iridium coins spilling into the dust-covered sidewalk.

The men gathered their booty as best they could with their clumsy power gloves and then dropped them into a retractable pocket of the armor. Each man gathered enough for a few rounds at the *Worm Hole*, the marine's bar of choice on Tiko III.

Before all the coins had been taken, Stryker knocked Klein on the shoulder piece, "Gimme a scan 'n commo check."

"Christ! Okay, just a minute," Klein scooped up a handful of coins and Stryker knocked them back into the dust.

"Now."

If Klein said anything in return, he didn't broadcast it. He hooked up the scanner unit once again, and turned his head to watch his fellow marines scoop up the loot.

There was a strange tension in the thin atmosphere of the dead colony and the muffled jingling of the scavenged coins in the thin atmosphere only accentuated the eerie silence. Klein finally broke it. "Christ, Sarge! There's fifteen fast movers comin' in at six o' clock! "

Stryker herded everyone into the crumbling bank and they dove behind the cover of the windows.

"What? What is it?" Hawkins shouted.

"Dunno. Shut up and be still," his leader barked.

Klein was still outside, trying to drag the heavy scanner into the building. The jack came out and the dish fell off into the dust.

"Damn!" he yelled in frustration. Graves leapt through the shattered window and chucked the dish back through. Klein yelled a quick thanks to the veteran and dragged the rest of the unit roughly through the door.

Graves was right behind him when there was a tremendous ripping sound, like someone had turned up the volume on a pair of shorting speakers. Ten sets of eyes watched as pieces of metal, blood, and bone showered the far wall of the bank and stuck there like bloody spittle on bathroom tile. Graves hadn't even had time to scream.

Shaick saw his long-time friend's remains sliding messily down the wall and stood up in fury. He raised the blaster and began spraying the empty street in unaimed, successive bursts. Hawkins reached up with his off hand to pull him down, but the Arab refused to budge.

Shaick stopped firing for a second, then broke the silence with, "What the —" There was another of the tremendous ripping sounds, and then Faysal Al-Sal Shaick joined his dead comrade in whatever afterworld awaited them.

Stryker could tell that his men were near panic. He scolded himself for getting caught with his pants down, but he didn't even know what the hell was being fired at them. No weapon he had ever heard of made a sound like that.

"How many, Klein?" Stryker screamed.

"I don't know! I can't get the damn dish back on!"

Stryker turned his head and saw the commo officer trying desperately to re-attach the uplink. It was covered in blood and gristle and the connections didn't seem to want to fit.

Jonn spoke into the suit's control mike, "Periscope." Instantly, an almost invisible fiber-optic cable rose from his helmet and peeked out over the window ledge. Half of his visor became a viewscreen filled with the image of the street, but there were no attackers visible. "Where the hell are they?" he grumbled in frustration.

The sudden excitement caused Jonn's breath to become heavy and wet. The condensation felt uncomfortable on his lip as he mouthed for the computer to switch him back to the open channel. "Hawkins. SPG at the building across from us. Duncan, same thing but use c-smoke. Fire, then break for the rally point on my mark. Do it!" There was some static on the line, something was interfering with the radio, but the message had gotten through.

Together, Hawkins and Duncan threw a self-propelled grenade through the window. Once the pin was pulled and the grip released, small fins emerged from the side of the can-sized grenade. Micro-thrusters kicked in and carried it into the side of the building opposite the bank. On impact, a high-energy laser superheated the hydrogen within the cylindrical device, exploding in a cloud of devastating plasma. The grenades were designed to kill, even through heavy power armor, but they served equally well as a distraction. The smoke round completed the diversion.

"Move!" Stryker screamed. The marines leapt through the window and into the street. "Fire!"

Seven blasters and two pulse cannons simultaneously opened up on the area across the street. Stryker had studied an old battle where so many rounds had been flying it had created an effect they called the "Hornet's Nest," and he imagined that if hornets ionized the air around them as they flew, it would look a lot like this. Finally, he gave the order to cease firing. The building looked like the surface of a golf ball with a couple of pulse cannon holes for good measure.

There was an open channel that all corporate marine forces monitored, and Stryker used this to challenge his enemy. "You've got four seconds before we open up again."

"One." Nothing.

"Two." More nothing.

"Thr—"

Duncan screamed. "Behind us! They're ..." Stryker saw Duncan squeeze the trigger on his blaster, but the power cord had fallen out of his weapon again and dangled by his knees. He was the farthest man on the left and facing the opposite direction, and whatever he was trying to shoot was out of sight of the others.

The ripping sound again; as if the thin air was being torn apart by whatever projectile was tearing through it. It barely caught Duncan in the right arm, ripping it off and sending hot blood into the cold atmosphere. He spun around with the impact of the blast and Stryker saw that the suit's sphincter system had already amputated the rest of the limb and sealed itself against the hostile environment. Four hypodermics secretly plied Duncan's skin and kept him from going into shock while numbing the pain and locally coagulating the blood.

It didn't really matter because the next blast caught him square in the face. Needless to say, there was no sphincter unit in the armor's neckpiece. The dangling cord of the blaster rifle lay in the congealing blood and dust.

Stryker had been running towards Duncan when he saw the helmet and its grainy contents spin away from their former owner. He stopped short, judging by Duncan's position that he could neither see or be seen by the mysterious enemy.

The corpse was still twitching within the heavy suit; Jonn imagined he could hear it flailing around inside. Duncan was the youngest of the company. Stryker had been whipping him into shape for three years now and he had become one of their best, and he had always been the quickest. *Not quick enough*, Jonn guessed.

"Everybody back to the ship!" It was Klein. Only Stryker could give the order, but before he realized what was happening, the others were hot on Klein's retreating heels.

Stryker's face contorted into hatred as he reluctantly followed the remainder of his fleeing squad. He spared one last look at the corner that hid Duncan's murderer and saw that there was a large amount of dust rolling out from behind it as if something large had moved up to the edge of the building. He thought he saw a stubby face peeking through the cloud and fired off a few rounds. Whatever it was withdrew and Stryker used the opportunity to beat feet.

As he ran, the image of the face began to register in his mind. It was … lumpy. There were grooves and tube-like shapes bound tightly to the front of the skull, but they didn't really look like the ceramic metal that most Brodie suits had. Of course there were other kinds of deep-space suits; a lot of shatrats even pieced together their own, but he had never seen any as grotesque as this.

His breathing was becoming heavy. The suit amplified his strength, but he was running fast and his breath was still condensing uncomfortably on the microphone. He spoke into the commo unit again and yelled for the squad to get into cover and form a defensive position. If they heard, they weren't responding. He was stirring up the dust as he ran and couldn't see a thing. Except the face. His mind's eye could still see that horrible visage.

Had he seen *jaws?* No armor he had ever seen had jaws. There was no point in it. What the hell would it have had jaws for? Did it have teeth? He hadn't seen any. Had he?

"Where the hell is everyone?!" he yelled over the open channel. There was no response. He was totally alone in a dead world. No one would have guessed that the battle-hardened commander of the corporate force known as the Wolverines had a serious phobia of being alone, but he did. Had they known, some psychotherapist in their cushy office would say that Stryker took solace in military tactics because they emphasized teamwork and working with others. All Jonn knew was that he was alone, and his own heavy breath crawling into his ears only made him feel more isolated.

He was only a quarter kilometer from the ship when ionized particles streaked through the air beside him. He leapt into some rocks and called up the periscope again. The dust trail he had made was already beginning to settle, and he could just make out the rest of the squad hunkering down in some rubble one hundred meters ahead. Something near the drop ship was firing at them.

He just bet it was those damn spiders. Maybe whatever was jamming their communications was jamming their friend or foe transmitter too. Stryker tried to raise the ship once more, but all he got was static.

There was a ripping sound again, and the ground beside him blew high into the air. It was now or never. The dust cloud from the explosion concealed him for the first few steps, and then he turned on his exhaust fans. The exhaust blew off a portion of the heating system's air supply and blew the dust behind him into great whirling clouds. That would conceal him from his attacker, but not from the damn spiders. He might have time for one quick shot before the auto-targeter switched to infra-red and picked him out of the debris. Milliseconds before his own HUD's targeter locked on the protruding head of the automated defense drone, Stryker eyeballed the shot and squeezed the trigger of his blaster. He ran straight for the ship, hoping the squad would follow behind. He kept firing as he ran, so that if he was missing he might at least confuse the spider's sensors by kicking up the rock in front of it. There was no way to be sure if he was successful, so Stryker held the trigger down until he was right on top of it. When he finally gained the lip of the dropship's crater, he saw the remains of the spider flailing weakly in the debris of dirt, rock, and metal fragments. Long cables spasmed dispassionately as legs clicked in and out of place.

The drop ship's turret was facing them, but fortunately the human crew was more selective than their automated servant. The deployment bay opened just as the remaining spider was retracted into its pod. Stryker signaled the squad in and threw several smoke and high explosive SPGs to cover their liftoff.

"Strap in!" yelled Fullerton, the female pilot. "Liftoff in five … four … three … two …"

SLAM! The hull of the drop ship took a tremendous hit. The twin turret cannons triangulated the trajectory of the attack and returned fire in seconds.

"One! Lift-off!"

The marines felt the heavy pull of an emergency launch. The ship was rocking back and forth from the recoil of the cannons and the almost automatic reaction of the in-flight stabilizers.

In a few more seconds the ship had cleared several hundred feet. The *Tyrannosaurus* wasn't hit again though the turret cannons continued to blast the landscape of New Akron. It never hurt to be sure.

Soon after, the marines were able to remove their helmets. Seven shocked and sweaty faces stared blankly at their leader. Three seats were empty, their straps swaying pointlessly with the motion of the flight.

Stryker wasn't sure who was responsible for the death of his men, but he knew that the sustained fire of the ship's cannons had killed at least as many of them in return.

Or at least he hoped.

But why the hell did their armor have jaws?

CHAPTER TWO

Tiko III

The boss was waiting for them when the drop ship docked on the mining asteroid/city of Tiko III. There were seven hundred and eighty-three registered citizens here, but only about a third were actual employees of the Tiko megacorporation; miners, corporate security forces, and bureaucrats. The others were support businessmen such as bartenders, surgeons, lawyers, trashmen, and the ever present and transient prostitutes, smugglers, and thieves.

The city itself was built beneath the surface of the asteroid in a series of tunnels and caves. Some of the mining structures remained on top, but these were used mostly for storage. It was far too dangerous to stay topside for any length of time due to the smaller asteroids that continually pelted the surface of the two-mile long rock.

The city had only existed for about six years, ever since a Tiko exploration team had discovered rich veins of iridium within the floating rock just on the fringe of the shatterzone. Several companies had competed for the rights to this particular area, and Tiko marines had fended off more than a few claim jumpers, particularly covert forces later linked to the Randall-Hollings firm.

The entire sector lay on the fringes of Consortium Space, or, that section of the universe that had so far been legally registered with the central civil government offices. The Consortium of Worlds had formed after mankind had developed the Quantum drive and before it contacted two other alien species in the Milky Way, the Glahn and the Ishantra. After a few tense situations and not a few bloody misunderstandings, the three species somehow banded together and established an intergalactic Consortium that would prevent any one race from trying to obliterate the other. The Fleet was their tool for doing so.

The Fleet held a tight rein over the Consortium's subjects; some said too tight, but it managed to limit the power of the ever growing megacorporations. Megacorps could own and rule entire planets, and were even able to write their own laws within certain boundaries. What they couldn't do was establish large offensive armies, "pirate" fleets, or anything else deemed dangerous to the Fleet itself.

Terrin Kelassiter was the Executive Head of one of these motley corporate cities. As corp types go, most citizens would have said he was better than average. At least he tended to leave the private businesses and visitors alone; unless they started trouble. Then Kelassiter was known to have an iron hand and an unforgiving will.

He was a handsome man with brown eyes and short brown hair that was long and always a little wild, like he dried his hair in front of the city's great oxygen fans. His cowboy hat and boots were out of place in the cramped confines of an underground city, but no one chided him for this idiosyncrasy.

His eyes had a certain wisdom that went well with

the wariness of his company sergeant, Jonn Stryker, but, other than that, the two men were in no way similar. Stryker was of average height and stocky build, while Terrin was slight of frame and stood well over six feet tall.

The lean one was waiting for his scruffy sergeant when he came storming down the drop ship bay. By the expression on Terrin's face, he had already spoken with the pilot of the *Tyrannosaurus*.

"What happened down there, Sergeant?"

Jonn pushed past him, "Read the freakin' report." He was a little sick of corporate officials after the sobering trip to New Akron, regardless of Terrin's particular personality.

Hawkins was the next out of the bay. His blonde hair was matted to his head with sweat and he ruffled it with his free hand as he approached his superior. "Might wanna leave him alone now, sir. We had a rough time down there."

Kelassiter whirled and yelled at Jonn just as he was about to leave the bay. "You're damn right you had a rough time down there! Three of my men are dead and I want to know what the hell happened!"

The sergeant paused for a second, letting the anger and frustration swell within him until it came boiling over the top of his blonde crewcut in waves of confused helplessness. "All right," he grumbled. "I'll tell you what the hell happened! Somebody else was on that gray hunk of dust and they ripped us a new asshole. Graves got nailed trying to drag Klein's worthless ass into cover, then Shaick lost his head and got hisself skragged. Then, while I'm trying to save everyone's bacon, Klein, the self-appointed God-Emperor of the freakin' Universe, tells everyone to get the hell out of Dodge!"

Klein and the others were standing at the foot of the bay door. Terrin turned to the communications officer, "Is that true, Specialist?"

The trooper stared incredulously at Stryker, then shifted his gaze towards Kelassiter. "I may have said something like 'Let's get the hell out of here' when ol' swifty was just watchin' us get mowed down, but I never gave any orders. Hell, nobody would'a listened to me anyway."

Stryker stomped towards the communications specialist and drove his fist down on Klein's chest armor, knocking the startled man to the hangar floor.

"Stryker!" Kelassiter yelled. "Help that man up and report to my office immediately!"

The sergeant looked Klein dead in the eye. His face was twisted with hate but his voice was flat and level so there could be no denying its sincerity. "If you had been doing your job from the beginning, none of those men would be dead."

There was a foreboding silence for an enormous amount of time. If looks could indeed kill, Klein would have been pulped.

"*Now*, Stryker!" Terrin demanded.

Jonn left Klein sprawled on the oily floor.

Most upper executives in megacorporate employ, particularly those in charge of an entire mining colony, had plush offices filled with luxuries and conveniences from any of fifty different worlds, but Terrin preferred to keep his room a little simpler.

Jonn didn't notice. He was still wearing his Brodie suit and cut a rather imposing figure in the understated room.

Terrin closed the door behind them and plopped down into his recliner. He propped his white cowboy boots up on the desk and folded his fingers into a steeple of flesh across his chest. "Now ... let's hear all that again, Jonn."

Stryker snarled and grumbled out a reply, "Klein was bitching when I told him to scan the area. Just before we got hit, he acted like he saw somethin' but he wouldn't say anything. He knows if we got unidentified blips on the screen that I usually put 'em down in cover for a while to check it out. Klein hates to waste his precious time hunkerin' down in the dirt for what's probably just some static charge in the wire, so he probably lied about what he saw. That gave whoever chewed us up time to close the distance and waste Graves and Shaick."

"Are you saying he ignored his machine?"

"No, not exactly. Anyone using good covering techniques usually just shows up for a second anyway. Klein probably got a glimpse of 'em and figured it was just static."

"How'd Graves and Shaick buy it?"

"Graves got hit while we were lootin' a bank machine."

"Didn't you set up a security team?"

"No. I didn't have any indication there was danger. Plus anybody on security doesn't get to grab credits."

"I see. What happened after Graves went down?"

"We got down inside the bank and seemed to be safe for the time being. Shaick went nutso on us and stood up firing at whatever was out there. I don't think he got any before he took it in the chest.

"I didn't wanna get pinned, so I had some of 'em throw smoke while the rest of us came out blazin'. There wasn't anyone out there, but we seemed to put their heads down."

Terrin grimaced. It was hard to place the blame here. Stryker had been around long enough to know a security team should always be placed prior to any action. On the other hand, given any warning by Klein, the sergeant could probably have handled anything that was thrown at them. He had before.

"What about Dunc?"

"The street was empty except for our smoke rounds,

and everything was fine 'til Duncan caught one of 'em sneakin' up behind us. It blew off his arm. He didn't go down right off so I ran over to help him, but they popped him again before he even hit the dirt. When I turned back around, Klein and the others were running towards the drop ship."

Kelassiter picked up a silver pen and began to write something on a notepad lying beside his expensive computer terminal. "Why do you think they ran?"

"I dunno. The second shot, I guess. There was a lot of smoke in the street and maybe they thought I bought it. Why don't you ask Klein? He was in the lead."

"You didn't try to radio them?"

"It wasn't workin' anymore, but the last thing I heard before we lost each other was Klein yellin' for everyone to scram."

"Was everyone's radio jammed?"

"I didn't know 'til I got back to the 'Saurus, but yeah. They were."

"What about the spider?"

"I dunno. Guess whatever jammed our radio blocked the IFF signal too."

Kelassiter spun in his chair and looked out of his third story window. Below him was Wiggle street, the central tunnel of the civilian sector of Tiko III. Numerous prostitutes, drug runners, pirates, miners, and workers filled the crowded space and conducted the business of their daily lives. Then an idea hit him.

He spun back around to face his friend. "Jonn, what about the comm unit? You know it stores all signals collected in the last twenty-four hours."

"Klein left it when we got hit. Pretty damn convenient if you ask me."

"I didn't. I probably would've dropped the thing too if someone was poppin' off pulse cannons at me."

Stryker raised his defensive stance a notch, "Wasn't pulsers."

"What then?"

"I dunno. Some kinda … rippin' thing."

"Ripping thing? What the hell does that mean?"

"Christ, I don't know. It sounded like it was rippin' the whole freakin' sky apart. A pulser'll rip open a Brodie if you hit it in the right place, but this thing popped Graves and Shaick like a rat in a microwave. I thought maybe it was some sort of area-effect device, but then it took off Dunc's arm like it was solid shot."

"The sphincter plates didn't save him?"

"Sure. 'Til the next round knocked his head off."

It was a rare sight to see Terrin confused. Stryker might even have enjoyed it under other circumstances. Frustration, like its sister, misery, loves company.

"I'll get some of the techies to look into it, Jonn. You want to bring Klein up on formal charges?"

Somewhere beneath the close-cropped hair of Sergeant Jonn Stryker, the gears of compassion kicked in. He had been given a second chance by Kelassiter once, and he guessed Klein deserved that much. And he really should have set up some security. But it was a hard choice for a man not used to admitting his mistakes.

"No. But put him on the street for a month and see if he can keep out of trouble."

"Done. Go shower and inform the rest of the company we'll have services for Graves, Shaick, and Duncan after dinner."

Stryker nodded and plodded his twenty-kilo boots out of Terrin's office and into the elevators.

Deep beneath the executive offices was the barracks of the Wolverines, Tiko III's only regular corporate security force. What they lacked in numbers, the forty marines, eight pilots, and ten service personnel made up for in experience and equipment.

There were four squads of marines. Each one was

composed of six privates, one technical specialist, two heavy weapons specialists, and a corporal who served as a squad leader. Over all of them was Sergeant Jonn Stryker.

Each man was assigned a Brodie Mark IV Deep Space and Armored Combat Suit, and a Kereketa Blaster Rifle with targeter link. The heavy weapons specialists carried the Kereketa version of the pulse cannon, while the communications man usually bore the heavy scanner-commo dish made by the Nere-Dorning company.

In the shower room of the barracks assigned to first squad, seven men washed off the sweat and grime that always accumulated beneath their power armor. There were usually ten steaming shower heads active after the return of a drop ship, but only seven hissed the scalding, recycled water this time out.

"Can you believe that jerk?" asked Klein. His red hair and beard hung low with the heavy water as he ran the yellow sponge across his muscular body.

The blonde haired Hawkins turned to face him and pointed an accusing finger. "You're the jerk, Klein! If you hadn't been belly-achin' about the damn dish the whole time, you might have seen them coming."

"It's not Klein's fault," the darkly complexioned Guibert chimed in, "Sarge shoulda put someone on rear security. Old man let his guard down, that's all."

Hawkins liked Stryker, and Duncan had been his best friend. His pointing finger traversed a line from Klein to Guibert, "That 'old man' could kick your butt from here to Teraxiter if he had the mind to do it, you sorry sack o' shit! And the last time he put you on security, you whined to Kelassiter that Stryker was cheatin' you out of the loot because you were stuck covering our asses!"

Guibert was more of an instigator than a fighter, and backed down. Klein picked up the banner and pushed

Hawkins back under the water.

"Look, ya rookie. When Dunc went down, Stryker just stood there. What were we supposed to do? Wait until he could come and cry over our corpses too?"

"He was trying to save Dunc's *life*, you stupid grunt!" Hawkins pushed Klein back, his fists unconsciously in the fighting stance they all had been taught at the corporate academy.

Guibert pushed Klein forward, "Little punk wants to fight, Steve."

Klein stumbled from the unexpected shove and slipped on the slick shower floor. The other men in the room laughed and sent the redhead's temper soaring to new heights. When he came up, he came up fighting. Hawkins got the wind knocked out of him as the frenzied Klein shoulder-charged him in the solar plexus. Both men went down again and all present heard a dull crunch. It sounded vaguely like the sound a watermelon might make if someone slowly pressed their fist through its outer shell.

Thick red fluid was quickly mixing with the steaming water of the shower and pouring gruesomely through the drain. The spectators were as surprised as Klein and Hawkins, and no one was quite sure who had broken what.

Hawkins was leaning against the tiled wall and rose up to look stupidly at his foe. When the bloody spittle dribbled from his lip, all knew that it was Hawkins' head that had cracked open on the ceramic wall.

Klein stood suddenly, dropping Hawkins and causing him to shampoo his blonde hair in blood and cranial fluid a second time.

"Call the medics!" yelled Simmons. "You're really gonna get it now, Steve."

Stryker was sitting by Hawkins' side when he finally came around.

"Hey," came a faint voice from the bandaged head.

"Shut up, kid. Doc said you shouldn't be movin' your jaw around. Klein's stuck with the street 'til we get this cleared up. Everybody said he started it. That sound right?"

Reluctantly, Hawkins nodded his injured head. His brain began to swim around and Stryker leaned forward and grabbed his hand. "Listen, troop, you gotta quit movin' your noggin around. Just tap once for yes and twice for no. Got it?"

Hawkins' lips trembled for a second before the nausea reminded him to tap his fingers on the metal bar of his hospital bed.

"I bet Guibert pushed him into it, didn't he?"

One tap. Stryker looked satisfied and shifted in his chair. It was obvious that he was through with that line of questioning.

"I need to ask you some questions about what happened at Akron. You up for it?"

One tap.

"Did you hear Klein order a retreat?"

Two taps.

"Did he yell for everyone to scramble?"

One tap.

"He say anything else after that?"

Two taps and Hawkins mumbled something about the radio blinking out.

"Yeah, I know. Just checkin'."

Stryker leaned back. Corporate code was a little gray in this area. Evidently, Klein had told everyone to retreat without actually ordering it. He had planned on going soft on the hot-tempered commo specialist, mostly for the platoon's sake, but after the shower incident he was going to chuck Klein out of the Wolverines on his fuzzy red ass. Unfortunately, Hawkins' story jibed with everyone else's and the most he could nail Klein for was cowardice in the face of the enemy and striking a fellow marine. That would probably only get him probation and a couple of weeks of duty as a street beater.

"Why'd you follow? Scared?"

Two taps. Hawkins struggled to speak and Stryker didn't stop him. "Thought you were dead."

"Dead?"

One tap, and he continued. "Saw Dunc go down, then ... dust and c-smoke everywhere. Couldn't see anything, but heard a second shot."

That's just what the others had said. A blinding cloud of that damn dust mixed in with the concentrated smoke, and then a second shot. The conclusion was inevitable.

Stryker nodded his head and rose to leave, but Hawkins moved with surprising speed and caught his wrist in a vise-like grip.

"Sarge," he whispered in painful breaths. "There was an ancient saying we learned at the academy. *Semper Fi - Do or Die*. It means we do the job ..." Murky saliva dripped from the corner of his mouth and he stopped to stab at it with his swollen tongue. " ...or we die trying."

"Yeah, kid. I know the —"

"No. I mean I stayed when the others ran. Not long, just enough to see ... it."

"It?" Stryker moved in closer to better understand the staggered speech of the delirious man. His eyes were wide and all he could think of was that damned face. *Why the hell did it have jaws?*

Hawkins had overtaxed himself. There was a loud, droning beep from the cerebro-monitor by the bed and the orderlies were surrounding them in seconds, pulling the struggling Stryker from the room as they tried to stabilize the marine's concussion.

"What did you see, Hawk? *What did you see?!*"

It took four orderlies to drag Stryker from the room.

CHAPTER THREE

The Worm Hole

The *Worm Hole* was the seediest bar on Tiko III. It was also the only registered bar in the whole city. A rival had opened a few years ago, but a freak accident with a mining drone had ended its potential in a few short weeks. No one had ever proven that the owner of the *Worm Hole*, Little Jake, had been behind it, but it was suspicious that his brother was the lead programmer in the corp's Automated Systems Department.

"Little Jake" was a misnomer for the 110-kilo, two-meter tall giant from one of the newer, heavy-gravity worlds who ran the bar. No one on T-3 (as the locals called their chunk of rock) was even close in height, weight, or raw strength. Over the years, most of the Wolverines had tried to best Jake's renowned physical prowess in arm wrestling, and some had even been stupid enough to fight with him. So far, the bartender was batting a thousand.

The balding giant saw Klein and Guibert stroll through the doors in their leather corpsec jackets. Both had obviously been put on the street beat, a common punishment for minor infractions within the corporate forces. Klein was known for his temper almost as much as Jake was known for his stature, but Guibert was the one Jake hated. Guy was one of those annoying men who took pleasure in getting others in trouble and rarely got personally involved.

But even he had money.

Klein slapped four coins down on the metallic bar and pointed toward the beer. Beer seemed to be one luxury even the frontier worlds of the Consortium seldom had in short supply. Food shortages, grain embargoes, and even law made beer brewing costly at times, but humanity never backed down from this one vice. It was rumored that the first thing early colonists did, even before establishing any permanent shelter, was look for grains that could be made into beer.

The two marines hopped up onto the barstools as Jake swabbed out two spotty mugs in the same fashion that men of his profession had been doing for several thousand years. Some things never changed.

"You on duty, Klein?" Jake ignored Guibert. He usually did.

"No. And who are you, my mother?"

Jake didn't bother replying as Guibert laughed loudly at his companion's retort. He poured two drafts and walked off towards another section of the bar.

"What do you think Stryker's going to do, *mon ami*?" Guibert asked and sucked the frothy head off his glass.

"Wipe that shit off your nose. What can he do? He's got nothing on me and no one really knows what happened anyway. Including me." Klein sipped at his beer and looked slowly about the room. "I just hope Hawk pulls through."

"That brat? He got what he deserved. It's not your fault he's got such fragile bones."

"He's one of us, Guy. You know, sometimes you make me really sick. Stryker's gettin' old. His time is up, but Hawk's got a future. He just needs to learn who to look up to around here."

From just behind Klein's ear came a low but powerful voice. It was Terrin. "Is that it, Klein? You cracked Hawkin's head open because he didn't show you enough respect?"

Klein didn't turn to face him, just lowered his head and sipped at his beer. "It wasn't like that, sir. It was an accident."

"I read the report, Specialist. But that doesn't change the fact that I've got an unknown threat near Akron and three dead marines. I don't need hot-heads like you putting more of my men in the hospital. You better hope for all our sakes that nothing more comes of this."

Klein nodded but Terrin was already out the door. Guibert yelled just as soon as he was sure he wouldn't be overheard by his superior, "Jerk."

"Shut up, Guy." Klein mumbled.

It wasn't easy being Jonny Stryker's fiancé (he hated "Jonny.") It was even harder when something was bothering him. Lucretia D'Atalack rubbed his sinewy back, but it was like trying to relax a rubber brick; the surface was soft but the damn thing just wouldn't bend.

He had already told her about Duncan, Graves, Shaick, Hawkins, and especially Klein, but there was something else he wasn't revealing. She could feel it just beneath the surface of his leathery skin. Her soothing touch was working wonders on him, but only time could heal the internal scars that Stryker bore. Still, she loved him, and she would try her best.

"Jonny, there's something else, isn't there?"

"No. Not really. I hear they got some new vid-slugs at Happy's. Want to check one out?"

"Why don't we just stay home tonight and watch what we've got?"

"Sure. Maybe I'll even make us some real food."

Lucretia laughed and slid around to his front. "That's okay, hon. My stomach still hasn't recovered from the last time you went in the kitchen. Let's just let the machine do it."

Stryker smiled in spite of himself and pulled her close. It was a rare sight for his harsh face, and Lucretia kissed him deeply for it. But somewhere in the process the kiss ate the smile, for when the silken-haired woman pulled away, his frown had returned.

Jonn stared for a while at her pale skin, jet black hair, and tired but pretty face. Her dark eyes were accentuated by the black gown she wore, as were her rounded breasts. She had been a working girl years ago, and prostitution was an acceptable occupation in certain parts of the universe, but Jonn grew jealous and offered to share his income with her. She had not argued, and the two had been together for the last three years.

"We still don't know what hit us." It was a question as much as a statement, and Lucretia felt that he somehow expected her to unravel the whole bloody mystery for him.

"What do you mean? I heard it was shatrats."

"Maybe, but I've never seen pirates as slick as this. And they had some sort of gun that ... *ripped* the air apart. It was weird. It had more punch than a pulser."

Lucretia placed her head in his clumsy hands, "At least you're okay, Jonny. I worry, you know."

"Yeah. I know."

But it had jaws!

And he just bet the damn thing had teeth too.

When Kelassiter returned from his uncharacteristic visit to the *Worm Hole*, Dr. Thaddeus Dumois V was sitting in his office. Several charts were sprawled across his desk, and the scientist's coffee mug had left a brown ring on a hardcopy of Stryker's statement.

Terrin sat in his high-backed chair and pulled the

report out from under the doctor's mug. The cold liquid ran down the papers and dribbled anxiously onto his lap. "Ah, shit, Thad," he grumbled.

Thaddeus was oblivious to the world around him. If there was ever a stereotypical "absent-minded professor," Dumois was it. Perhaps the only striking difference was that Dumois was bisexual. On his home world, most everybody was. Terrin had heard that the mutation rate on Silentius was extremely high and that those who could reproduce paired diametrically for population purposes, and heterosexuality had never really caught on there. Silentius could be a fun place to visit if one had the right attitude about such things.

At any rate, Thaddeus was holding up several charts Terrin knew to be their little section of space just inside the shatterzone. The 'zone was a sea of asteroids and energy that that many people thought defined the limits of traversable space. Ever since the creation of the Quantum drive, it had been possible to travel incredible distances in a relatively short amount of time, but even the universe seemed to have an edge. Several companies and even the inter-galactic Consortium of Worlds had attempted to penetrate the swirling shell of rock and debris, but with little success as yet.

The discovery of the "shattered zone" had sparked a number of philosophical debates back on the home worlds. The crystal sphere theory of the ancients had even been rekindled and modified. What most intrigued the questioning minds of the known universe was: what was *beyond* the edge of the universe?

Some said that beyond the shatterzone, as it came to be called, was simply another section of the universe much like our own. Others believed that past the impenetrable barrier of spinning rock were the Heavens, and that man was not meant to venture any further. As was typical with human beings, this had been the cause of several minor wars.

The 'zone was large enough to exert a gravitational field, and would sometimes "catch" a large asteroid between it and a nearby system. This allowed some rare rocks to hover in a relatively stable position, and this was where the money was. Many of these contained rich veins of rare or precious minerals, while others could be used as defense stations or research platforms for whatever corporation settled them. Kelassiter's asteroid was the third such colony established by the relatively new Tiko corporation; hence the creative name of Tiko III.

Terrin blotted off what coffee hadn't already seeped into his shorts and sighed. "What is it, Thad? More 'rats?"

This sector of the shatterzone was known for its large iridium deposits. Iridium was currently a hot item on many markets, and pirates tended to prey upon any stray ship that attempted to transport the ore back to the core worlds. These unscrupulous individuals had been dubbed "shatrats" by someone, long ago.

"Hmmm," Thaddeus muttered and stared at the executive over his gold-rimmed glasses. "Actually, no. It appears as if something has come through the 'zone."

Kelassiter's eyes doubled in size and his jaw hung slack in his handsome skull. "Someone got … *out*?" he stuttered.

Thaddeus waited just long enough to enjoy the importance of his knowledge before speaking, "No. Something came *in*. Toward us."

Terrin leaned back and thought about this. He never actually considered that someone or something might be peering in at them from the other side. It felt a little creepy, kind of like being a fish in a tiny aquarium, and the blurry shape on the other side might be the guy with the food or a hungry cat. It was impossible to tell which.

He had heard rumors of "bolter" aliens — strange species that claimed to have "run the 'zone" fleeing some unnameable horror. But he'd always put that into the same category as space legend. There were plenty of alien species he'd never heard of on this side of the 'zone, for God's sake. He didn't need to make up more.

"What was it? A ship?"

"Yes, small and silver, but it seems to have been destroyed shortly after emerging from the 'zone."

"By what?"

"Not sure. It seems Hollings got nervous and …"

"Hollings?" Terrin interrupted.

Thaddeus nodded, "Yes, it came through in Hollings' sector."

"Oh, great!" Terrin despaired. Trouble between Tiko and Randall-Hollings went way back, especially between Terrin and Todd Hollings himself. The two had come into conflict twice: once over the rights for this rock and the other for some stolen cargo that Todd somehow wound up with. The latter had led to a generous helping of bloodshed before Fleet came poking around and a truce had been declared. For them.

And now there was this nightmare. Kelassiter was sure Hollings would salvage something useful off that alien ship and find a way to turn it against him. Whether it was new weapons or figuring out how to get *back through* the 'zone, Terrin was sure it spelled trouble for him and his isolated city.

"How'd we find out?" he sighed.

Thaddeus folded up the charts and adjusted himself in the uncomfortable plastic chair. "The usual."

Terrin grinned; he still had his ace-in-the-hole. The "usual" was an agent known only to himself and Thaddeus. She was extremely good at her job, and always managed to smuggle out Hollings' best kept secrets. Neither of them knew exactly what position the spy had managed to secure for herself, but it didn't really matter. Dreama Collaris was one of the best deckers corpsec had ever trained. Given a halfway decent cyberdeck and a safe terminal to plug in her cerebral jack, Dreama could run the virtual reality of any ship's computer. Any data stored in the massive electronic vaults of Todd's planetary cruiser, the *Constantine*, was vulnerable to her ethereal grasp. And, if Todd planned on attacking, Dreama would alert them well before the threat materialized.

Hollings was much higher than Kelassiter on the two companies' respective corporate ladders and didn't stay in one city for long. He preferred to travel about the inner rim of the 'zone in the company's flagship, the *Constantine*. It was here that Terrin's spy lurked.

The nearest of Hollings' colonies was thirty light years away, but the *Constantine* had ventured out of system two weeks ago, presumably to corner a particularly nasty band of shatrats that had hijacked several of their cargo ships. Consortium law demanded that Terrin allow them to continue the chase. This kept companies from sheltering pirates within their various spheres of influence.

Kelassiter folded his hands behind his head and peered off into infinity. He couldn't help but smile a little. He was actually beginning to love these little *tête-à-têtes* with Hollings. Terrin had come out on top more often than not, and adversity was indeed the spice of his life. And, of course, it was possible that Hollings' scavengers had found no more than a recipe for alien stew amid the wreckage of the dead ship.

Still, he was dealing with something totally unknown, and that made him a little uneasy, even though it made for one hell of a game. Maybe Todd would even give him some real competition this time.

But he doubted it.

CHAPTER FOUR

Virtual Mousetrap

There was a pulsing corridor of light just ahead. She was close. The sentinel patrolled the hall as usual, checking the doors and rattling his golden key ring around his virtual finger. This was always the hardest part.

In the real world, Dreama's deck received the signal that told it to switch the Pickpocket program into memory. The Cyrus Stealth Package had to be downgraded in order to make room for the memory-hogging patch, so Dreama would have to manage some of the sneaking part on her own.

But that's what she did best.

In the virtual reality of the *Constantine's* computer, in the section dedicated to data collection, Dreama's projected image darted down an artificial corridor and whipped the key off the key ring as it spun about the sentinel's finger.

This would have been impossible in the real world, but this was all representational. In reality, Dreama's Pickpocket program had patched itself into the intruder protection program and teased out the various binary codes that would allow her system into the various sections of the ship's computer.

The section she was particularly interested in was the Scientific Investigations unit. She was sure there had been a lot of activity here after the weird ship burst through the 'zone, and this would be where all of the notes were recorded.

Physically, this department was located near the bridge, far away from the Sanitation and Recycling offices where Dreama Collaris worked for and spied on the Randall-Hollings flagship, the *Constantine*. She couldn't have gotten close if she'd wanted to. But in cyberspace, she could go wherever she pleased. If she wasn't caught.

The sentinel never knew what hit him. She had cut it close before, but this run was going off without a hitch. Only a few more nodes and she'd be in the main system.

She had sent the initial news of the incident to Kelassiter in the last garbage dump almost two months ago. The *Constantine*, like other ships of its size, recycled about 85% of its garbage. What wasn't recycled was jettisoned twice monthly. Such a regular schedule made it easy for Dreama to deliver her information back to Kelassiter. The system was simple; she always attached the microdisk to flashlights, slug-playing personal music systems, or other electrical devices. Once the package was jettisoned, it was a simple matter for one of Tiko's courier drones to follow the garbage trail and activate a specially fitted electro-sensor to find the item. Of course, the batteries in the host device would have worn down by the time the drone arrived for pickup if Hollings didn't meticulously keep on schedule.

The biggest problem Dreama had faced so far was that she kept running out of penlights, radios, and alarm clocks. After a brief plea in one of her messages that the clerk at commissary was getting suspicious, Terrin had paid an "Aunt Sara" from the human core worlds to constantly send her gifts. If Dreama allowed anyone to get to know her, they would have thought she was hell on slug players. And she didn't even own any music.

Now it would be almost two weeks before her next message could be sent, and another week or two for the pick-up drone to make it all the way back to Tiko III. It normally took even longer, but Hollings was chasing a band of shatrats that just happened to be leading them closer to the Tiko sector. Dreama couldn't help but wonder if the pirates were secretly employed by her boss, and, if the truth were known, her lover.

Leaving the virtual hallway, Dreama used the "keys" to open one of the airlock-style doors. Beyond it was a shoreline Dreama knew to be a representation of old Athens, from Terra. The construct, the electronic representation of the Automated Systems computer, looked like a shimmering Acropolis sitting on the edge of a violent ocean.

It was standard policy to let corporation techies recreate their segment of virtual reality to better suit their personal tastes — as long as they paid for its use. Supposedly, this prodded their creativity and increased their productivity. Katanopolis Andropopolous just thought it was prettier.

"Kat" had traced his lineage back to the ancient country of Greece on the humans' core world of Earth. When he wasn't studying quantum physics or probability theory, he would read about his ancient ancestors and their society. He was particularly fond of their architecture, and had completely reprogrammed the ship computer's virtual simulator to fit it — once he made Chief Theorist and Head Technician aboard the *Constantine*.

Dreama saw the image of Katanopolis standing on

the cliff face overlooking the crashing waves. If it would have done any good, she would have pushed him off. It was possible to kill someone in cyberspace, but Dreama wasn't here to burn out the doctor's overstuffed brain.

There was a hole in the center of the Acropolis that led into the drearier heart of the system and the valuable data files beneath. She had been down it twice before, once only two days ago, but Kat's presence made her nervous. He was probably one hell of a decker himself, and getting spotted would ruin any future raids even if she managed to escape. Still, if she backed out now, she would just have to break through everything again.

Kat was standing with his back to the Acropolis, seemingly thinking about something very deeply. That was a little odd in cyberspace, but Dreama supposed it was just representative of inaction. Maybe he was doing some serious number-crunching and the computer had to put him on hold for a while. It was as good a bet as any, and she made her dash for the stairwell.

Dreama's virtual self slipped in quietly. Her image in the network was that of a bag lady, a parody of her position within the sanitation department. Katanopolis didn't seem to see her, but the image was so convincing that Dreama wondered if he might actually be able to smell her.

Underneath, the stairs ended in a short hallway of doors. Some of them were relatively bland and featureless, but the one on the end was white and graven with the contrasting Greek images of Homer and Ulysses. Beyond the electronic lock, a virtual portrayal of a password system, was Kat's personal journal. Anything the professor cared to relate while in the node would be transferred to this file.

Dreama took one last look behind her and tried the keys. As she suspected, none of them worked. Reluc-

tantly, Dreama erased her stealth package and downloaded the memory-gluttonous Master Lock program.
In cyberspace, the Bag Lady whipped a silver skeleton
key out of a large satchel and rammed it into the stone
door. The lock clicked open.

Dreama entered the dusty chamber and saw a large
tome lying open on a stone desk. An inkwell rested
beside the ancient book, and Dreama could see hundreds of tiny scrawl marks on the vellum pages. She
switched out the Master Lock and loaded in a copying
utility. The image of the Bag Lady pulled a spy camera
out of her oversized bag of goodies and began flipping
through Katanopolis' journal.

The handwriting would have been hard to read; it
was probably coded, but Dreama had a top of the line
translator that she would use back in the privacy and
safety of her own room.

She had almost finished when she noticed that the
last entry had not been encoded. She stared for a
second in disbelief, and the Bag Lady's jaw sagged
noticeably. The letters read:

LOOK BEHIND YOU!

Dreama turned. Katanopolis and two technicians
were standing behind her. She tried to jack out. The
Bag Lady ran through the men and crashed through
the door. She climbed out of the hole and stumbled
across the Athens countryside until she reached the
main system door that seemingly hung suspended in
mid air. Dreama leapt through into the drab hallway,
and was astounded to find that the tall, dark-haired
Greek still walked casually beside her.

"It's no use, my dear. We've already got you. We've
had you for the last four seconds, actually, but we
wanted to see exactly what it is you were after."

The Bag Lady reached the outer circuits of the
computer and instantly vanished into the much larger
general system where her virtual image shimmered

into nothingness, but it was too late. As Dreama awoke into the real world and shook off the trauma of jacking out, she saw that she was indeed surrounded by Hollings' security troops.

They were standing in her bedroom, their blasters pointed nonchalantly in her general direction. It was several moments before Katanopolis himself arrived in the flesh. His bearded face emerged at the edge of her door, and the scientist's concerned look suddenly changed to satisfaction. He had suspected that the pretty sanitation worker was the spy that had evaded security for so long, but the Bag Lady routine had thrown him a bit.

The decker looked nothing like her virtual image. Both were of average height, but Dreama had long red hair and deep green eyes as opposed to the Bag Lady's dirty brown hair and black eyes. Her body, like her wavy hair, was currently hidden beneath the drab gray of the sanitation uniform. Katanopolis was visibly excited just the same.

"Oh, my dear. You are in such trouble now."

CHAPTER FIVE

Wriggle Street

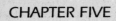

Klein talked casually with Vanessa, his favorite prostitute, on the bustling and overcrowded Wriggle Street. She was tall with a vaguely Oriental cast and she wore a long blue dress and dangling gold earrings. Her make-up was thick, but her honeyed words were even thicker.

She smiled seductively at the man she sometimes loved, and more often hated, and said, "Max will be in next week."

"Yeah, so?" Klein grabbed her by the waist and pulled her close. He and Guibert were wearing the Tiko street-beater uniform; Brodie skirmisher vest, tan pants, bright orange corpsec soft cap, and a genuine leather jacket — a sure mark of wealth or corporate favor.

"So ..." she nibbled on the policeman's ear. "He's short on men. Something got one of his ships and wasted half the crew."

Vanessa had been trying to get Klein to sneak away from Tiko and join up with Max Hunt, a bounty hunter/pirate/mercenary of the most dubious nature.

And, of course, she would accompany him. Hunt's people, the Jaegers, weren't known for their social skills, but they were probably the most successful and, correspondingly, richest band of over-armed hoodlums in this tiny sector of Consortium space.

Vanessa had been raised on a military colony where all of the citizens were required to fight in times of need. Those times had been frequent, and Vanessa was a hardened veteran by the age of sixteen. When her colony had finally given it up, the orphaned girl drifted from city to city and planet to planet until she finally wound up on Tiko III.

Max Hunt, on the other hand, was from a society where women were ornamental and thought of as relatively useless for anything but making babies. That's why Vanessa needed her on-again, off-again lover. Hunt would sign on an experienced marine in a second, and Vanessa was sure she could manipulate Steve into bringing her along. Once she was in, she could prove herself "under fire," and wouldn't have to depend upon her boyfriend's benevolence.

Klein pushed her back against the plasteel wall of her apartment building. "You want to join up with someone who just lost half his crew?"

Guibert snickered. Vanessa hated to be laughed at. If it wouldn't have gotten her in trouble, she would have disemboweled Guy in a second.

"It's just bad luck, honey," she said as she slipped her arm back around Klein's shoulders. She pressed her barely concealed breasts against his chest, and rubbed her long-nailed fingers across his neck.

Guibert would have instigated a fight between the two lovers if he hadn't secretly wanted to join up with the Jaegers himself. "Come on, Steve. Let's go to the *Hole*. We'll be off duty by the time we get there."

"Yeah. Sure." Klein gently pushed Vanessa away again and backed off. "Wanna tag along, Van?"

Tag along, she thought. *Not 'Do you want to go with me?' No, that would mean that we were together, in public, and that I wasn't just some whore that you can see whenever it's convenient.* "No thanks, Steve. I've got work to do."

Prostitution was acceptable on some worlds, and Tiko III was no exception. Vanessa, however, wasn't particularly proud of her newest occupation.

Klein and Guibert continued down Wriggle Street towards the *Worm Hole*. They had some time to kill, and the two men stopped in front of the flashing video monitors of *New You*, a cybernetic enhancement shop specializing in out-patient modifications. The monitors portrayed the transformation of a scrawny young man wearing thick glasses into a hulking brute with silver eyes and a very lethal-looking cybernetic claw, the Slasher Personal Retractable Protection System 4000. The last clip in the video showed the young fellow exacting revenge on those who had provoked the changes in the first place.

What they didn't say in the ad was that the poor schmuck would have shelled out about three years' salary for the replicating muscle cells, Slasher 4000, and Nere-Dorning optical housing (not to mention whatever was in them). He also would be thrown into the nearest Consortium or corpsec iso-cell for about fifty years for his troubles — if some bean-counter didn't decide to shove him out an airlock to save credits. *Some bargain*, thought Klein.

Guibert laughed and saw that Klein hadn't enjoyed the video. "What's with you lately, man?"

Klein was staring morosely down the street. Vanessa was talking to some kid, and disappeared with him into her apartment. "Nothin'." He turned back to face his companion. "Doesn't it bother you that some of our buddies got slagged the other day?"

Guibert turned his head and popped a couple of peanuts in his mouth. "Yeah. That crazy Arab owed me money."

Klein reached over and grabbed Guibert by the collar, grumbling in a low, angry, voice, "He gave his freakin' *life* for a friend, mate! It's a lot more than some would do. Present company included."

Two policemen arguing on the street attracted some attention, and Guy started to feel a little uncomfortable. His voice softened as he avoided Klein's intense gaze, "Hey, I'm sorry, man. I'm just dealing with it in my own way. Okay?"

Guibert wasn't stupid. His only thought about the incident on New Akron was that he was glad it hadn't been him that had gotten ripped apart. This wasn't the first time others had noticed his selfishness, but he had watched enough vid-slugs to know how to act.

Steve released his sometime friend roughly. "All right, let's go get a drink."

Out of his right eye, Klein saw a flash of motion. With veteran quickness he threw out his foot and tripped a dirty teenager who was running past. The youth sprawled into the street and an electric delivery cart had to swerve to keep from running him over completely, but still managed to thump loudly into the side his head.

"There aren't that many carts here, kid. You must be pretty unlucky." Klein reached down to help, and saw the contents of a spilled handbag beneath the wounded man. "You don't look like the type who carries a purse, matey." Klein chuckled and pulled a pair of plastic handcuffs from his belt hook. A woman was just running into view.

"Oh …" she panted. "Thank you, officer! I thought he was going to get away with all of my money!" She managed to stop her headlong flight by impacting with the smiling Guibert, who dutifully put his protective arm about her slim waist. The 'woman' was actually a girl. She wore a tattered longcoat and a green jumper, and her curly golden hair needed a good combing. Dark patches of dirt on her cheek helped blur the line between her obvious poverty and her budding beauty.

Klein didn't imagine the boy would have gotten much from her purse.

The brown-haired youth looked up from his position on the ground and smiled at Klein. He wore a beige jumper, patched here and there with rags of all colors, almost matching his prey in economic appearance. "Hey, corp-sucker. You just screwed up."

Klein was looking into the youth's narrow eyes, trying to decipher his meaning when he heard the sound of Guy's pistol being drawn from its holster. Even as he turned his head, he realized he had been had.

The girl was pointing Guibert's pistol at Klein, and waved it as he reached for his own. "That pistol's happy where it's at," she smiled.

The boy seemed to disagree and carefully reached for it, never losing eye contact with the red-haired officer. Had the con artist known Klein better, he wouldn't have liked what he saw in those glistening orbs. It was excitement.

In an instant, Klein wrapped his right hand around the boy's throat and rolled him into his grasp. His left hand, in an amazing across-the-waist draw, held the blaster. He was just raising it up to the boy's head when the girl fired.

There was a loud crack, and Guy was unsure who was the most shocked; the girl, for having pulled the trigger, or Klein for having his thigh ripped open. The hyper-accelerated particles struck him in the left half of his pelvis, just missing the struggling shield he was attempting to hide behind. The shock of the injury knocked him backwards with a painful scream.

Wriggle Street finally took notice and most of the citizens leapt behind carts or into the doorways of the various shops and apartments. Things had gone bad for the two thieves.

Guy stared stupidly at the girl. It still hadn't registered with him that she was in on the scam. The boy jumped up from Klein's bloody body and towards her.

"Cripes, Tally! You shot him!"

Guy's stunned mind finally recovered and he moved towards the couple.

"St-st-stop or ... I'll shoot ag-again!" she stammered.

CRACK! Klein, apart from being a hot-head, was a tough individual. He couldn't quite sit up on his shattered hip, but he still managed to roll over and squeeze off a shot that creased the girl's earlobe and shoulder.

She was in too much shock to scream, but dropped the gun and began to walk away, cupping the pulpy remains of her ear in her sieve-like hands and trying to blink away the previous few seconds of her life. The boy was also confused, and shifted his gaze from his fleeing companion to the marines before his "fight-or-flight" synapses finally kicked in. He overtook the girl in seconds and grabbed her by the arm, practically dragging her to one of the few alleys leading off of Wiggle Street.

"Call it in, you ass!" Klein managed to grunt through gnashing teeth.

Guy shook his head and grabbed the comm unit out of its holster. "Officer down on Wriggle, in front of *New You*. Get medtech down here and seal off the street. Two perps; one male in a beige jumper and a blond female in a green jumper and longcoat.

"*Sacre Bleu*, Steve! She really screwed you up!"

• • •

Tally and Rygil ran down the loading plank of the *Distant*, a tramp freighter bringing supplies to the Tiko chain. Tally was still trying to rub her nonexistent earlobe and Rygil was desperately trying to figure out how their simple scam had gone downhill so quickly. They lived in a squalid little apartment in the cavernous section of Tiko III called the Hive, but they were nowhere near there now. Rygil had thought to steal a couple of blaster pistols and sell them to the many mercenaries that frequented the city. With the funds from their heist and the other junk they'd stolen in the last few months, they had hoped to buy an economy class ticket to one of the larger worlds. Preferably one with more opportunities for their constant cons and scams.

The two had met on the streets of some run-down city on a backwater planet when they were very young. Life had seemed to be a contest between those who had and those who took, and Tally and Rygil considered themselves some of the best takers in the galaxy, but they had never actually had to shoot anyone. It was bound to happen, and they knew it, but it was a shock just the same. It didn't help any that *they* were almost killed themselves.

A cargo handler was pushing out a plastic crate labeled "Vid-Players" when he saw the couple hiding in the shadows of the loading bay. He could just make out that one of them was doubled over against the wall, and the other seemed to be soothing him or her. "Hey, are you two okay over there?"

Rygil was in a near panic himself, and was surprised to see the cargo worker twenty feet away. He grabbed Tally and dragged her back out into the street. The people had just started moving again when the two bandits emerged. Someone screamed, and the crowd dove back into their hiding places. Things were not going well, Rygil thought.

At the far end of the street, the one that ended with the corporate offices, the blast doors opened and a half squad of marines, five men, walked out. Someone shouted "Over there!" and pointed at Rygil and Tally, who was mumbling something about her earrings and trying to get the blood off of her hands.

"Shit!" Rygil yelled. He would be trapped if he didn't act fast. An abandoned electric cart was idling nearby, and he rushed toward it, dragging Tally with his off hand. The cart wasn't particularly fast; the marines could probably outrun it, but that wasn't what he was interested in. What he wanted was a distraction.

The marines were already running towards him and waving their pistols. In a few seconds, they would be in front of the huge glass windows that held back the waters of the *Critters'* two-thousand-gallon aquarium.

Rygil jumped into the cart, leaving Tally standing in the street, and stepped with all his weight on the accelerator. Someone yelled for him to stop and fired off a warning blast. The cart screeched forward and Rygil had to fight to get it on the proper course. Another shot rang out as the marines realized his plan, but Rygil managed to get his head down and roll out the far side without getting hit. He lay on the street and watched as the cart smashed into the front of the aquarium wall and ... bounced off.

The marines laughed and walked towards him. If he were to even breathe fast, they would probably turn him into a squishy pile of jelly. Suddenly, there was a brittle, cracking sound and Rygil saw the face of the lead marine contort into a twisted mass of aggravation. He looked to the aquarium face and saw a hairline crack ominously release a few drops of salt water onto the rocky street.

The crack suddenly branched like black lightning up the glass and the water rushed in rivulets. Rygil jumped to his feet just as the aquarium shattered and filled the street with two thousand gallons of water and hundreds of flopping fish.

The sudden dousing of the lead marine wasn't enough to cool his temper. And Stryker had always hated fish.

It took Rygil and Tally about an hour and a half to make it back to the Hive. The walk usually lasted about fifteen minutes, but the Wolverines were everywhere and Tally was rather easy to spot with her ragged ear and blood-drenched longcoat. It wasn't that there weren't lots of places to hide in the overcrowded city; back tunnels, alleyways, and rock formations dotted Wriggle and the adjoining streets, it was just that it was so damn *small*.

The oxygen ducts were the safest route Rygil knew. The corporation manufactured breathable oxygen by some process that neither of the two thieves understood, and pumped it into the ducts which writhed like worms just beneath the surface of the underground city. One of the larger tubes led into the Hive, and relatively close to their cell.

Space was always at a premium in the colonies, especially in the asteroid cities where the rock dictated the shape and size of the settlement. Thus were born the hives. A hive consisted of hundreds of crudely carved cells in which civilians and corporate employees could live. They were relatively cheap and a good sized cavern wall could hold over a hundred families. Access was provided by a mobile elevator system which traversed the length of each wall, sort of like a sliding ladder in front of a library bookshelf.

Rygil dragged Tally toward one of these lifts after emerging through the nearby oxy-fan. He figured corpsec had already made a quick check of this area by now and he could walk quickly but quietly to their barren apartment.

"Where are we, Ryg?" Tally asked as the lift carried them to the fourth level.

"We're home. You all right?"

"I think so," she stared away uncertainly. "Did you find my earring?"

"No." He dragged her into the cell and sat her down on the tiny cot they shared. "Listen, Tally. I've been thinking. Maybe we should sign up with Hunt and his group when they come around next month."

The Jaegers! You know how I feel about killing, Rygil." Tally looked out of the cell door and back towards Wriggle Street. "Do you think I killed him?"

"Nah. Marines got doctors that can fix anything. You probably just made it real hard for him to take a shit for the next week or so. Don't worry about it."

"What makes you think they'd take us anyway?" She was still rubbing her mangled ear.

Rygil stood abruptly and headed for the sink. His pride had been hurt. He considered them two of the finest thieves in the galaxy, Tally was a little more realistic. "I heard they needed some people. It's good timing is all."

Every cell had a tiny kitchen area with a molecular accelerator (for cooking) and portable distillery (to recycle bodily fluids). Rygil turned the faucet handle and watched as murky brown goop dripped into the pot he had planned on making coffee in. "Damn it, Tally. Didn't you get this thing fixed?"

"No, stupid. We're poor, remember? What am I supposed to pay with, my good looks?"

That hit a sour note with Rygil; they had discussed Tally becoming a prostitute, or rather she had, but he had strictly forbidden it. Neither had any claim over the other, but he remained adamant on the subject. Tally had only mentioned it to get him to prove his jealousy anyway. Jealousy often substituted for love in their relationship.

"Damn!" he shouted as he threw one of their two pots into the sink. "We're never going to get off this rock."

Tally laid back on the cot and continued to rub the remainder of her ear. She had almost completely forgotten about the incident in the street. She was like that.

"Sure we will, Ryg. One or two more good heists and maybe we could even get a ticket to Teraxiter."

Rygil placed his hands on the sink, stepped back, and let his upper torso fall between his arms in a sort of stretching motion. "You mean the place where all the corp-jerks go on leave? Hmmm. That would be a good place to go. Lots of boozed-up miners and paper-pushers looking for a place to spend their cash. Yeah. We could do pretty well there." His voice betrayed his renewed enthusiasm.

"There's a Teraxian ship that tunnels to all the corporate outposts and ferries people back around the system. I heard it's going to be stopping here soon; maybe we could hitch a ride."

Rygil stood and walked over to his best friend and constant companion. She scooted over to share the cot and they lay there with their arms around each other, looking out over the dim lights of the dreary sprawl below. The gleam was back in Rygil's raccoon-like eyes. "Yeah, Tal. I think this is gonna work out. Why, I bet Teraxiter is just full of suckers."

CHAPTER SIX

The Tourister

The *Tourister* wasn't full of suckers. It was full of bodies. And pieces of bodies.

The ship was owned by a transport company that circled one small portion of the frontier, a portion that happened to include the Tiko and Randall-Hollings chains, among others. Once its rounds were made, the vessel deposited its cargo on Teraxiter, a jumping-off point somewhere between the outer worlds and this section of the frontier. Gambling, whoring, and almost anything else made the planet attractive to bored corporate workers who spent most of their time in the mines or stuck behind a desk typing in mundane paperwork.

The *Tourister* was usually permeated with drunkenness and laughter. Now, the blasted hulk of the luxury liner drifted in cold silence.

A Randall-Hollings marine was the first through the breach. They hadn't *made* the hole, but they were using it for a door since the ship's automated systems weren't functioning. The *Constantine* had picked up their distress signal several hours ago, and they had just now arrived to attempt a rescue.

Scorch marks surrounded the hole, and it looked as if the attackers had entered via the same breach. The scout cautiously entered the room beyond the makeshift entrance and saw that there were more of the burn marks inside. Other than that, the chamber was barren and he quickly moved through to a doorway on the opposite wall. After signalling to his remote guide that he was moving on, the scout stepped into the bluish hallway.

Almost instantly he leapt back into the first room. The larger half of a steward's torso spun slowly in after him, the head and most of the limbs seemingly ripped off from the pulpy stumps that remained. The scout wanted to vomit, but that could be extremely dangerous inside a sealed suit, so he swallowed his stomach's physical protest.

The scout pushed the gruesome body aside and watched as it floated casually into the nearby wall. He returned to the hallway, but the sight that awaited him was a shock to even his veteran eyes. There were more bodies, and pieces of bodies, floating and spinning through the corridor. The weightlessness accounted for the floating, but what was moving them around? He looked around and saw that the oxygen and heating units were still functioning on emergency power. The air currents they produced were randomly catching the bodies and blowing them about like ping pong balls in front of a hair dryer.

The crystallized pools of buoyant blood he had seen before, and carefully avoided the grotesque obstruction. The remains looked like civilian passengers or *Tourister* crewmen. There didn't seem to be any remains of the attackers. They would have taken some losses, even against the lightly armed security men. *Ah*, he thought, *the pirates must've taken their dead with them. To cover their tracks*. That made a little more sense.

"Hendrickson? What is your status?" the receiver in

his ear cracked.

"Cripes, Sakk! You scared the shit outta me! I'm just entering the first hallway."

"Proceed. Left, then another left. Then straight until you see the lift shaft."

Hendrickson could imagine the guide, Sakk, sitting in the safety of the search and rescue vessel attached like a leech to the outside of the *Tourister*. She would be staring into a screen filled with the vector image of the ship, guiding her scout to the bridge. Hendrickson's mission, in lieu of rescuing survivors, was to recover the black box, a record of the last few days of the crew's lives. Some record of the attack would no doubt be recorded there, and Hendrickson's boss, Todd Hollings, could prove his right to salvage.

Sakk watched as the yellow blip that represented Hendrickson maneuvered towards the lift. The penetrating sensors of the S&R ship gave her a perfect blueprint of the *Tourister*, and she used this to maneuver her marine through the maze, much like a child playing a video game.

"You should be able to see it now. Are the doors open?"

Hendrickson was standing in the middle of the main corridor on the fourth level. The lift doors were indeed ahead but looked as if they were blown open by the same weapon that had left the scorch marks in the other rooms. More of the mangled corpses bobbed about the hallway, and Hendrickson used the tip of his laser to knock them away.

"Yeah. Something's blasted 'em off the track, but the cables inside look like they're intact. Car's smashed at the bottom, so there shouldn't be any obstruction. Switch to level three on my mark. Three … two … one … switch." He stepped out into the shaft and used the dangling cables to propel himself upwards.

Sakk lessened the intensity of the scanner and instantly brought up the image of the next level of the cruise ship. He was moving up fast, so she quickly flipped through the next eight levels until she came to the end of the lift, where the bridge and the valuable black box would be. The elevator itself probably wouldn't have gone this high unless one had the proper clearance card, but the ghostly crew of the *Tourister* wasn't arguing.

The penetrating scanners couldn't tell the difference between flesh and steel, but the thermal imager could. None of the *Tourister's* current occupants were emitting heat, so Sakk was surprised to see three red dots hovering just near the lift shaft where Hendrickson would emerge in less than three seconds.

"Hendrickson! Hold your position! There's three blips two levels above you!" There was no reply. Had he heard her message? Was she too late? No, his yellow signal was still moving up the screen. "Stop! Hold your position! Can you hear me? Acknowledge!"

She was screaming at him. The other guides surrounding her leaned over in their chairs, watching excitedly. One of her friends switched on the video channel and Sakk's screen filled with Hendrickson's view.

The micro-camera was mounted on the left side of the marine's helmet, so Sakk could see almost all of that Hendrickson could. There was a body pinned to the wall by some sort of jagged, short pole. The head hung limply from the neck, and it was turned so that Hendrickson and the attendant guides could see it plainly. The expression frozen on that face was one of stark terror, and it would remain in Hendrickson's nightmares forever.

Most of the hair was burnt off and the body was still smouldering slightly; this accounted for the blip on Sakk's screen. It was very strange for a body to be burning in the icy vacuum of space, but nearby oxygen tubes were still spraying the corpse with the flammable gas, feeding the consuming flame.

"Somebody's ... pinned him to the wall," the marine muttered. "With the base of a chair."

Now that he had said it, it was obvious that the post of a crewman's seat was rammed through the man's chest and stuck in the wall behind. Hendrickson wondered if he had caught fire before or after being pinned, and decided that it must have been before from the expression on his face.

He pulled on the cable and propelled himself onwards. His scout armor brushed the corpse, and pieces of charred meat spun into the oxygen stream. Sakk heard a murmur over the comm as Hendrickson pulled himself over the lip of the floor.

"More bodies in here," he said. Sakk and the other guides saw through the video link that several of the officers were impaled, mangled, or tied by sparking wires to the computer screens and consoles of their ruined helm. It was a gruesome sight, and Holling's marines were silent for some time. Sakk jumped when Hendrickson finally spoke again. "Somebody must've been pissed off."

"Yeah …" Sakk whispered.

All of them had seen bodies before, many in worse shape than these. They had seen the innards crystallize in the icy coldness of space, and they had seen the frozen, floating blood pools hovering near their ruptured hosts. But never, in all of their collective experience, had they seen such a morbid display of deliberate malice. Whoever had done this had gone beyond revenge; beyond sending a message; they were just plain *evil*.

• • •

Hollings could be a little like that. Todd leaned back in his chair twelve hours later and watched the vid-slug that had recorded Hendrickson's entire exploration.

"Damn, those critters are mean."

"Yes," replied Katanopolis in a contemplative voice. He rubbed his bearded chin, it was a habit he had picked up from watching too many slugs about scientists. "And quite powerful, it seems. Perhaps they are more dangerous than we had originally guessed?"

Todd spun around in his plush chair and faced the white coated Chief of Technology. "You aren't getting cold feet on me now, Kat?" he grinned.

"No. It's just that I would have expected them to lose a few of their own in the fight with the *Tourister's* security forces."

"Oh, come now, Kat. Those Teraxian rent-a-cops only have pistols. But I'd bet a couple o' thousand creds our boys could've handled this with McGinleys and pulsers. Plus, we're smarter than those half-wit bureaucratic stooges."

That seemed a dangerous conclusion. "What makes you say that, sir?"

"Look how they tore into the *Tourister*. No commander in his right mind would send his men through a hole that size. A couple of men with adequate weaponry could have covered that hole for days." Todd stood up and walked to his private bar. He poured himself something that Katanopolis didn't recognize, and swallowed it in one quick gulp.

As he did so, Kat thought that perhaps his employer was right, but he could also think of two other reasons why the beings they had been studying for the last two months might have taken such a tactical risk. Either they were so quick that they felt they could exploit the breach before the dimwitted Teraxian forces could react, or they were so powerful the risk was inconsequential.

"Did we ever find out anything about the Akron attack?" Kat asked.

The overweight Hollings gulped down another of the strange drinks. "Yes. Seems the Wolverines are down by three, " he snickered. He was going to come out on top of that smart-ass Kelassiter this time.

Even if it killed him.

CHAPTER SEVEN

Tiko's Fury

K elassiter was a little nervous when Thaddeus brought him the drone's report. "Looks like another iridium deposit, Terrin."

"How big?"

"Big enough to go after."

"I don't know. We're looking a little weak right now with four marines out of action."

"Didn't you put in for replacements?"

"Of course, but it's going to take a while for the courier to get there, and then the damn transport has to make it all the way back out to the butt end of the galaxy!"

The scientist pushed his glasses up onto his nose, ignoring his boss's misdirected aggravation. Science had long since eliminated the need for such devices (except as an affectation), but Thaddeus Dumois was a little strange. Science was his life. He lived, breathed, ate, and drank the mechanical, geological, and physical wonders of the universe. He had invented several gaseous detection instruments, and even helped develop the Nere-Dorning optical enhancers. He had trained at the Tiko Academy for the Development of General Science, a school designed exclusively for their scientists who would be stationed aboard remote stations and constantly be called upon to explain, in layman's terms, virtually every scientific oddity that could occur in the isolation of the colonial frontiers. Thaddeus Dumois was a genius, and Kelassiter couldn't have functioned without him, but he had one particularly unusual character trait.

He was techno-phobic. When his overtaxed eyesight finally gave out at the tender age of twenty-two, he had simply gone to the academy's hospital to buy a cyber-optic system that would replace, and even enhance, his normal vision. Dumois paid for and reported for the surgery, but found himself in an inexplicable state of panic when the med-tech had shown him slides of the procedure. Pictures of surgeons carelessly removing his *own eyeballs* and stuffing the exposed optic nerve into the new mechanical housing painted the viewscreen of his brain with bloody terror. Thad had called in a lot of favors to get a pair of bi-focals made that weren't fitted *behind* the iris.

Kelassiter knew the story, the scientist had gotten drunk one night and spilled his whole psycho-history. Terrin looked at his ill-sighted friend and smoothed back his hair. "How big?"

Thad flipped through a print-out, stabbed at something with his pen, and answered, "Probably a hundred thousand tons or more of impure iridium. Definitely worth checking out."

Kelassiter stood and jammed his hands into the back pockets of his slacks, then turned and looked out over the busy ants of Wriggle Street. The extra profit would do wonders for his city and his career, maybe even net him a better post back in the inner worlds. "Okay. I'll authorize an armed recon of the rock to get a better estimate of its tonnage. But this time I want the whole company out."

Thaddeus was horrified. He was no tactician, but it didn't take a genius to figure out that if all the marines were out on a mission there would be no protection for the city itself. "The whole company? We'll be wide open for attack!"

"Yes. But I don't want an understrength force out there when we still don't know what hit us on Akron. And besides, we've still got the automated defense systems and the militia, and I'll double the fighter patrols."

Thad looked away, a little confused. He saw the wisdom in concentrating the exploration team, but couldn't help feeling a little uneasy. He didn't trust the automated defenses — several torpedo-firing pods secreted about the surface of the rock — and had even less faith in the militia — the city's miners armed with spare blasters and Brodie skirmisher armor. Kelassiter obviously felt that this was enough, and Thad had no real platform of experience to argue from, but it frightened him just the same. But then again, so did his toaster.

Terrin placed his hand on the one-way glass, and stared hard at the rabble below. Two men were fighting over a woman outside an off-duty station nearby, and one punched the other hard enough to send the man spinning to the ground. "Well, maybe we should keep one squad, at least."

Stryker was coating the inside of his armor's visor with an anti-fogging solution when his intercom sounded. It was Terrin.

"Jonn, get your boys ready. I've got a job for you."

"Be there in five," he grumbled.

It was his job as a crusty sergeant to grumble about any work that passed his way. If the truth were to be told, however, he was ready for some action; and possibly another chance at whomever had jumped the Wolverines on New Akron.

Five minutes later, he was in Terrin's office.

"Looks like we found some more of the heavy stuff, Jonn."

"Great. I'll get second squad ready." He turned to leave; the briefing would be downloaded into the *Tyrannosaurus'* computer before takeoff, so he had little else to discuss with his boss.

"Actually, Stryker," Terrin halted him with his 'I've got a surprise for you' voice. "I want you to take them all. Or, at least, all but first squad. I figure they need a break."

Jonn turned and leveled a hard gaze at his employer, trying to fathom the reasoning behind his order. "That's nuts. The *Constantine* is hardly a day away. Hollings finds out we're gone, he'll jump you like a sailor on a two-credit whore." Colorful expressions were also in his job description.

"Maybe. But he's not going to find out. I'm not going to log it in for another day and first squad won't even be told you're gone."

"They'll figure it out when they haven't seen us for several hours."

"I'm sure, but by the time they do and word gets out," he narrowed his eyes sharply, "*if it gets out*, you should be on your way back home."

"Assuming nothing happens to us."

"Actually, Jonn, I'm kind of hoping that it does."

"Thanks."

"I've got confidence in your ability to handle it, and I hate not knowing."

"Not knowing what?"

"What hit us on Akron."

"Recon by fire, huh? Sounds wonderful."

Terrin just smiled.

• • •

In two hours, the last three squads of the Wolverines were strapping themselves into the *Tiko's Fury*. The corvette class assault ship was big enough to carry the entire company and armed to the teeth with four Titan ship-to-ship torpedoes, no less than eight pulse cannons, and four heavy lasers to slow burn a hole into an enemy's side. The sudden loss of interior atmosphere could be devastating to the crew inside, which was, after all, the real object of the fight.

There was a metallic "clunk" somewhere outside as the magnetic anchors were released and the *Fury* lifted itself out of the city's launch bay. "Flight crew to exploration party, ship is now en route to target. Prepare to accelerate."

Stryker and the rest steeled themselves for the sudden kick of the *Fury's* thrusters. Once it was two miles beyond the slowly spinning city of Tiko III, all four of its burners kicked in and thrust the ship into the clutter outside the first layer of the shatterzone.

The trip would take several hours, and the marines did what men of their profession had been doing since they were first transported in ships 800 years ago. They slept.

Stryker never dreamed. He didn't have enough imagination for it. But he did have nightmares. In his tortured mind, he saw Lucretia returning to the streets, like Klein's girlfriend, Vanessa. The two women had actually been friends once. *Or had they been something more?* The idea at once excited and disgusted him, and the cerebral folds of his mind flipped over to unveil a new horror.

Kelassiter hated Todd Hollings. Everyone knew that. But what if he had sold out to the corporation he represented? What if he had sent the Wolverines to some worthless hunk of rock so that the gluttonous fingers of Hollings could encircle Tiko III and leave a slimy trail across its rocky exterior? In Stryker's troubled mind, he could just see his boss standing there with a grin spread from ear to ear and a handful of cartoonishly oversized credits.

But Jonn had known Terrin for years. He would never sell out his own city. *Would he?*

Next fear. He was standing on New Akron. Graves had just exploded, and Shaick was in the process of flipping backwards in a vibrant display of gore. Duncan ran towards him, but something in the nearby smoke, something with jaws, was grinning at him. There was a ripping sound and Duncan's arm whirled slowly through the air, landing ghoulishly in the thick dust of that damned moon. The veins didn't realized they weren't supposed to be working anymore, and sucked up some of the powder. *NO!* Jonn screamed, *If the dust got pulled up to Duncan's heart, it might kill him!* But that was silly; the arm wasn't even attached anymore.

Then the shoulder sphincters amputated the remainder of the stump and sealed the suit off from the environment. Except … they didn't seem to be working quite right. The sphincter hydraulics must be ruptured because the blades couldn't cut through the arm, it was more like they were … *gnawing* … through. There was a white piece of bone poking through the blood and meat of the arm, and the sphincter couldn't seem to cut it. Duncan was screaming inside his suit but the mike wasn't on. Stryker couldn't hear it, but it was deafening just the same.

Why don't they blow his head off? He knew it was going to happen; why didn't they just go ahead and get it over with? Duncan ran towards him, that damned sphincter still chewing on the unbreakable bone. He made it all the way to his commander and stretched out his good hand in a desperate plea for help. The hand thumped on Jonn's armor and somehow left a palm print even through the suit's metal hide. Duncan's pain must have been unbearable. *When does he get his head blown off?*

The wounded marine reached across his chest with his good hand and grabbed the bone with the vice-like grip of his power glove. The inaudible scream grew louder and Duncan's fear-stained eyes locked with Jonn's. He pulled on the bone, trying to let the suit seal before he lost all of his internal pressure and exploded like microwaved meat. The bone fed through the jaws of the sphincter, but it was taking the rest of his clavicle with it. Duncan cried tears of salty blood now and the crimson drops ran over the white of his exposed teeth. There was a crunching noise as he finally pulled his shoulder through the hungry maw.

Stryker couldn't watch the horrible spectacle anymore. He screamed and raised his blaster to Duncan's faceplate, usually a black mask though it was somehow visible in Jonn's nightmares. The men screamed together, primally, each knowing what must happen next and raging against whatever entity had decided this fate. Finally, Stryker raised his rifle to Duncan's head. The marred barrel scratched against the clear plasteel in a cacophony of screeching helplessness, slowly drowning out their bonding screams before deluging them in complete silence. Jonn drove his eyes shut, ground his teeth together, and pulled the trigger.

But there was no sound.

When he pried his eyes open millennia later, Duncan's head was still spinning through the air, his dead eyes staring deep into his leader's soul. *Why did you kill me, Sarge?*

And he *had* killed him. Hadn't he?

Suddenly, Klein was there. Standing in his face and yelling at him. "Why didn't you set a guard, Jonny? You screwed up, old man!"

Stryker had no answer. He wanted to run and hide, but then he'd be alone again. And anything was better than that.

• • •

"ALERT! ALERT!" There was a whining of high pitched sirens and the scream of the *Fury's* pulsers

71 ∎

firing at some unseen enemy.

Stryker woke in a cold sweat. His visor was still up, but a corporal named Juslk reached over and slammed it into place.

"Something's got a lock on us, Sarge!" the man beside him yelled.

"Whatta we do, Ryk?" screamed another.

Marines hated ship-to-ship battles. They had no control over the situation. All they could do was sit and wait for a torpedo or a laser to blow a hole through the wall and whoever was sitting there.

BOOM!!

Something rocked the rear of the *Fury*, probably a near miss by a torpedo. The pilot was swerving back and forth and the hull was sustaining multiple shots from some sort of mass projectile weapon. It sounded like someone had thrown a garbage can over the marine's heads and was beating it with an iron pipe.

Stryker still hadn't escaped the grip of his nightmare, and was growing more and more confused. Everyone was shouting at him to do something, but what the hell could he do strapped into a seat?

"Seal your suits," was all he could manage to get out. Most of them had done that already.

All of a sudden there was a series of holes in the hull of the ship and the oxygen and heat fled through the breach in a stream of cowardly white mist.

The alarm was whining on and off; the pilot was jerking around and losing the enemy's lock occasionally. It didn't seem to matter because there was a second burst that sheared off the rear of the *Fury* and took most of fourth squad with it.

Stryker saw the burning chunk rip apart and eight men scream for help before they spun out of sight. And there wasn't a damn thing he could do.

The icy vacuum of space was full upon them now, but the sealed armor protected the marines from its deadly embrace. They sat in silence now, desperately trying to figure out what they could do, but they were helpless in this sort of combat.

There was something bright behind them, a flash of light against the inky blackness of space, and something large and blue streaked through the opening made by the previous hit and exploded in their midst. Every man there expected to die from the blast, but it was the hundreds of tiny seeker heads that emerged from the missile casing that actually did the job.

Before they died, the marines tried to brush off the deadly limpet mines, but it was too late; the seeker bomblets struck home and stayed. There was a rippling explosion, starting with those spheroids nearest the missile and ending with those which had to fly toward the rear to find their unwilling host.

Stryker wanted to cry, but dead men shed no tears.

The pilots were still trying to maintain control when the bio-sensors connected to their passengers went blank.

"Tiko III, this is the *Fury*; we are under attack." The message wouldn't reach Tiko for another hour, but the communications officer knew that Kelassiter would want to know what happened in the last few moments of their lives. "Ship is breached and on fire from unknown missile type and multiple projectile hits; probably mass drivers. The cargo *is* lost." The other officers looked gravely at their friend, finally acknowledging the fact that the entire marine platoon had been destroyed. "Crew will eject in fifteen … fourteen …"

Everyone on the bridge locked their restraining straps into place and mumbled their individual prayers.

"… thirteen …"

SLAM! Another missile crashed into the side of the ship, just behind the sealed bridge.

A lieutenant screamed, "The lock's jammed! The pod won't disengage!" The bridge was designed to disengage from the rest of the ship and serve as a makeshift escape pod. But the young lieutenant's console clearly showed that the locking mechanism had been fouled, possibly welded together by the last hit.

"... twelve ..."

The lieutenant screamed, "Stop counting, damn it! I told you it's fraggin' jammed! We're dead! Dead! Dead! *Dead!*"

The commo-officer looked dumbly at his companion and turned solemnly back to his recorder. "Damn you, Kelassiter. Damn you."

Those were the last words he ever spoke.

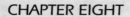

CHAPTER EIGHT

Samaritans

T he *Constantine* was less than half a light year away when its sensors picked up the high-speed distress beacon of the *Tiko's Fury*. The technicians on the bridge weren't surprised when their boss ordered them closer to the battle. They even bet amongst themselves whether Hollings would salvage the wreckage or strike another blow against Kelassiter by helping the attackers. When the *Constantine* finally arrived and dispatched a salvage tug, several crew members were out a month's pay.

Hendrickson always got the shit jobs. He *was* a very good scout, and he often paid for it by getting the toughest assignments. Maneuvering around in deep space and asteroid tunnels without a tether was considered one of the toughest.

Apart from being stealthy and alert, Hendrickson was blessed with a slender and muscular body. His armor was the McGinley Mark VII, one of the latest in scout armor design. It was lightly armored but bathed in a black masque of sensor- and light-reflecting paint and electronics, and it was thin enough that the man inside could be surprisingly agile. It fit Hendrickson perfectly.

His guide, Sakk, watched as he exited the hatch of the tug. He would be the hands, she the eyes and ears. Attached to his suit was a Jenner Personal Thruster System which shot flame out a traversable nozzle and thrust Hendrickson in whatever direction he wished to go. In this case, it was the wreckage of a Tiko corvette wedged deep inside a mammoth asteroid. What remained of the vessel had skidded along the jagged rock, and somehow wound up 200 meters below the surface in a deep hole. His velocity was increasing as he headed towards the wreck, and Hendrickson guessed that it had a modicum of its own gravity. "This sucker's huge."

Sakk answered, "The asteroid? Yeah, scanner says it's made mostly of iridium. It's even got some gravity. Must be worth a fortune. Say, did we do this?"

"Don't think so," Hendrickson answered as he glided towards the wreckage. "We didn't have any fighters out. Must've been pirates. Or an accident."

Hendrickson eased over to the hole and quickly thumbed the joystick that turned the propulsion nozzle up. This sent him into a steep dive and the scout was soon whizzing towards the cold hulk below. He had to be extremely careful; the asteroid's gravity wasn't enough to seriously interfere with his flight, but it might throw off his balance and cause him to slam into the jagged rock, an event which might pop open his lightly armored scout suit.

He could just make out a few lights here and there and saw a mass of tangled bodies lying in the rear of the hull. These he ignored for now and headed straight for the bridge. It was easy to get around the wreck; it had lodged sideways and probably would have fallen had there been any more gravity here. As it was, the metal hung loosely on the jagged walls of the tunnel, so he could move around inside if he was careful.

The pilots were smashed against the stone and their blood had already frozen in crystalline sculptures about their mangled forms, forming what looked like giant red pancakes. Hendrickson reached in and turned off the distress signal. Hollings had been very clear about that, he didn't want Tiko coming around until he had gotten a chance to either salvage it or "rescue" any survivors.

The golden rule of salvage was that if there were any survivors, the ship had to be turned over to its owners — minus fees for towing and medical costs. If there were no survivors, then any and all parts of the vessel were eligible for selective reclamation. Needless to say, there were surprisingly few survivors of interstellar mishaps, but lots of salvaging.

Strangely, however, the boss had been very clear on this one. Any survivors were to be brought back onto the *Constantine* for immediate medical care. Hendrickson guessed this was to appease Kelassiter after the recent war, maybe to lull him into a false sense of security or some other executive bullshit.

He triggered the joystick again, gently this time, and slowly floated up to the peeled hull. "It's a mess in here, Sakk."

The guide shifted her glance from the vector image of the hole and the floating green blip that was Hendrickson, to the video monitor above. Her screen was filled with the sight of Brodie suits blasted, melted, punctured, singed, shattered, and ripped. It was grisly, but nothing compared to the *Tourister* massacre they had explored last week. She looked down at the screen again. There was Hendrickson, the moving green blip, but what was that red thing? "Shit, Hendrickson! One of 'em's still alive! Better grab him quick, the heat scan's weak!"

The scout pulled away several bodies before he

came to one that was relatively whole. The name on the suit said Juslk and identified him as a corporal. Hendrickson leaned towards the faceplate and saw that the tiny light from the bio-monitor said that the bloody thing inside was still alive. Barely. The scout rarely got to save lives; he was usually ordered to take the salvage instead. This was an entirely different feeling, and he decided he liked it.

"It's okay, buddy. I'm gonna get you out of here," Hendrickson said though he knew the marine couldn't hear him. There were several small holes burned through the breastplate, right in the thickest part of the man's armor. Fortunately for the victim, one of the sliding plates within the thick chestpiece had done its job and sealed the breach from the icy vacuum around him. Inside the expensive armor, it was the numerous auto-injectors, heart massagers, and auto-docs that had kept the man alive.

Hendrickson grabbed the man by the arms and thrust upwards. Several more of the corpses slid off as he did so, resettling into a mass of twisted metal, flesh, and icy blood, and soon the two men were rocketing back toward the tug.

Two hours later, the tug had finally managed to maneuver the mag-cables down into the hole, and Hendrickson had attached them to the strongest remaining sections of the hull. Since the craft was pulled straight up, the bodies remained in the cup-like rear hull rather than falling slowly back towards the dense asteroid.

In the medical bay of the *Constantine*, Randall-Hollings med-techs fought to save the life of Corporal Juslk. Several of the internal organs in his torso had flash-boiled and been blown apart by the hydrostatic shock of the penetrating explosive, and his ribs had turned into shrapnel factories. The medical bay on the *Constantine* was state-of-the-art, but nothing short of a miracle could save Juslk. The doctor pumped his heart full of electricity via a wire inserted directly into the myocardium, but it was no use. The marine died without waking.

Just as the technicians finished washing off the dead man's blood, Todd Hollings appeared. He walked confidently into the emergency room, grinning from ear to ear and wiping some sort of grease from the corners of his mouth. "What's the situation, Doc?" he asked the head clinician.

"Well, sir," the surgeon looked at an LCD clipboard and traced his stylus across several lines of information. "Looks like he was a corporal. Corporal Hezzerat Julsk. Been in the ..."

Hollings went pale. The doctor, a man named Tryuis, began to get a little worried. His boss was known for his sudden and inexplicable temper tantrums.

"CORPORAL? What do you mean, *corporal*?" he was stammering like a child. A very powerful, and very dangerous child.

"Well s-sir, that's what the ID chip says ..."

Hollings turned and threw his forehead into the tiled wall, leaving a trace of blood there. An awkward period of silent tension passed while Tryuis and his assistants watched their exalted superior stalk about the room, mumbling something about sergeants and Brodie armor. Finally, Hollings seemed to decide something, wiped the blood from his forehead, and spoke. "Okay," he said with renewed calm. "How is he?"

Tryuis gulped. It was obvious that Hollings had wanted this man alive. How would he tell him that he had died only moments before? Tryuis guessed that Hollings had wanted to extract information for an impending attack or some such corporate nonsense, and he was going to be very upset when he learned he had missed his chance by mere minutes. No doubt Hollings would take out any anger on the bearer of this disappointing news. Tryuis bit his lip and looked nervously about the room. With a sudden snake-like smile, he turned to his medical assistant. "Carl, please inform Mr. Hollings of the patient's current state." The doctor looked rather pleased with himself.

Carl's eyes got as big as saucers and his stomach felt like it was turning inside out. Hollings turned and stared him dead in the face, just daring him to tell him that the marine was dead.

"Well," Carl began, "the patient has suffered a serious rupture of the sternum and massive damage to the internal organs, particularly those centered around the cardial region. Emergency procedures were effected to stop the bleeding in this area and synthetic blood producers were introduced into the patient's system to replace the enormous amount lost." He smiled at Tryuis.

Hollings growled and shifted his gaze towards the doctor again. "I didn't ask for a first-aid lesson, you pencil-necked freak. I want to know how he is!"

Tryuis was paler than Hollings now, but could see no other way out. "He's dead, sir."

Carl tended to Tryuis' nosebleed as Hollings ran screaming down the hall.

The tug had finally pulled the wreck into one of the huge repair bays of the *Constantine*. Four salvage specialists were beginning to strip off whatever they felt might be of use, and two orderlies were just now dragging the mutilated marines from their cold mausoleum.

Graz looked at the carnage and pointed at one of the corpses. "Cheez, Hank, lookit this one. Sumpthin's attached itself to his groin here and blown it clean open."

The other one turned casually and looked at the mess, "Yuck. Looks like his arm's gone too."

Graz nodded his head but then leaned in closer,

"No. I think it's just caught in this jagged metal here." The orderly grabbed hold of the wall and attempted to bend the steel outwards, but it was far too strong. "Hand me the saw, Hank."

The other man handed him the blade and stood back, munching casually on a chocolate bar. Graz cut into the trapped appendage and watched as the tool ate through the heavy alloy of the suit and the tender flesh of the arm within. He was greeted with a sickening spray of warm blood.

"Ah, cheez, Hank. This one's ..."

They looked at each other, dumbstruck. After all this time, there was only one way the marine's blood could spray.

"He's still alive ..."

CHAPTER NINE

Flashback

After the blast, Stryker could see hundreds of limpet-like spheroids leap from the missile housing and attach themselves to him and his men. Their visors concealed it, but the sheer terror on the faces of the men revealed that none of them had ever seen this type of weapon before. They had tried frantically to peel them off, but the devices had exploded seconds after contact and blown a shaped charge through the thick armor of the marines' suits.

Stryker went in and out of consciousness as the *Fury* continued to be blown apart before finally slamming into an asteroid. He could tell they were scraping rock because the ship's walls were being peeled back by the rough-hewn walls. Georges was still strapped into his seat when a jagged slab tore through the wall and ripped his pinned body in half. His warm blood had frozen in seconds and left a disgusting but eerily beautiful ice sculpture sweeping from the shattered remnants of his suit and corpse to the rear of the craft.

Then Stryker closed his eyes and allowed himself to slip into unconsciousness.

Reflexes caused him to turn into the wall, away from the explosion, and the mysterious flying mines had attached themselves mostly to his right side. He had seen one on his arm, two on his chest, and three on his leg and thigh before their collective blasts knocked him into a semi-aware state. Now there was a dull, throbbing pain slowly coursing through his body, but he was so pumped full of drugs he could hardly feel his teeth chattering.

Teeth chattering? he thought. That didn't make much sense. The Brodie suit could protect a man for several weeks in absolute zero. How could he be cold? There was really only one explanation. His chest must be so ripped up that the sealant system had been slow in covering the damage.

The extending plates that formed this system were tucked away in several locations, forming a redundant patchwork. The system was "smart," and could figure out exactly where a breach had occurred, activating only those plates necessary to quickly re-seal the suit. Of course, in the five or six seconds the metallic web had formed, Stryker's chest and upper body had already felt the effects of severe frostbite. The heaters were working overtime to keep him alive, and they would continue to work for several hours, but now, Jonn felt like he was sleeping naked in a freezer.

He attempted to raise his head, but someone was lying on his helmet. He was pretty sure he was upside down because he could feel the blood rushing slowly but surely towards his head. There was also a wet pool resting around his hairline, and it occurred to him that there must be gravity where the ship had finally landed; probably generated by the dense, iridium-filled asteroid they had come to investigate.

"Tudsl …" he tried to speak but nothing much came out. It felt like there was a large amount of fluid built up in his throat and lungs. He tried to cough it up, but …

83 ∎

AAAAH … his mind screamed as the pain wrenched through the barrier of narcotics. His lungs nearly burst from the effort and threatened to escape his chest cavity by the most violent means possible if he were to dare try that again. *Oh God, someone please help me!*

Mercifully, the suit shot him full of tranquilizers.

But that didn't last long. He was losing blood somewhere, he was sure of that. The coagulants administered by his armor should have stopped it a while ago, but something must have gone wrong.

There was still nothing to see and his body was trapped in a painful, contorted position. The only thing he was sure of was that he was upside down. He knew this because the pool around his head had now crept past his forehead.

And then it hit him. He was *alone*. The others must all be dead. He hadn't felt any movement in the last three hours save for *his* occasional flopping around like a fish out of water. His commander's armor was six-tenths of a millimeter thicker than the others, maybe slightly more than the shaped charge of the mysterious mines could penetrate. In spots, at least.

He was guessing about the three hours; it was hard to tell in the fleeting bits of consciousness allowed him, and the HUD was off to divert more power to the heating system. Regardless, Jonn felt like an eternity had passed since almost thirty of his friends had died screaming and helpless in the back of the *Fury*.. Maybe, his tortured mind screamed, he would soon feel the firm hands of a rescue worker dragging him from the wreckage.

Or maybe not. Maybe he was going to have to sit here for hours, hanging upside down and freezing and bleeding to death while some donut-eating tug-captain made his way across the sector to the crash site. Or maybe they wouldn't even find him at all. Maybe the wreck had drifted into the 'zone and no one could get to it.

Jonn thrashed again, writhing like a worm on a hook. But the movement told him something. His right arm was caught in the metal wall of the ship. He had seen the wall behind him rolling up like a carpet just before he fell unconscious, and now realized that it must have rolled his arm up with it. It felt like it was twisted around several times, and he knew he would be screaming if his veins weren't full of pain-killers.

And then there was the cold. The air from the heater was only lukewarm now; power must be getting low. There was no way of telling how long it would last without the suit's near omniscient interface. Maybe it was better that way. He wasn't so sure he wanted to know just when he would die. But the waiting was nearly as painful. In the meantime, all he could do was pray that someone would save him in time.

Before the damn heater finally gave out.

Just don't let me die alone! Please don't let me die alone!

Stryker passed out again.

When he awoke, he felt sure that several hours had gone by. The liquid in his helmet was up to his eyes now. It had slowed but never stopped. He imagined the flow had lessened because he was slowly freezing to death and the blood was moving a little more sluggishly now.

Suddenly he felt a jolt! Something had bumped into him! *Thank God someone else is alive! I'm not alone anymore!*

Nothing else happened for a while, but Jonn waited anxious and blind for any sign of salvation. And then … LIGHT! Someone had shone a light directly into his right eye! (He couldn't seem to open the other one.) *Someone is rescuing us!* Jonn wanted to open his eyes again, but the light had seemingly blinded the one eye he could get open. Seconds passed like hours and his screaming mind told him to open his damned eyes or they were going to think he was dead and leave him, but it hurt *so* bad.

There was another bump. He could stand it no longer and forced the cooperative eye open. Someone was moving around above him, hovering. The figure was illuminated in some sort of brilliant glow. Was it a search light, or ... was it something else? The way it flickered, and cascaded in mote-filled rivulets of light, it almost looked like ... *Is that an Angel? Am I dead?* Stryker didn't really believe in God, not like most people seemed to anyway. But now that he was seeing an Angel, he was more than ready to change his religious beliefs.

But ... where's its wings? And why does it have a thruster? He would've laughed at this if his confused mind wasn't begging the world to make some sense and get him out of this jagged metal coffin.

Now Jonn saw the figure rummaging through the flesh and steel carnage that had been his friends. It moved a little closer, and Jonn's straining eye made out its features clearly. *That's no Angel! It's a marine! And oh, sweet Christ, he's one of Hollings'!* The attack didn't seem like their work, and Jonn had never seen a missile full of self-propelled limpet mines before. Besides that, he knew he had been out for quite a while already, and that also indicated that Hollings wasn't behind the attack. Otherwise, they would have been on top of the *Fury* hours ago.

Stryker fought to keep his cowardly mouth from calling out, to scream for help, to cry like a baby if the scout would take him out of here, but he knew better. If there was any way he was going to survive this, he would have to wait on Kelassiter. If Hollings' men found him alive, they would shoot him on the spot just for the salvage rights. And that was assuming it wasn't them that had attacked the *Fury* in the first place.

Tears of frustration rolled up Stryker's face and added to the growing pool in his helmet.

It was an hour before Jonn felt the wreck being dragged from the asteroid. It took another forty-five grueling minutes to maneuver the ship through the tunnel before the *Fury* finally cleared the last turn and pulled free of its jagged prison. Stryker was thrown over into a new position by the maneuvering, and the pool around his head was tilted at an angle that made it rise over his eyes and stop just short of his nostrils. It seemed to be made mostly of blood, but there was something chunky and cold mixed in with it that settled uncomfortably between his eyes.

The ship was getting jostled around and the sickening soup occasionally lapped up and ran down his nose. Each time he blew it back out, causing shards of pain to shoot through the cartilage of his nose and slam him back into a delirious stupor.

Oh God. Oh God. Oh God. Stryker had suddenly become very religious. He was very close to drowning in his own treacherous blood. *How much longer can this go on?*

The coldness must have gone away since Jonn could no longer feel anything in his chest. That or it had frostbitten him into numbness. He didn't really care to dwell on it, the blood surrounding his head was the immediate concern.

After the fourth blood-sneeze, he felt the ship settle into its final position. If things were happening like he thought, the *Fury* was now hanging from a salvage hook in one of the *Constantine's* enormous repair bays. He knew it would be a while before the salvage teams got to the bodies, and passed out.

The last time Jonn awoke, two RH crewmen stood over him. He could just make out their voices, but had no idea what they were saying because the drying blood had caked in his ears. Had his head not been tilted at just the right angle, Jonn would have drowned long ago.

He tried to move his arm but felt it still caught up in the wreckage of the near wall. One of the workers pointed at it and said something to the other. The second man was eating some sort of candy bar, and shrugged nonchalantly. Then he reached out of Jonn's sight, and handed the first man something that looked like a ...

oh no. oh no. oh no.

... saw.

CHAPTER TEN

Hollings' Relief

The slave-girl bled from more places than she cared to think about when a low beep sounded from somewhere in the darkened room. Her sweaty tormentor rose from the bed, wrapped a towel around his flabby gut, and walked to the ship's intercom.

"What?" Todd Hollings demanded in a guttural growl.

Dr. Tryuis' shaky voice crackled feebly over the line, "We've found another survivor, Mr. Hollings, a sergeant named Jonn Stryker. We've stabilized him, but he's a real mess and the repairs will be expensive. How shall I proceed?"

There was a long pause as some recessed part of Hollings' scheming mind recalled his original intentions, plans he had scrapped upon hearing of the previous survivor's demise. Now a grin seeped out of his fleshy face, finally exploding in a blinding display of white teeth and pink gums. "I'll be down shortly. Signal Dr. Katanopolis to join me in the sick bay. Immediately."

"Yes, sir." Dr. Tryuis hoped he wasn't going to be punched in the nose again.

The marine was a mess, but Hollings was sure it was that bastard Stryker, Kelassiter's favorite engine of destruction. One eye had been pulped along with most of his face, his right arm had been amputated (and recently, it seemed), and his pelvis looked like jelly; but the son of a bitch was still alive.

That was all that Dr. Tryuis got to see before Katanopolis and Hollings ordered him from his own operating room. He wasn't sure what they had planned for the unfortunate marine, but they wore the perverted expressions of little boys dissecting a live frog.

• • •

The waiting was killing him. Terrin paced back and forth, anxiously awaiting news from the salvage and rescue ship he dispatched hours ago. The courier carrying the distress beacon had tunneled in and broadcast its warning, but no subsequent messages had been sent. And that was a very bad sign.

Terrin knew he had really blown it this time, and now Jonn and the others were most likely dead. If the salvage ship didn't send back some good news, Kelassiter would most likely have to evacuate the city. Fast. He flipped open the intercom and spoke softly to his long time friend, Thaddeus Dumois.

"You think it was Hollings?"

Dumois was in the deep space transmission room, alone. He had dismissed the two regular operators so that he might keep the *Fury's* fate from the rumor-hungry technicians. "Who knows? It's a little bold. We prove he did it and Fleet would revoke his mining rights."

"Then who?"

"Pirates, maybe?"

"I don't think shatrats could get near the *Fury*."

"Yes, I'm sure you're right."

Terrin nodded in his lonely office. But did Dumois' voice sound just a little doubtful, like he wasn't sure whether to believe the word of a man who had just destroyed most of his city's defense force?

"Ah, there's no sense crying about it 'til we hear from the rescue ship."

Thad heard Terrin rise from his creaking recliner, and then the sound of ice falling into a glass. He could use a drink himself, but he was afraid the ice maker would tear his hand off.

Two and a half hours later, the tired scientist noticed he had tapped his fingers until the nails had began to bleed from the cuticle. He rose to call for some disinfectant when the voice of the salvage captain finally sounded from the ether. Terrin also listened from the darkness of his office.

"It's bad, Mr. Kelassiter. Looks like the *Fury* smashed into an asteroid; there's wreckage all over the place. The *Constantine* is picking up the pieces, but I can't be sure they're responsible. The *Fury* could have gotten away from a flagship in a heartbeat. I'm about to initiate contact with the Hollings ship, but I wanted to send this message before. Just in case."

Terrin and Thad knew what that meant. Captain Jameson wanted to give them a spot report before contact just in case the *Constantine* blew the tiny tug out of the sector. It was impossible to tell if Hollings was behind the attack or just happened to be in a convenient location for the clean-up, but either way, Tiko III was virtually defenseless.

And Todd knew it.

Hollings and Katanopolis were still in surgery when the bridge received Captain Jameson's transmission.

"Ahoy, *Constantine*. Under treaty of the Consortium of Worlds, the crew of the rescue ship *Searcher* welcomes you into the Tiko corporate sector."

"Ahoy, *Searcher*, this is *Constantine*; Captain Nichols on the bridge."

"*Constantine*, we've lost a small vessel somewhere in this area and request your assistance in finding our ship and crew."

"A small ship?" Nichols chided. "Haven't seen anything like that around here ..."

Robbie Jameson grimaced. Nichols was playing a game with him. The surly veteran could see right through the act; Nichols wanted him to admit to losing a corvette. Unfortunately, Robbie wasn't known for his tact. "Okay, Captain Nichols, then how about a fully armed corvette-class attack vessel? Does that ring any bells?"

"Ah yes, that's a little clearer. We have the wreckage hanging in our salvage bay right now. I'm afraid there isn't much left."

Robbie fumed. Nichols wasn't volunteering any information — he wanted to humiliate his rival and Robbie would have to go along with it, but he didn't have to like it.

"Are there any survivors?" he grumbled. He knew there wouldn't be; it interfered with the salvage rights, but he had to ask.

"That's a negative, *Searcher*."

Robbie's heart sank. He knew the answer before he asked, but it hurt just the same. Several of the dead men, including Jonn Stryker, had served with him before he had been relegated to command of the rescue ship because of his age.

"Who's responsible for this?" There was rage in his voice, but it was unfocused. Strangely, Robbie doubted that Hollings was behind this. For one thing, he doubted that they could have pulled it off. The *Constantine* was certainly heavy enough to take out the *Fury*, but it was far too slow. A corvette could easily leave a ship of the line in the space dust long before her missile decoy pods and shields gave out.

"Not sure, *Searcher*. We found her this way. One man lived for a while, but our med-techs couldn't pull him through."

Sure, Robbie thought, *especially after they put a particle stream through his brain.* "Roger. We want the bodies."

"Of course, *Searcher*. We'll be happy to accommodate our friends at Tiko Corporation after the remaining armor and cybersystems have been removed from the corpses. All according to Consortium Salvage Law, of course."

It was butchery, pure and simple, but Consortium law came down hard on the side of the finder. Robbie's snarl betrayed his true feelings, and he could just picture Nichol's amused smirk, "Roger, *Constantine*. We'll wait."

"It could be a while, *Searcher*, would you like to get off that rat-trap and relax in our lounge for a few hours?"

Robbie just turned off the mike.

When the courier returned to Tiko III the second time, it only confirmed Terrin and Dumois' worst fears.

Thad tripped the return circuit and sent the drone tunneling back to the *Searcher*. The coffee on the console had grown cold an hour ago, but he poured it down his gullet in one quick swallow. His bandaged hand flipped on the intercom to Terrin. "Why?" he asked quietly.

There was no response. Kelassiter lay in his dark office with his leather boots perched on one end of the couch and his throbbing head on the other. Several Venusian Moonrises usually eased this sort of pain, but not today. Cheap booze wasn't going to stop it, but it was a good place to start. Terrin and Dumois had monitored the conversation and sat in their respective rooms in abject silence. Everything was over. Tiko III was Hollings' for the taking, and Terrin had lost one of his best friends in a bone-headed maneuver that a kindergarten kid wouldn't have tried. Terrin had made his career on gambles like that, and he guessed it was only a matter of time before the odds caught up with him.

But why did others have to suffer? He asked himself this again and again before finally rising from his leather chair and draining his last Venusian Moonrise. Terrin threw the glass into the sink, not caring if it broke, put on his ten gallon hat, and headed out of the corporate offices for the *Worm Hole*.

Dumois was just turning the commo room back over to the technicians when he spotted his boss from the other end of the hallway. Terrin stopped and looked pleadingly at his friend, but Dumois could offer no help and scurried away to his chambers. The executive's hat seemed to suddenly gain weight and force his head down towards the plush red carpet.

"I'm so sorry, Jonn. So sorry."

CHAPTER ELEVEN

Home

Captain Robbie Jameson and the crew of the *Searcher* waited for seven hours before Captain Nichols established communication again.

"Ahoy, *Searcher*, this is the *Constantine*."

Robbie jumped in his seat, startled from the sudden noise interrupting what had been a tense silence. The bridge had been a maelstrom of swearing and rage for the first three hours, but now things had settled into a dismal quiet. "Ahoy … *Constantine*." He said it slow, pronouncing each syllable through gritted teeth.

Nichols sounded amused. "It seems we have a survivor for you after all. We didn't find him 'til late; his bio-monitor must've cracked in the accident. I'm afraid this spoils our salvage rights, but we've already cut your corvette into little tiny pieces."

Robbie's jaw dropped three inches. This was unheard of. Because of the Consortium's salvaging laws, finding survivors was a very rare thing. For a corp run by Todd Hollings, it was an impossibility. Yet it had just happened.

Robbie was speechless.

"*Searcher*," Nichols broke the silence, "we assume you would like the remains of your ship and crew?"

"O-Of course," Robbie said hesitantly.

"Okay, Captain. We'll send a shuttle with your men in it and jettison the wreckage. Is that agreeable with you?"

What the hell is going on? he thought. "Roger, *Constantine*. You want to tell me why our boy pulled through?" It was a terrible breach of etiquette, but Robbie wasn't much for manners. Besides, something was really rotten here.

Nichols chuckled. "Not my decision, Captain. I'm just a ship jockey."

Twenty minutes later, the *Constantine* jettisoned a large cargo net full of the dissected remains of the *Tiko's Fury*. The *Searcher* cautiously approached the bundle, and harpooned it with towing cables for the long haul home. Once that was finished, Robbie signalled the *Constantine* and watched as a tiny shuttle issued from the gargantuan flagship and docked with his much smaller vessel.

He couldn't help but be nervous. What if this were all some elaborate trap? One squad of marines could easily take out his unarmored crew of five. But why would Hollings go to all this trouble to take out a simple rescue ship? It didn't make much sense, and Robbie assumed he was just paranoid. But if Hollings did try something, Jameson wasn't going down without a fight.

He and his bosun would greet the medical crew in the hallway leading to the airlock. They heard the boarding tunnel lock into place, and saw the green "All Clear" light illuminate as air rushed into the sealed chamber. The strap was already dangling from the holster of Robbie's blaster, and now he fingered the safety to the "off" position.

The wheel that would open the door began to turn.

If Robbie saw anything that looked like a weapon …

The door swung open and Robbie drew his pistol, instantly dropping into a firing stance. The long wait had gotten to him more than he realized.

The Hollings med-tech inside nearly had a heart attack as he dropped the front end of Stryker's plasma-tube. The thick casing cracked at the edges, and a gush of warm, red goo spilled onto the entryway around Robbie's feet.

"Oh my G … I'm sor … I …" was all the captain could manage to get out.

The goo was actually bacteria-saturated plasma. It greatly accelerated healing, provided oxygen to the lungs, and was filled with cannibalistic micro-organisms that prevented most infections from setting in. Of course, to affect the internal organs, the thick jelly was circulated through the lungs like air where it would slowly work its way into the bloodstream and throughout the rest of the body. It also contained a powerful anesthetic since breathing jelly could be rather unsettling to an already traumatized patient.

But it wasn't powerful enough to keep Jonn under when the tube cracked open on the airlock floor. He opened his eyes and mouth, but could only see a red blur and feel a thick, bitter fluid oozing around in his throat and lungs. His eleven-hour delirium wasn't over, and he thought that the rising blood in his helmet was finally drowning him.

The top of the tube was still intact, but one of Jonn's arms now shot through it, sprinkling shards of thick glass over the med-tech who had dropped it.

The medic's jaw dropped four inches. Vat tubes were made tough for just such an emergency. The man inside must be incredibly strong.

Jonn's arm continued to flail about the jagged hole he had made in the tube. The broken glass ripped his flesh and peeled it back from wrist to elbow. Beneath the slimy coating of blood and plasma, Robbie and the medic could clearly see ... *metal!*

"For God's sake, son! Help him!" Robbie screamed, but the medic, Carl, was still wary of the pistol. "Damn it!" Jameson raised his weapon and the med-tech dodged back against the side of the hallway.

BLAM! BLAM! BLAM! Robbie carefully blasted the remaining casing away, allowing Jonn to spill out of the tube in a wash of jelly, glass, and blood. Carl jumped on the marine almost immediately. Skillfully, the med-tech shoved a needle into Jonn's left arm and rammed a tube down his throat.

"What the hell are you doing?" Robbie screamed again. The rest of the crew was now poised behind him, weapons drawn and leveled.

Carl thumbed the tube in Jonn's throat and depressed the trigger on a micro-vac. "If you're going to shoot me, I suggest you wait until I get this jelly out of your friend's lungs or he's going to drown. This stuff bleeds oxygen in the open air and ..." SMACK! Jonn's flailing arm blindly smashed into Carl's nose, adding yet another shade of red to the ooze below.

Robbie and the bosun jumped into the mess and grappled with Stryker's metallic limb. With their help, Carl finally pumped the jelly out of the marine's lungs and shot him full of tranquilizer.

A short while later, Carl and Robbie placed Jonn on a treatment bed aboard the *Searcher*. Jameson was impressed by Carl's nosebleed and his ability to ignore it while fighting to save a man's life. He appreciated it even more when he learned that the nose was broken. But he still couldn't figure out why Jonn had lived. Hollings was either very afraid of Kelassiter, or he had something more devious in mind.

Terrin and Dr. Dumois were waiting on them when the *Searcher* touched down on Tiko III. Robbie and the bosun wheeled Stryker down the loading ramp, and the rest of the crew went to supervise the handling of the *Fury's* wreckage.

Terrin stopped the gurney and looked Jonn over. He was a mess. "Why'd they let him live, Robbie?"

"I don't know, boss. I don't know."

• • •

Almost two weeks later, while Jonn was still in the hospital and Terrin and the rest of Tiko III waited for reinforcements, a tiny shuttle materialized within the Tiko corporate sector.

Two fighters were waiting at the projected arrival point to escort the shuttle home. One of these was piloted by Hrajis Nuyt, an Ishantran. He was Tiko III's top fighter pilot, and Terrin trusted him and his wingman Zak to the most important mission they had flown in four years of service; escorting in the thirty-three corporate marines that would replace those lost in the wreck of the *Fury* and the attack on New Akron.

The sensors on Hrajis' glowing green instrument panel cast an eerie glow upon his black visor, but showed only minimal activity within the sensor's limits and none within threat distance. He and Zak had been waiting for nearly thirty minutes now.

But the black ship had been there for hours. Its crew sat in silence, carefully monitoring their reflective signature. They knew that the shuttle would have to be dealt with first. It took ship computers several minutes to calculate a new jump point, but all of them carried an emergency backtrack button which took the last safe jump point from memory and could throw the vessel back to it in an emergency. If the shuttle wasn't destroyed in the first salvo of missiles, it would vanish and the pirates wouldn't get a second chance.

A small patch of star-speckled blackness wavered and three different ships watched as the shuttle materialized. There was no need for the assassins to warn the shuttle by locking on it with their laser designator, the passive seekers at the tip of the missile's warhead could recognize complex images and fly undetected without it. The pirates fired, and thirty-three young marines, many of whom had never kissed their first girl or fired a shot in anger, perished in a silent flash of light that gutted the shuttle like a fat fish.

The now-open launch bay doors of the pirate ship ruined its electronic invisibility, but it didn't matter. The ship rotated and quickly fired another salvo of ship-to-ship missiles at the fighters.

Hrajis' monitor flickered and alarms blared at the incoming threat. "Launch decoys, kid!" he shouted at Zak.

A metal device floated out of the rear of Zak's fighter and headed towards the last detected threat. The "bullet" consisted of a chemical thruster, a magnetic detonator that would explode if any large mass of metal, such as a missile, passed by, and a radio override that detected the unique signal of a tiny transmitter within every Tiko ship. The radio kept the decoy from exploding too near a friendly vessel, but the assassins had fired too quickly and too close. The missile streaked by the decoy, leaving it unharmed, and slammed through Zak's cockpit.

Hrajis screamed with rage and fired his own missiles at the near-invisible attackers, but they had already activated their own decoys and the weapons detonated harmlessly.

Now the pirates returned fire with a new weapon, this one a long blue torpedo. It raced towards Hrajis' ship, but his decoy effectively detonated and the torpedo vanished in a flash of light and hurtling debris. Hrajis smiled with relief, and prepared to escape. He didn't like running away, but Kelassiter had to know what happened.

But then he saw something strange. The debris of

the torpedo seemed to be racing towards him! The Ishantran watched with horror and confusion as hundreds of tiny limpet mines locked magnetically to his hull. There was a rippling explosion and the cockpit was shredded into metal confetti.

But Hrajis lived. The mines ruined his ship and the ejection system instantly threw him out into the void. He was spinning slowly, fighting to maintain consciousness but he realized his thin protective suit had been pierced by the explosion. Air and pressure raced out into the vacuum, and Hrajis felt his body slowly and painfully expanding.

He saw his enemy maneuver in front of him. As he suspected, it was a stealth fighter. *But only Fleet is allowed to have those* — had Hollings somehow turned the military arm of the Consortium against the Tiko Corporation?

Hrajis screamed in defiance at his unknown murderers, and burst inside his suit.

CHAPTER TWELVE

Rejection

The saw, the limpet mines, the wreck of the *Fury*, severed arms, drowning in blood, and Duncan's screaming face haunted Jonn's mind for the next three weeks. The med-techs had kept him in an artificially induced sleep while the worst of his wounds were healing. This spared Jonn a great deal of physical agony, but kept his mind in a drugged delirium that only heightened the intensity of his nightmares. Overall, he would have preferred a couple of aspirin and some company.

When Jonn was finally allowed to awake, Terrin was by his side.

"Welcome back to the land of the living, Stryk."

Jonn turned his head slightly, angling to get a better look at Kelassiter. It was obvious he was having trouble focusing with his right eye. He reached up to rub it and almost knocked himself out when his cybernetic arm overcompensated for the movement.

"Easy," Terrin said as he grabbed Stryker's arm and eased it down onto the bed. "You've gotta get used to your new self, old buddy."

"Whaddya mean 'my new self'?"

"You were pretty messed up from the ambush ..."

Jonn sat up suddenly, causing a rush of nausea and pain to rise in him.

Kelassiter winced in sympathy but could only watch. "We know what the pilots saw — Hollings gave us the black box. What did you see in the back?"

"I dunno. Some kinda' heat-seekers or somethin' kept hittin' us 'til they ripped a hole in the rear. Then they put one right up our tail, landed it right in between us. Only this one didn't just explode. It popped open and hundreds of little mines leaped out and clamped onto our armor. I was sure they'd kill us all." Stryker looked around the sickbay, realizing that he was the only patient.

"You're telling me somebody shot an *anti-personnel* weapon into the *Fury*? And then didn't even bother to capture the ship?"

Jonn shrugged as he flexed his new arm back and forth, attempting to adapt to the strange power stored within the alien appendage. "Not anti-personnel. *Anti-marine*. Those things were designed to go after — and *through* — armor."

"That doesn't make any sense. Someone wanted our marines dead, yet ... there's been no follow-up. This whole thing reeks of Hollings, but he's come out cleaner than Dumois' lab coat. According to the pilots, whatever hit you had to be a stealth ship, but the Consortium would make the R-H Corporation a fading memory if it was discovered they had them."

Stryker was experimenting with his mechanical eye now, feeling the strange sensation of being able to touch his eyeball without wincing. "Is Fleet pissed at us?"

"If they were, we'd know it."

"Must be pirates, then."

"Then why didn't they hang around to salvage the ship?"

"Maybe they got scared off when the *Constantine* started movin' in."

Kelassiter was becoming more and more frustrated. The game was beginning to get a little too dangerous. "But where did they get that kind of firepower? No pirates in this sector can afford experimental missiles and stealth ships."

Stryker grunted, a signal that this was Terrin's problem. He was just supposed to shoot whatever his boss pointed the finger at. "How many of us made it through the wreck?"

Terrin turned his gaze to the floor. His silence confirmed what the empty medical bay had hinted at. "Must've been your armor."

The commander's version of the Brodie deep space suit with its extra degree of protection had saved him. Designed to protect the commander of the squad, with his extra comm packages and sensor unit, it kept him alive. His duty was to keep the other marines alive.

Jonn didn't want to dwell on it. His nightmares had taken care of that for the last month. "How long've I been out?"

"A little over three weeks. It would've been shorter, but I didn't want to put you back in the vat tubes."

Jonn shivered visibly and nodded his head in embarrassed approval. "New-bees here yet?"

Terrin sighed and furrowed his brow in aggravation. "No. They were due in a week ago, but something happened."

"What?"

"They ... got ambushed too."

"Christ, Terrin! And we haven't been invaded yet?"

"No," he shrugged. "The *Fury* and the shuttle could only have been hit by pirates, and they might get lucky and take out a ship from time to time, but they don't usually go invading whole cities."

"Then it has to be Hollings. Maybe Todd's built

some stealth ships."

"Come on, Stryk. Not only would Fleet wipe him out in a month if he broke the ban, but Dream —" Terrin caught himself, *"our spy* on the *Constantine* would've heard about them by now."

Jonn almost laughed; it was no secret to him where the love of Terrin's life had vanished to over six months ago.

Jonn flexed his new arm again, the tubular bulge of the metal hydraulics visible just below the thin syntheflesh. There were several jagged scars scattered about the length of the limb, and some of the skin was missing from the accident with the plasma tube. Around his shoulder was one particularly nasty line of white tissue that seemed to circle all the way around his arm. Jonn remembered the two salvage workers, the one stuffing a chocolate bar in his mouth and the other with the … saw.

He sucked in a deep breath and leaned back against the starchy pillows. A metal platter held a glass of water and some pain relievers and he suddenly swept them off onto the floor and held the reflective surface to his face. His right eye was a monstrous mockery of what Jonn thought it should be. A metal ring surrounded the socket, and a glassy, bulbous monster poked grotesquely from it as if it were trying to free itself from the prison of his skull.

"Geez, Terrin. How could you do this to me? You know I hate this junk."

"We didn't do it, Stryk. It was Hollings."

There was a flash of darkness within the twisting tunnels of the marine's mind. He barely remembered Todd Hollings standing over him, covered in blood and … *grease*. And there was another man, a doctor. They were pulling something out of him, something red and wet and slimy like liver. He remembered the pain, and the fear, but not the details. And why were they laughing?

"What's wrong?" Terrin interrupted.

The marine shook his head, bringing him quickly out of the flashback. "Nothin'. What else'd they cut out?"

Kelassiter stood and shoved his hands into the back pockets of his gray jumper. "Your groin's shot, and they had to give you a new bladder and some other junk down there. Most of your chest rotted from frostbite and got replaced by syntheflesh, and the upper half of your skull is laced together with plasteel strips. The eye's full of enhancements, a top-of-the-line model — Hollings said it was all they had — and your kneecap's been replaced with a plastic plate. Other than that, you're perfectly normal."

Jonn felt violated and ashamed. It wasn't easy losing pieces of one's body to intrusive metal monsters. "Get the hell out of here."

Terrin left.

The corporate head of Tiko III strolled through the halls of the administrative complex situated at the end of Wriggle Street. He had been watching the early detection probes for over three weeks now, each day expecting the follow-up attack that would finish his tiny colony for good. But nothing had happened.

The offices were quiet lately, word had finally gotten out about the *Fury* and everyone was blaming it on Terrin. Worst, Kelassiter had to agree with them. Only the militia and the automated defenses remained to protect Tiko III from whatever had picked off its defenders.

He entered his office and poured the three parts vodka, one part tomato juice, and one part orange juice that made a Venusian Moonrise. He had seen a lot of that particular astrological phenomenon in the last three weeks, and hoped he would be around to see a few more in the future. The exhausted executive had just started to feel the effects of his drink when a tinny voice sounded over the intercom.

"Sir, we've received a courier transmission from the Randall-Hollings ship, *Constantine*. It's directed specifically for you Mr. Kelassiter, shall I transfer?"

Terrin rattled the ice in his drink and wiped the cold perspiration from the glass onto his brow. His first thought was that this was *it*. *Hollings was calling now with his ultimatum. 'Surrender or be destroyed, Kelassiter!' But then why the hell had he waited three weeks?*

Might as well get this over with. "Yeah, patch it through." The communications viewscreen slowly rose from Terrin's black desk and the pudgy face of Todd Hollings began to materialize within its glass confines.

"Hello, Terrin," he said with a smug look. Grease pooled in a fold of his chin and slowly dribbled out onto a napkin tied about his neck. Terrin could see the remains of a Grazzian *rogulet* waving about, complete with bite marks and the protruding leg bone of the rare bird.

"How are things?" Todd managed to get out between juicy bites. "And how's your boy — that Stryker fellow? Did you get our bill?"

Of course Terrin couldn't answer. Not now, anyway. The courier would take almost a day to get back to the last plotted position of the *Constantine*.

"Why did we go to all that trouble, you ask? To show you that we harbor no hard feelings since our last little spat. And then there's Stryker himself."

Terrin's expression changed from anger to confusion.

"When that particular threat is destroyed," Todd tightened his smug smile into one of pure hatred, "I want to be the one who pulls the trigger."

This came a little closer to satisfying Terrin than the "kindness-of-our-collective-hearts" explanation.

"Anyway," the slob continued as he settled back

into his plush chair, "we'll be leaving the system now just to let you breathe a little easier. We've finished dealing with the pirates who've been troubling us of late and wish to return home. You must be a little nervous after losing so much, and I'd hate to worry you." Todd leaned back and slurped up a slimy tendon. "You know how I'd hate to see you sweat, Terrin."

Click.

Todd's greasy smile disappeared in a staticky point of white. Terrin leaned back, propped his boots upon the mylar desk, and pushed his favorite ten gallon hat down over his eyes. It was time to think.

● ● ●

Stryker knew what would make him feel better. It was time to see Lucretia. The medics released him with a warning about moving around too much and he headed straight for his barracks. There, he changed clothes, had a quick shave, and doused himself in Lucretia's favorite cologne. He passed by the empty beds, open closets, and empty footlockers of the Wolverines, when it finally hit him that his friends were gone forever. Jonn had lost a lot of companions in his corporate military career, but never an entire platoon at once.

Or at least, most of the platoon. Klein sat playing solitaire on a cot as Stryker passed by. Klein looked straight into Stryker's mismatched eyes accusingly.

"What happened, Sergeant?"

"Whattya mean, Klein? You know what happened."

"No. I mean who did it? And why haven't we gotten any replacements?"

"They're comin'. You know how slow corp is."

Klein nodded and seemed to relax his gaze a bit. "The Jaegers are here."

"Yeah, so?"

"So, maybe we could hire them on 'til the new-bees show up."

"Since when did you become the freakin' boss around here? Yellin' 'retreat' gave you a little taste of authority 'n now you want it all! 'Zat it? You wanna be the damn leader, Klein?"

Steve glared at his superior. Jonn was being unfair and the bastard knew it. He was just looking for someone to take his anger out on, but a fight would only get Klein deeper in trouble, so he backed down. Besides, Stryker looked a little crazier than usual today.

Jonn stormed out of the barracks and through the doors of the executive building, where he emerged onto the upper end of Wriggle Street. Most everyone knew Jonn here, and his strange new appearance drew uncomfortable stares.

"Nice skinjob, Sarge." It was Guibert. He had emerged from the *Worm Hole* with one arm around an orange-furred whore that Stryker had never seen before.

Jonn continued on his way, frustration welling up within him like disassembled parts that never fit back into the box they came in.

"Lucretia's gonna love that shiner," he heard as he continued down the street.

Tears of grief and aggravation started to well in his human eye. Only the thought of reaching the sympathetic arms of his woman carried him through the crowded street. He finally made it to her apartment and flipped on the intercom.

"Luce?" he called softly.

There was no answer, so he called once again. The tears in his good eye picked that moment to stream down his face in a salty torrent. Jonn stabbed at them with his hands and found that syntheflesh was about as absorbent as skin. Someone on the street was watching him and Jonn quickly turned his embarrassed face to the wall. He had never cried before. His eyes had watered from pain or smoke, and he had certainly known heartache, but he had never actually *cried*.

"Luce?" he called again.

Finally, a voice sounded faintly through the electronic link. "Jonn … I'm …"

He heard a soft creak, like weight shifting on the spring of a bed in the background.

"I'm with someone."

No words could describe the feeling in Jonn's stomach and heart. Everything had been lost. His companions, his *flesh*, and now the woman he loved. His mechanical hand gripped the handle of his blaster all too easily.

Jonn had no idea who or what he was going to shoot, but he knew he was going to blow a large hole in something.

He reached into the pocket of his slacks and took out a corpsec passcard. The thin skeleton key could open almost any door in the city, and Lucretia's was no exception. He stormed through the small entryway and burst into her bedroom with his pistol drawn.

Sitting on the edge of a bed Jonn was all too familiar with was Lucretia. She wore some cheap jewelry he had once bought her, an expression of shame, and little else. Behind her, still lying half under the sheets, was a man Jonn recognized from a year-old security briefing.

"Max Hunt? Of all the people you could dump me for, you choose the biggest pirate in the galaxy?"

Stryker pointed at him with the pistol and Lucretia screamed. "Oh my God, Jonn! No!" She stood and blocked her lover, hoping that Jonn wouldn't risk firing through her.

Hunt was no stranger to the situation. The seven-foot tall black man jumped to his feet and flung himself across the room in an attempt to grab the marine's weapon. Before he made contact, Jonn grabbed him by the throat and rammed his bald head halfway through the cheap plaster wall the apartment.

Lucretia stood and tried to cover her nakedness with stained sheets. Her shock and disgust was significantly harder to conceal. "Y-you're a monster, Jonn! A monster!"

Stryker smiled for the first time in a month. Everything he had suffered had weighed upon him like a lead collar. Now the collar had broken from its own weight and crashed upon his bloody feet. Lunacy was the easiest, and the last alternative.

BLAM! BLAM! BLAM! Jonn fired three holes in the plaster around Hunt's body, cackling maniacally as the humiliated mercenary danced in panic. BLAM! Jonn shot the expensive sound system he had installed last Christmas, and sparks leapt from the ruined unit as it protested its electric death.

Lucretia stared in horror at the man she had loved and been foolish enough to cheat on. He was no longer the scruffy but loveable commander of security, he was pure insanity and violence wrapped in an elastic wrapper of skin and metal and syntheflesh. But she had known that for some time, hadn't she? Couldn't she tell by his grotesque new appearance and the terrible nightmares he had recounted in his drugged sleep over the last three weeks? Hadn't that been the reason she had sought comfort in the arms of a stranger? Or was she just making sure that someone was going to keep her in cheap jewelry and wine?

But her reasons didn't matter, not now. All that mattered was that Jonn was going to kill Max if she didn't do something. "STOP IT, JONN!" she screamed. "You are not Jonn Stryker! You're a monster! Look at yourself!" She pointed towards a mirror hanging just over the nearby sink. "Look! See what you've become!"

Stryker looked into the mirror and saw the mad

stranger that stared back at him. Tears leaked from one eye and blood from another. Jonn's mind, his rational thinking self that had been honed to think in the midst of bloodshed and violence, fought to free itself from the stranger prison of rejection and heartache. It almost didn't register what the cybernetic eye instantly focused on.

Hunt had freed himself from the wall and grabbed a heavy iron chair. The mercenary brought it down hard, hoping to cave in the jealous lover's head, but Stryker dodged with surprising quickness and the chair smashed down into Lucretia's vanity. Make-up and myriad products understood only by women scattered across the floor.

Jonn smashed his fist into Hunt's jaw, the barrel of the pistol adding to the mercenary's pain as the jagged tip ripped out a chunk of flesh just below the eye. Max staggered back, holding his wound.

"Please, Luce," Jonn pleaded, turning his back on his opponent.

She simply dropped her head, staring down at the bed on which she stood. Suddenly, a new voice entered the scene, "Freeze, Stryker!" It was Guibert — he was leaning in through the hole in the wall Hunt's head had made and pointing his blaster at his sergeant. He seemed to enjoy the situation.

Jonn turned to the voice, ready to bash in another head, but Guy was looking at him funny, shifting his glance from Jonn to a spot behind. Stryker finally caught on and turned just as Hunt swung the chair again. The mercenary managed to hit him this time.

CHAPTER THIRTEEN

New You

Four hours later, Jonn woke once again in the sick bay. Probing fingers told him that a thick bandage was wrapped around his head, and he saw a bladder full of ice dying on his pillow. Jonn wiped off some of the condensation and rubbed it across his parched lips. He was really getting sick of sick bay.

It wasn't long before Kelassiter came down. Stryker saw him flash his pass at the guards (as if they didn't know who he was), and walk into the room. Characteristically, he shoved his hands into the back pockets of his jumper and stared out the plexiglass into the infirmary. Terrin's hell would have been a place without pockets and windows.

"You really screwed up this time, Jonn. I can't believe you tried to kill someone over a *woman*."

"If I'd tried to kill him, there'd be a seven-foot-long corpse in your morgue."

Terrin turned, throwing his hat on the end of the bed. "You don't get it, do you? Max Hunt might be the only thing that saves our collective ass around here. The Wolverines are all but dead, our only corvette's in a million pieces, and *you* just pissed off the only armed group of men that might throw in with us."

"Didja ever think maybe Mr. Wonderful is behind all this? Whatever hit us on Akron wasn't no corp. No corp armor I ever saw had jaws."

"Jaws? What the hell are you talking about?"

Jonn shrugged and picked up the ice pack. He rubbed it around his forehead for a while before he finally decided to let his boss in on the secret. "I don't know. I saw one. Just a glimpse when they waxed Duncan. It looked like jaws or somethin'."

"You mean sculpted into the armor? Like for effect or something?"

"Prob'ly. But they sure looked real. And they were drippin'. Slobberin' or somethin'." Stryker's tongue felt swollen and he was having trouble talking — Kelassiter was having even more trouble understanding him, especially the bit about the jaws.

"Let me get this straight … you're telling me some sort of …*animal*… killed Duncan, Shaick and Graves?"

Jonn turned his head and shot cold daggers into Kelassiter's heart with his gaze. "I didn't say nothin' about no freakin' animals. Animals don't carry guns that rip the air apart and then turn you into jelly. Ask Hawkins. He says he saw 'em too."

Terrin shoved his hands back into his pockets and turned back towards the window. He was sure Jonn had finally flipped.

"I think you need some time off, Jonn." It was a hard decision. There wasn't much protecting Tiko III now, and Jonn was the finest commander under fire that Terrin had ever known. But it seemed that a choice had to be made between Max Hunt's Jaegers and one experienced, though wounded, man.

Jonn nodded. He had expected as much.

• • •

Guy and Vanessa were waiting for Klein at the *Worm Hole* when his shift ended.

"Hey, Stevie-boy!" Guy seemed unusually cheerful.

Klein presented the opposite picture. His face had been fixed in a perpetual scowl ever since the attack on New Akron, and the fight with Stryker had tightened the scowl into something even less pleasant.

"*Sacre Bleu*, are you ever going to quit moping?" Guy had already bought the three of them a beer and slid one down toward Klein as he arranged his stool.

"Yeah. Sure." He grabbed the beer roughly, spilling froth and amber liquid on the already dirty bar. In one swift chug, he finished the drink and tossed the stein to Little Jake.

"If you came here to get drunk, Klein, you can just go ahead and toss yourself out," the bartender spoke.

"Just give me another drink before I trash your whole stinkin' place."

Jake looked deep into his customer's eyes. What he saw there was anger, hate, and a whole lot of pain. He poured Steve another drink and tried to understand why he was giving in.

The marine seemed to settle down after this small victory and dropped his orange jacket on the stool. He took his seat and looked casually at Vanessa.

"What are you doing here?"

He hadn't meant it insultingly, and she somehow knew it. "Hunt's here. And he wants to talk to you."

Steve's ire rose once again. "What'd you tell him?"

"Nothin'. Just that things were going to shit around here and you and Guy might be interested in jumping ship."

"You stupid whore! Kelassiter hears that and I won't live to see another day!"

Vanessa withdrew into herself. This wasn't going well.

"Oh, calm down, Steve." Guy interrupted.

"Kelassiter isn't going to hear about it, and even if he does, it's just talk."

"Talk's enough to get you hanged, boy."

"If that's true, then you might as well go talk to Hunt."

Klein swallowed another beer and stared at the motley collection sitting against the far wall. The Jaegers wore Kimbo-Miyaga quilted armor covered in a loose amalgamation of whatever they had managed to scrape up over the years. The biggest man, Hunt himself, wore only leather pants, a brown vest over his ebony skin, and a red bandana around his bald pate.

With a shrug, he stood and headed towards their table. Guy followed behind, but signalled Vanessa to wait. "Let me set this up, okay? Then you'll get your chance."

Vanessa didn't trust him, but had little choice but to agree.

"So," Max smiled at the red-haired marine. "Guibert tells me things aren't going so well here."

That much was true, and Klein shrugged noncommittally. He looked for a chair and saw none, then stared hard at the nearest pirate.

The man started to say something when Max kicked him under the table. "Let our new friends have a seat," he grinned.

The pirate reluctantly stood, and Klein plopped down in his chair. Max filled up a mug for each of them, and Guy scurried off to grab another seat. He returned quickly, and started the conversation that would lead to their desertion. "Max, this is Steve. Steve — Max."

"I know who he is," Steve spat and drank from the mug. "Good beer. You must be rich."

Max smiled. "We do all right, Mr. Klein."

Guy looked around the room and leaned in to speak more quietly, "Look, Max, if we do this, we're going to have to do it quick. Before Kelassiter finds out and has us shot for desertion."

The giant nodded. Guy saw that he and Steve had locked gazes, and were sizing each other up in some sort of mental duel. Max responded without breaking the stare, "And the girl, Vanessa?"

"Yeah, she's coming too. At least for now. She'll tell Kelassiter otherwise. We can always dump her somewhere."

If Steve heard his partner's last comment, he didn't say anything.

• • •

Jonn managed to get out of sick bay for the second time today, and was looking for something a little stronger than aspirin to cure his aching head. He had never felt such a strong urge to get roaring drunk, but he supposed that his brain demanded some reprieve from the recent past.

As he descended Wiggle Street, he couldn't help but notice the flashing television monitors of *New You*. The screens pieced together the story of a man horribly burned in a mining accident and showed the restorative cosmetic powers of syntheflesh.

A veil parted in Jonn's mind. *Of course!* He could simply have his new cyberware cleverly tucked away and be his old self again! Then Lucretia would want him back and everything would be right with the world!

Jonn knew there were flaws in his plan, but he was getting desperate. His world had crumbled in front of his one good eye, and nothing made much sense any more.

He burst through the doors of *New You* and glanced about the room. A male receptionist was stationed at a long, curved, white desk. Immediately in front of him was the heart of *New You*, a computer imaging device. Jonn approached the computer, looked into it, and nearly jumped when his face suddenly appeared on the screen. The hideous cybernetic eye was there, frozen in time as it tried to crawl from its jagged metal housing. But that would soon change.

The orderly shuffled some papers and dropped them into something hidden behind the counter. "Can I help you, sir?"

"Uh? Oh, yeah. I wanna get …" he pointed quickly and noncommittally to the embarrassing eye, "this hidden. Or tucked away, or something. Can you do that?"

It was obvious his client was shy, and the orderly seemed to enjoy it. "Oh, certainly, we can get rid of almost any unsightly blemish or condition. That's a real poser, but I'm sure we can do something with it." He grinned from ear to ear, watching Jonn's shame with glee. "Would you like an internal optical device to replace what you have now?"

"Um. Yeah. Internal. Can you make it look like …"

"Real? Of course! Though some marines prefer to leave such things visible. It tends to scare off the bad guys, I've heard."

"No. I want it to look real. I've got some other stuff, too."

"Ok. Let's just take care of that eye first." The orderly touched the computer image of Jonn's eye and both watched as it was carefully cut away, leaving a large white space in the corner of Jonn's head. Next, the orderly touched the image of the other eye, and after the computer had scanned and removed it, dragged it across the screen into what looked like a silver tray. There he hit "Copy," and sent it back to its original position. Then he hit a button labeled "Flip-Horizontal" and placed the inverted copy into the white space left by the mechanical eye. Finally, he pressed a button called, "Fill and Complete" and the few white pixels left uncolored began to shade themselves in Jonn's dark skin tones.

Stryker watched with the fascination of a six-year-old — another reaction the orderly seemed to enjoy. Jonn was not in love with mechanical toys and tricks, but was still amazed by the things they could do sometimes.

"How does that look, sir?"

Stryker saw his old face staring back at him from the monitor. The new eye didn't look quite right, but that was only because it was a symmetrical image. "Yeah!" He was excited, soon he would be his old self again. "Uh, how much does this cost?"

The orderly punched in some numbers on the monitor and Jonn watched as the screen flashed two thousand credits, the equivalent of about two months of his pay. He could afford that, especially since he didn't have to support Lucretia anymore. *But isn't that why I'm doing all this in the first place?*

He pushed the doubts out of his head. He was going to do this, and now, before the nagging questions raised themselves back into his conscience.

Then he thought about the other surgery that he would need. The scars on his right pectorals had healed into a squirming mass of syntheflesh, and that would have to be smoothed. Then there was the arm. The ruined syntheflesh was already beginning to rot and needed replacement. The kneecap and the pelvis could stay, but other parts important to any future romance would need some work.

After a brief and embarrassing talk with the orderly, Jonn was told that all of his operations would cost him just over half a year's pay and require two days in the *New You* clinic. He thought it over and paced around the room, rubbing his crewcut hair and staring at the meticulously clean white floors. He pretended to mull it over, but the decision was already made.

"I'll take it." Jonn wasn't sure if that was the right

thing to say but he got the message across. The cost was enormous, both in monetary terms and, in some Faustian way, the amount of his soul he was trading to have his anatomy altered with synthetics. But it felt so good to resolve the world's problems in the flash of a credcard. Jonn smiled, he was going to be himself again. He wanted to tell the orderly that is was actually the "Old You" that he was after, but he couldn't stand to see the bastard smile anymore.

"Do I pay now?" he asked, hardly able to conceal his elation. *Just two short days and I'll look like myself again!*

"If you like, sir. Or you can spread the payments out over the three-month period."

This was great! He didn't even have to pay right away! He had three months to … *the* three months?

Jonn's heart began to sink in his chest. "I thought you said this would only take two days?" he asked warily.

"That's right, sir."

His heart rose again. It fluttered expectantly in his throat.

"But we only have one surgeon and our waiting list is booked for the next three months."

Thud.

Jonn could bear no more. Sinewy arms hung limply by his side, and it required a Herculean effort to replace the impotent credcard in his wallet. Neck muscles failed, and his scarred head lowered slowly toward the gleaming floors of *New You*. Jonn turned his back on the flashing monitors, the grinning orderly, and the soul-stealing computer.

The *Worm Hole* had swinging doors in the entranceway, something that Little Jake had insisted on having after watching too many Westerns on his slugplayer. Stryker pushed through these swinging anachronisms and was greeted by the sight of Max

Hunt and his gang of mercenaries. Klein and Guibert sat with them, but Jonn hardly noticed. His attention was locked on the man that had ruined his life.

Everyone in the room had heard of the embarrassing fight in Lucretia's bedroom, and a tense silence settled over them as Jonn looked over the Jaegers. To everyone's surprise, he walked brazenly toward their booth.

"You men have permits for those weapons?" he grumbled. The mercenaries on Jonn's side of the table parted so that Stryker could face Hunt alone. Even sitting, the seven foot tall giant cut an imposing figure next to the squat and stocky marine.

"Get out of here 'fore we bash your head in again, ya freak!" one of the men taunted.

Jonn's gaze remained leveled at their leader, his weapon hand rock steady and hovering just inches away from his blaster.

Max had been in a lot of firefights, and had fought with and against many fierce opponents, but never had he seen such calm in the face of potential danger. Stryker looked pained when he entered, but now the threat of violence seemed to *soothe* him, to focus all of his frustrations into one dangerous mass of adrenaline pumping neurons.

The men sitting at the far ends of the table stood, ready to deal with any threat toward their captain. Other patrons also began to rise; some carelessly knocking over their chairs in an effort to remove themselves from the danger zone.

There was a tense silence as mental gears clicked in Hunt's head. Finally, he spoke. "It's okay, boys. Sergeant Stryker here has every right to check our permits. I'm sure you'll find everything is in order, Sergeant." Hunt managed not to break the stare as he slowly dug out his wallet and flipped the four-year-old Tiko permit onto the table. Stryker picked it up, shook off the liquid it had picked up on the messy table, and seemed to examine it. Hunt was quick to notice that Jonn's eyes never actually focused on the license, but remained locked with his own instead. The corporate man ignored the other mercs' licenses.

Stryker dumped the slimy paper back onto the table and suddenly walked away, seating himself at the bar. An audible sigh filled the room, and soon the sounds of chatter, small talk, and innuendo had returned to the bar.

"You're picking on some tough guys today, Stryk," Jake said and greeted his friend with a frosted glass of beer.

"I've seen tougher."

"I've heard rumors Kelassiter's thinking about hiring them for a while. Any truth to it?"

Jonn sipped at his beer and shrugged a "Who knows? I'm just a grunt" at the bartender.

"I'm sorry to hear about Luce, buddy. You know what they say though, once a whore ..."

Jonn stopped drinking and stared up at the bartender with his human and cybernetic eyes.

Jake knew he had said enough.

Max threw a pair of dice on the table and grimaced as they stopped in a pool of spilled beer, stopping on the wrong numbers. One of his men gleefully grabbed a credit from the boss's pile and added it to his own.

Max leaned back. He was tired of this game. Klein and Guibert had gone for a walk so that the Frenchman could talk his companion into deserting the Tiko corp. Max wasn't so sure he wanted anyone who had to be talked into joining. But the marine was a good man to have around, and he had to think of the Jaegers.

The man who might put an end to his plans was across the room, downing glass after glass of the cheapest stuff in the house.

"Look at him, boss. He's gettin' drunker 'n a skunk."

"It hurts a man when he loses what he's found."

Oleg, the man who had won the credit, frowned in confusion.

"The whore," Hunt explained, "the one I was paid to sleep with. She said Stryker didn't have much else but the corp, and now that's about gone, too. He's had a rough couple of weeks."

"I heard he got trapped in a wreck for eleven hours," a squat mercenary chimed in.

"Yeah. He was the only survivor," added another.

Oleg held the coin up to the light, squinting with his one good eye. "I don't trust a man who survives what no other does."

Hunt nodded in agreement. "Perhaps it would have been better if he'd just died."

"He's *gonna* die the way he's packin' the booze away!" said another of Hunt's men. "Why the hell does the bartender keep givin' 'em to him?"

Jonn swayed on his stool as Klein and Guibert returned to the *Worm Hole*. They crossed to the Jaegers' table, and greeted the others with a short nod of the head.

"Klein's up for it," Guy said as he poured himself a drink from one of the Jaeger's pitchers.

Max looked to see Klein's reaction, but he was busy watching his sergeant. "We better get him outta here 'fore he falls off that stool and breaks somethin'. God knows I'll get blamed if he does."

"Ah, leave him be. It'd serve him right. Maybe he'll break his fraggin' neck," Guy mouthed through the head of his beer.

Klein turned his head and for the first time took a hard look at the captain of the mercenary group he had just agreed to join. He didn't care for freelance mercenaries, but he noticed something that helped ease his conscience. Hunt didn't seem to like Guibert's last remark, either.

Max nodded towards Stryker, and he and Klein stood and crossed the bar. With a hint of sympathy, the two men put their arms around the drunken veteran and carefully dragged him off the stool. Fortunately for them, Jonn was beyond holding a grudge.

They carried him all the way up Wriggle Street and into the silent barracks of the Wolverines. Klein poured a glass of water and set it and some pain killers beside Jonn's bed, then he and his quiet companion returned to the *Worm Hole*.

CHAPTER FOURTEEN

The Traitor

I t was shortly after midnight. The simulated day and night cycles had long put most of Tiko III to sleep, making it easy for the traitor to steal his way unseen down the back alleys that paralleled Wriggle Street, and make his way to the main entrance of the iridium mines.

He walked up to the booth that housed the night watchman and the entrance to the main airlock. When he knocked on the booth's door, the old man inside was caught napping and hurried, embarrassed, to open it. As soon as the lock clicked out of place, the traitor shoved the door open and pinned the watchman against the wall. The man wheezed once before the blaster was shoved deep into his gut.

The traitor ignored his blood-spackled clothing and moved to the airlock control. Every morning, Tiko's miners passed through this checkpoint on their way to the airlock and the mines beyond, and the nearby sensors kept a record of every time it opened or closed. These were disabled in minutes, and the traitor quickly donned one of the miner's deep-space suits.

He stepped through the airlock, and left Tiko's womb through her rocky umbilical cords, finally emerging onto the surface of the slowly spinning asteroid.

It was a long walk to the first missile pod. The traitor heard his heavy breathing within the suit and smelled the fetid cloth of the face mask where countless miners' breath had condensed and hung there in a smelly pool of liquid stench. He ran across the rough surface in measured leaps, always careful not to lose his footing. He had to work without a safety tether to get where he was going, and it would be easy to leap too hard and hurl himself out into space.

Thirty minutes later, the traitor reached the ship-killing missile pods that protected Tiko III from invasion. The first was well hidden in a natural niche of rock, but Tiko had no secrets this man wasn't privy to. He quickly removed the suit's mining laser and burned through the rear access panel of the launcher. Every circuit in the corporation's defense computer should have surged with warning signals and flashing alarms, but there was nothing, only the routine transfer of countless data signals and binary communions with other ignorant machines. The traitor had guaranteed the system's blindness earlier.

As he looked at the racks of automated missiles, he vowed that Tiko would pay for their faith in oblivious circuitry and steel over honest flesh and blood. With reckless abandon, the traitor began gutting the launcher of its missiles like a pumpkin on Halloween.

Only a few more to go, he thought.

CHAPTER FIFTEEN

Going in Cold

Dreama sat on her cold metal cot deep within the brig of the *Constantine*. It was almost time for the guard to bring her dinner, and for an attempt at saving Tiko III. And Terrin.

She hadn't realized how much she loved him until Katanopolis had imprisoned her and she began to wonder if she would ever see his silly cowboy hat and leather boots again. Hollings promised her a quick death after certain experiments had run their course, but she believed her hero would overcome the slimy toad and free her from this sterile ship. She could almost imagine a stellar horse carrying him across the sector.

But the spark of hope waned after the first three weeks, and dwindled in size from a bonfire to a flickering match in the week after. She wasn't giving up, though, not yet.

Her cell was barren, save for a plasteel commode, a metal cot, and one synthetic pillow and quilt. There was a ventilation shaft on the wall above her uncomfortable bed, but it was far too small for anyone to fit into. She had an idea about it though, and dinner would provide her with the key to challenge it.

Hollings kept everything on a tight schedule, and dinner came promptly at six p.m. Dreama thought it ironic that Hollings demanded such a perfect environment when the man himself was usually covered in grease and sweat.

The guard that brought the food was a young man with dark hair cut just above the scalp. His jaw was angular and square under the red cap that denoted his cadet status in the corporate marines, but his eyes betrayed something a little softer. The inexperienced youths in the corporate military were often given such jobs as guarding and feeding prisoners.

"Hey, new-bee. What's for chow?"

The cadet seemed embarrassed. She knew he had been watching her through the narrow door window at night. He slid the platter through a slot in her door, and watched as she grimaced at the thick broth, stale slice of bread, and glass of murky water that was to sustain her.

"No meat?" she whined.

The cadet shook his head, a little embarrassed at the spartan meal, and quickly disappeared from view. His over-polished boots clacked loudly as he hurriedly walked back down the corridor to his guardpost.

Dreama could care less about the distasteful fare; what she really wanted was meat — because then they would have given her a knife, and a knife could make a wonderful screwdriver. Now, a spoon would have to do.

She grabbed the tool, grimaced at it, and stood on the cot under the ventilation shaft. The spoon wouldn't fit in the small screws that secured the vent cover and Dreama cursed in frustration. She sat back on the cot and fumed for a while before an idea finally hit her. Dreama hopped off the bed and raised the commode lid, wedging the tip of the spoon in between the hinges. She lowered the lid, sat, bounced roughly upon it, and then removed the spoon. To her relief, the tip had flattened into a makeshift screwdriver.

She stepped up on the cot again and the spoon fit snugly into the slot of the screws. In a few short minutes, she had removed the cover and reached into the ventilation shaft. Her hand explored the tube, carefully searching for an opening somewhere in the thin synthemetal before she found a gap where two sections of ductwork joined. Her fingers were calloused from the sanitation job, but they maintained their sensitive touch and she slipped them into the crack. Luckily, she found what she was looking for.

She wrenched her hand back out of the duct and pulled a long wire from a socket beneath her curly red hair. Dreama guided it through the gap in the airshaft and jammed the sharp end into a data-line strapped conveniently to the underside of the ductwork.

As she had suspected, Todd Hollings' ship had the latest in heating and cooling systems. Sensor cables led to the end of the vent, feeding constant temperature readings into the main control unit. This was what she had tapped into. Dreama couldn't get her physical form out of Todd's barren prison, but her virtual self could ride the datacord all the way into the ship's central computers.

Everyone with a data-jack also had a tiny translator inside their skull. This was the gizmo that transformed computer-generated binary signals into the electrical impulses used by the human brain. Dreama's translator had its own central processor and storage facilities that could be used as a "bare-bones" cyberdeck, but using it to raid a ship's mainframe was kind of like a using an airgun to take down a whale. Dreama had told Terrin she was the best decker in the sector, now she was going to have to prove it.

With a slight turn of the socket, the jack was activated and millions of brainwaves were converted into computer readable signals. The metal prison cell began to fade and Dreama felt the familiar pull of the electronic world concealed beneath shielded cables and guarded mainframes. Dreama had never felt so free after four weeks in a cramped prison. She raced down the electronic pathways and burst through the drone sensor cable into the heating and cooling system.

She materialized as herself; there wasn't room in the tiny translator for the disguise program that turned her into the Bag Lady. Not that it mattered — stealth and disguises weren't going to help her anymore. She had to find out what she needed and send it to Terrin fast, and damn the consequences.

There was a sentinel blocking the path that led to the central computer. It saw Dreama enter the virtual chamber, scanned her, and quickly pulled the alarm. It would take only seconds for the *Constantine's* technicians to jack in and investigate.

Programming on the fly was the toughest thing a decker could attempt. She didn't have to spell out every line of code, the computer could write that based on her conception of the sub-routines, but she did have to think up each part of the program in a logical order. Since mistakes in the computer's translation would be common, each segment had to be reduced to its most essential and simplest element. This is where the talent came in.

Dreama visualized deleting the sentinel's programming. All sentinel programs were protected against such things by a "flag" that marked them as non-erasable, but there were ways around this, and Dreama quickly made a list of several possible commands. Fortunately, one of them worked and the sentinel went down in a flash of extemporized code.

The rise of the mega-corporations had actually made

some things easy for the electronic thieves that crept through their data-networks. All sentinels had to be licensed, and each reproduction of it cost money. That's why the less important areas of the *Constantine's* mainframe were protected by the low-cost, and consequently less intelligent, intrusion countermeasure programs. Dreama knew things wouldn't be so easy closer to the heart of the system.

She leapt through the unguarded doorway of the temperature system and streaked down the central datapaths. Another quick improvisation and Dreama concocted a program that virtual reality depicted as a battering ram. She exploded through the first few datalocks, the "battering ram" overloading local circuits with garbage so that the system had to devote extra processor time to clearing up the mess. As she had predicted, the *Constantine's* mainframe ignored the usual password routines when the local processors were overloaded. Of course, such a brutal method left an easily traceable trail all through the computer, but Dreama wasn't worried about subtlety.

She crashed through the last seal and floundered in the gigantic central node of the *Constantine's* computer. A hastily envisioned scanner program helped her find the adjoining cell with the highest security level, and she once again filled the processor with garbage to penetrate what she hoped was Todd Hollings' personal records. The door to the cell shimmered, giving up its invisibility as the system stole its energy, and Dreama dove through. Then she stopped. She had expected a sentinel on the other side, but not one as deadly as the Medusa.

The Medusa was a high-end, artificially intelligent sentinel with much more processor access than usual. Its main attack program was to "lock up" invading entities by piggybacking onto their signal and sending a hardware-crashing virus into their deck, or in

Dreama's case, her tiny translator. Once that was done, the human technicians could dispatch corporate security and easily arrest the physical form of the data-thief. The "lock" was represented in virtual reality by the Medusa's mythical ability to turn its victims to stone. If Dreama was hit by her lock, however, there was a good chance the overload would fry her brain instead of just freezing her.

The thing was recessed in an alcove just inside what appeared to be a private study. Dreama was literally at its feet when she materialized in a hectic jumble of half-run programs and confused virtual images. The Medusa waited exactly two point three seconds for a deactivation code, and then came to life. Its figure and face were beautiful, and it wore a sparkling, sheer nightgown — Todd's preference, Dreama guessed. But atop its head were dozens of tiny green snakes, all writhing in a chaotic pattern of idleness. The eyes of the Medusa seemed devoid of any intelligence until the two point three seconds were up, then the lifeless orbs transformed into those of a serpent and locked onto Dreama's image. With a terrible hiss, the Medusa bared her fangs and one of the hideous snakes shot towards its prey.

Dreama instantly recognized the Lock and Trace program it was running, and managed to sever the link by running in a tight circle and dropping what the computer's virtual interpreter called "litter" on her trail. In reality, Dreama had retraced a particular data path and then filled it with garbage the second time through. This momentarily confused the guardian when it tried to identify variables by their contents and coordinates. But such an expensive sentinel would only fall for this trick once.

There was a journal lying open on what had to be Todd's desk. Dreama wanted to grab it but knew that it was bait in a particularly fatal trap. It would take several seconds for her to download whatever files it represented, and the Medusa was in no mood to wait.

Dreama took advantage of the thing's temporary confusion and burst back into the core of the system just as the virtual images of two technicians came on-line. As she expected, the Medusa was right behind her and lashed out with one of the venomous serpents. A quick dodge managed to get a stunned technician nailed by the creature's fangs and a blue glow shot through the telescopic reptile and zapped the unfortunate man into paralysis.

Dreama and the second technician couldn't resist watching the mythical gorgon in action, and both were surprised by what they saw next. The official purpose of the Medusa sentinel was to catch and detain unwanted visitors in virtual reality. But this one kept attaching her horrible living hair to its paralyzed victim, relentlessly repeating its virus program in the unfortunate man's physical terminal. Then, the snakes began to recoil, slowly dragging the Medusa towards its prey. Dreama knew that this meant it had successfully tracked the rival decker to his entry point, and the guardian now had a direct link to his unprotected brain. The Medusa bared her fangs as its voluptuous body entwined with the technician's, and it ripped out his throat in nanoseconds. Dreama and the other decker watched with horror as the snakes wormed into the image's ears, nose, and throat, turning his head into a twisted mass of virtual jelly.

But the thing was only supposed to catch and hold its target, not fry them. Dreama knew that such a grisly representation could only mean that a fatal surge of electricity had been sent up the unfortunate guard's jack and fried his brain to a crisp.

The other guard disappeared in a flash of light as he jacked out of the dangerous network, leaving Dreama as the malfunctioning creature's only possible target.

While the thing continued its brainburn, Dreama leapt back through to Hollings' study and tried to download his journal into her translator's tiny storage facility. She had to hurry; it wouldn't take the Medusa long to finish its victim, and then it would come looking for her.

But how could she defeat it? Dreama wasn't sure she could crash it even if she did have her cyberdeck. Without it, it was virtually impossible.

Downloading the journal gave her a moment to think about it. *Wait, how was the "real" Medusa defeated? Something about a mirror?*

She was almost finished when the Medusa entered the chamber. Its reptilian eyes and bloody fangs could only mean one thing: it was out of control! Programs of this complexity were prone to crashing and Dreama's off-the-cuff decking was probably the cause. With a little luck, the creature would have disappeared or locked into some repetitive pattern, but Dreama's luck was all bad. This thing wasn't going to capture her like it was supposed to — it was going to kill her. If the death of the supposedly allied technician hadn't been proof enough of the creature's intent, the maniacal look in its yellow eyes was.

The sentinel paused for a moment, scanning the room again until it found its opponent. This gave Dreama just enough time to finish stuffing the journal into her bag, but she was sure it was going to be garbled at best.

The Medusa closed for the kill. There was no way past it and no weapon available to combat it. *What was it about the mirror?*

Dreama had never studied Greek mythology in school, but some legends live forever. She remembered hearing about the gorgons, and even seeing a movie or two about them, but there was no mirror or polished shield in virtual reality. There were only lightning fast attack and defense programs, and Dreama was all out of both.

She prepared to die ...

I tried, Terrin; I tried.

Dreama froze in place, waiting for the snake to fill her with a venom that would fry her overworked translator and turn her brain into stew. Two of the things raced toward her.

And missed completely.

"Right here, you stupid program!" she yelled in anger.

And then it hit her. The Medusa was analyzing data and using it to decide its next action. The last time it had attempted to strike her, she had dodged and the technician had been hit instead. The Medusa was playing it safe this time and struck to either side, but it hadn't considered the possibility that she might not move at all!

Priorities! Dreama had an idea. It wasn't a mirror, but it might as well be. All sentinels had one simple line of programming that forbade them from attacking themselves, or, in technical terms, the program couldn't address the buffer that it currently resided in. But, if the Medusa's priorities were to first check its own position, and *then* anticipate its target's actions, Dreama could "step" into its coordinates and cause it to attack itself. Of course, she would have to be there when the program launched the snakes and gone before they arrived, and that would require a lot of speed and even more luck.

But Dreama knew how to even the odds. It was already recovering from its last mistake as she darted past and hurled her virtual image back into the core of the computer. Frantically, she looked for a security slave node. The Medusa slithered in angrily and reared to attack. Dreama finally found what she was looking for and pulled the ship's emergency alarm.

All over the *Constantine*, alarms sounded, lights

dimmed, airtight doors closed, and power was diverted to the flagship's weapons. And then Dreama's desperate gambit paid off. The computer devoted most of its processor power to targeting systems, reverse triangulation programs, deflection angles, and the million and one other tasks that it monitored during a combat alert.

The Medusa slowed to a crawl.

Dreama stepped in front of the thing, urging it to attack before the computer figured out what was going on and returned it to full power. The tangled mass of snakes reared back as one and Dreama awaited the sentinel's targeting check. As the things launched, she quickly moved herself into the Medusa's place, stepping inside the creature and melding her virtual flesh with its own. The snakes arced back around in search of their prey, and Dreama exited her host like an exorcised spirit. The snakes locked onto the Medusa, and bit deep.

The Medusa screamed in stylized agony as the other serpents began to wrap themselves around her bloody throat, bite deep into her eyes, and burrow hungrily into her exposed ears. Long-nailed fingers tried to pull the creatures from its head and shoulders, but the Medusa had no defense against its own powers. Screaming and kicking until the last data bit was visible, the compnode's guardian went down in a writhing mass of virtual serpents and representational blood.

The maneuver was a million-to-one shot, and the timing it required near impossible without diverting the processing power of the central computer. But Dreama had done it.

Dreama stumbled into communications circuits just as the surviving technician appeared with reinforcements. She pulled the remains of Todd Hollings' journal out of memory and dumped it in a ship-to-ship courier system. With a triumphant grin, she punched in Tiko III's transmission code and hit a large red button labeled "Transmit."

The data was still in memory, and Dreama read what she could before the inevitable security technicians arrived. She didn't like what she saw.

Dreama collapsed, falling off of the cot and landing with a crunch on the metal floor. Her arm screamed at her to get off of it, and she flopped over like a wounded animal. She knew it was broken, but it had been worth it. She had a much better idea of what Todd Hollings was up to, and now Terrin would, too.

The first journal entry that had caught her attention was about the ship that had burst through the shatterzone months ago. Something had destroyed it, but Todd wasn't saying what. According to Hollings, their sector was plagued by a particularly savage band of pirates in the month following the event. The shatrats' favorite tactic seemed to be attacking ships that had suffered an accident. A distress beacon activated anywhere in the sector seemed to draw them like flies to honey. But, unlike other 'rats, these pirates seemed satisfied with making the kill—very little was salvaged from the defeated hulks.

Between this and the last "disagreement" with Kelassiter, Hollings couldn't afford to lose much more, and had announced that he would seek out the thieves with his flagship, the *Constantine*. Only one month later, his war ship had supposedly chased his quarry into the Tiko sector.

Dreama thought about the list of plundered ships between Todd's announcement and his arrival in Tiko space. Why would fleeing pirates have sacked ships *behind* the *Constantine* if she was pursuing them? And also, there was something familiar about the ships reported destroyed. The *Gloria*, the *Mon Toaralla*, the

Benri Solaar; she was sure she had heard these names before. But where?

After arriving in Tiko space, Todd had recorded the attacks of three more ships. Two were more of Hollings' fleet but one was the Teraxian cruise liner, the *Tourister*. The *Constantine* had picked up her distress beacon but waited four hours before it had reacted. Almost as if Todd had wanted to visit it *after* the pirates had struck.

Dreama hadn't had time to read the last few sections of Todd's journal thoroughly, but mostly they dealt with the *Tiko's Fury* incident and how Todd had watched as Katanopolis butchered Jonn Stryker on the operating table. He thought it was particularly funny that Katanopolis had done everything without anesthesia.

The last few pages of the journal was about some group called the Lost Sheep, an unregistered mercenary gang working out of Teraxiter. They had been hired to ambush something, but it wasn't the *Fury*, so Dreama had skipped over it.

But the whole tone of the journal was strange, as if Hollings had wanted to keep a log of his schemes, but wanted to insert a touch of plausible deniability if it fell into the wrong hands. There was something written between the lines; something tangible that would tell her everything that Todd was up to, but Dreama couldn't quite put her finger on it. But Terrin would. The courier would deliver the journal to him in a few short hours and he and Dumois could figure it out in no time. And then he would rescue her. She was sure of it.

Footsteps reverberated down the hallway, breaking her train of thought. It hadn't taken Katanopolis long to figure out who had made a shambles of his system and destroyed the expensive Medusa program. Dreama rolled over on her injured side and saw the accompanying cadet's flushed face as he fumbled with the door — he was obviously having trouble with the passkey.

"Hurry up, you dolt!" came the unmistakable voice of Dr. Katanopolis.

Dreama smiled. They were too late. Terrin would fix them, she thought, and passed out.

Katanopolis glanced at his injured prisoner and immediately shifted his gaze to the ventilation cover and the four tiny screws lying on the metal cot. "That bitch!" he yelled and kicked the young woman in the ribs. Katanopolis stood on the bed and looked into the shaft. Seeing nothing, he jammed his hand into the vent and found the sensor cord through the gap. He could figure out the rest.

The scientist leapt from the cot and landed beside Dreama's inert form. He crouched and grabbed her soft red curls in his tightened fist. "Wake up, you red-haired bitch!" A few quick slaps reddened Dreama's cheeks before finally bringing her around.

"You're screwed, greaseball," she moaned. She was half-delirious from falling off the bed and breaking her arm. Katanopolis' constant smacking wasn't helping much either.

"I am not Todd Hollings, little slut!"

Her vision cleared a little but she still felt a little giddy. Pain had that effect on her. "Oh. Then you must be his pet scientist. How'd you get off the leash, Kitty Kat?"

The cadet wouldn't have thought it possible, but Katanopolis' face turned an even deeper shade of red. He reached into Dreama's hairline and started feeling for her cyber jack.

"Oooh, that feels good. A little lower please."

Katanopolis found the jack and stretched the cord to its limit.

"Aha!" she said for him and giggled.

"Arrgh!" Katanopolis ripped the cord out of her head, causing rivulets of blood to leak from beneath her hairline where the jack had been secured to the translator. He smiled at the spectacle and eagerly awaited his prisoner's scream, but none came. She was beyond that now.

"Too late ..." she whispered weakly as her dark and heavy eyelids began to close, "too, too late. Terrin's gonna get ya, Hollings, and your little Kat too."

The scientist stood, furious. The delirious girl continued to lie giggling feebly on the floor. He kicked her once more, harder this time and heard the satisfying sound of breaking ribs. With a contented smile, Katanopolis grabbed the cadet and left the tiny cell.

Dreama heard the door slam shut and two sets of boots clapping on the metal corridors. The sounds reminded her of the silly sound the news station on Tiko made just before they came over the vid channel. She remembered watching the news every day during the fight with Hollings over their mining rights, and had followed Stryker's exploits as he and the Wolverines destroyed the *Laverne*, the *Georgia*, and the *Mon Toaralla*.

The *Mon Toaralla*. *That* was it. Hadn't Todd reported it plundered on his way to Tiko space? How could that be when Stryker had gutted it months ago? Dreama blinked her eyes in determination, fighting the urge to pass out from the ache of her broken arm and a new pain growing hotly in her ribs.

Then it hit her. Hollings wasn't chasing pirates into the Tiko sector, he was *leading* them in! It made perfect sense. Todd couldn't deal with this threat, so he was going to let Terrin do it for him.

But why would the pirates keep following if there was nothing but burned-out wrecks to prey upon? Something was terribly wrong, something that Todd had been too afraid to write in his most personal journal, that hidden something that kept eluding her.

Dreama tried to rise and felt a series of sharp pains

in her side that threw her quickly back to the metal floor. She wasn't sure how badly she was hurt, or why she was having trouble staying conscious, but the sudden pain did manage to give her one clear thought. One word could be changed and everything would fall into place.

Pirates weren't chasing the *Constantine* halfway across the system.

Aliens were. Aliens from beyond the shatterzone.

CHAPTER SIXTEEN

Stowaways

When Stryker awoke the next day, he wasn't certain which hurt worse, the concussion or the hangover. He slowly turned his aching head and noticed the water and pain killers resting on the night stand. Someone still loved him.

A trembling hand slowly traversed the cavernous distance between the bed and the table and grasped the tablets. He didn't feel like rolling over to use his other hand, so he simply dumped the pills into the water and weakly grabbed the glass. Stryker finally sipped the now tepid water, and streams of it dribbled from the corners of his mouth. Standing up didn't seem like such a hot idea, so he laid his head back on the pillow and closed his swollen eye. The mechanical one never closed, but kept a vigilant watch over its sleeping master. At least it was smart enough not to process images to his brain when he slept.

Again, nightmares. Terrin making love to Lucretia in the corporate office while Jonn hung upside down in a pool of his own blood in the remains of the *Fury*. Max Hunt and the Jaegers hiring out to Tiko and betraying them as the *Constantine* approached with guns and missiles blazing.

But the worst: Jonn clunking down Wriggle Street in front of its laughing citizens and indigent population, walking on two metal legs jammed together in a back-alley chop shop. Arms made of rusted iron and nauseating joints made of red slime; hot oil and blood working as one in a dubious alliance. One eye the size of a hubcap with a red-veined orb jerking spasmodically around the jagged metal frame; the other … human. Jonn's eye. Jonn.

He was in there somewhere. He was sure of it. If only he could find some small scrap, some tiny portion of the tougher-than-nails marine that had won this chunk of worthless rock from Todd Hollings.

Jonn's dream self ripped off a shiny metal plate over his leg, watching as it tore loose from the snapping skin beneath, trying to find himself beneath the metal monstrosity of his body. He pulled out the cybernetic eye in a long cord of pulpy red cartilage, stringing out of his head like scarves in a magician's sleeve. He threw it on the ground and watched as the bloody eyeball whimpered and crawled out of its metal housing. It had wanted freedom above all else, but would now die without Jonn to feed off of. Lousy parasite.

Jonn continued to tear away the metal attachments as the citizens of Tiko III looked on. Rotting pectorals bulged out from beneath leathery syntheflesh and came off in bleeding strips of muscular gore. The mechanical arm pulled loose of its bony socket and snapped where the idiot salvage crew with their damn candy bars had sawed it off.

Eventually, Jonn Stryker was little more than a limbless mass of flesh and blood, helpless and alone amongst the crowd.

He awoke again, the pasty taste of the pain killers and near-vomit crawling out of his mouth and sneaking up his nostrils. Jonn managed to raise himself slightly, but had to hold his head for a full minute when the sudden rush of blood threatened to overwhelm him. Eventually, he limped over to the shower and cleaned himself up.

He felt like hell, there was no denying it, but a thought managed to cut through the nausea when he finished his shower. There was a shuttle bound for Teraxiter in just four short hours. Jonn could easily board it and have the surgery he desired performed while on his forced vacation.

He didn't remember the nightmare, not consciously anyway, but he was somehow less concerned about his cyberware now, as if part of his psyche had resolved something it wasn't letting him in on. Still, it would be great to get it looked over and tucked away.

His excitement grew into fervor — he couldn't wait to get away from this place, for a while anyway. He quickly stuffed some clothes and other junk into an over-the-shoulder bag, threw on his tan duster, and was just headed for the door when there was a gentle knock from the other side.

"Who is it?" Stryker barked. He wasn't in the mood for another visit from Terrin, Klein, Hunt, or most of all, Lucretia.

"Hawkins, Sarge. You all right?"

Jonn opened the door, blocking the light behind him with his massive figure.

"Sorry, Sarge. I thought you were probably sick — after last night, I mean."

Jonn said nothing.

"Anyway, I just … you going somewhere?"

"Teraxiter. I'm on leave for a couple a' weeks."

Hawkins looked surprised. "You mean *now*? With all the trouble and everything?"

Jonn nodded, and Hawkins finally guessed that this wasn't Stryker's idea. "Oh, I guess after the fight and all."

"Yeah," he answered. It was embarrassing and he quickly changed the subject. "How's your head?"

"Oh, fine. The vat tube healed it up in a couple of days."

Jonn shivered at the thought of the plasma tubes, and shifted his weight anxiously, signalling that he wanted to leave.

Hawkins finally caught on and moved out of the way. "Have a good trip, Sarge."

"Yeah, kid. I will." Jonn walked past the marine and headed quickly for the door before remembering what he had been wanting to ask him for a month. "Hawkins, did the boss ever ask you about what happened on New Akron? Not the attack itself, but what we saw in the smoke?"

"Yeah, I told him about it. But he thinks some pirates just had it sculpted into their body armor. Some kind of trademark or something. He's probably right, and I can't really remember it too well after getting my head cracked open and everything."

Jonn sighed and walked out the barracks door. It would be the last time.

• • •

Rygil didn't know, and Tally wasn't about to tell him. He had enough to worry about what with trying to get them on the shuttle and all. Besides, she was tough, and she could probably even get it fixed on Teraxiter without Rygil ever knowing. She carefully put on her ragged longcoat — that didn't hurt too bad — and then picked up the shoulder bag and carefully placed it over the wound. It felt like wearing starched wool on a sunburn, but she could bear it for a short while.

Tally hadn't told Rygil that the shot that had torn off her ear had also nicked her shoulder just above the left collarbone. It had seemed like such a scratch at the time. But over the last few weeks, as they had waited on the *Tourister*, a Teraxian cruise liner which had never arrived, the nick had gotten infected from her dirty clothes and grown into a greenish boil the size of a golf ball. Rygil was too preoccupied with the disappearance of the *Tourister* to have sex in the last two weeks, and so he hadn't noticed. Prophetically, their ship hadn't come in.

Finally, a Tiko supply shuttle had docked and the captain announced that he would take passengers in light of the cruise ship's disappearance. Supply shuttles weren't the ultimate in comfort, but it would get them where they were going.

Tally was walking out the door of their cell when it burst.

Rygil heard it from clear across the room. It sounded like a kid popping the wrapping that came around sensitive electronics; like bags of thick liquid bursting in quick and random succession.

"What the hell was that?" he asked angrily, thinking that she had broken one of their few belongings.

Tally turned her smudged and dirty face towards him in dull shock, and collapsed on the barren floor of the hive. Rygil dropped his things, and grimaced as something she had dropped shattered. Quickly, he crossed the room and knelt roughly beside her. He saw a wet stain peeking out from under her tattered longcoat and pulled it back. Some sort of murky, yellow fluid was seeping through the thick green fabric of her filthy jumper.

With more care than Tally would have thought possible, Rygil pulled back the dirty garment and saw the deflated sack of skin still oozing its odorless pus. His mouth curled in revulsion and his first thought was to yell at her for not telling him. Then he realized that yelling was probably the very reason she hadn't.

There wasn't time to do anything about it now, even

if he could. The shuttle was leaving in fifteen minutes and Rygil still had to sneak himself and his unconscious companion onto it. Tears of frustration began to well in his eyes.

Then Rygil had a thought. It made him feel a little dirty, but his mind couldn't help but conceive illegitimate ideas. He could use Tally's wound to get them on the shuttle.

It was hard getting her down the lift that ran the face of the Hive, but it was even harder dragging her all the way down Wriggle Street. Tally didn't weigh much, but Rygil wasn't very strong, either.

The commercial docking bay, like nearly everything else on Tiko, led directly off Wriggle Street. Rygil struggled down the public access ramp and could see the owner of the *Worm Hole* arguing with what was obviously the captain of the Teraxian shuttle.

"You bring me this cheap shit again, and I'll toss your worthless ass off this asteroid."

"Look, Jake, I'm sorry. The *Tourister* was bringing your regular stuff, but it got waxed and this was all the hooch we could find on such short notice. I thought I was doing you a favor."

Jake shook his head and acquiesced. "All right. I'm sorry to hear about the liner. Anybody know what happened?"

"No. The whole planet's buzzin' about it, but if anybody knows anything, they ain't talking."

Rygil stood by the pair until they took notice, Tally still hanging limp in his arms.

"Christ, son. What's happened?" the freighter captain asked as he ran towards them.

"Sir, I … we … "

The captain and Jake helped Rygil lower Tally to the hangar floor. The blood from the busted infection had caked convincingly in the pit of her collarbone, and the captain brushed her hair out of the mess.

"We were robbed," Rygil finished. "Two men took the money we were going to use to book passage back to Teraxiter." He rubbed her rosy cheek and tried his best to look concerned, yet brave. "She's okay, sir, just a scratch."

The captain looked around in concern, trying to spot the alleged thieves. Unfortunately, he couldn't see past the forest for the trees. "We better get you on board before they come back. Are you going to be okay?"

Rygil didn't answer, but looked with concern at his lovely companion.

The normally stern captain bit Rygil's bait down to the proverbial sinker. "You two work for Tiko?"

Rygil half-nodded, hoping that was the right answer.

"Well, go ahead and get on board. We'll fill out the paperwork and take the fare right out of your pay, okay?"

Rygil smiled from ear to ear, "Yes, sir, thank you. I'm sure there won't be any problem."

Little Jake frowned doubtfully and went to inspect his cargo.

The captain seated Rygil and Tally in the small passenger section. There were two other men and eleven women on the transport. The shuttle captain didn't know it, but no Tiko employees were allowed on leave until the marine's reinforcements arrived. He needed every available member of the militia until then, and some of the non-committed civilians were taking that as a sign to flee the ship before it sank.

Rygil stretched comfortably and noted with smug satisfaction that the seats adjacent to them were empty. The cabin was mostly dark with the majority of the light pouring in through the entranceway. Rygil was just about to close his eyes and drift off to sleep when he saw a stocky silhouette block the feeble illumina-

tion. The figure handed the captain a credcard, some
sort of license, and then pointed to the blaster on his
massive hip. He wore a brown longcoat, a white shirt
buttoned up to his thick neck, blue pants, and heavy
black boots. His hair was cut close to the scalp, forming
a sharp "v" between his narrow eyes, and the face was
lined and hard. The stranger stepped into the cabin
and grimaced at the fleeing civilians.

Rygil just *knew* he was going to sit next to him.

Tally slept for most of the first day. She always slept
with a determined look on her face, as if the world
would just have to wait until she finished sleeping
before it was allowed to hurt her again.

Stryker was returning from the toilet when he noticed the beads of sweat rolling down the sleeping
girl's forehead. He saw the dried stain on her jumper
and took a long sniff at the air. "Infection," he said and
nodded towards Tally.

Rygil sat up and looked nervously to see if the crew
was around. "Um. She was only wounded yesterday."

Stryker sat in his seat and leaned his crew cut head
back against his raised arms. He closed his eyes and
sniffed the air once again. "Bullshit. It's infected. A
long time. Maybe two, three weeks."

Rygil was amazed at the stranger's perceptive powers. "Oh, you mean the shoulder? Yeah. Nasty infection. She, uh, it happened in, uh … "

Jonn turned his head and looked disapprovingly at
the skinny man with the brown bowl-cut hair beside
him. He decided that whatever the jerk had obviously
been up to, it wasn't his concern. He was on vacation.
"Better get it treated. I've seen it before and it's only
gonna get worse."

"Uh, yeah. Thanks, I — we will." Rygil turned
uncertainly in his seat and looked at the crusty stain on
Tally's shoulder.

The thump was no louder than someone carelessly dropping their carry-on bag, but Stryker awoke with adrenaline pumping through flesh and metal. Something was about to happen. He could *feel* it.

The other passengers remained asleep, and the skinny youth that had lied about his girlfriend had accidentally rested his dirty head on Jonn's shoulder. Jonn shrugged off the weightless cranium with a disgusted look of contempt and watched as the disoriented man awoke.

"S-sorry … " he moaned.

"Shut up. Something's happening."

The passenger section of the shuttle was in the middle of the ship, between the small cockpit and navigation room, and the larger cargo section behind them. Several rows of seats sat in the middle of this segment and the aisles ran around the outer edges. Straight ahead and to the center was the door to the bridge, and the bathrooms and cargo entrance sat directly opposite to the rear.

Stryker unbuckled his restraining belt and shrugged off his nylon duster. Rygil checked on Tally, and then turned to see Jonn's heavy blaster pistol near his face. The marine's hand was hovering over it like a vulture and his vein-ridden neck was craning to somehow help his ears hear through the bridge doors.

"What is it? What's wr-*ummph.*" A strong hand, a *very* strong hand, reached behind the marine and clamped over Rygil's jaw.

"Everybody wake up," Stryker commanded in a quiet voice that somehow managed to rouse most of the passengers from their sleep.

He moved like a sinewy panther towards the bridge door and placed his ear against it. There was a dull thump and Stryker leaned back against the wall adjacent to the doorway.

The door began to move. The passengers shrank in

their seats and watched intently, afraid mostly of Jonn and his blaster, now gripped tightly in his mechanical hand. The doorway opened and a great deal of smoke billowed out, obscuring the bridge beyond. The air smelled of burning flesh.

CHAPTER SEVENTEEN

Firefight

Through the smoking doorway stepped a man in a rag-tag collection of plated body armor. His headgear was scraped together from several sources and looked like a biker's helmet with a hockey mask thrown in for good measure. In his hands was a short and lethal-looking blaster rifle, but the barrel had been sawed off so that the hyper-accelerated particles would spread out over a larger area, much like an old-style shotgun.

Rygil slid over and covered Tally with his body. They were only four feet from the pirate. The brigand lowered his weapon and pointed it at the lovers. Tally finally awoke from her delirium and screamed in her defender's ear.

Before she could complete her scream, a strong hand reached out from the smoke behind the pirate and grabbed him by the throat, jerking his head back as the barrel of a blaster pistol wedged itself in under the rear of his helmet. There was a loud crack and the pirate was dead before he had a chance to scream.

The marine holding the corpse spun in place and

used the dead man as a shield. Blaster holes soon ripped into the corpse's jury-rigged armor, and Jonn calmly returned fire into the smoky bridge.

There was a brief silence afterwards, and Rygil saw something small and yellow roll out of the smoke, emerging just past the marine's legs. It was cylindrical, like a tapered can, and the blonde with the blaster didn't seem to notice it. Suddenly, Rygil's mental synapses fired and told him what the device was. He leapt off of Tally and grabbed the grenade. He was about to lob it back into the bridge when …

BOOM!

Stryker was knocked to his left, wedged between the wall and the still-dripping corpse that had been his shield. Rygil was rolling around on the floor in shock, his hands a bloody mess of charred meat and bone.

"Everybody *down*!" commanded a voice from the smoky bridge.

Stryker was still stunned. It took him a few moments to realize that he had been hit by a concussion grenade, and he wasn't sure if the blood that had ruined his white shirt was his or that of the brainless stooge lying on top of him.

Then two more men ran into the room and crouched beside the door, ready to blast anyone who wanted to be a hero. No one fired this time, and another man walked casually into the room. His helmet was off, and his shiny head was hairless save for a black length of pony tail tied tightly at the base. A waxed moustachio was the only other visible facial hair. His skin had a yellowish tinge to it, and the eyes were slightly sloped. A dozen earrings dangled from his stumpy earlobes, and he carried what looked like a crossbow.

Jonn was playing dead, now thankful that his cybernetic eye remained open so that he could take in the pirates without their knowledge, though it was hard keeping it still. Every time he tried to adjust his view he could feel the damn thing start to rotate.

At least, it seemed the blood and gore were mostly from the man on top of him. Jonn felt a little bruised, but nothing serious enough to mess with his reflexes. One of the men who had crouched beside the door was probably watching him — it was hard to tell with the helmet, but Jonn still figured he could nail him before he squeezed his trigger.

"Good evening, morning, afternoon, or whatever it is in your particular day-cycle, ladies and gentlemen. I am Captain Bernard and these are my faithful companions, the Mongols. Please don't consider us pirates. We like to think of ourselves as independent customs agents. And it is our 'custom' to take everything you own." Bernard laughed heartily and muffled guffaws could be heard from beneath his lackey's helmets.

Jonn snuck a look at the young man who had saved him from the full effects of the concussion grenade. He was leaning against the wall opposite Jonn, just in front of the other crouching guard. They obviously didn't consider him a threat with his wounded hands and the telltale trickle of blood leaking out of his ears, a sure sign that his eardrums had burst from having a concussion charge explode in his face.

"Now, if you will kindly place all of your belongings in the first row of seats, I will gladly rid you of them." The pirate captain bowed and signaled for another man from the bridge.

Jonn flexed his fist, delicate sensors reassuring him with the simulated feel of the blaster in his mechanical hand. It was going to be easy, but he wanted to know how many there were before he blew their heads off.

"Safurio, grab Teller and Gentry and start unloading the cargo."

To everyone's surprise, the blonde in the green jumper, the one who had slept the entire trip up to now, started giggling.

"What's the matter with you, girl?" Bernard glared and waved his crossbow in her direction.

The giggling grew to laughter.

"Are you mad?"

"Is that your best, 'I'm a tough pirate — fear me everyone' voice?" she mocked in between snickers.

Bernard fumed, his skin turning a shade darker as shameful blood wormed into his cheeks.

That's it, girl. Distract 'em. Jonn thought. He carefully shifted the corpse and was alarmed when a fresh pool of pulpy blood spilled out of the helmet rim and dripped noisily on his soiled shirt. Fortunately, no one seemed to notice.

"What kind of an idiot are you?" Tally asked.

Bernard started visibly shaking. "What do y — ? How dare — ?"

Rygil felt the blood drain from his face, leaving it a pasty white. *What in God's name is she* doing? It had to be the infection; it had driven her mad.

Bernard looked uncertainly at his men. He was being humiliated by a child, a *female* child, and had to do something quick. An evil smile grew on his face and he placed his foot upon Tally's armrest, leaning in towards her with the crossbow, the antiquated bolt pointing at her chest. Tally seemed to grow suddenly afraid and shrink back in her seat. Bernard's confidence returned and he locked eyes with the cowering child. Her lips began to tremble and tears welled in her eyes. Bernard was sure she was about to beg him for forgiveness.

But suddenly, Tally could hold back no more and gave up the ruse, her lips and nostrils flaring as unbridled laughter screamed past her teeth like a runaway locomotive.

Bernard withdrew in confusion at the mad child at his feet. "Stop that!" he said.

It was too much. The other passengers couldn't help

but laugh at the pirate's feeble command.

Tally barely managed to speak over her uncontrollable laughter, "What kind of an idiot robs a shuttle *after* it's made its delivery?"

Bernard's eyes grew as big as his Oriental face would allow. Now even his men were starting to chuckle. Just as he was about to nail Tally's golden curls to the back of her seat, he saw the girl's face change and tighten into the most determined look he had ever seen. He was confused just long enough to see her look up at him, curl one corner of her lip into a deadly serious smile, and reach up to his right ear. Tally grabbed a handful of the pirate's dangling earrings and pulled hard, causing bright streamers of blood to streak down the pirate's bulging neck.

Stryker knew better than to look a gift horse in the mouth and fired one shot into the breastplate of the man covering him. The force of the blow knocked him back though it hadn't penetrated the armor, but it was all the break Stryker needed. Another shot rang out and he caught the opposite guard in the kneecap, exposed by his crouched position. The man doubled over and Jonn tapped him again in the back of the neck as he fell.

The first man was trying to roll back onto his feet when Jonn nailed him in the bottom of the boots, another spot armor didn't protect. The man screamed and rose to grab his shattered heels. Jonn caught him thrice in the helmet, the third bolt finally bursting through the faceplate and turning the man's skull into a pasty mix of plasteel and gore.

Bernard recovered quickly and bolted low for the cargo door. Jonn would have hit him had Tally not lunged for Rygil just at that moment, blocking his shot. And that was one little beauty Jonn wouldn't have risked hitting for the world.

Bernard made it to the cargo bay by scurrying

behind the rows of seats, and screamed for the men he had sent to secure the cargo. Jonn rose, letting the corpse slide ingloriously off him, and winked at the concerned faces of the man who had shielded him from the concussion grenade, and the girl that had given him the distraction he needed.

Rygil was still partly in shock and looked at his lover with stunned confusion. She gave him a "I-don't-know-I-just-did-it" shrug and motioned for him to crawl out of the aisle into the protection of the seats.

Jonn walked casually past them and checked the power meter on his pistol. The concussion grenade had shredded his light shirt and exposed the mangled conglomeration of syntheskin and cybernetic arm beneath, and his chest was covered in something chunky and red.

Tally and Rygil looked up at him in amazement. Power and confidence oozed from every pore of the marine's skin, and every joint of his metallic arm. His perpetual scowl had been replaced with a look of familiarity. Tally recognized the look, though she had only known it once in her lifetime. Jonn was *home*.

He walked with powerful steps around the right side of the aisle, firing steadily as he advanced. The shots impacted with several cargo containers and the rim of the open doorway. Jonn wasn't hitting anyone, but the racket was keeping the pirate's heads down as he advanced. When an accelerated particle took off a chunk of metal doorway, it gave a man a lot of incentive to remain hidden.

Jonn suddenly stopped firing, "Throw out your weapons. Now."

To Rygil's surprise, one of the sawed-off blasters sailed out of the room and landed at Jonn's feet. Everyone heard "What the hell are you doing?" from the cargo bay and a sharp twang, and then one of the pirates ran through the doorway, a crossbow bolt sticking harmlessly from his armor. He tried to run past Jonn, but a quick elbow to the chin clotheslined him to the carpeted floor. Stryker placed his foot on the struggling pirate and fired a few more shots into the cargo bay.

The pirate had one grenade on him and Jonn bent down to grab it. It was a Kereteka concussion weapon, the kind the Wolverines sometimes used when they didn't want to blow a hole in an airtight environment. Without standing, he thumbed off the safety switch, pressed the activation button, and held it for two seconds before sidearming it into the darkness. Stryker pulled the dazed pirate up to him for cover, then waited until the blast rocked the cargo section. Shrapnel had torn open the man's armor and stunned him into unconsciousness, so Jonn grabbed his makeshift shotgun.

Quickly, Jonn walked into the smoky cargo bay and turned off the lights. The cybernetic eye clicked into nocturnal life, and Jonn could see the pirates' body heat emanating from behind a large container. They couldn't see him from their position, but he could overhear Bernard urging his men to counterattack.

Jonn shut the door behind him and sealed them in more complete darkness. His eye was seeing everything in infra-red, something Stryker was used to after years in Brodie power armor. He inched in further and saw one of the faces rise above the container, hopelessly trying to see why the door had closed.

"Where is he?" whispered Bernard.

"I dunno, boss. I can't see nothin'. I think he locked us in or somethin'."

"Ah, good. Then we shall prepare to re-establish our position." Bernard tried to speak eloquently, hoping to soothe his men into acts of bravery that might save his own life.

Jonn watched as one of the pirates stood and lifted

his face mask to wipe perspiration from his brow. A brief flash of light was the only visible sign of Jonn's blaster, and the sweaty pirate dropped quickly to the floor.

"What was that?" Bernard screamed. "What happened?"

No answer. Jonn slid forward with his back against the wall. He could see Bernard, the other pirate, and the rapidly cooling corpse. Bernard was reaching over to the dead man. Jonn saw him touch the man's leg and shake him.

"Safurio?" Bernard whispered. He removed his glove and ran his hand up to the dead man's helmet. Something warm and wet greeted his probing hand and he quickly withdrew it. "Ugh!"

Stryker couldn't help but snicker. He saw the orange heat signature of the remaining lackey turn and point his blaster in his direction, and quickly moved out of the firing arc.

"Captain! He's in here with us! He's locked himself in here with us!" Panic had set in and the pirate called Gentry stood and ran for the door.

Jonn pushed a stack of boxes and watched as they fell in front of the blind bandit, sending him sprawling and causing his weapon to slide out of his clumsy hand.

Gentry felt his jaw come down on the corner of something metal. It felt like his teeth had shattered against each other and he thought his tongue might have been in between them when it happened. "Mmmph-gurgle," he pleaded, confirming his guess. He started to cry and felt around for his weapon. He knew it was over when his hand rested on a leathery boot.

"I'd've let you live, but you killed the crew. An eye for an eye, buddy."

Bernard heard his last crony scream until Jonn's

blaster cut it short. Sweat was dripping down the brigand captain's cheeks, cheeks that had grown fat off of loot too easily taken. He thought about surrendering but wasn't sure if the maniac with the pistol would let him. Bernard felt the other pirate's blaster lying at his feet, and he quietly took it. "What do you want?" he called to the darkness.

He was answered with a disturbing chuckle. Jonn didn't want this to end so soon, but he realized more of Bernard's buddies might be entering the ship even now. "Throw your bow and arrow out here, Mr. Customs Agent."

"Then you will kill me?" Bernard thought that by pointing out the lunacy of this particular policy, it might change.

"Yep."

Bernard was quiet for a while, and he was having trouble breathing.

Jonn was leaning against the door, waiting for the pirate to stand so that he could finish this, when the crossbow flew out over the box Bernard was hiding behind.

"Okay, I surrender. There's no need to shoot, Mister."

Jonn smiled. Bernard's voice was too calm — he wasn't giving up yet.

"Turn on the light and I'll surrender." Bernard waited a few moments and heard something bumping around in the darkness behind him. "Mister? Did you hear me? I said turn on the lights and I'll give up." There was a scraping sound from near the doorway, but no reply from the marine. "Mister?"

Suddenly the lights came on. Bernard jumped to his feet and pointed the blaster towards a figure standing near the cargo doors. He screamed in defiance and emptied the weapon into the target, riddling its skirmisher armor with craters and cracks.

Skirmisher armor? Bernard thought as he saw the last sight of his life: Jonn was standing beside him with the crossbow pointed at his head.

Jonn walked towards the sliding door and looked at the corpse he had propped up. Bernard had ripped it apart with the improvised scatter-gun, and Jonn inspected the weapon approvingly.

He opened the doors and walked cautiously into the passenger section, making sure that no more Mongols had entered the ship. He stopped at the head of the aisle and looked at Rygil and Tally. "Good work. How're your hands, kid?"

"Huh? Oh, they're … okay. Uh, fine … *sir*." Rygil's hands were bloody and a lot of skin was missing, but the damage was superficial. He'd be all right.

Stryker smiled a "thanks" and looked toward the bridge. He could see the crew sprawled across their chairs, but the room was otherwise empty, so he moved on. In the ceiling was the pirate's entry hole, a rough cut circle leading to a short airlock tube that connected the shuttle with the pirate's parasitic vessel above. Jonn knew that pirates usually boarded with their entire crew since no one wanted to get left behind and miss out on potential loot, but it didn't hurt to be sure.

He started to crawl up into the chute and stopped. With a quick glance around the dimly lit cabin, he found the distress beacon and thumbed it on. Then he crawled up into the darkness above.

CHAPTER EIGHTEEN

Interlude

On a viewscreen never seen by human eyes, surrounded with scavenged machinery and blue illumination, a red dot appeared and began to beat like a tiny, throbbing heart. Four individuals covered in stolen body armor turned in their ill-fitting chairs and leered hungrily over the pulsing dot. Their dark armor was covered in rounded segmentations, and reflected the blue lighting like the carapace of crawling millipedes caught in the beam of flashlight.

Leathery fingers topped in stained ivory claws tapped on the screen as one of the creatures needlessly pointed it out to his companions. There was a grunt of satisfaction and the beings began to program the strange computers that drove their warship. They sped towards the wounded Teraxian shuttle, one of them picking a wet morsel of black food from his oversized jaws.

On a viewscreen mounted in the circular bridge of the *Constantine*, a tiny red blip appeared. A technician busy with other things finally noticed it and called for his superior. The senior man walked over, gave a noncommittal look and thumbed the intercom, setting the dial to Todd Hollings' private channel.

"Mr. Hollings? Bridge to Mr. Hollings."

The technician heard the intercom flip on and a feminine whimper end abruptly in the background. "What is it?" he demanded breathlessly.

"It's, um … you wanted to know if any distress signals were activated in the sector, sir."

Silence.

"*Well?*"

"Yes! Umm, yes, sir! About a day out of Tiko sector, Mr. Hollings."

"Good," he slobbered. "I'll be right down."

CHAPTER NINETEEN

Near Miss

The pirates had breached the bridge in the typical fashion. They came in hard and fast and locked onto their prey with metallic grapples, then rammed a boarding tube through the "skull" of their victim. This penetrated just deep enough for a tracked laser torch to revolve about the interior of the tunnel and cut an airtight entry into the shuttle. After that, well-armored men had dropped down the tube and easily dispensed with the relatively defenseless crew.

Jonn reached the top of the airlock and listened. When he was as sure as he could be that no one was covering the entrance, he stepped up another three rungs, but kept his body bent so that he could spring through the hole in one quick movement. With a surge of energy from his powerful legs, he jumped through the hole and rolled behind the first cover he could find, an improvised control panel for the extended boarding tube.

He was in some sort of work bay. Welding torches, crates of bolts and scrap metal, and boxes of stolen goods lay haphazardly around a rectangular, dingy white room. There didn't seem to be anyone present and he quickly scrambled to the doorway. A short hallway led to another section of the ship, and Jonn could hear someone moving around, possibly flipping switches by the clicking sounds he heard.

"Go close the hatch, Marty. I'm not gettin' anything."

"Screw that. Bernard'll kill us if we leave 'im!"

"He's already dead, lunkhead!"

"How do *you* know?"

"We ain't heard from 'im in twenty minutes!"

"I'll go look, okay?"

"Yeah, sure, you do that."

Jonn smiled as he heard the owner of the reluctant voice stand and turn into his hallway. He stood quietly and concealed himself just inside the door of the repair bay. The pirate entered the room and crouched, covering the boarding chute with his weapon. Fortunately, he wasn't wearing any headgear and Jonn quickly grabbed him from behind, covering the pirate's mouth with his vice-like cybernetic hand. With a quick twist of the head and a bone-wrenching pop, the thief dropped to the floor in a rubbery heap.

"Marty? Marty? Izzat you? What happened?"

Jonn knew he should have lowered the body to the ground, but he couldn't resist a little psychological warfare. The pistol was a conventional slugthrower — Jonn's favorite type of weapon. Unfortunately, he figured one of the pirates ought to live so that the authorities on Teraxiter could clear up some of their other cases with his confession. He stepped into the doorway of the bridge and smiled at the remaining pirate.

"Who the f —" was all the man managed to get out before Stryker cold-cocked him in the jaw with one quick jab of his artificially enhanced limb. *Maybe this cyber-junk isn't so bad after all*, he thought.

The black warship slid through space on the track of its prey. The distress beacon of the shuttle guided it in like a wounded fish calls sharks. The leering creatures within salivated at the excitement of a fresh kill, and loaded their weapons with terror shells — large-caliber explosive rounds molded in sharp ridges to make a ripping sound as they tore roughly through an atmosphere. They knew they were close … but still out of sensor range. The beacon guided them like a lamp on a black night.

The pilot stabbed an oversized claw into a bowl of slimy eel-like creatures and dropped the wriggling thing into its gaping maw. It was only an appetizer.

Jonn sat in the pilot's chair and familiarized himself with the jury-rigged controls. The pirates had taken an average ship and modified it with everything they had stolen over the years. On the floor were several components surrounded by tools and technical manuals. Evidently, not all of the scavenged pieces worked properly.

The navigation computer had several pre-set destinations programmed into it, and Jonn quickly found the button that would steer it and its ruined host towards Teraxiter. Fortunately, the oversized Q-drive of the pirates was geared to carry more than one ship — probably so they could tow hulks back to their secret base for easy plunder.

Tally stood and walked cautiously to the bridge of the shuttle despite Rygil's protests. She saw the scorched circle in the ceiling and the tunnel leading off above it. Dead crewmen continued to smoulder and Tally almost vomited at the hideous smell. Although she had never seen one before, she knew that all ships carried a distress beacon. She looked at the complicated panel of flashing lights, dials, meters, and switches and finally found one labeled "Emergency Only." She opened the safety cover and flipped the large red switch beneath, hoping it was the right one. A flashing light on the console suddenly died, but Tally didn't notice as she ran from the stinking room and smoking corpses. It never occurred to her that Stryker had already turned the beacon on.

Not too far away, the creatures' leathery faces froze in anger and frustration. The one closest to the monitor smacked the casing, but it was no use, the red dot had disappeared. The others cursed him and sat back in their uncomfortable thrones. There would be other prey. There always was. The masters had taught them that.

• • •

In his office on Tiko III, Terrin Kelassiter was still trying to come to an arrangement with Max Hunt, the leader of the mercenary group known as the Jaegers.

"Look, Terrin, the way I see it you don't have any choice. Any Tom, Dick, or Sherry could come whizzin' in here and roll you over like a fat lady on her first date."

Kelassiter breathed a laugh and stared at the seven foot mercenary. "Yeah, but that's not going to happen because they know Fleet and the rest of the Tiko corp would come out here with guns blazing and take it right back."

"Then why do you need me?"

"Insurance, Max. Just to prevent some fool from trying it in the first place."

"Which fool are we talking about? Hollings?"

"That's a possibility, but I don't think so. If he was going to try something so stupid, why hasn't he done it already? We've been defenseless for over a month now, and its probably going to be another two weeks before a relief force shows up."

"Who, then?"

"Pirates, I guess. They're the only ones that gain anything from attacking our ships, and they wouldn't stand at a chance at invading an entire city."

Hunt wasn't convinced. "There are ways of getting your colony legally, you know?"

"How's that?"

"Act of God. If something unusual happens, like, say, the colony's wiped out by a plague or swallowed by an exploding star, and the system is left vacant for more than three months, the first person to establish another claim gets territorial rights."

"Sounds like you've been reading up on Consortium Law."

Hunt smiled. "Laws are a good thing to know when you're in my line of work."

Terrin chuckled again and went to the worn spot on the carpet in front of his window. A militia man on the street below was fighting with his partner over what looked like a spilled ice cream cone. Terrin shook his head and sighed, "Okay, Max. Fifty thousand credits for two weeks, double if anything more dangerous than the flu hits us. I get you, your men, and the ship."

Hunt stood and bowed with a sweep of his long arms, "We are yours to command, my Captain."

"You did what?" Guy shouted over the din at the *Worm Hole*.

"We're going to hang out here for another couple of weeks. 'Case anything happens."

"*Sacre Bleu*, Max! Terrin's sure to find out about us by then!"

The black giant drained a cup of beer and then wiped his mouth with the back of his hand. "I wouldn't worry about that too much. Your boss is over a barrel, and I get to spank him."

Klein had been silent up to now, but he was glad to know Tiko wouldn't be left unprotected. "What do you think's going to happen, Max?"

"Don't know, Steve. But something will. I'd bet money on it."

And Max never bet on anything he wasn't sure of.

CHAPTER TWENTY

Teraxiter

Almost eight days later, just above the atmosphere of Teraxiter, Jonn contacted the orbiting Fleet outpost and turned over the pirate ship and her dead crew. The lone survivor was dragged screaming curses from the bridge, a broken jaw garbling his fruitless protests.

The other passengers were still sitting in their seats when Jonn and a Fleet officer entered the room. The officer, a man named Tallard, listened to Jonn describe the attack with a look of reverent disbelief. Tally couldn't help but stare in awe as Jonn led the captain about the scene and explained to him how he had slain an entire band of pirates as casually as she might eat her morning breakfast.

When they returned from the cargo bay, Stryker led the captain to the front of the passenger section and pointed at Rygil.

"This guy saved us all," he said with a smile. "Tried to return a concussion grenade, but it went off in his hands. He damped the impact enough that we weren't all knocked out."

The captain looked confused for a moment, his mind trying to register what had happened. "Medic," he finally said. A corporal in a red Fleet uniform stuck his head in the door and Tallard pointed out the primitive bandages on Rygil's blasted hands. "Fix this man up."

Stryker pointed at Tally, "Her, too."

After a cursory glance at Rygil, the medic examined Tally and spotted the wet stain beneath her jumper. He tried to pull the material back to look at the wound but found that it was stuck fast. Tally looked away embarrassed and the medic brushed some of the crusted pus from the edge and squirted the rest off with a small pump of water. He realized that the wound had been there a while, and looked to his captain to report it, but his questioning gaze never made it past Stryker. Soon, Tally's shoulder was wrapped in sterile bandages and treated with topical antibiotics. Rygil's hands, though limp and near skinless, were also re-wrapped in plasma treated bandages, and the medic told him they would be functional in a day or so.

Stryker pointed at Tally as the medic finished his duties, "This little girl smarted off to 'em after the blast. If she hadn't distracted 'em, I wouldn't've been able to skrag 'em."

Captain Tallard rubbed his smooth chin and looked at the dried blood splatters covering the shuttle floor. He wondered if the other passengers realized just how dangerous their situation had been. One man with a blaster and two kids with a little bit of guts had managed to take out an entire band of pirates. Granted, the pirates seemed to be somewhat incompetent and Stryker was an experienced marine, but the sheer superiority in weapons and armor should have decided the matter ... at least according to everything he had ever been told by Fleet.

Tallard decided he had been behind the helm too

long. The blood on the floor and the insane man with the blonde crewcut reminded him that war wasn't fought between the pages of a Fleet battle manual. It was fought between men of flesh and blood and bone and iron. He was very glad he rarely had to draw his weapon.

A short while later, the passengers of the shuttle were transferred to another ship and held for questioning. There was a tense moment when it was discovered that Rygil and Tally had no current identification, but their actions in the attack caused Captain Tallard to give them the benefit of the doubt, and they were soon released.

Stryker seemed to become gloomy after the excitement died. Tally told Rygil that he looked like a child whose toys had been taken away. Jonn saw the couple looking at him and tried his best to smile. He had scorned the skinny little man when he had boarded the shuttle. With his bowl-cut hair and dirty jumper he looked like just another lazy civilian who never appreciated the sacrifices made by the marines. They were a miserable lot, civilians; no discipline or purpose in their life. All they ever wanted to do was get rich and fat without doing any of the work. And when someone got screwed and came looking for payback, it was Jonn and his men that would have to save their pimply white asses.

There were some that Jonn considered worth protecting, some that worked within the system to make it as bearable as possible for everyone else. Terrin was like that, but most of the executives would sooner soak a planet in red blood than watch their corporate ledgers fill with red ink.

Jonn looked at Tally again. She was tidying the bandages on Rygil's mutilated hands, and kissing his fingertips tenderly. They were laughing, each pointing out how stupid the other had been in the attack a week ago.

In that moment, Jonn suddenly remembered why he had become a marine in the first place. All of the civilians weren't money-grubbing executives or lowlifes living off the tender underbelly of society. There were some that were innocent, like this young girl and her boyfriend. They had risked everything and asked for nothing.

As a soldier, Jonn sometimes found it hard to sacrifice his men — men that had trained hard and sweated blood — to protect a bunch of generally ungrateful civilians. Why should those that have proved their worth die to protect the ignorant masses? Since armies had existed, men had asked themselves these questions, particularly as they become more and more isolated from the population they were supposed to protect. Now, a simple smile dappled across the honey lips of a blonde-haired child had put everything back into place.

Tallard broke Jonn's trance and started going over the facts of the attack one final time. After an hour of his redundant questions and Stryker's repetitive answers, the passengers were escorted down to Teraxiter.

Teraxiter was about the size of Mercury and had blossomed into a dirty but profitable jumping-off point between the frontier worlds and beyond. It only had one inhabited continent, also named Teraxiter, which was about the size of the Terran continent of Australia.

The sky was black and grimy, and the streets were filled with urchins, prostitutes, cyberleggers, and gangs, but the bars and casinos somehow managed to stay filled with hundreds of corporate miners, paper-pushers, and terminal-slaves.

All of the major companies in the area owned bits and pieces of the continent, and the spaceport at Gonqlin was no exception. Jonn stepped off the shuttle and grimaced at the gigantic red "R-H" plastered in neon lights above the terminal entrance. Rygil and Tally were already at the door and boarded a skimmer. Both waved goodbye and the girl blew Jonn a kiss as the vehicle glided out of the pick-up area.

It was drizzling rain today. Actually, Jonn couldn't remember a day when it hadn't rained on "the holiday planet." Someone had told him that the enormous amount of unchecked air pollution, combined with the cheap terraform job, kept the planet continuously wet and miserable. And, as usual, everyone here seemed to get a taxi but Jonn.

A half hour later, Jonn finally managed a ride in a filthy hover-cab whose driver reeked of cheap cigars. An endless trip across the rainy city later, he checked into one of the cheaper hotels and dragged his tired body up to his leaking room. The bed could've passed for a pool. A rat scurried into a crack in a wall covered in mildewed wallpaper, and the bathroom was best left to the imagination.

Jonn stood in the doorway a long time before he finally entered and tossed his single bag onto the worn sofa. There was a vid-phone on a rickety table beside it, and Jonn sat to begin the lengthy process of scanning the computerized phone book for registered cyber-surgeons.

There was a branch of *New You* located in Gonqlin, but he had already decided against that particular clinic. It was still morning on Teraxiter, and Jonn started making calls to several of the registered hospitals specializing in cyberware and plastic surgery. After speaking with six different businesses, Jonn found that the shortest waiting list was two weeks long.

He leaned back on the couch and glanced about the dirty room. He could've afforded better but it might have eaten into the money he had set aside for his surgery. And he was going to have it. *One way or another.*

He took off his clothes and stood in front of the cracked mirror that topped the room's dresser. His pectorals were still a crawling mass of flesh, and the hideous eye continued its spasmodic dance across his face. The knee and groin looked like a patch on a pair of worn out jeans, and his arm was still covered in hanging flaps of rotting syntheflesh highlighted by peeking bands of steel and hydraulic tubes. He couldn't stand to look at himself anymore, so he pulled his clothes back on and headed for a bar.

The thought of getting smashed was appealing to him, but not nearly as overwhelmingly obsessive as it had been after the incident at Lucretia's. That had been a stronger and somehow stranger urge — almost as if he had been *ordered* to get drunk.

A quick walk down the street put him through the doors of the *Pirate's Den*, a crowded bar full of people from most every walk of life. Jonn grabbed a seat near the back of the bar. He wanted nothing more than to be alone in a crowd of people.

The first drink he ordered was Terrin's favorite, a Venusian Moonrise. He was just about to order a second when two men stalked a pair of girls into the ladies' room. Both of them wore ragged black tank tops and the leather pants that were all the rage amongst Teraxiter's gang population, but what really caught Jonn's attention was their cyberware. Virtually every portion of available flesh was wired, hooked, gouged, or otherwise invaded by plastic tubes and metal sockets. One of the men's hair was spiked up in black points jingling with tiny chains and fishing hooks, and the other was bald save for several tattoos and a battered chip holder. Two chips were visible in the device, tiny cartridges with skill-enhancing programs wired directly into the brainstem. Just under this, the words "Lost Sheep" arched over his ear in large red letters. Jonn just bet that wherever the punks got their cyberware, there wasn't a two-week waiting list.

He stuck his credcard in a slot on the table and

poured the melting ice from the drink into his mouth. Then he stood and quietly left the table, casually crunching the cubes between his teeth as he headed towards the toilet.

The men had cornered their prey in the tiny bathroom, and several other girls quickly fled the area, leaving their sisters to their own fate. Jonn quietly pushed the door open and saw the punks forcing the women up against the tiled walls. One of them was bleeding from her mouth where the punk with the spiked hair had obviously hit her, and he licked it from her neck with a crenelated, synthetic tongue.

Jonn stepped into the room and cleared his throat to get their attention. "Oh, is this your boyfriend?" said the one with spiked hair.

Jonn just stared at him, feeling a cool breeze of natural confidence waft over him and carry away his anxieties. The right corner of his lips rose involuntarily into a wry smile.

The second thug, the bald one, released his victim and pulled a knife from his pocket. His eyes had a sharpness to them that revealed his fear, but bubbles raced up a thick amber tube behind his ear and artificially quelled it. Jonn knew the drug; most Brodie suits injected it into the wearer's system during combat. The user would become more confident in his ability and his fear could be channeled into energy that gave him increased speed and agility. But it didn't compare with experience and real confidence.

In one quick move, Jonn reached past the first man and grabbed the other thug's wrist, twisting it backwards. There was a sharp snap, and the knife dropped to the ground as the youth fell back onto a toilet seat — the drug and the pain sending contradictory emotions to his stunned mind. The other one's souped-up reflexes helped him get in a single punch before Jonn's elbow caught him in the temple and sent him crashing to the ground.

The woman whose mouth was bleeding spat out a tooth and kicked her attacker in the ribs. She grabbed her friend and dragged her out the door, turning to Jonn just before they left, "Thanks a lot, he-man, but we could've done just fine without you. Don't expect any favors."

"Sorry. Didn't mean to help you or anything," he mumbled.

When the women left, Jonn grabbed the one on the toilet by his over-sized nose ring, and tore it and the middle lining out of the punk's nose. "Where'd you get all this junk?" Jonn asked after the kid was finished screaming.

"*Schiess*, man! You ripped off half my fraggin' nose! I ain't gonna tell you *jack*, you lunk o' ugly."

Jonn saw a bulge just beneath the thin fabric of the man's tank top and ripped the fragile shirt open. As he suspected, the nipple had been pierced and another ring dangled from it. This one looked like a coil of barbed wire, he thought. *Probably some sort of fashion statement about oppression or something.* Jonn stuck his smallest finger in the hole and tugged slightly, threateningly.

The man's eyes grew wide with the anticipation of pain. Suddenly, he realized there was a way to avoid it. "*Schiess*, man. Everybody knows about Hacksaw. Ain't no secret. Just go uptown under the old *Costa del Sol* hotel. Hack's got a chop shop under there. Just don't tell him who sent ya. Check?"

Jonn smiled a "thanks," and ripped the barbed ring out of the man's chest.

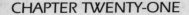

CHAPTER TWENTY-ONE

The Undercity

Jonn rented a red cycle for fifty creds and headed down into the undercity. It was starting to get dark now and the city lights refracted strangely beautiful in the oily drops of rain. The heavy wind whistled over his crewcut and whipped at his duster. He had a blaster jammed into the waist-line of his denim pants, and a simple white t-shirt covered his scarred chest.

Jonn was getting that feeling again, the feeling that soon there would be violence and blood and pure, genuine adrenaline — not the heavy, synthetic stuff that the Brodie suit was always shooting into his veins.

The surgeon called Hacksaw would be the nucleus of a cyberlegging outfit. Jonn knew all about their kind. Bodysharks, zipyanks, ghouls; they went by a score of different names but their operation was always the same. When they saw someone with cyberware, they'd follow him, drag him into some dark alleyway, and rip, cut, or tear his stuff out. Of course, the donor rarely survived the process.

The doctor would have a street clinic known only to

a few privileged clients, and would reinstall the stolen parts cheaper and faster than any registered hospital could. A good surgeon could install electric claws, small caliber slugthrowers, and even such bizarre devices as monofilament whips and razor wire. This was all illegal under local corporate law, but that's what made the business so profitable.

The surgeon would be surrounded by a bunch of chipheads — burnt-out gang members who did the actual stealing and protected the surgeon from other cyberleggers. The inevitable confrontation with these flunkies brought the smile to Jonn's face.

Downtown was exactly what he had expected. Seemingly deserted high-rises towered above the dirty slums below, and the refuse of an uncaring population huddled in its cold and rainy streets. There was a dirty smell here, but it was something thick and oily that crawled out of his nose whenever he tried to catch and identify it.

The address of the *Costa del Sol* was still in the electronic phonebook, and Jonn rolled down the side alley that would take him there. The dead sign of the hotel was only a few blocks away and Jonn took careful notice of his environs as he began to slow. The architecture spoke of something, a neighborhood once filled with happy faces excited about their lives on a new world. How many people had come to this planet looking for work and wound up living in a rat-infested hell-hole like this? How many corporate employees had lost their savings in the casinos and bars and become trapped here forever?

The bike was attracting some attention from the locals, but Jonn didn't care. He welcomed it. The thought of violence took his mind off the gray poverty around him. He wondered why he hadn't noticed all this when he and Lucretia had visited before, but he supposed happiness had blinded him to the truth. He thought it felt a little like being an executive in one of the planet's mega-corps. As long as he was happy, everyone else must be too.

Stryker pulled up in front of the *Costa del Sol* and cut the bike's engine. A few faces tried to look disinterested as they leered out of the surrounding doorways, and gunfire sounded sporadically in the distance.

The hotel had been one of the city's first. Now it was a firetrap and a haven for rats and anyone who couldn't afford a cardboard box. A rusty fire escape hung down over the entrance where several youths bristling with grotesque metal, boiling tubes, and sparking wires sat. There were four of them, and Jonn noticed that two had the distinctive bulge of a firearm under their syntheleather jackets. Three were looking at each other and Jonn and trying to figure out just why some idiot had just delivered them a brand new motorcycle. The fourth was a little cooler and picked his teeth with a long, razor-sharp talon that slid silently from his knuckle.

The one with the talon wore a gray shirt and black syntheleather pants. Black hair hung down over his eyes and wallowed around his shoulders. "You loco?" he asked.

Jonn ignored him and looked up and down the street, trying to discern if the gang had any other members posted in less obvious locations. "Hacksaw," he finally demanded.

The youth stared at him for a moment, and then looked away ignorantly. "Don't know no Hacksaw, brother. 'Fraid you musta come all the way down to the Shits for nuthin'."

Jonn looked at the filthy alleys and saw a rat nibbling at the fingers of a drunk or a corpse. "They call this the Shits, huh?"

"Yeah. 'Cause that's what everybody down here's

got. The water's bad, the food's bad. Even the air'll give you the runs."

Jonn grunted in amusement. "Tell Hacksaw I'll be back tomorrow at eight. I want some surgery done and I've got the money."

"You look like you already got some surgery there, Steel-eye."

Jonn ignored the comment. "Eight o'clock. Tomorrow." With that, he kicked on the ignition and slowly turned the bike in a tight circle. When he was facing back towards the upper Gonqlin, he twisted the accelerator and left the Shits behind.

The *Pirate's Den* was as good a place as any to kill the rest of the night, and Jonn got roaring drunk on beer and whiskey. Tomorrow night, he would be himself again.

CHAPTER TWENTY-TWO

Lost Sheep

Tally and Rygil ran down the dark alley and almost screamed when they saw it was a dead end. They turned just in time to see their four pursuers stumble hastily in behind them, sealing off the exit.

The punks stopped when they saw the trap their quarry had blundered into and casually rearranged their leather jackets and dangling chains. One of them whipped out a comb and ran it through his greased hair, and smiled evilly at the beautiful young girl he had cornered.

Rygil stood in front of her and threw up his bandaged hands as if to fight. The gang members roared in laughter and Tally felt her face flush red with anger and frustration.

The one with the comb flicked a thumb over the teeth and watched the grease fly off in the Teraxian moonlight. "Look here, boy, why don't you just run along and leave us this tender morsel? You don't have anything we're interested in."

Rygil knew better than to return the thug's banter —

it would only rile them more, but Tally wasn't as placating. "Frag off. I wouldn't touch you for all the money on Teraxiter!"

The thug acted hurt and turned a sad face to his laughing companions, "She don't want to bump-bump with old Skraz, fellas. Well, I wouldn't want to upset you, little girlie, so I'll just do it when you're dead, okay?"

There wasn't much Rygil could do. The men weren't after their money; it was painfully obvious that they had none. The only thing Rygil and Tally had that was worth stealing was their flesh and blood and self-respect.

A bum stirred in a filthy pile of garbage and an empty bottle rolled out into the moonlight. Rygil leapt for it and smashed off the bottom on the dirty street. With one quick slash he sliced open the nearest thug's sleeve. Bright blood spilled out of the synthetic leather and the startled hooligan staggered backwards.

The leader, the one who called himself Skraz, growled with delight and shot himself full of Quickill and adrenaline as claws slid out of his knuckles. The other men rushed to his side and pulled knives from their boots and jacket.

"That's the spirit, boy!" Skraz howled as Rygil waved the dripping bottle at him.

One of the thugs lunged to his right and grabbed Tally by her golden curls. Rygil panicked and attacked with everything he had, swinging the improvised weapon in a wide arc of crystal pain. Skraz took a cut across the face and grimaced as the shard scraped across the bone beneath his teeth. The remaining thug dodged in under Rygil's swing and rammed his metal knuckles into his kidneys.

Tally dug the heel of her boot into the thug's arch but he only yelled and butted her on the back of her skull with his forehead. Blackness started creeping into her vision, but her body continued to struggle. Rygil was on his knees in front of them, feebly stabbing at the dancing figures which eluded him. Skraz stepped on his flailing arm and Tally heard the sound of breaking glass and bone followed by a pitiful scream that quickly dwindled into a low moan.

One last blow to the back of her head caused wet rivers to seep down the back of her jumper. Skraz had Rygil by his moppish hair and was feeding him something, threatening Tally if he didn't swallow.

Mercifully, she fainted.

There was darkness, penetrated occasionally by grinning faces and reeking breath. There was pain. The back of her head was throbbing and wet like a bruised melon. She felt someone grab her, touching her in places only Rygil had before. But this time it wasn't with the smooth caress of a lover's touch, it was with a bestial mauling as cold as the metal of the hand that did it. Then, the feel of ripping flesh and a dirty pain. It started low and worked its way shamelessly up her spine. Tally felt tears running down her face, or maybe it was the hot saliva of one her tormentors. It really didn't matter which any more.

The moon had moved out of the tiny alleyway when Tally awoke. She could only see the wall of a building stretching above her as she lie on a cardboard box beneath it. Directly across rose the wall of the other building that bordered the cul-de-sac. That was all she could see without moving her head. She tried to raise it and felt her hair crunch as it pulled free of the crusted blood that matted it to the wall. The pain was no longer intense, just a dull throbbing that only got worse as she attempted to rise. Her feet were dangling off the end of the box and the shredded remains of her jumper hung limply around them.

In the street was Rygil. He was lying on his face in

a pool of blood that had attracted most of the vermin away from her. She slid off the box and felt a rough, scraping sensation deep within her womanhood. She held herself in a vain effort to stem the pain, and looked closer at her lover. His mouth was a blasphemy of torn flesh and drying blood. Tiny shards of glass coated his lips and Tally realized just what it was the thugs had made him eat.

A loop of something white and viscous protruding from beneath his sternum told her the rest. Slashers, the common name given to those maniacs with cybernetically attached claws, often gutted their victims as a sign of their status.

The punk that Rygil had sliced across the arm was lying against the wall nearby. Tally turned cold eyes upon him and tried to understand why he had died. He had been bleeding too heavily, she guessed, and death had been certain in the undercity where there was little medical care and even less sympathy. His companions had gutted him and ripped out every last bit of the dead man's cyberware. Tally was short on sympathy herself. The eyes and jaw had been removed, and something rectangular had been ripped out of the right side of his skull. The only thing left was a red tattoo arching across his blood-encrusted scalp. It read "Lost Sheep."

Tally pulled the tattered jumper up around her and held it to her bruised breasts. She stared in hatred at the corpse for what seemed like hours, and finally kicked it in the chest. It felt good, and the throbbing pain seemed to ease. She wanted to cry, but she was all out of tears. She kicked him again and felt something snap inside the rib cage. Again and again, she kicked the mutilated body, no anger or hatred visible on her bloody face, only passive apathy.

She had managed to put her foot through the man's chest when the Teraxian police finally arrived.

CHAPTER TWENTY-THREE

Adoption

S omeone was pounding on his door. But who the hell even knew he was here besides Kelassiter? Jonn rose and slipped the blaster out from under his pillow. He jammed it down the back of his boxers and walked carefully to the door.

"Yeah?"

"It's the police, Mr. Stryker. May we come in?"

Jonn was still half asleep and wondered why the hell the police cared if he messed with a local gang of small-time zipyanks. He opened the door slightly, saw that the voice did indeed belong to a policeman, and stepped back. "What's the problem, off—"

Between the uniformed men was Tally. She had been cleaned and bandaged, probably by a police medic, but the bruises and lacerations told Jonn that her first night on Teraxiter had met with disaster.

"Christ, come in!" Six arms helped Tally into the broken sofa at the foot of Jonn's bed. "What happened?"

"We're not sure, Mr. Stryker. She wouldn't talk to us for hours, and then she only gave us your name. We looked you up in the central registry and hoped that you'd know her."

"Yeah, yeah, I know her. Where's her boyfriend?"

"We found two corpses at the scene, Mr. Str—"

"*Scene?* Scene of what?"

Sheer presence forced the leading trooper back a step. "T-the scene of the murder, Mr. Stryker, in the downtown section. One of the corpses was a member of the Lost Sheep, and the other had no identification."

Jonn looked down at Tally and the emotion called helplessness, something he was getting all too familiar with in the last few months, slipped into his eyes. "Rygil?" he asked her. She blinked slowly, and Stryker knew the answer to his question.

"Will you be taking care of the girl, Mr. Stryker? She seems to have no money or identification and the city—"

Jonn whipped his head around and stuck his finger in the policeman's face. "Don't you say another word to me, you half-ass rent-a-cop. Yeah, I'll take care a' her." *And them, too*, he thought. "Where do these Lost Sheep hang out?"

"Well, sir, perhaps you don't understand. The Sheep are the largest gang in the city. They've got their hands in a little bit of everything, including some off-planet pirating. Even if you are a licensed mercenary, w-which you seem to be, I wouldn't go stirring up that bunch if I were you."

"If you stuck-up *pinheads* had been down there doing your fraggin' *job* and not bein' so afraid of gettin' your soft little hands dirty, you wouldn't have gangs like that!"

The policeman was young, inexperienced, and could have been dead at Jonn's feet in a minute, and he knew it. But Stryker had hit a nerve, and he was going to stand his ground, even if it killed him. "Look here, Mr. Stryker. We patrol the downtown as much as we can, but the damn mega-corporations have their own marines in their sections, and we aren't allowed to go in unless asked or we see a crime in progress. The officers that went in the Hollings' sector risked their jobs *and* their lives by going in when they saw the girl kicking some chiphead's heart out!"

Jonn backed down a little, calmed somehow by the trooper's outburst. "The Hollings' sector, huh? As in Todd Hollings?"

The officer wiped the sweat off his brow and wallowed in the relief of Jonn's reaction. "Yes, sir. The Randall-Hollings corporation owns that section of the city. Their marines didn't respond to the scene, so we took the liberty of escorting the girl to the hospital."

Jonn turned his head back to Tally and looked at the spoiled face of innocence lost. "Hollings. Now why does that make sense?" he grumbled.

• • •

"Damn it, Thad! Open the fragging door or I'm going to blow it open!" Kelassiter kicked the door with his genuine leather boots and banged on the facing with his fist for the fourteenth time. Finally, the red panel slid aside and the scowling figure of Dr. Thaddeus Dumois appeared centered in the doorway.

He gray hair was frazzled in every direction, like he had been rubbing his pink hands through it repeatedly. His bifocals rested in the time-worn red cradle on his nose, and the fingers of his hands were locked together in contemplation. "I've been checking our equipment."

Terrin had asked him to run a check on all the equipment since the security guard had been found dead in the airlock to the mines, and now it seemed Thaddeus had found something. By the look on his face, Terrin was almost afraid to as what.

Thad turned away and headed towards an antique table in the middle of his cluttered living quarters. A well-used sofa served as his bed by the blanket and pillows there, and the table in front of it was covered with several days worth of empty and half empty plates. The desk was covered with calculators, pens, and charts and printouts all stained with the telltale circle of a coffee cup. "Everything seems to be working just fine, and nothing unusual has occurred. Except for when you turned off the airlock alarms just after the guard's death."

Terrin gasped. Thad was accusing him of treachery. "Wh-what are you talking about? I was sound asleep when all that happened! Why the hell would I turn off the alarms?"

"You tell me, Terrin." Dumois whipped a taser out of the pocket of his labcoat. One bolt from the device would paralyze Terrin for fifteen or twenty agonizing minutes. "Only you *can* turn off the alarms. Remember? The foreman, the night watchman, and two other miners have bypass keys, but it takes three of them to override you, and I'm not ready to buy into the conspiracy theory just yet. So that just leaves the eye scanner, something that only recognizes your particular retina pattern."

"But why the hell would I want to go outside the airlock, anyway?"

"That's a good question, perhaps Jonn could figure it out, but you sent him away. Funny that. First, almost our entire marine platoon gets slaughtered, and then our veteran commander gets exiled to Teraxiter. Very suspicious, if you ask me." Dumois reached his off hand under the desk and pressed an orange switch.

"Thad, how could you think I'd sell us out?" The scientist shook his frazzled gray head mournfully.

Two minutes later, Guibert and Hawkins appeared at the scientist's door. Guy saw the taser in Dumois' hand and instantly drew his blaster, leveling it at the scientist's chest. "Drop it, Doctor!" he yelled.

Terrin turned and signaled for the marine to put his weapon away. "Dr. Dumois believes I've sold us out to Hollings."

Thad fingered the taser nervously, as if it might accidently shock its user, and held up a fan of paper, "The retinal scan was used to turn off the airlock sensors just after the guard's death. Only Mr. Kelassiter can do that alone."

Guy eased his blaster back out of the holster. "You are accusing Mr. Kelassiter of treachery?"

Thad nodded his head.

Suddenly, Guy leaned forward and brought the grip of his handle crashing down on Terrin's ten-gallon hat. "That's good enough for me," he grinned.

Hawkins and Dumois were in shock; neither of them had expected Guy's reaction. If they had known that he was preparing to desert, something that could easily get him executed, they would have understood his zealousness to create confusion in the corporate hierarchy.

Terrin shook his head slightly, as if confused, and dropped to his knees. Red juice trickled down his forehead, and Terrin stabbed at it with his fingertip, as if confirming that it was indeed blood.

Hawkins didn't know what to do. If Dumois was accusing Kelassiter of treachery, then there must certainly be something to it. But Terrin was the boss and out here on the edges of known space, he was more than the CEO, he was God All-Mighty himself. He was still in shocked confusion when the grinning Guibert clubbed God a second time.

Thaddeus woke up an hour later than usual the next morning. He didn't trust alarm clocks, of course, and his body's normally foolproof system was thrown off by the stress of his unintentional *coup d'etat*. When he finally managed to crawl off his sofa, he picked at some breakfast, and began to work on the case against his friend and superior.

He threw on his wrinkled coat, grabbed a cup of coffee, and left his dingy quarters for Terrin's office upstairs. He started with the drawers and other conventional hiding places, and finally — reluctantly — opened the computer terminal secreted in Terrin's desktop. He hunt-and-pecked through endless files ranging from Klein's reprimand to Stryker's phony "Request for Leave," to the dubious decision of sending out the entire marine company on a routine investigation of potential mining assets. Taken as a whole, the events of the last month were devastatingly incriminating.

Dumois diligently printed out each of the files and added them to an ever-growing pile. He finally stopped after three hours of sifting through the hundreds of other bureaucratic reports. Thad rose from Kelassiter's uncomfortable chair, stretched his scrawny arms, and looked about the room one last time for anything he might have missed.

A tiny light blinked silently on a black machine, but Thad had no idea what it was for. He made a mental note to have one of his junior technicians investigate it, but he was too techno-phobic to mess with the machine himself. So he stretched once more, grabbed his coffee cup and his pile of evidence, and headed for his more familiar sofa to sort things out.

The light on the ship-to-ship courier system continued to blink long after Thad had drifted off into disturbed slumber. It was Terrin's "red-line," a very expensive and private system for sending and receiving messages not meant for other ears. The blinking light meant that it had recorded a message, and only awaited the touch of a button to divulge the contents of its memory buffer.

If Thad had been more familiar with the common tools of the executives, he might have found Dreama's desperate transmission, the one she had almost died trying to send. He might have figured out the extent of Hollings' plan, and he might even have saved his city.

But he didn't.

CHAPTER TWENTY-FOUR

Costa del Sol

T ally was in the shower when he left to buy her some new clothes. The green jumper, still crusted with blood, went into a dumpster on the way out. He called the Teraxian police from a payphone and found out that Rygil's body had already been disposed of in the city's crematorium. The dead weren't particularly good for business, and the standing policy was to dispose of impoverished persons quickly and cleanly. Jonn could think of worse ways to go.

He bought his guest some clothes at a thrift store nearby. He didn't know anything about style or fashion, so he grabbed something simple and walked back to the hotel. She had just stepped out of the shower when he returned. Out of the steamy white room stepped a battered and bruised young woman that little resembled the girl Jonn had seen earlier. Where the towel didn't cover her tender flesh, Jonn could see long red streaks, as if she had rubbed herself raw in the shower. He figured she had a lot of memories to wash off, and handed her the packages. The brown jacket, black shirt, and blue jeans that she finally chose made her look more mature than the one piece jumper she had worn on the trip to Teraxiter, and Jonn had to watch himself to keep from admiring her in a way neither of them was ready for. He had never seen her cleaned up, and Tally couldn't remember the last time she had done it properly, but both silently decided it suited her well.

"They've already … um … cremated him."

Tally nodded slowly, trying to accept that her lover no longer existed. And she hadn't even been able to tell him good-bye.

"Are you … hungry, or anything?" Jonn suddenly felt stupid. He had just told her that her boyfriend had been turned into ash and now he was asking her if she was hungry.

To his surprise, she nodded.

The two walked out of the grungy hotel and wandered into one of the nicer restaurants on the block. Tally remained speechless throughout the expensive meal, and ate slowly but heartily. Jonn couldn't help but notice how beautiful she was. He guessed she was about twenty-three, but her eyes could have been a thousand for all the pain they held. He didn't think they had looked that way before.

Even with the scabbing wounds, the long tear at the corner of her mouth, and the swollen blue eye, Stryker couldn't help feeling attracted to her. She caught him looking at her once, and he shamefully looked down at his tasteless food and avoided her gaze.

"Thank you, Jonn." Her voice sounded a thousand years older than the last time he had heard it.

He pretended to look to his right, hiding the side of his face with the mechanical eye like a teenager with an embarrassing pimple. "For what?" he said through a mouth full of steak.

She didn't answer, but he understood — it was for

letting her be alone with him.

Tally had been with the police the entire night and hadn't slept since the shuttle from Tiko III. When she and Jonn returned to the hotel, she crawled onto the soggy bed and fell fast asleep.

That suited Jonn just fine. He quietly slipped on his duster and strapped the blaster pistol to his thigh. Before he left, he locked the door.

Again he mounted the scooter and headed into the undercity of Gonqlin. It was 8:14 pm by the watch set into the bike. Jonn had wanted to scout the place out early and look for the trap that the gang would no doubt set for him, but the long dinner with Tally had put him behind schedule.

He rolled down the street and saw that the same group of toughs was sitting in the recessed entryway of the dilapidated hotel. For some reason, the sign was on tonight and four of the letters actually lit. Jonn was surprised that the building even had electricity, but then figured it must have some power if it was being used as a makeshift hospital.

The four at the door and who-knew-how-many-others hiding in the dark alleys of the dirty street weren't the real problem. Jonn figured he could take them if he had to, or at least blow his way past them and through the door. Only one of them, the one that sported the claw, even had any kind of armor on, and that was little more than a padded jacket similar to the kind worn under power armor.

Killing everyone in sight, however pleasurable, wasn't going to work if he was going to have some jerk operate on him, however. Somehow, he had to impress them, bribe them, or terrify them into a submission so firm that he could trust them while under anesthesia. Jonn remembered the surgery on the *Constantine* well, and he wasn't about to go through anything like that again.

195 ■

"You back?" said the thug with the claw.

"Yeah. Hacksaw ready for me?"

"Now what makes you think I know anyone named Hacksaw?"

Jonn heard a movement behind him, some amateur flicking the safety off a weapon in the darkness. He took a wild guess and hoped he was reading the signal right. "Sign's on. That means you're open for business."

Claw looked around, checking out the surroundings for any sign of trouble. "How you know that, psycho?"

"Look, chiphead, I've got a couple o' thousand credits I want to spend on some tech. You gonna help me out or you gonna sit out here and jerk me around all night?"

The thug looked around one last time, then pursed his lips and nodded his head. "Okay, maniac. Let's see some money."

"Give me a break, pinhead." Stryker stood off the bike and walked up to the steps, towering over the sitting slasher. "Half now, half when it's over and I'm walkin' outta here."

The slasher stood. "Let's see the half, then."

Stryker threw a thumb at the bike. "Get it yourself."

Claw nodded at one of his companions and the boy walked over to the scooter. In the single compartment, he found a bag of credits.

"Wanna count it?" Jonn asked.

"Naw, man, we'll check it while you're under. You try and stiff us, we'll just cut you up. Got it?"

"Yeah. Now get out of my friggin' way."

Claw led Jonn into the hotel and through the decaying halls of the first floor. They passed the elevator and the youth knocked twice on a door labeled "BASEMENT." A return knock sounded and the door opened, revealing a guard armed with a submachinegun.

Jonn and his host walked down the dingy stairs into a darker room illuminated only by a candle flickering on a rickety plastic table. Claw directed him to sit at one of the three chairs, and took another for himself. After five minutes or so, the door to a well-lit room opened and a burly man wearing a white lab coat splattered with blood entered. He slipped off a pair of dripping latex gloves, threw them sloppily onto the table, and took the remaining chair. Stryker thought he looked a little like an evil version of Thaddeus Dumois. Graying hair jutted out from under a surgeon's cap, and beady eyes locked on their patient with a look that was somewhere between a concerned nurse and a hungry vulture.

"What can I do for you, Mr. ...?"

"Jones."

"Ah, yes," he grinned knowingly. "I think I treated your brother last week. Must be an awful lot of you Jones boys on Teraxiter."

"Yeah, dozens." Jonn felt a sickness roil inside his stomach. He wasn't sure if he would live through this even if the gang didn't try to kill him. "I want this packed away," he pointed to his eye. He pulled his shirt off and displayed the rotting syntheflesh of his arm and chest, "and this patched up." Jonn didn't figure the knee was worth messing with, but he had a real problem. A simple skinjob wasn't going to be worth nearly as much as his mechanical eye, so the cyberleggers would probably just kill him and take it *and* his down payment instead. The solution was that he would have to add another enhancement, something expensive that could be the first part of a larger system. That way, the thieves would keep him alive in hopes that he would come back for more. Business was business, after all.

"I'm working on an entire system. Arms, legs, spine, intradermal plating. The works. 'Course I can only afford a couple a' pieces at a time," a brainstorm hit him, "as my merc contracts pay off." Mercenaries were notorious for looking after their own and even the Lost Sheep might be reluctant to make a new enemy, especially one that might refer his friends to them in the future.

"So what do you want to add today?" Hacksaw smiled.

He hated to do it, but there was little choice, "Another arm?"

"We might have one of those at the moment. It's expensive, though, probably thirty thousand at least, depending on the manufacturer."

"That's fine. I can cover that now and get a good start on saving up for the next one."

Hacksaw stared hard at his potential client. Stryker hated this con-man crap. It was Kelassiter's game, not his. Jonn would much rather have put the slasher's head through a wall and ripped off little bits of Hacksaw's flesh, but that wouldn't get him what he wanted. "Okay. It's going to take about four hours and two days in the vat."

"No. No vats. I had a bad experience in one of them once."

"Okay," Hacksaw shrugged, "it's your misery."

The table felt strange after Hacksaw placed the breather up Jonn's nostril. Jonn saw a knife glisten under the hot lamps and felt a slight sting under his armpit. Delirium hadn't quite given in to unconsciousness when Jonn saw a long strip of flesh being peeled off a metal arm.

He dreamed again. This time, Todd Hollings was raping Tally at the end of an alley while a couple of the Lost Sheep made Rygil chew glass. Rygil looked up at him and reached out a bloody, bandaged hand, but Jonn knew he couldn't help.

What was Todd's part in all this? How was he

hooked up with the Lost Sheep and what was it that was gnawing at the back of Jonn's mind, some tiny detail he had overlooked? *There's something about the slasher. What is it?*

Then he was looking over his body as it lay on the operating table. The surgeon was taking some sort of tool out of his dirty black bag. Of course, it was a hacksaw. Jonn saw the doctor grab his arm and place the blade just over his shoulder, but this dream was getting old and he forced himself on to the next terror.

Tiko III was a smoking ruin. The *Constantine* was blasting chunks of the asteroid into space dust, killing everyone within the sealed city as the oxygen and pressure rushed out like vented steam. Klein and Guibert were the first to explode, their eyes popping out of their skull like fleshy mortars. Terrin and Dumois ran screaming into the street and were slagged by the *Constantine's* pulsers before the icy vacuum could claim them. Hunt and Lucretia were banging away and laughing at Jonn, and exploded in a mass of tangled wet redness.

But Hollings wouldn't attack Tiko III now. *Would he?* Todd hadn't been directly linked to anything that had happened in the last month, but then why did his name keep floating up like crap in a backed-up toilet? Jonn knew the greasy bastard was somehow to blame for every dirty, painful, thing that had happened to him, to Lucretia, to Terrin, and to Tally and Rygil in the last month. He just had to figure out how, and then there would be hell to pay.

The nightmares were mercifully short this time.

Hacksaw's voice wafted into Jonn's consciousness, "You sure jump around a lot for a fella under anesthesia. You're all fixed up, though."

Jonn heard the snap of rubber gloves being pulled off the surgeon's hands. He opened his left eye and squinted under the bright light.

"Let me turn that off for ya," the surgeon offered. "Ya can't open the other one for about a week, and them bandages on your head need to stay there about as long. They're treated with most of the same stuff that's in the vats so they'll heal pretty quick, but only if you don't break the airtight seal, so don't mess with 'em."

Jonn rose and rubbed his head. Miraculously, it didn't hurt.

"You're shot full of pain-killers right now, friend. It'll ache in the morning though, you can trust me on that one." Hacksaw turned and grabbed a bottle of pills from a nearby table in the dingy operating room. "These'll help a little bit, but watch out or you'll be takin' 'em for the rest of your life. Oh, an' don't flash 'em under the cop-dogs' noses, eh? Don't need any o' that attention."

Stryker stood and looked around for his clothes. In the corner were his things, wadded inelegantly but with the blaster, sans power clip, lying on top. Dressing was out of the question. His entire chest and both arms were bandaged, and he could feel the thick stitches rubbing just beneath the surface. His spine felt a little sore and he was glad that Hollings had already replaced it with one that could bear the power of his new arms.

Hacksaw held a small silver sphere up to the lamp and looked it over through squinting eyes. "There was somethin' a little strange in your chest, young fella. Near the heart."

"What's that?"

"I've got no idea. Some kinda silver ball or somethin'. I couldn't figure out what it did, so I plucked it out. Kinda recon by fire," he laughed.

Jonn failed to see the humor in his joke. "Maybe you oughtta put it back?"

"Nah. It's not important, or you'd'a been floppin'

around an hour ago."

"Thanks, doc," he bit.

"That's one hell of an eye-piece, too. Who makes it?"

Jonn hadn't really even considered the fact that cyberware had brand names. "I don't know. It was all they had at the time. Or at least that's what they said."

"Well, you're all done anyway. You can come back by if there's some sort of problem. I'm here most every fourth and fifth day from noon on. Skraz'll let ya by a little easier next time."

"I'm sure he will, doc," Stryker finally grinned.

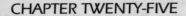

CHAPTER TWENTY-FIVE

Last Respite

Hendrickson was lucky. After the two salvage bozos took Jonn Stryker's arm off, he'd scooped the marine up and carried him into the infirmary. He hadn't had any idea just how happy he had made his boss until Hollings himself gave him a one-month leave on Teraxiter.

The event itself was a little strange. Todd wanted him to save one of their greatest enemies, and then rewarded the man who did it. Six months ago, Robbie would have been summarily executed instead, contract or no. But he wasn't one to look a gift horse in the mouth, and was on board a lightning-fast medical shuttle to Teraxiter one week later. The craft was small and almost as fast as the messenger couriers, but it had still taken over three weeks to reach its destination.

He couldn't help but wonder where the *Constantine* would be when he returned. It was sitting just outside the Tiko sector now, almost two weeks away from the asteroid-city itself. Everyone expected Todd to attack, especially after the ominous trip into Tiko sector, the destruction of their only corvette and marine platoon, and Todd's general malice towards Terrin Kelassiter. But nothing had happened.

Yet.

Oh well, Robbie Hendrickson thought as the shuttle entered its final approach to the planet, *it's not my problem now.*

• • •

Stryker returned around eleven the next morning. He unlocked the door with his key and tried to be as quiet as possible in case Tally was still sleeping.

The sunlight was just peeking through the tattered curtains as he entered, and pooled across the girl's nubile form. Tally rose, still wearing the black shirt and jeans from the night before. She looked around, confused for a moment, and then did the most beautiful thing Jonn had ever seen. Tally rolled over on her back and sat up, arching her spine and raising her arms in a long yawn. Her round breasts poked through the thin fabric of her blouse, and a bright gleam peeked out from under her naturally shaded eyelids. *God*, he thought, *is this what Rygil woke up to every morning?*

"Ohhhhh," she moaned. "What time is it?" A clock sat on a simple white table beside the bed and Tally turned it towards her. "Hmmm. Eleven." She yawned again, a little less spectacularly this time. "Where did you sleep all — Oh my … *Jonn*! What happened?"

He was draping his shirt and jacket across the bed when Tally noticed his bandaged head and chest. "Nothin' serious. I went and had a little surgery done."

She looked away from him, trying to decide how she felt about this. "You went and got … *more* of that … stuff?"

"No. I had it tucked away. Hidden."

The blonde curls swung playfully as she turned her head back around and sighed with relief. "Good," she said without thinking. "Not that … I mean it wasn't …"

"It's okay, kid. I hated it myself. Want some breakfast?"

"You mean lunch?" she smiled, relieved.

"First meal of the day, I call it breakfast."

"Everybody else would calls it lunch at eleven o'clock," she toyed.

"I'm not everybody else."

"No. You're certainly not."

Jonn had never seen anyone recover from tragedy so quickly. Not even, he hesitated to admit, himself.

The walls of the restaurant leaked with Teraxiter's ever present rain, but at least the plates and glasses were free of the crud found elsewhere. Lunch, or breakfast as Jonn insisted on calling it, consisted of oily Teraxian salmon and *hunj*, a local jelly spread over the grainy bread that had somehow permeated the city of Gonqlin. Stryker caught himself wolfing down his food as he had so many times in the mess hall with his buddies, and then thought better of it. He saw Tally eating even faster and with less grace than himself, and she looked up embarrassed. It was too funny for either of them and most of the *hunj* and its associated bread wound up flying back onto the table as Jonn and Tally burst out in laughter loud enough to annoy the couple next to them. It was the first time Jonn had done more than chuckle in years. He had almost forgotten what it felt like. Unfortunately, his head and side weren't in as good a mood and began to throb with the pain of yesterday's operations.

Jonn's laughter slowly dwindled into a moan and he downed a few of the painkillers Hacksaw had given him with a glass of pulpy juice. The woman sitting next to him looked strangely at the pills, and Jonn realized for the first time in his life he was doing something extremely illegal. This only made him start laughing again. The renewed pain almost forced him to down another of the soothing narcotics, but Jonn figured this was a vicious cycle and managed to ride it out with a grimace and another shot of juice.

When they had settled down and finished the rest of their overpriced breakfast/lunch, Tally tongued the last drop of juice from her glass and set it on her empty plate. "Jonn?" she said and scrunched her eyebrows in determination.

He wiped some jelly from his mouth with the back of his hand, "Yeah?"

"I know you think 'cause I'm laughing and stuff that I don't think about it, but I do."

She caught him off guard with the sudden change of tone, and he recoiled into his normally quiet self.

"You've done everything for me, even though Rygil and I used to run from you guys on Tiko. We even shot someone once."

Jonn looked aside for a moment, *that* was where he had seen the boy. The thought of the *Critters* aquarium bursting all over the floor made him laugh once again, a little less painfully now that the drugs were kicking in. He still hated fish, though, and stabbed the last bit of salmon from his plate with vengeance.

"So you know I have no money, and there's no way I can ever pay you back."

He shrugged and curled his lips into a "who cares?" smile.

"But I want one more thing from you, Jonn."

He looked a little surprised and then nodded eagerly. He was terrified that she was about to leave and he would never see her again. Anything she wanted that prevented this from happening was no less than a miracle to the lonely marine.

"You have to teach me how to use this." From under the table, Tally pulled Jonn's blaster.

"Cripes!" he whispered through a mouthful of *hunj*. Despite being slowed by his bandages, Stryker managed to throw his dirty napkin over the weapon and pull it under the table before too many others had seen it. "How the hell?" he patted his waistline and found that, indeed, the weapon had been stolen from him. "How did you ..."

"That's how we got by, Rygil and me. Now it's just 'and me,' and I'm going to have to learn to use a weapon."

Stryker looked about nervously. A couple of Jortusians from the next table were watching them, and though he had a permit for the weapon, the Teraxian police wouldn't look kindly upon him waving it about in public. "You don't wanta do that, kid. I can get you a job back on Tiko or somethin.' It wouldn't be much, but it'd pay the bills and put some grub in your gut."

Tally looked frustrated, as if she didn't know what to say next. Jonn figured that Rygil usually did most of the talking once Tally's big brown eyes had failed. But in those eyes, Jonn saw a glimmer of himself. It was something frightful and alien to the childlike face that surrounded it, and Jonn knew that Tally hadn't wanted the gun for personal protection.

"Don't lie to me," he grumbled and lowered his head back over the remains of his meal. "You want to kill the guys that skragged your boyfriend."

She turned away and faced the leaking wall, watching as the rivulets slowly tore away the paint and revealed the ugly stone beneath. Some dying part of her tried to correct him, but she knew he was right.

Her silence was all the answer Jonn needed. "Thought so."

She turned back towards him, pleading. "It's just one of them, Jonn. A slasher. He calls himself Skrag or Skraz or something. I know I can find him. Just one time and I'll give it back and never ask you for anything again."

Jonn studied her with his human eye and saw the shame that had twisted her once smiling face into a mask of hate. She wasn't just going to kill Skraz, she was going to murder every Lost Sheep she could find until either they, or more likely she, was dead.

"Forget it."

The hate dripped off her face and resentment took over. "Then I'll find another way."

Jonn ate the last crumb of his toast and then it hit him. "Did you say 'Skraz'?"

It was against his better judgement, but if he didn't help her get over this, she was going to go do it on her own and would probably wind up much worse than raped and beaten for her troubles. He tried to tell himself that perhaps her spoiled innocence would return once Skraz was dead, but he knew from personal experience that the pain and the urge to inflict it only grew more insatiable afterwards.

They transferred to a room with two beds on the second night, and Jonn couldn't help but slowly and surely fall in love with a girl young enough to be his daughter. For three days, he showed her every combat exercise his healing body would allow. She already knew a few hand-to-hand moves, mostly throws that used the opponent's weight and momentum against him. She had learned those the hard way and Stryker worked on combining her natural style with a few offensive maneuvers that would keep the attacker down once she put him there. The last day, he took her downtown and taught her how to fire the heavy blaster. He also picked up a spare from some local urchins, and several of the twenty-shot energy cells that powered it.

By the evening of the fourth day, Jonn felt ready to remove his bandages and help an innocent young girl kill her first man.

Tally gently cut the dressing from his chest and Jonn noted with pleasure that he could feel the cold steel of the scissors against the artificial flesh. The ribs and collarbone on his left side were still heavily bruised, but Jonn seemed to be able to move his new arm with only a minimum of soreness.

After Jonn played with his arm for a few minutes, he pointed at the lights. Tally turned them off and carefully slit open the bandages that covered his cybernetic eye. Turning off the lights was actually useless — the cybernetic eye had built-in chromatic sensors that darkened instantly in bright light.

Jonn saw his surroundings blink into existence and gave the mental command that switched his eye into infra-red mode. Tally showed up as a brilliant orange, yellow, and red splotch while the overhead illumination glared blazing white. In low-light mode, he could make out the slight bulges of the artificial veins in his new arm even though the curtains emitted only a tiny slash of illumination. He rose, switched modes again, and threw open the curtains. The telescopic enhancer seemed to work fine as he zoomed in on a passer-by below, and Tally watched in fascination as the lens of his eye extended and recoiled to enhance and reduce the magnification level.

The flesh around his eye and the sensitive nerve cords leading into his brain were the reason for the bandages. Had Jonn not given it time to heal, the tiny servo motors that rotated the eye would have ripped the cord right out of his cerebellum. The device still didn't look quite right; the "white" part of the eye was actually silver and the pupil and cornea were solid black, but at least the jagged socket and frame had been removed and a simple pair of sunglasses could hide it altogether.

Jonn put on his jeans and the syntheleather jacket once again and jammed the blaster into his waistline. Tally wore a similar outfit and tied her hair back around her head. The spare weapon that Stryker had given her fit snugly down the front of her jeans, and was almost invisible when she buttoned her brown jacket over it.

"You sure this is what you want?" he asked before opening the door.

"Yes. But how are we going to find them?"

Jonn frowned. "Don't you mean 'him'?"

"Yeah, 'him,'" she confirmed.

Jonn shrugged and the unlikely couple walked down to the street where they rented the red bike once again. He made her wear a helmet this time so that Skraz wouldn't recognize her before she could get close enough to kill him.

As they made their way downtown, Tally leaned forward and shouted in his ear, "So how are we gonna find him? It's not like he'll have a big sign over his head or anything!"

Stryker couldn't help but smile a little.

●   ●   ●

Vanessa was Terrin's first visitor. He was sitting on his cell's metal cot with his trademark boots propped up on the uncomfortable looking steel toilet. A plasma bandage was wrapped around his head, and he looked generally miserable.

It wasn't a good time for introductions, but Vanessa wanted revenge.

"Mr. Kelassiter?" she asked.

He nodded.

"I wanted to talk to you about Guy Guibert and Steve Klein."

He nodded again. The name "Guibert" didn't seem to sit well with him by the snarl on his lips. "Yeah?"

"Well, sir ..." she stammered. Vanessa had never talked to an executive as high up as Terrin Kelassiter before. She wasn't really afraid of him, especially since he was behind bars, but it was a little unnerving just the same. "Well, it's kind of hard to say, but ..."

"How did you get in here?" Terrin interrupted.

"I told the guards we had a … *relationship*."

"What? That's ridiculous. Everyone on Tiko would know if I had a girlfriend."

Vanessa flushed red. "I didn't mean *that* kind of relationship. I'm …" this was getting harder with every word, "a prostitute."

"Oh. Great. Just great. Now I'm not only a traitor, I'm a lecher too. Things just couldn't get any better."

Vanessa looked down at the floor. Anger was overcoming her shyness and she was about to say something when the man behind the bars seemed to notice.

"Hey, I'm sorry. I didn't mean it like that. I've just got a lot on my mind. Besides these bandages," he laughed. "What'd you want to tell me?"

"Well, you know that the Jaegers are in port?"

Terrin nodded.

"Klein and Guibert are going to go with them when they leave. Guy was at the *Worm Hole* getting plastered, and said that now that you *and* Stryker were out of the way, nothing could stop them."

Kelassiter frowned and leaned back against the wall by his cot. "What am I supposed to do about it? I'm a prisoner."

"I don't know," she seemed embarrassed, like this hadn't occurred to her. It made her feel stupid and she started to leave.

"Wait," Terrin halted her, "what's all this to you?"

Here was a question she could answer, and Terrin saw the look of a woman scorned. "I was supposed to go too. But they cheated me. I'm as good a fighter as any of the Jaegers, but Guibert told them I'd be the ship's *whore*!"

Terrin saw that Guibert had smashed the girl's dreams like he had smashed the back of his head. "I wondered where he got the balls to hit his boss. Guy's usually just an instigator." He leaned back on the cot and wished he had a window to stare out of. "Go on back and pretend like you haven't told me a thing. I'll be out of here as soon as Dr. Dumois figures out what's going on, and I'll take care of things. Especially Guibert."

Vanessa nodded and walked out of the brig.

Robbie Hendrickson couldn't believe it. No sooner had he exited the Gonqlin spaceport than Jonn Stryker whizzed by him on a motorcycle. The look on his face meant that something was about to happen, and Robbie decided he wanted to be there when it did. Stryker was practically a legend amongst his marine company, and Robbie had felt a certain amount of pride when he had carried him into the sickbay after the salvage idiots had cut his arm off. Now he might have a chance to see the legend in action.

There was a girl with him — she was fumbling with some sort of pistol stuck in the front of her pants — but Robbie barely even noticed.

CHAPTER TWENTY-SIX

Costa del Sol (Two)

T he plan was simple. Stryker and Tally would pull up in front of the doorsteps and she would empty her blaster into Skraz and turn him into a big greasy, bloodstain. Of course, as an old core world historian had once said, no plan survives contact with the enemy.

They stopped the bike in front of the hotel and there were indeed four punks sitting on the short concrete steps, but Skraz wasn't one of them. A girl with leopard spots dyed into her short hair had seemingly taken his place. She wore a black tank top, rounded plastic glasses, and tubes that shot out of her neck and disappeared into her left breast. A Trinity submachinegun lay within easy reach. The others didn't seem to be armed, but their bulky jackets and metallic limbs could easily disguise most any type of weapon.

"Wattcha want?" the girl with the spotted hair hissed. She arched her neck as she spoke and revealed fleshy slits along its length, almost like gills.

"Where's Skraz?"

"Anything Skraz can do for you, I can do better."

"I doubt it. What's your name?"

"Ripper. You the dude what got the arm the other day, right?"

"Yeah. I need to see Skraz. You gonna tell me where I can find him?"

"S'pose so. Come on, and bring your squeeze. This ain't no place for a woman."

Stryker climbed off the bike and followed the hulking female through the double doors. Tally hung onto him closely and tried to hide the bulky weapon in the front of her tight pants.

"Skraz is workin' the downstairs today." Ripper led them to the stairwell and knocked three times. There was an answering knock, and the door opened. The guard posted there wasn't Skraz, but what he wore sent a chill down Stryker's plasteel plated spine.

He had dirty hair that strayed in all directions and a host of cybernetic apparatus that led in and out of several festering sores around his neck and ears. He wielded a scattergun and pointed it up at the roof as Ripper passed. On his arms was the same sort of quilted jacket that Skraz had been wearing, the type usually worn under powered armor. Over this he wore an extremely thick chestpiece made of black plasteel. Now Stryker knew what had been bugging him since he had first seen the slasher named Skraz. Where the hell did punks like these get ahold of expensive Brodie undersuits?

And more importantly, why did the breastplate worn by the door guard have the word "Wolverine" printed just above the left breast?

Of course! Everything made sense now! Captain Tallard, the Fleet officer who had taken the last of Bernard's pirates into custody had told Jonn that their parent gang, the Lost Sheep, had an off-planet pirating operation. And it was this same gang that seemed to have the run of Todd Hollings' corporate sector planetside.

Now the final clue was right before his eyes! The chestpiece could only have come from one place: New Akron! All of the powered armor from the wreck of the *Fury* had been returned once the salvage rights had been forfeited, and the armor his outfit had worn in the previous conflict with Hollings had been gray. That meant that the punk guarding the door could only have scavenged the undersuit and the chest plate from the three bodies left on New Akron.

Stryker grabbed the man's shotgun by the barrel and rammed it back into his nose. Ripper turned just in time to pop a razor sharp claw from her knuckles, and caught a boot in the chest that knocked her down the concrete stairs. She flipped over several times, accenting each tumble with a sharp snap, and landed in a crumpled heap at the bottom.

The guard was still holding his broken nose when Stryker sent him sprawling down after Ripper. He heard a sharp crack and turned to see Tally firing back toward the doorway where Ripper's friends were already trying to get in. Somewhere below, he heard the operating door creak open hastily and then slam shut.

"Hold 'em!" he yelled to Tally as he leapt down two and three steps at a time. He turned the corner at the bottom just as someone threw a bolt loudly into place on the other side of the operating room door. The bolt was probably metal but the door was only thin wood and Stryker hurled his heavy body through it.

He crashed through in a wave of splinters and instantly rolled to the left to avoid the rounds that hit above and to the right of him. At the apex of his roll, he stopped and mistakenly plugged the startled Hacksaw and an unfortunate patient who happened to be in the way. The doctor turned into a bright red mist and the patient convulsed spasmodically, but Skraz had already bolted past Jonn and through the remains of the door.

"Shit!" Stryker yelled and scrambled to his feet to give chase. "Tally! Comin' up behind you!"

Skraz's footsteps echoed loudly as he ran up the stairs. There was a burst of gunfire and then two loud cracks from a blaster. Skraz slid down the stairs just as Jonn turned the corner. He was also wearing one of the scavenged breastplates and the blasts had only stunned him and knocked him off his feet. Stryker looked up the staircase and saw Tally still pointing the blaster down at them as she sat on the top steps. He grabbed Skraz's Trinity and quickly pulled the clip, checking to see how many rounds were left. It seemed near full and he looked back up toward Tally just as the punks from the doorway rushed her from behind.

"Down!" he yelled and fired over her head. One of them danced their way into the hail of bullets and his momentum carried him over Tally's head and down the stairs. Jonn stood on the growing pile of bodies and continued to spray sporadically at the doorway. He felt a sharp pain in his leg and looked down to see Skraz raking his cybernetic talons across his hamstring. Faster than the slasher could have believed possible, Jonn raised his massive leg and smashed his foot down into the murderer's jaw, sending teeth, tongue, and blood cascading over his neck.

Tally spun and was now lying flat at the top of the staircase, pointing her pistol at the entrance. Footsteps resounded from every corner of the hotel as the members of the Lost Sheep converged on the action. "Jonn! There's more of them! A lot more!"

Stryker looked around for a second exit and saw that there was none. The number of voices and plodding footsteps convinced him that they were thoroughly outnumbered. A retreat was in order. "Get down here, now!"

Tally lifted her feet and let herself slide down the steps rather than giving the horde a chance to pop her in the back as she stood. Jonn admired the maneuver and emptied the rest of the submachinegun through the open doorway to cover her retreat.

When Tally hit bottom, he grabbed her and ran back through to the operating room. The door was a shambles, so Jonn ripped the table from the floor and levered it up against the frame. "That oughtta hold 'em for a while. Least 'til we figure a way outta here."

"But how are we getting out? There's no other door down here! We're trapped!"

Stryker checked the ceiling, hoping to see a venti-lation shaft or those cheap tiles that often concealed a crawlspace beyond, but it was no use, the basement's roof was solid concrete. He looked down at Tally and saw the fear in her eyes. "Maybe the gunfire'll draw some rent-a-cops, kid."

Hendrickson's cab lost Stryker, but managed to spot the bike he had been riding in front of the *Costa del Sol*. The cab stopped and the driver was reaching around for Robbie's credcard when gunfire erupted from the hotel. "Forget it, man!" the cabbie yelled as he floored the accelerator. Robbie jumped from the ve-hicle and rolled on the dirty street, somehow manag-ing to hold on to his small bag. He wasn't so sure tailing his corporate rival was such a hot idea anymore.

Stryker had pulled the remaining furniture into the corner, forming a small arc that might or might not protect them from the firearms the gang seemed to be carrying. It wouldn't help much if they came up with anything bigger, though.

Jonn threw the empty machinegun into the corner and drew his own blaster. He checked its power sup-ply, then looked about the room for some way out. "Shit!" he exclaimed.

"What? What is it?" Tally was crouched behind the makeshift barricade, just waiting for someone to stick their head through the door.

"I should've dragged Skraz in here. He might know a way out or at least made a good hostage."

"You think they give a damn if he gets hurt? They'd just as soon rip his junk out as help him," Tally screamed.

"It's worth a try, girl," he snarled. "It's all we've got."

To Tally's horror, Jonn jumped over the overturned filing cabinet in front of him and rushed the table that covered the doorway. He listened for a second and pulled slightly on the heavy barricade. Bullets stitched through the thick wood, some penetrating through and narrowly missing the marine's head. Jonn looked discouraged and glanced about the room. The body of Hacksaw's patient was lying on the floor where it had fallen when Jonn had turned over the table, and he picked it up with one massive arm. Bullets were still striking the table as Jonn ripped off his duster and wrapped it hastily around the bloody corpse. Then he stepped over it and put his back against the wall nearest the gap, somehow managing not to get shot in the process. With a quick glance at Tally, he fired two shots through the widened crack. Instantly, every weapon in the room fired, splintering the table and causing it to teeter. Jonn let the door fall and dropped the corpse into the opening.

Someone yelled "I got him!" and rushed forward.

Jonn spun into the doorway. One of the toughs ran headlong into the massive marine and Jonn slammed the barrel of his blaster into the man's gut and pulled the trigger. Before the youth could scream, Jonn grabbed him by his greasy spiked hair and used his body as a shield against the others. Four stunned gang members caught hyper-accelerated particles to the head and chest while Jonn's unwilling shield turned into a grisly mass of twitching gore.

Most of the others routed, their leather-clad legs

disappearing up the stairs just as the power pack in Jonn's pistol beeped empty. One of the Sheep was still alive and had dropped his weapon when his elbow was shattered. Jonn dropped the corpse he was holding, ran forward, and kicked the survivor squarely in the jaw. The punk toppled backwards and slammed his head on the concrete floor as Jonn rushed the stairwell and sorted through the pile of bodies. As Tally had suspected, no one had bothered to drag Skraz out of the danger zone.

"Get up, filth," Jonn growled as he grabbed him by the back of the jacket. The Sheep were already regrouping upstairs and a particularly brave soul leaned in the doorway and raised his pistol. Stryker's new arms gave him incredible strength and he managed to pull Skraz up just in time for the bewildered slasher to catch the round in his stolen and ill-fitting chestplate.

Skraz's jaw was hanging limp and pieces of bone and teeth could be seen matted to the bright blood. Jonn manhandled him back to the operating room and tossed him through. Someone ran down the stairs behind them, howling like a dog. Stryker grabbed an almost ancient pistol from the floor and shattered a kneecap before its owner had turned the corner. As Jonn stepped through the hole and slammed the table back into place, he heard the man's howl turn into a whimper.

Hendrickson peeked in the hotel doorway and saw over thirty street urchins pushing their way down a dark staircase. Someone with heavy boots was walking down the steps opposite him, and Hendrickson ducked back into the shadows. Robbie looked across the smoky entrance hall and saw black leather boots descend from the carpeted stairway that led to the rooms above. Their owner was big — probably hooked up on steroids since childhood or a native of a world with much heavier gravity. He wore gray form-fitting pants and a dirty tank top covered in some kind of vehicle grease. Smoke from a huge cigar obscured his features, but Hendrickson could see a black mohawk and a set of silver eyes that gleamed as they caught the dim red light from the flickering sign outside. Metal skulls dangled from his earlobes, and a thick tube exited his ear and disappeared into the pit of his collarbone. Huge knives the size of Robbie's forearm were strapped to his thighs, and a single shot rocket pistol dangled carelessly from a studded leather belt. In his hands was a rifle, the kind that fired ten-millimeter rockets. That thing could punch through Brodie Five's, and Hendrickson seriously doubted that Stryker was wearing anything more than ballistic nylon.

The man stopped at the top of the basement stairs and looked into the darkness with his metallic, pupil-less eyes. Robbie could feel them wash over him, switching from infra-red to low-light in an attempt to see him better. The man flicked off the safety of his launcher and pointed it toward Robbie, but the scout was already out the door.

Hendrickson bolted out into the street and tried to figure out what to do next. He wanted to help Stryker. He didn't know why — Hollings probably wanted him dead again by now, but Robbie felt some sort of kinship with the rival marine. But what could he do? He had no weapon, and the guy with the rocket launcher probably wouldn't hold back if he saw him again.

But he had to do something. Robbie finally made up his mind and leapt for a ladder attached to the rusty fire escape in front of the *Costa del Sol*. It somehow managed to support his weight, and he pulled himself quickly up the iron rungs. At a window on the second story, he slipped inside and entered a long hallway. Numerous rooms led off from each side, and he opened the first one he came to with a determined kick. As he had suspected, at least some of the gang was living in the condemned hotel.

Junk was lying everywhere. He saw magazines, hotplates for cooking illegal drugs, and other garbage strewn about in the haphazard way of spoiled children. With a look of disgust, he grabbed a stained sleeping bag and set it on fire with one of the many cigarette lighters lying about the floor. In seconds, the supposedly flame-resistant material was smouldering brilliantly.

Robbie ran down the main staircase dragging the makeshift weapon and watched as the carpeting behind him began to catch fire. When he finally hit bottom, he ran to the basement stairs and tossed the burning bag down onto the backs of several of the crowded gang members. Hendrickson couldn't help but watch as the blazing synthetic material of the sleeping bag glued itself to the punk's blistering flesh. Some of them attempted to run back up the steps and lost their footing on the cramped stairway, causing them to ignite others as men and women became trapped under the falling barrage of screaming flesh. As Robbie had hoped, the inhuman screams and the terrible smell panicked the others. Those that were actually in the room realized that they were trapped and began to push their way back up the stairs, feeding those nearest the bottom into the burning mess above.

Suddenly, a sprinkler system long thought dead activated and dumped brownish water from the ceiling. The plastic sleeping bag that wasn't supposed to burn and the syntheleather jackets it had ignited weren't greatly affected by the trickle of water, but were doused just enough to let most of the screaming masses flee past. Hendrickson stepped aside as the herd rumbled by, and stumbled back into a dark corner. When the fleeing gang saw the burning carpet on the stairs beginning to spread to the hotel's walls, their rat-like instincts told them to abandon the building.

Hendrickson turned back into the basement doorway and saw the mass of smouldering bodies near the landing. The crowd had only passed them at the expense of those that were pushed into the flames and momentarily suppressed them, but now these unfortunate few were only adding to the blaze. Robbie didn't see the guy with the rocket launcher anywhere, but the growing fire forbade him from exploring further. Stryker was on his own.

They heard the hundred or so footsteps on the stairs, and then they heard the screaming and smelled the burning flesh, but Tally and Stryker still had no idea what the hell was going on beyond their makeshift barricade.

Jonn was just about to stand when the table he had replaced in front of the door exploded in a mass of splinters and smoke. After a moment of silence, a massive figure stepped into the doorway, silhouetted from behind by a bright mass of burning corpses. The sprinklers had put out the man's cigar, and he spat it at the two figures huddling behind the barricade. Stryker heard the distinct sound of a bolt being retracted and quickly fired a shot from his pistol into the man's chest. His shirt and a layer of synthetic flesh exploded in a bloody, tattered mass, but the man barely flinched.

Stryker couldn't act before the man pulled the trigger again and another rocket slammed into the wall behind the barricade, knocking him forward into the room.

Jonn played dead as the man stepped forward. Fringed leather boots sloshed in the growing puddles near Jonn's head as the man looked over him and the unconscious girl now buried under the barricade. He switched his mechanical eye to infra-red, and could see the man's heat signature through the synthetic eyelid Hacksaw had given him. He watched the giant step forward, and saw the red-hot barrel of the launcher poking Tally's colder form.

Jonn took advantage of the distraction and leapt from the floor, blindsiding his huge opponent and smashing them both through the overturned chairs and filing cabinets that had buried Tally.

They rolled back and forth, Jonn feeling thick wooden splinters driving into his side while the other man barely seemed to notice. Stryker rammed his fist again and again into the man's gut, but it was like hitting a bag of flour. It had to be intradermal plating. The most expensive and dangerous cybernetic operation available was to have thick, rubbery plates inserted over the major muscles. This usually covered the chest and arms and could stop most anything short of a blaster. Jonn knew his fist wouldn't even cause a bruise.

Tally awoke as the two men thrashed about and scrambled out from under the debris. She rolled over on her side and pulled the blaster out of the water around her. The big guy managed to snake out a boot quicker then Jonn could believe, and snapped Tally's firing wrist in one easy kick.

She screamed and fell back into the corner, holding her fractured limb. Somehow, Jonn and his opponent got separated and both rolled onto their feet, crouching like jungle cats as each looked the other over. Jonn saw the cybernetic adrenaline booster set into the man's head, and knew just why he was so quick.

The only light came from the burning bodies outside, but it was more than enough for both men's cybernetic eyes to give them almost total visibility. Jonn saw the bullet wound in the big man's chest and the blackness of the rubbery plates beneath. These and the man's blinding speed made Jonn feel truly outclassed for the first time in his life.

The man went for the gyro-pistol on his waist. Jonn threw himself forward and just managed to latch onto the man's studded leather bracelet before he fired. The shot went off and the rocket went wild, sinking into Hacksaw's dead gut and exploding with a muffled charge that blew innards and fat across the room.

The man dropped the empty pistol and crashed his other fist into Jonn's jaw. Stryker felt the bruised flesh around his eye scream with resentment and he fell roughly to the wet floor. A follow-up kick caught him in the ribs but somehow failed to break anything. Jonn caught his opponent's boot as it withdrew, and pushed, sending the giant back into the waiting room where he landed with a watery splash.

Muddy water ran down Jonn's face as he stalked through the door after his foe. The man smiled, wiped some blood from his lip with the back of his hand, and drew one of the oversized knives attached to his thigh.

They danced in a circle, the giant slashing cautiously as Jonn dodged and leapt away from the blade. There was no sound from upstairs. They were alone, two men made of metal and flesh in a battle that only one would walk away from. Jonn was increasingly aware that it wasn't going to be him.

Tally stumbled in the next room. Jonn was only distracted for a moment but the big man acted quickly and cut him sharply across his mechanical eye. The flesh around the orb stung, and a real eye would have been dripping down his face now, but the cybernetic invader wasn't even scratched.

An idea suddenly formed in Jonn's mind, something brought on by the cut across the eye. He wasn't using his resources to their full advantage. The man stabbed, and Jonn dodged aside with a quickness surprising for his bulk. That wasn't what he was waiting for.

His grinning opponent stabbed again. *Damn it, slash at me, you moron!* Jonn thought as he retreated once again. Finally, it happened. The man slung the knife in a wide arc and Jonn caught the knife on his forearm. A warm spray splashed his face and he saw a long swath of skin peel away in front of the razor sharp blade.

But it was only the artificial lubricant between the synthetic skin and the metallic arm beneath that was "bleeding" out. There was no pain and no real effect on the metallic limb beneath. He latched onto his adversary's knife arm with his blocking hand and bent it in at the elbow, driving the knife deep into the man's groin.

"Betcha don't have any armor there," he whispered as the giant sank to his knees in the bloody water.

Jonn turned around as Tally walked through the door carrying the oversized launcher that the man had dropped during scuffle. "Come on, kid, let's get the hell —"

"JONN!" she screamed.

Stryker turned and saw that his opponent had pulled another knife and was poised to cleave Jonn's head open with it. Stryker leaped to the side just as Tally squeamishly pulled the trigger on the appropriated rocket gun. A ten-millimeter missile whizzed past his ear as he dove aside and lodged with a wet thunk in the giant's chest. The man panicked and grabbed the still-burning missile by the tail fins. It seared the flesh from his enormous hands as he tried to pull it free, and was almost out when the rocket finally exploded inside his sternum, cracking it open like double doors thrown wide.

The giant was still standing and leering madly at the ceiling when Jonn kicked his carcass into the burning bodies at the bottom of the staircase.

"Let's go," Stryker commanded.

"What about Skraz?"

"Oh, yeah. I almost forgot," he grinned.

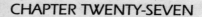

CHAPTER TWENTY-SEVEN

Seven Marines

S tryker dragged Skraz over the splintered fragments of the door to the operating room as Tally peeked around the corner and up the stairwell. "I don't see anybody," she whispered.

Jonn walked to the bottom of the steps and Skraz's head caught on the rough concrete with a dull smack. Stryker released his collar and the punk lay squirming in pain from the blow to the head and the broken jaw. Jonn looked about the flooded room and visually sifted through the human detritus. Several weapons were still lying about, and he grabbed a Yuniki flechette gun.

He climbed the staircase with slow but confident steps, and saw only the smoky entranceway upon reaching the top. "Bring Skraz up here," he commanded to Tally.

"How?" came an excited whisper, "I can't carry him!"

Stryker turned his head back toward his companion. "I broke his jaw, not his legs."

"Oh, yeah!"

Skraz was less than pleased to stand with most of his jaw hanging three inches lower than it should have, and would have been even less happy if Tally wasn't still wearing the helmet that disguised her true identity. "Get up," she said and poked him with her blaster.

Skraz scowled at her through broken teeth, "Skwu yoo, bithe."

BLAM! Tally surprised herself by pulling the trigger. When she opened her eyes beneath the dark visor of the helmet, Skraz's hand had a hole in it big enough to see through. His eyes were blinking in shock and she kicked him in the leg. "I said, get up. Now."

Jonn saw Skraz walking deliriously up the steps and heard the gang members yelling and screaming in the nearby street. Smoke still clouded most of the entrance, so Jonn switched his cybernetic eye into infrared mode. If there had been anyone hiding in the dark corners of the burning hotel, the heat-sensing eye would easily have picked them out.

"Now what?" asked Tally.

"Yoo-wuh twappthed. Theaw-uh ain't no bakth way outh," Skraz taunted.

Stryker sneered and walked over to where he could peek into the street. The eye showed him several orange and red blobs running around and taking up positions in the ruined building across from them. "Then we'll have to go out the front."

Jonn took the rocket rifle from Tally's shoulder and checked the ammo counter; there were three rounds left. He looked past the smoke with the cybernetic eye and saw that a ground car had just pulled up in front of the hotel. "Follow right behind me. Got it?" he yelled at Tally.

She nodded and Jonn pulled back the charging handle that prepared the rifle for firing. He raised it to his shoulder, flicked a toggle switch to short range, and fired the round through the driver's side window. A lifetime in the marines had taught him accuracy, and the vehicle's driver disappeared in a flash of light and a cloud of blood.

He fired the second round into the building across the street. Two thugs kneeling in a broken window were blinded by the flying debris, and vanished behind their cover. The final round went into the stunned throng of milling people. Few were truly injured but the explosion put everyone's head down and allowed Jonn to run safely to the car window. The driver had vanished from the sternum up and a wounded passenger was frantically trying to brush blood and brains out of his matted hair. Jonn fired the flechette pistol and caught him in a spray of diamond shaped slivers, perforating his neck so badly that it nearly toppled off the trembling corpse.

Stryker threw open the door and yelled for Tally, then dumped the driver's lower half out into the street and climbed into the mobile charnel house. Tally barely managed to push Skraz into the back seat as Jonn floored the accelerator and shot through the crowd of wounded gang members.

He was just starting to feel safe when Tally screamed. "Jonn! They're following us!"

A glance in the rear view mirror showed five punks following on motorcycles, and several others crammed into a beat-up land rover. That vehicle, like this one, was constructed from the frame of a luxury model but had been modified for life on the streets. Chicken wire covered the windows and the bumpers were covered in crudely fashioned steel spikes.

Someone from the rear car fired and Tally whirled around to return it. The helmet was restricting her movement in the cramped cab, and she dumped it at Skraz's feet. Shocked realization grew in his face and he was just about to say something when bullets started tracing up the trunk of the vehicle and forced both their heads down. Tally had to kneel over him and could smell his stinking breath through the bloody wreckage of his jaws. It was a sickeningly familiar smell and she fought hard to keep from retching. She braced her arms on his bent form and pushed herself up to fire, mashing his injured jaw into his leather clad knee in the process.

Stryker looked in the mirror and saw her firing from the rear window. "Keep your head down, kid! I'll get us outta here."

Tally ignored him and took aim at the pursuing car. She could see a figure leaning out of it, trying to steady his firearm as the vehicle swerved beneath him. She fired four times before the thug managed to balance himself enough to get off a burst from his own weapon. The burst sprayed the hood and she was forced to duck back behind the seat. The slasher moaned as his jaw was driven into his knee once again.

"I can't hit him with this thing!" she yelled at Stryker. "I need one that fires lots of bullets at once!"

Jonn smiled a little and nodded. "All right, hang on!" He slammed the brakes hard and the pursuing car rammed into them, throwing the man hanging out the window into the street. Stryker hit the accelerator again and Tally rose in time to see the thug still spinning down the pavement. One of the bikers couldn't avoid the whirling body and flipped end over end when it got caught up in the spokes of his wheels.

The battle-crazed girl in the back laughed triumphantly and fired the blaster four more times, finally hitting another biker before the pistol beeped that it was empty.

Hendrickson avoided the Lost Sheep by stealing Stryker's forgotten motorcycle. He sat in a nearby alley until Stryker finally made it out of the burning building, stole a car, and rammed it through a crowd of stunned gang members. Now he had two options. He could join in the chase and risk his ass to save Jonn Stryker's life a third time, or he could find a dreary hotel and spend his leave on wine, women, and gambling. It wasn't a difficult choice.

He kicked the starter and roared out into the street. Here and there a street lamp actually worked and Hendrickson could make out four cyclists and one vehicle pursuing Stryker and his friend. He caught up with them just as a shot from Stryker's car killed another of the bikers.

There were still three cyclists, but the car was his greatest concern. One good swipe from the heavy vehicle and he would be little more than a fading skidmark on the greasy streets of the undercity. Fortunately, they were all so preoccupied with Stryker that they hadn't seen him yet.

The bike's accelerator was on the right of the scooter and Robbie had to wield the blaster with his left hand. He drove up beside the driver's window and fired three times, missing his target but causing the vehicle to careen into another of the bikers, who was ground to a messy death beneath its furious wheels.

The driver recovered quickly and swerved back toward Hendrickson, jumping the curb and trying to flatten him against a nearby wall. Robbie twisted the brake and sparks flew as the car scraped the gray brick, narrowly missing the front of his scooter. The car was directly in front of him now, and someone in the back raised a scattergun to the rear window. Robbie ducked and the shot whizzed over his head. He knew that the weapon would have to be pumped before it could be fired again, and returned fire with his off hand. The shot missed the target but glass fragments blew into the man's eyes and put him out of the fight.

Hendrickson faded to the right of the car and fired

through the passenger's window. The blast hit an already dead passenger, but a second shattered the driver's leg. Still, the man drove on and managed to raise his own weapon. Robbie slowed suddenly and the shot only creased his left biceps.

The last biker finally heard the shots and dropped back between Robbie and the car. The driver waved his weapon furiously, trying to get the motorcycle to move so that he could get in another shot. Unfortunately, the biker didn't understand and only looked at him in confusion. Hendrickson smiled at the bewildered punk and kicked his bike toward the speeding vehicle. The man pulled the cycle down with him and both skidded in front of the car where they were melded into a hot mess of metal and flesh.

The remaining biker threw himself onto the back of Stryker's car. He saw that the girl was out of rounds, and thought that he could peel off the chicken wire and climb in through the back window before she could reload. He pulled himself into a sitting position and stuck his fingers through the wire, but the girl was looking at him strangely, like he was stupid. With a mighty tug he pulled on the chicken wire just as Tally kicked at it with her foot. The screen gave more than the thug had compensated for, and he flew backwards where the trailing vehicle claimed its third victim.

The driver of the car fired four more rounds at Hendrickson. The last caught the marine in the left shoulder and his bike banged roughly into the wall where he tumbled, rolled and crashed to a painful halt.

The driver's attention was riveted on Hendrickson as he slammed spectacularly into the wall, and he noticed the cargo truck in front of him too late. The driver might have been able to stop if it weren't for the ever-present Teraxian rain.

CHAPTER TWENTY-EIGHT

Prisoners

Hendrickson's right arm was broken. He threw it out to catch himself when his bike careened into the wall but he was moving a lot faster than he realized, and the muscular limb snapped grudgingly against the wet brick. He felt a sharp stinging in his leg and pushed off the wreckage of the bike. The flesh was scraped off and still hung from the wall in long, gooey peels, but it seemed the damage was superficial, though painful.

More bikes were coming up the street and Robbie played dead. They either didn't fall for it or didn't care though, and he was quickly surrounded by leering faces marred by the gang's characteristic cyberware.

"Get up," one of them said.

The throng of smelly delinquents picked up Hendrickson's broken body and sat him roughly on the back of a bike. Then they bound his hands and tied him to the driver so that he wouldn't fall off as they rumbled back into the Shits.

"Where to now?" Tally asked Stryker once they had

cleared the undercity.

"I dunno. I wanna find out how this jerk and his friends managed to get ahold of our armor. And then I'm gonna get me some payback."

"Whath yoo talkin' 'bout, thsyco?" Skraz muttered.

Jonn pulled off another of the downtown exits and parked the battle-wagon under the ramp. Then he turned in his seat and grabbed the prisoner roughly by the collar. "You know *exactly* what I mean, filth. Where'd you get this?" A stubby finger poked the chestpiece right above the letters that spelled "Wolverine."

"I don'th know. Thum of the big boyth goth ith off-planeth. They juth gave ith to me and Jeffth causth we wath on guard for Hackthaw."

Stryker thought a minute before he understood everything Skraz was telling him. Evidently, those in the gang who were in on the off-planet pirating had picked up the armor and given the scraps to some of the more important stooges below them. What Skraz hadn't answered and probably didn't know was whether or not the pirates had simply scavenged the body suits or had actually been in on the attack. Again, nothing pointed directly at Todd Hollings, but Stryker thought it curious that the gang that wound up with the goods just happened to be *his* pet monsters.

"Where can I find them?"

"Who?"

"You know who, chiphead. The big boys. The ones that gave you the armor."

"Go thwcoo youthelf, ath-hole."

Jonn reared back and smashed his fist into Skraz's broken jaw.

The pain Skraz felt was unbelievable. Teeth ground on bone, trapping sensitive nerves between. "Thit! Thit, man! Thop it!" he cried. "Whatevuh, juth thop ith." His tear-ducts had been removed when his low-light eyes had replaced his originals, but he was crying just the same. "Ith an old hanguhout ath the spathe porth. On the eath thide!"

It was all Stryker needed to know. "Whattya wanna do with him, Tally?"

Stryker saw that she was a little shocked by his question, evidently she had forgotten why they had come here in the first place.

Skraz flushed and looked at the beautiful girl he and his friends had ruined. "Lookth, baby, I'm thorry about that stuff. Ith wathn't nothin' perthonal."

Tears held back for too long finally cascaded down Tally's battered face. She thought of Rygil, chewing *glass* to save her life. She remembered the shameful feeling when they had ripped her clothes off, and the horror of the first …

She stopped thinking and the tears dried up. She had changed, and this new person didn't cry as easily as the old had. Now there would only be vengeance. She raised her weapon to fire …

SNAP! Jonn twisted Skraz's neck like the lid of a jar. It popped loudly and the rapist twitched for several minutes before dying.

Tally stared at him angrily and threw the gun onto the seat.

Jonn wanted to tell her that he had done it for her, to stop her from doing something she would regret for the rest of her life — but no words came. He *couldn't* have let her do it, and he *shouldn't* have stopped her. Stryker was tired of these no-win situations.

Robbie didn't know there was a back way into the Randall-Hollings' spaceport, and he didn't know about hangars twelve through twenty. Nine of these ancient structures sat in an isolated row in a disused section of the two and a half mile square spaceport of Gonqlin. Two of them, buildings thirteen and fifteen, may have been forgotten, but they certainly weren't abandoned.

Dozens of bikes were parked in a column just inside the gargantuan hangar, and the catwalks were crammed with even more leering criminals. The interior was modified with ramshackle aluminum walls that formed apartments and what looked like a mess area, and the amount of work that this had taken told Hendrickson that his boss was well aware of the hangar's occupants.

One of his captors was an obese man named Yuri, and he slid a long, sharp knife out of his plastic boot. To Robbie's relief, Yuri cut the ropes that bound him to the man in front. "I'd hate to be you," he grunted.

Hendrickson thought he'd give it one last try, "Look, I work for Hollings, you moron. So you better turn me loose right now or the corp's going to come down on you like acid rain."

Yuri smirked, "You don't work for anyone, anymore."

They led him to a crude aluminum apartment and threw him inside. He sat for a long while before the doors opened again and a young girl entered. She wore a dirty pink skirt and a white blouse that barely hid her developing womanhood, and carried a length of pipe, a t-shirt, and a pair of scissors. Hendrickson almost pissed his pants before he realized she was going to set his broken arm.

"What's the point if they're just going to kill me?" he asked.

The girl shrugged and tried to avoid eye contact. "I dunno. They didn't want you all busted up when *she* gets here."

"Who the hell is 'she'?"

"Gallacia. Our boss. She's cool, but really scary. I'd sure hate to be you."

Hendrickson was beginning to agree.

He spent the rest of the day in weary delirium. No one bothered him after the girl set his arm, but they were clearly gearing up for something big. He could hear the gang moving their bikes around and clearing the garbage and debris from the center of the hangar. It seemed that the Lost Sheep weren't often visited by this Gallacia person, whoever she might be.

Robbie was asleep when the chain that locked his door was noisily removed, and still groggy when they dragged him out into the center of the hangar. The gang members were all sitting around the floor, leaning against the walls, or dangling their legs casually as they sat upon the catwalk that circled the perimeter of the hangar. There were more of them now, almost a hundred, he guessed. The bikes had been moved outside and the floor was cleaner, but the corners were still piled high with the refuse of the undisciplined thieves. They dragged him into the middle of the hangar and a bright light shone down on him from above.

High overhead, stationed on the rear center of the catwalk, was one of the strangest creatures Hendrickson had ever seen. It wore a long blue robe suggesting it was a female, and had scarlet, leathery, streamers that ran elegantly from its skull like the scales on the back of a lizard's head. The face was greenish and shaped somewhere between a reptile and a humanoid, but the eyes gleamed a brilliant yellow.

"She" was surrounded by six men in McGinley battle armor, the kind worn by Hollings' marines. It was dark black in color and probably coated in reflective paint. Etched across the left breast of each man were the words "Black Sheep" — evidently the personal bodyguards of whatever weird creature was leading this bunch. Six suits of this armor would've cost a fortune, and Robbie finally realized just who was footing their bill. They operated out of the Hollings corporate sector, at least some of them lived in Hollings' spaceport, and they even wore the same type of armor worn by Hollings' marines.

Sometimes, Robbie really hated this corporate bullshit.

Now the gang's boss dropped her robe and revealed a silver body entirely encased in gleaming metal. The joints were covered in a flexible metallic cloth that hung in loose folds and accented her lizard-like appearance. This had to be Gallacia.

All those present became quiet as she raised a silver arm, and then leveled a pointed claw at Hendrickson. "Who are you?" she demanded, "And why did you and your friend attack our hotel?"

Robbie wasn't quite sure what the hell was going on. Why did he merit such a prestigious death?

"You are wondering why we go to such trouble?"

Robbie had only thought it, and wondered how the thing had so easily picked up on his confusion. Then he felt something green and slimy slithering through his mind, eating out everything he knew about the attack at the *Costa del Sol*. *She's reading my freaking mind!* He knew telepathy was possible, but had never actually experienced it. He tried to fight her, tried to hide Stryker's name from the thing in his mind, but the more he fought the harder it became, and finally the name Jonn Stryker burst from every curved passage of his gray matter, literally *feeding* the mind-reader everything Robbie knew.

"Get out of my head, you freak!" he shouted.

Someone in the crowd threw a tin can that bounced painfully off the side of his head and angry murmuring rose echoed from the aluminum walls.

"Silence!" Gallacia commanded. "He is of no use to us now. He has given us the man's name but knows no more. Kill him."

Hendrickson felt a panic rising within him. *Knowledge is power*, he remembered hearing once. *Find your enemy's weakness and exploit it*. Nothing brilliant came to mind however, so Hendrickson settled for satisfying the most obvious question. "What's the big deal? So we offed a couple of punks and ruined a chop shop."

Gallacia had donned her robe again and was about to leave when Hendrickson spoke. Now she turned and her slitted eyes widened with hate. "Because he killed my lover!"

Robbie saw her hate and frustration and finally came up with a plan. It wasn't a very good one, but it was all he had. "You mean the big, stupid-looking guy with the mohawk? *That* was your lover? I don't know which one of you had to be more desperate."

"You seek to goad me into personal combat? Is that your ploy?"

Hendrickson decided he hated mind readers.

"Then so be it. I will satisfy my hunger in one way or another, human. If I cannot sup on the pleasures of the flesh, then I shall dine upon it in a more direct fashion." Gallacia hissed and bared two rows of sharp, metallic teeth, and to Robbie's surprise, a whip-like tail slashed out from behind her and cracked loudly against the catwalk railing, cutting it easily in two.

She walked eloquently and waved for one of Robbie's guards to free him from his bonds. "You will wish you had allowed yourself to die quickly, human."

The man beside him cut his ropes and whispered, "I'd hate to be you, man."

He wished they'd stop saying that.

It wasn't hard coming up with disguises. Two hours of walking around the undercity was all it took to get a new bike and some of the heavier leather jackets that seemed to be popular with the Lost Sheep. One of the gang members even had a scattergun which Jonn told Tally would "shoot lots of bullets at once." They didn't have the trademark cyberware of the gang, but a pair of sunglasses and a bad attitude worked just as well.

It was just after dark when they arrived at the

spaceport. They weren't having much luck finding the row of hangars Skraz had told them about, but Gallacia's entrance was better than a road map. Her entourage passed through a previously locked gate at the far end of a little-used runway, and Jonn wouldn't have spotted them if not for his low-light eyes.

He followed them carefully, always staying at least one hundred yards away and keeping himself and the bike behind whatever cover he could find. If he could see them, there was a good chance they could see him. The bikes and the hover car that led them gave off a lot of heat, so he switched his vision again, this time to infra-red. Now he didn't have to spot them directly, he could simply follow the trail left by their exhaust.

After zigzagging through a maze of abandoned buildings, the procession drove into an open hangar filled with what Jonn saw as dozens of glowing orange splotches. There were at least twenty bikes and four cars parked just outside, and Jonn quietly parked theirs out of sight. The lead car and its escort also parked quickly, and hurried inside. Stryker shrugged to Tally and they casually inserted themselves into the crowd once the attention focused on the silver-skinned woman and her bodyguards.

These "Black Sheep" were wearing black armor, but it was McGinley, not Brodie, and that told Jonn why the salvaged Tiko pieces had gone to those lower in the gang's hierarchy.

The weird woman and her bodyguards climbed a catwalk and stood before a waiting throng of people. The crowd grew quiet and four gang members dragged a dazed man from a makeshift prison. His arm was crudely splinted with a pair of lead pipes, but he seemed otherwise healthy.

Jonn and Tally watched quietly as the woman called Gallacia questioned her prisoner, but were shocked when she revealed that Jonn had killed her lover.

Stryker was still trying to figure out how the prisoner knew his name when the man taunted the reptile woman into single combat.

Now Gallacia circled about the wounded marine like a hungry animal. Hendrickson primed himself and felt a surge of natural adrenaline shoot through his system. He waited for her to drop her guard — to drop her silver talons for even an instant so that he could drive in and snap her gleaming neck.

She lowered her hands and Hendrickson leapt for her throat, but the mind-reader tricked him and jumped aside, smashing his broken arm with her whip-like tail and laughing as red blood spurted in ropy jets.

Robbie had read about weapons like this. The tail was comprised of a series of metallic tubes strung over a long cord that could be directed in any direction by a small motor attached to its base. Each tube would be covered with raised ridges cut to razor sharpness by a laser, and these could rip through metal and bone like a hot knife through butter. He didn't have a chance.

Fortunately, Gallacia was savoring her prey's demise, and Jonn had a few moments to act. He whispered to Tally to sit still and slipped back outside to the vehicles. The gang's motorcycles were the internal combustion type, and Jonn pulled off his undershirt and stuffed one end into the fuel tank. Fortunately, one of the cycles was equipped with a cigarette lighter, and he quickly fanned the other end of his shirt into flames. Then he fired his blaster twice and jumped on one of the gang's bikes and rode it through the hangar doors. "Fleet!" he shouted. "Fleet marines! Hundreds of 'em!" To punctuate his words, there was a loud boom outside, followed shortly by a series of chain reactions as the booby-trapped bike and its neighbors began to explode.

The Lost Sheep trampled each other in their haste to get out the back doors of the hangar as Gallacia futilely screamed for them to stand and fight. Only her six armored guards, the Black Sheep, held their ground.

Hendrickson took advantage of Stryker's distraction and leapt at Gallacia again, catching her from behind. He brought the iron pipe strapped to his arm down on her skull, but it felt like hitting a rock with an aluminum bat.

Gallacia responded by wiggling her snake-like tail up between his legs and smashing it into the back of his skull.

Stryker had a clear shot at Gallacia now and fired the flechette pistol, cursing as the diamond-shaped rounds bounced harmlessly off her metallic skin. He felt a quick stab into the recesses of his mind and the woman glared at him in fury.

"You! You're Stryker! You killed my lover!"

Jonn snarled as his brain was raped, and charged her with the bike. Blaster fire erupted from the catwalk as the Black Sheep attempted to stop him but cut short as he got closer to their leader.

Gallacia nimbly jumped aside, anticipating Jonn's charge, and whipped her tail at his crewcut head as he passed. Jonn didn't have to read minds to see what was coming, however, and managed to duck before the metallic cable cracked over his skull.

Tally pulled her weapon and opened fire on the armored bodyguards as Jonn once again left their leader's protective radius. The scattergun didn't have a prayer of penetrating their thick armor, but the startled men immediately ran for cover as the shots rattled noisily off their suits.

Jonn whirled the bike again and made another pass. He felt cold fingers massaging his mind and tried to push them out. But Gallacia had been doing this far longer than Jonn, and once again avoided the kick that he had planned for her.

How do you hit someone who can read your freakin'

mind? Jonn thought.

"You can't, murderer!" came a mental cry.

Ah, then guess what I'm gonna do next, bitch?

"I don't have to guess, you idiot! I'll pull your mind apart and rip your heart out when I'm through!"

Stryker whirled the bike around just as he was about to hit the far wall. Tally was near him, and a pile of junk momentarily protected him from the fire of the Black Sheep. He sat calmly on the bike, smiling at the mind reader and revving his engine.

Gallacia probed again, and found Jonn's mind a terrible whirl of thoughts and ideas. He was going to attack again, but even he didn't know what he would do when he got there.

Jonn rushed forward and let his battle-honed reflexes take over. Gallacia panicked and snapped her tail prematurely. Stryker leapt from the bike and dragged her metal carcass to the concrete floor. The tail snaked out from under her but Jonn grabbed it before the motors could give it the dangerous momentum that could tear his head off. The syntheflesh on his palm bled artificial blood from the sharp ridges, but there was no pain, only a slight tingle sent up the neural cables that alerted him when something was wrong.

He yanked hard and wound the cable about Gallacia's throat. The skin there had been replaced by metallic fibers, but the tail could wear through it easily if Jonn yanked hard enough.

A click on the catwalk reminded him that he wasn't alone and he rolled over, keeping Gallacia's struggling form in front of him. "Go ahead and shoot if you wanna see the snake lady dance," he challenged.

The Black Sheep stopped and stared at each other, unsure of what to do.

Jonn leaned into Gallacia's ear and whispered, "Tell them to drop their weapons or I'm gonna yank on the bottom of your tail and your head's gonna go spinning off like an ugly top."

The guards did as they were commanded and Jonn tugged threateningly on Gallacia's tail. "And one more thing. Get the hell out of my mind."

CHAPTER TWENTY-NINE

The Raven

Tally gathered up the blaster rifles and forced
the six guards to remove their power armor. They couldn't just strap it on themselves — the powerful strength-increasing joints could
rip an arm off if the suit wasn't customized.

Hendrickson finally regained consciousness and
tried to figure out why Gallacia's bodyguards were
naked and he wasn't dead. Then he saw Stryker. "Oh,
my God. Saved by Jonn Stryker himself. That almost
makes us even."

"Huh?" Jonn grunted dumbly.

"You don't know me, Sergeant, but I know you. Do
I ever." He sighed and rubbed his aching head. "Right
now, though, I think we better get the hell out of here
before more of these jerks show up."

Jonn could hear the rest of the gang already starting
to filter back in. Tally threw the blasters into the back
seat of Gallacia's car, and Hendrickson quickly loaded
the McGinley armor into the trunk.

One of the bodyguards sneered at them, "We'll find

her, you know. And when we do, you'll wish you'd killed us."

Stryker couldn't agree more. He shrugged and opened up with the flechette pistol. Two dove over the railing to escape the bursts and cracked their necks and back on the concrete below. The other four did a frenzied dance of death before toppling or slumping through the railing and joining their companions.

Gallacia turned her head as much as possible and stared at Jonn in shock.

He grinned, and dragged her to the car.

Tally was driving and Hendrickson was in the passenger's seat, leaving Jonn and Gallacia to cram into the back seat with the pile of captured weapons. Ten minutes later, Tally maneuvered the car back through the bustling spaceport and into a nearby parking lot. She stopped the car and turned off the thrusters, allowing it to settle gently on the skirts that surrounded its gigantic fans.

Jonn still held Gallacia like a ventriloquist, threatening to yank the razor-sharp tail across her throat if she tried to escape. "Now, let's have a little talk. And none of that telepathy shit."

"I'll tell you nothing," she spat.

Jonn sneered and pulled on the tail. The barbs tore into her neck and droplets of blood oozed out of the metal cloth. "I think you will. It's just a matter of how much pain you have to suffer before you do."

Gallacia closed her eyes and probed each of their minds, hoping for something to help her out of this situation.

Tally had been physically raped and wasn't about to let anyone enter her mentally. She leaned over the seat and jerked out one of the leathery fins that topped the alien's skull. Blood dripped down her face in sharp contrast to the stainless steel of her cheeks and forehead.

"Now," Jonn said softly, "where'd your choir boys get the armor?"

"That's no secret, you twit! Everybody knows we hire out to Hollings Corp. Sometimes he pays us in goods instead of cash."

"Not that, the black stuff your urchins were wearing at the chop shop. The ones that say "Wolverines" on the breast."

"How the hell should I know where my children get their playthings?"

"Because it could only have come from one place. Who hired you to attack Tiko marines?"

"Take a wild guess."

That answered the main question, but there was still one more thing that Stryker had to know.

He looked about nervously, almost embarrassed to ask the next question. "Tell me about the ..."

Hendrickson and Tally noticed the change in his tone and turned to look.

"... jaws," he finished.

Gallacia gaped at him in confusion. She reached into his mind and pulled out the image of the thing in the smoke. This time, Stryker didn't fight her. He offered her the vision eagerly, hoping that there would be some explanation. But he could feel her fondling it uncertainly, as if it was as confusing to her as it was to him. Finally, she shook her head and said, "You can yank my tail all you want, but I don't know anything about this."

Stryker ground his teeth together and shrunk from Tally and Hendrickson's stares. He knew she told the truth, her cerebral probe proved it — but there was still some missing element that he couldn't figure out. He now knew that Hollings was up to something, and that meant he had to get back to Tiko III, but it wouldn't hurt to stop by New Akron on the way.

He pulled on his captive's tail once again, "Where's your ship?"

"You *are* crazy!" she gurgled.

"That's what we're gonna find out."

The *Raven* was parked in an obscure hangar that looked a lot like one of the fuel warehouses that dotted the spaceport's acreage. Stryker suspected that this was so Hollings could allow the pirates to dock their ship here without getting in trouble with the local officials. Fortunately, there were only two guards, and the confiscated blasters finished them in a hurry.

Inside the hangar, Stryker marveled at the pirates' ship. It was built like a corvette and outfitted for cargo to boot. The oversized engines were well suited for the quick escapes needed for smuggling, and its color was the dull black of its namesake. The sensor-absorbing paint and the conical superstructure of the ship were enormously expensive and highly illegal by all but Fleet stealth fighters, and again spoke of the gang's patronage under the Hollings' corporation. Coupled with the latest in electronic jammers, the ship could be practically invisible to most sensors until its weapons fired.

Gallacia unwillingly fingered in the code for the gangplank and it lowered smoothly down to the concrete floor. Tally and Hendrickson carried the heavy armor from the car to the ship while Stryker kept his stranglehold on the silvery pirate.

"You know how to fly this thing?" Stryker asked Hendrickson.

"Yeah, probably."

Hendrickson disappeared into the cockpit and Jonn looked around for something to secure his prisoner with. Tally offered him a length of steel cable, and he quickly looped it about Gallacia's hands and feet.

"They're here!" came a yell from the bridge.

Stryker felt the ship start to taxi and ran forward. Hendrickson hit a switch on the control panel and the hangar door slid open. Some of the gang had come to check their ship, and thought about trying to stop it. They changed their minds quickly when Hendrickson opened the forward weapons bay.

"By the way," Stryker grunted, "who the hell are you?"

Hendrickson smiled and sped the sleek craft down the runway. When the *Raven* started to rise, he retracted the landing gear and shoved the thruster lever to FULL. "I'm a Randall-Hollings marine," he grinned.

Stryker sat and snarled at the man piloting their stolen ship. "What do you mean, you're a Randall-Hollings' marine?"

"Which word didn't you understand?" Hendrickson chided dangerously. Then he saw Jonn's face and decided he had better explain. Quickly. "Look, I'm a scout aboard the *Constantine*. I'm the guy that pulled you outta the *Fury*."

"Nobody pulled me outta the *Fury* 'til some slob cut my arm off."

"Yeah, I know. I missed you the first time, but I stopped those salvage jerks from finishing you off just to keep their jobs. They were going to let you bleed to death, but I was still floatin' around on my Jenner and happened to see the ..." he paused, trying to read Stryker's reaction, "... blood spray. I tried to save your corporal before that, but he didn't make it." Robbie shrugged and pretended to look over controls he didn't understand. "Actually, I'm surprised the boss let you live. He really hates your guts, you know?"

"Yeah, I know."

A full day after the *Raven* blasted out of the Gonqlin spaceport, a reluctant communications technician aboard the *Constantine* knocked on Todd Hollings' door. "What?" came a grumbling voice from a speaker nearby.

"Sir, we have a ..."

"Speak up, you sniveling dolt."

"Um, yes, sir. There's been some trouble on Teraxiter. Some of our, um, *special agents* have reported that their ship was stolen."

There was silence for a moment as Todd figured out just who those *special agents* were. "That stupid bitch! Does she know how much that damned thing costs? Let them deal with it."

"Sir, they have no other way off-planet. Bernard's crew was taken over a week ago."

"Oh, all right. Have some of our fighters go and look for it. I don't know how we're going to find it, though." The technician heard an angry sigh. "The damned thing's practically invisible, and the silver bitch *loses* it!"

"Actually, sir, it was stolen."

"Well, aren't you a genius? *I know that, you idiot!!*"

"N-no sir, I mean, stolen by someone in particular." He saw the chance for another angry rebuttal and hastily added, "Someone we *know*, sir!"

"Well, are you going to tell me, or do I have to guess?"

"It was Jonn Stryker, Mr. Hollings."

Todd's grimy face grew even paler in the utter darkness of his pristine room. If Stryker was aboard the *Raven*, then he knew *everything* and was racing back to warn Kelassiter even now!

But that was okay. It didn't matter anymore if Kelassiter and his pet stooge knew every sordid detail of the plan that would kill them *and* turn Tiko III over to the Hollings' corporation — it was too late for them to do anything about it! Todd wasn't thrilled about having to fight Jonn Stryker, but he was prepared for that, too.

CHAPTER THIRTY

Return to New Akron

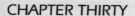

New Akron lay halfway between Teraxiter and the Tiko sector, and it took the *Raven* only three days to get to the ruined colony. Robbie coasted the craft down to the moon's only city, and Stryker pointed out a familiar spot for him to land. They descended in a whirling cloud of dust that turned the ship's inky blackness into a mottled gray. If a moon could be mummified, Robbie thought it would look a lot like this.

He, Tally, and Stryker donned the captured power armor. Jonn had adjusted the armor in transit, and it fit each of them better than he would have thought. To be safe, Jonn checked over the dangerous suits one last time, and the three stepped into the airlock.

Stryker looked out over the dusty ruins of the city where the chain of events that had ruined his life began. He was apprehensive about something, like he was about to learn some dark secret better left hidden, but he had to press on. Jonn believed it was better to fight the danger he knew than the one he didn't, even if that meant sticking his neck out occasionally.

The three stepped into the airlock and waded out into the thick dust. A rush of oxygen accompanied them, and the flying sediment obscured their vision. With heavy footsteps, Jonn, Tally and Robbie trudged out of the thick cloud and headed towards New Akron.

Up ahead was the macabre crater where the Akronites had begged to be shuttled off the dying planet. Jonn saw where Hawkins had disturbed the dust, and recognized ten sets of footprints still leading into the colony. They followed these all the way past the ruined supermarket to the bank where the first attack had occurred.

Graves' body had finally fallen from the wall and pooled in a dusty pile of bone and metal beneath — there was no chance his armor had been salvaged. Shaick was missing altogether, and there were obvious drag marks where the pirates had carted him away. Jonn would have guessed that the Arab's armor was beyond repair, but knew it might have looked much worse than it actually was. Still, the pirates' weapon had quite a punch. That reminded him to ask Gallacia what kind of arms Hollings was supplying them with when he got back to the ship.

There were bootprints all around the area, and Jonn inspected them closely. Some were obviously made by the Wolverines, but the thick dust told Jonn that others had passed by later. These fresher prints weren't rounded or ridged like armored boots, but long and wide instead. And Jonn didn't even want to think about why they had three toes.

He wandered over to where Duncan's corpse rested half-buried in the dust. One arm still lay in the street, and his bloody, shattered helmet was covered in a large pile of dust. He knew Duncan's armor would have made perfect salvage, especially since the thieves were only using the chestpieces and not trying to wear an entire suit.

So why was Duncan still wearing his?

Jonn had seen at least two of the Wolverines' breast-plates on the Lost Sheep, and had assumed that they were salvaged from New Akron. But there was only one suit missing. Where had the extra chest-piece come from?

He almost slapped himself for being so stupid. Gallacia admitted to attacking Tiko marines, but not necessarily on New Akron. There was one other place the pirates could have stolen the valuable armor. The missing shuttle. He'd heard everything had been re-covered from that debacle, but he hadn't actually seen the salvaged material.

Jonn ran past Hendrickson and Tally and bolted for the *Raven*. His startled friends followed clumsily be-hind but couldn't quite keep up, and Stryker reached the ship well before them. He fingered in the code for the airlock and it opened slowly. He didn't wait for it and jumped through before the gangplank touched ground. Jonn stormed into the cargo section while the suit continued to adjust to the new environment, and threw open the door to the weapons bay. One wall was taken up by a rack of ship-to-ship missiles that fed into the launcher above, and another wall was comprised of sensors and damage control devices.

He knew there had to be one more bay somewhere. The gunner's chair was equipped with a device that fired something not labeled on the master circuits, and Jonn thought he knew what it was. If he could only find the damned thing.

He stomped his foot in frustration and heard a metallic rattle as the floor plating shook. With renewed vigor, Jonn stepped out into the hall and pulled the heavy grill up with his powerful arms. There, he found what he was looking for — a newly added launch tube. Stacked in the feed tray was a long torpedo that ran the length of the hall and disappeared under the cargo hold. It was blue, and Stryker just bet it was full of spheroid limpet mines.

So that was it. Hollings wasn't stupid enough to build his own stealth ship — Fleet would make his company a bad memory if they found out — but he had hired and outfitted a deadly gang of pirates to do his dirty work for him. Hollings could probably get away with this since he owned the spaceport that the pirates worked out of, and because Teraxiter was so far out on the frontier.

All this could only mean that Todd did indeed have his sights on the Tiko sector, and Jonn began to regret wasting the three days it had taken to get to New Akron. If only he hadn't had it stuck in his head that the Lost Sheep's armor came from Duncan or Shaick, he might've pieced things together sooner and been able to beat Todd to Tiko III.

But someone *had* attacked them on New Akron, and someone *had* taken Shaick's body. And he just bet that it was somebody with jaws. He still didn't know how New Akron fit into Hollings plan, but once he got to Tiko, he planned on beating the answer out of him personally.

The *Raven* was now ready to streak back towards Tiko III in an effort to thwart Hollings' impending attack. Hendrickson piloted the ship, and Tally was in the cargo section keeping an eye on Gallacia.

Robbie punched in the navigational coordinates for the quantum drive and the tiny red screen before him printed the words, "FROM: NEW AKRON TO:____?" He turned to Jonn with a look of mild surprise. "See that?" he pointed. "Navigational computers only give you the sector coordinates unless you tell it the *name* of a place instead."

"Yeah, so?" Jonn grunted, eager to get moving.

"The universe is too damn big for the computer to store the name of every shithole moon, colony, or village. So, navigators usually give the computer a name instead of looking up coordinates every time they want to go somewhere. Somebody's told it that these coordinates are called New Akron."

Jonn still didn't get it.

Hendrickson sighed, "This ship has been here before."

Stryker left Hendrickson at the controls and ran to the cargo bay. Gallacia was still lying on the floor and he smashed her silver-plated head with the butt of his blaster. "You were here before. Tell me about it. Now!"

Gallacia hissed and bared her teeth, only to be clubbed on the head again.

"Now!"

"Hollings!" she screamed. "Hollings had us drop something on the planet while you and your stupid marines were playing in the dust!"

Jonn gritted his teeth and spoke evenly through them, "I won't ask twice. What was it?"

"A distress beacon! He told us to drop a distress beacon!"

"Why?"

"I don't know! I swear! He just told us to drop it and get the hell out of there!"

The ship started to rock, Hendrickson had punched in the coordinates for Tiko III and the auto-pilot was lifting off. "It's doing it on its own!" came a faint yell. Robbie desperately tried to understand the controls before him, but the high-tech ship was beyond his limited experience. "I don't know how to stop it!" he yelled.

Jonn grabbed Tally and threw her into the hallway that led to the bridge. "Tell him to keep going and get us out of here." With that, he slammed his fist into the door control and the thick panel slid shut, sealing the cargo bay from the rest of the vessel.

Jonn stuck his suit's helmet back over his head and

dragged Gallacia to her feet. With a strength born of four weeks frustration he threw her across the bay where she collided painfully with the far wall. "That was for New Akron!" he yelled.

He stomped across the room and backhanded her with a monstrously strong arm, "*That* was for the *Fury!*" She stumbled to her knees and looked up at him. Blood streamed from her mouth where one of the cheek plates had cut into her jaw muscle, and one protecting her skull was dented like an old can.

Then Jonn grabbed her by the throat with his left hand, and hit the button that opened the airlock with his right. The *Raven* was almost fifty feet off the ground now, and her powerful thrusters were kicking up years of dust and death. Gray swirls licked the interior of the cargo bay as Jonn held the kicking pirate by her slender, bloody throat. She hissed and spat and managed to work her deadly tail free, but it was no use. The razor sharp coils were useless against Jonn's armor.

Stryker screamed with her, locked in a bitter duet of frustration and rage. He staggered nearer the open door, and held the frantic pirate over the edge. She clawed at him until her gleaming nails broke and left long greasy trails down his visor. Finally, Jonn's powerful hand unlocked from around her neck, and she plunged into the thick silt below. Through the thickening swirls, Stryker could just make out her wiggling form as she convulsed and trembled from the damage of the fall. She would die there, from suffocation or her broken back; it really didn't matter which.

"And that one was for me," he said.

The Quantum drive of the *Raven* was just preparing to collapse the inertia fields around her and ride them to the Tiko sector when Jonn returned to the bridge.

"Look, Jonn. I'm in this up to my neck now. I've stolen one of the boss' ships, hooked up with one of his two greatest enemies, and now I'm helping warn

Kelassiter of his attack. I go back there now, I'm a dead man."

"What are you tryin' to say, marine?" Jonn grumbled.

"I'm saying I'm on *your* side, okay?"

"I won't turn down free help. That leaves you, me, and about seven other marines to defend the place from whatever Hollings' comes up with. Oh, yeah, 'n a dirt-bag mercenary named Max Hunt."

Hendrickson gulped. "Max Hunt? Of the Jaegers?"

"Yeah, what's so special about him?" Jonn scowled.

"He was on board the *Constantine* three months ago!"

CHAPTER THIRTY-ONE

Promises Kept and Broken

The *Constantine* had just exited Tiko space when the courier caught up with it. Terrin Kelassiter appeared on the video-communications display, and pleaded desperately for Todd's help. Tiko III was being invaded by some unknown force, and they were completely defenseless. Todd quickly dispatched a reply courier, and stoically agreed to honor Consortium law by coming to their aid.

The transaction was recorded and broadcast throughout the entire ship as the *Constantine* turned about and headed back toward Tiko III.

Two senior technicians had helped Katanopolis splice together the bogus tape, and the forgery team sent it to their ecstatic employer. The Consortium would someday examine the transmission and test its authenticity, but Katanopolis assured Hollings that the tape would be lost long before then.

It would take the *Constantine* five days to reach Tiko III from its current position. Long before that, a courier containing a pulsing distress beacon would race to Kelassiter's city and throw itself into the city's iridium mines. With any luck, the aliens would swarm down once again, and the traitor's sabotage would prevent the automated defenses from destroying their ship. By the time the *Constantine* arrived, the aliens would have destroyed the defenseless colony and Hollings' crew would have only the minimal task of finishing whatever remained. He had to insure that his allies were exterminated — it wouldn't do if Fleet later managed to communicate with them and found out about the distress beacons, but it was worth slaughtering an unknown invader to get his hands on the iridium-filled Tiko sector.

Only two things could go wrong; Kelassiter could somehow defeat the aliens, or they could fail to attack altogether. But the meticulous Hollings had planned for this, also. If either circumstance occurred, one handpicked squad of marines would descend and annihilate every living being on the asteroid. Of course, that squad would later have an unfortunate accident themselves, but again, this was a small sacrifice when compared to the enormous profits at stake. Todd hoped that this second plan wouldn't be necessary — it wasted valuable resources and would make things a little tougher to prove to Fleet — but Todd was sure he could catch and kill enough of the aliens to make it look convincing later on.

"Course plotted to Tiko III, Mr. Hollings. Estimated time or arrival is one hundred-fourteen hours."

Todd leaned back in his plush chair and chortled at his pet scientist.

Soon after Katanopolis grew tired of his boss' greasy adoration, he strolled down to the fourth level of the massive ship and headed for the brig. The young cadet was on duty again, and the scientist casually ignored him as he made his way to the prison cells.

Dreama's broken arm hadn't healed quite right and

there was a bloody rough lump where her rib had been snapped. Despite her constant aching however, she smiled spitefully as the tall Greek strolled into the room.

He looked down at her for a moment, then placed his hands behind his back and stared at the ceiling, as if trying to remember some trivial message he was supposed to deliver. "Let's see. I was supposed to tell you something. Now what was it. Ah, yes! Do you know Terrin Kelassiter, little spy?"

Dreama's smile wavered a little.

"Yes? Well, I'm afraid he's had an accident. Seems a terribly vicious group of previously unknown beings has attacked Tiko III. They ate him, I believe. Yes, that was it. Ate him alive." He paused to let his words sink in, then continued. "Or at least, they will." He looked at his watch, "In about four days."

Raw hatred shot from Dreama's eyes and slammed Katanopolis in the gut. He was surprisingly afraid — there was something in that stare that meant business. He had wanted her to sweat out the next week, worrying futilely over the inevitable, but now he was beginning to regret telling her. But she couldn't do anything about it, *could she?*

Katanopolis regained his composure, "I'll be back for you later, little girl. I'm going to show you Kelassiter's head, and then I'm going to kill you." He stormed out of the brig, and hated himself for his fear.

Almost five days later, the *Constantine* and the *Raven* unknowingly raced each other back to Tiko III. Hollings' flagship had a head start, but the stolen pirate ship was much faster, and both vessels neared the city within hours of each other.

The drone smashed into the iridium mine three days before either ship arrived, but the creatures from beyond the shatterzone were slow to respond this time around. The courier's beacon beeped and whined for three days, but Tiko's equipment failed to detect it, again thanks to the actions of the traitor.

But days later, the alien ship did appear, and the curious beings inside it were once again drawn to the distress beacon. They were well aware that someone was leading them deeper and deeper into some sort of trap, but after a lifetime with their former masters, it took a lot more than the frail small creatures on this side of the 'zone to frighten them.

One of the beings poked a thick finger at an indentation and the sensor began to show the warm lifeforms that lived near the pulsing beacon. They were growing tired of playing the game with Hollings' derelict hulks, and the promise of fresh meat made their oversized jaws drip with thick saliva.

The leader of the pack, the warmaster, rose and went into the ship's den where the others lay lazily about, pawing through the junk they had collected in their most recent hunt. They were a servitor race, long ago enslaved by another, and the pack had adapted their masters' cruel behavior well. Escape hadn't been easy, and the warmaster had soon plunged their stolen craft through the shatterzone to elude pursuit and inevitable retribution.

The pack was trained from birth to hunt, and their ship, weapons, and armor had been provided by their masters. The warmaster had proven the strongest of his litter, and he commanded his surviving brothers with bestial authority.

His speech sounded like a cross between heavy breathing and a low growl as he prepared them for the hunt. One of them ran a black claw down the face of a long-dead tourist and licked his jagged teeth with delight. He asked if this were to be another useless foray without meat. The warmaster roared that it was not, and reprimanded him for his impudence.

Then the warmaster told the others of the upcoming feast, and promised that they would no longer play the tiny creatures' game. Now they would destroy everything they could find and then see what came to save it.

And then they would destroy that, too.

The others approved.

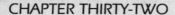

CHAPTER THIRTY-TWO

The Warmaster

The warmaster studied Tiko III and drooled at its inviting geography. Many tunnels and caverns made up the underground complex. It was perfect. The pack could enter under cover and trap their prey in their underground hive. There would be no escape.

His body was tall and covered in leathery brown skin scarred by years of battle and abuse. His claws were enormous compared to his lean form, and the knobby talons were almost as long as his slim skull. Jagged teeth extended from his lower jaw in a menacing underbite, but it was the eyes that were most disturbing. They were a glossy black, totally devoid of any form or feature like others of his race, but there was something unnatural — almost *non-living* — about them, and even the masters had been unable to fathom the mind that lurked beneath those black orbs.

The armor disguised his true features and made him look more like the carapace of some giant, two-legged beetle. It was glossy black and horribly decorated with ridges, spines, and grooves designed to instill terror in the being's prey. Even the headgear had the creature's oversized jaws sculpted into it for this purpose.

The weapon he chose was one Jonn Stryker was already familiar with. The end was tipped with a barbed spine that functioned like a bayonet, and a long ridged cord hooked into an ammunition pack strapped to the warmaster's back. The rounds it fired were shaped to produce a ripping noise as they traveled through any sort of atmosphere, and were fitted with explosive tips far more powerful for their size than anything humans had yet invented.

It was going to be a glorious feast, and he promised the pack they would kill well.

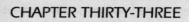

CHAPTER THIRTY-THREE

Fishing

Peter Vasiliovich, the foreman of the iridium mines, entered the airlock to gather up his men and send them to lunch. He waved to the new guard as he entered the airlock, and flipped on the light attached above his faceplate. The tunnels were lit by a few random electric torches set at intervals along the walls, but their pale glow did little in the twisting passages.

Peter walked on into the tunnel and felt an ominous chill run up his spine. But why? Peter had walked these tunnels for years now. He knew every branch, every vein, and every vertical climb in the system, and other than careless accidents, there had never been anything to be afraid of. Yet the chill remained, just the same.

It was well over a half mile to the section where the work crew was stationed today. At the end of the first hall, an umbilical tether stretched out into the darkness. It led all the way to today's work site, and each man was connected to it by his own individual cable. Peter grabbed one of the sliding rings that allowed them to maneuver freely up and down the tether's length, latched it through one of the eighteen foot personal cords, and started pulling himself forward.

He followed the line through a twisted section that went perpendicular to his previous path, and had to pull himself through the narrow opening to enter the tunnel above. The tether felt strangely loose as he pulled himself up its length. He tugged a little and felt it give, hoping that it hadn't snapped somewhere, but there was definitely weight on the other end — it just seemed … *lighter*.

Down the next twisting passageway, he felt the line suddenly go taut and jerk frantically, like a fishing line suddenly hit by a hungry fish. *The boys're playing a joke*, he thought; that's what it had to be. Peter smiled and laughed to reassure himself, but it sounded ominously false and alone.

He came to another vertical section and the line once again went slack, as if the imaginary fish had dropped the hook. He poked his head through the hole, and started to climb through when a rush of rock and other debris tumbled eerily down the tunnel he had entered. There was no air here, yet somehow, something similar to a blast of wind had just swept over him.

He climbed on through and continued to pull himself towards the work crew by the yellow tether. Something was whirling down the passage, something long and cylindrical, like one of the laser-torches carried by the miners. It whipped by, still spinning lazily and propelled by unseen currents that couldn't possibly exist in the vacuum of the mines.

Peter felt a desperate sense of urgency and pulled himself on once more. A cold sweat broke on his brow and the suit's internal heaters blew it into his eyes. There was no way to rub them through the visor, so he tried unsuccessfully to blink the salty sting away. Around the next corner, several torches, burnt cables, and other debris had caught as they had been blown by the mysterious wind. The stuff was pooled there like detritus washed up on a beach after a storm. There were other things caught on the rough wall, but they were at least partially hidden by the gloom, and Peter's subconscious wouldn't let him look deeper. He noticed that the lights had died here and the only illumination was provided by the probing beam attached above his head.

The darkness and a growing realization caused adrenaline to shoot up his spine and pool uselessly in the sagging lobes of his brain. But he was almost there, there was no turning back now.

Peter grabbed a rocky protrusion and spun himself around the last corner.

The bodies of the miners were everywhere, their mining suits torn open like bags of bloody potatoes. Matted strands of the thick material splayed jaggedly from their red wounds, and meaty innards leaked out to crystallize in the icy cold. Visors were shattered inwards, turning the men's faces into frozen stews of pulpy meat and splintered plastic. Arms and legs were torn from their sockets and still floated about the room in a macabre dance of spinning horror.

Peter felt his breakfast crawling up his throat. He tried to catch it at the gullet but the warm spew squirted through his gritted teeth in a chunky gush before he could stop it. The acidic fluid floated about the inside of his helmet, clinging to his face and clogging his nose and eyes. He tried to clear them and managed to snort most of it from his nostrils, but the sudden rush of air only spun the thick matter around again.

Something was heading towards him, something big and black and glossy moving from the shadows past the miners. He caught a glimpse, but the vomit quickly forced him to close his eyes. Panic overtook him and Peter beat at the air, trying to turn himself in place and escape, but his flailing fist caught in the tether. The motion sent the foreman and his dead crew racing toward each other, and they met in a grisly tangle. Painful glimpses through his biting stomach acid showed Peter dead faces peering in through his dripping visor. Outstretched hands, brittle arms, stiffened legs, and twelve tangling tethers caught him in a ghastly wrestling match that he couldn't win. He squirmed like a fish that had swallowed the hook and fought to get free. Terrible glimpses of something black and massive and terrible only increased his panic.

He still wasn't free when it reached him. Peter finally ignored the streaming corpses and pulled on the far side of the tether, rocketing himself down the corridor with his knotted friends in tow. He didn't dare look back for fear of tangling himself further, but instead kept grabbing at the life line, working himself back along its length at a frantic pace.

He was doing well until he reached the first hole. There was no way he could crawl down through it with the mass of bodies still attached. He reached into the pocket of his dead crew chief and pulled out his lasertorch. He hoped that his previous effort had bought him some time — he knew there would be no second chance. But eighteen years of mining experience made quick work of the interfering safety cords, and Peter shot through the hole without his gruesome companions.

His panic made him push through too hard, and he slammed into the opposite wall of the next tunnel. Something wrenched in his ankle and pain surged up his nerves and shot through his mouth in an angry scream. Strands of vomit still floated about the helmet, and the rush of air once again forced the acidic juice into his nose and eyes. In desperation, he tugged with all his might on the tether and shot himself forward again, but his blindness betrayed him. Peter smacked into a rocky outcropping and he heard the visor crack. The heaters whistled through the fissure and his oxygen was blown through in precious spurts, but the floating vomit froze in the cracks and stopped most of the escaping air. He blinked his eyes clear once again, but this time frozen shards of vomit tore into them and lodged painfully beneath his lids. There was no way to dig them out while in the suit, so he fought to lock his eye muscles open. Through blinking, bleeding eyes, he spared a glance back to the hole through which he had descended.

The thing dropped through like a stone, body parts and debris following in its wake. Peter could barely see his own hands for the blood, tears, and vomit, but he believed he would have seen those jaws even if he was blind.

Tug after tug after tug, he rocketed onwards, but the thing was lumbering after him, propelling itself by the rough walls.

Peter reached the second crawl and shot through, smashing his shoulder and knee in his haste. They weren't broken, but the pain was unbearable and tiny holes leaked precious heat into the void. He felt his leg veins expand in the sudden depressurization, and rich blood hardened around his stinging flesh. He bounced off the opposite wall on both feet and felt the injured knee throb in protest, but he ignored it and grabbed the cable again.

He pulled … and almost instantly shot backwards! The smaller cord that attached him to the main tether had caught on an outcropping near the last hole, and it had snapped him back elastically. Peter cried and twisted in midair, floating helplessly below the treacherous snag. A horrible ridged face with gleaming silver teeth leered at him like a cat that had caught an unwary fish in an aquarium. A spiked hand reached through the hole and stuck in Peter's shoulder, breaching the mining suit again and impaling him like a wiggling frog.

But Peter wasn't done yet. He still had the torch and applied the concentrated beam to the creature's claw. It recoiled in surprise, and Peter desperately sliced through the snagged cable with his makeshift weapon. He kicked at the rim of the hole and launched hurriedly away to the far wall. After another painful slam into the rough rock, he started pulling himself forward. With hands and feet he crawled the length of the passage, propelling his slowly exploding body toward the city by rough handholds in the wall. Peter knew he would be dead now if the freezing blood hadn't matted the suit to the ruined flesh beneath.

He shot over a connecting passage and glanced backwards again. The creature was nowhere in sight! Tears of relief tried to push past his freezing eyeballs and finally squirted out in a salty mist.

Ahead was the airlock door and Peter rocketed toward it, slamming against the solid steel so hard that his neck popped painfully. The blow knocked him back and up, away from any handholds, and ripped the suit from its makeshift seal. Peter floated in the middle of the wide passageway, slowly realizing his helplessness as his delirium began to clear. He was revolving slowly, and saw the creature above him. He hadn't lost it after all, it had just been above him. There was nothing he could do. He couldn't reach the walls to run anymore, and the suit had blown open anyway.

The thing vanished from sight as Peter's eyeballs finally hemorrhaged and burst in a viscous slime that hung over his protruding and bloated tongue. Blood vessels exploded in his brain and internal organs popped flaccidly.

At least it *didn't get me*, he thought.

CHAPTER THIRTY-FOUR

Hunters

T he new guard heard a thump on the airlock door. He rose with a start, remembering that it was time for the foreman to return, and started the depressurization process. A few minutes later, he spun the silver wheel that opened the airlock and listened as the bolts slowly wound out of the door frame. Before they had cleared, however, someone kicked the door roughly, as if trying to open it but not realizing that the bolts were still in place.

"What the hell are ya *doin'*, Pete?" the guard yelled. He started to spin the wheel again and heard what sounded like muffled breath. "Pete? Quit foolin' around in there."

He waited and listened, a bad feeling settling over him. It hadn't been so long ago that another guard had been killed in this very room. "Pete?" No answer, but he was sure he could hear the faint sound of breathing from the other side. "Aw, hell, Pete," he finally decided and gave the wheel one last spin.

The door creaked open, and the guard saw the black spike for only a second before it poked through his

269 ▪

skull like an eggshell and scrambled the gray matter inside.

The warmaster growled into his transmitter and slid the tiny corpse off his gauntlet. A few seconds later, the warship fired a burrowing charge into the asteroid where the sensors showed its main power plant to be buried. It was time for the assault.

Guibert was on shift with Hawkins when all hell broke loose. Suddenly, they felt the city quake and heard the muffled rumblings of a huge explosion somewhere beneath them. Glass panes shattered from the buildings and the people on Wriggle Street stumbled helplessly to the ground. Moments later, Tiko III was plunged into darkness and a wailing siren bleated out its death throes. Red emergency lights flickered on and cast the city in an eerie glow.

Guibert was the first to his feet. "*Sacre Bleu!* The power plant must've exploded!"

Hawkins rose to his knees and stared dumbly at the dark tunnel that led to the iridium mines, "G-Gu-guh-Guy ..." he stuttered.

Guibert spun around and saw a trio of black-suited individuals loping in the pale red light. "It's *Hollings*! They're attacking!" He drew his pistol and fired a shot down the alley at the figures, but they dove into the shadows and disappeared. Guibert did the same and flipped out his radio. "Control! Get me someone in charge! We're being invaded. They're coming through the mines, I've seen six so far ..."

Hawkins backed slowly up the alley and watched as several more of the creatures spilled out of the tunnel. One of them roared and aimed something towards him.

Guibert saw something rip through the air and split the young marine like a melon, the round passing through his unarmored flesh and exploding against the opposing building. Guy had heard that sound before.

"*Sacre* ... Get *Hunt*!" he screamed into the transmitter. "Did you hear me?! Get the Jaegers down here! Now! And tell them to bring everything they've got!"

Max and his band were enjoying a game of *jostis* at the *Worm Hole* when the lights went out. Kelassiter had given him a radio before being imprisoned and the communications technician's voice came blaring through.

"Mr. Hunt! Mr. Hunt! It's the Hollings corporation! They're attacking! Guibert says they're coming through the iridium mines!"

The radio was loud in the stunned silence of the room and the technician's plea threw the room into panic. The mid-day patrons of the *Worm Hole* scampered through the darkness and poured out into the street, screaming their impending doom and panicking those around them.

Hunt waited until the mob had passed and signaled for his mercenaries to follow him.

Steve Klein followed Max and the others out of the bar, but then slipped off into the darkness. In the distance, he could hear Guibert trying to quell the panicking citizens as they swarmed their houses in an attempt to hide or gather their belongings, but he turned and ran the other way, toward the corporate offices. The doors to the complex were locked shut, and he yelled for the terrified militiaman to open them.

"I-I'm not supposed to open the blast doors, Mr. Klein!" the frightened voice pleaded.

"Look, laddie," he spoke evenly, "how am I supposed to get to my suit if you don't let me in?"

"Um, yes, Mr. Klein."

The doors opened and the red-haired marine rushed inside. The barracks were straight ahead but he turned left and headed for the brig instead. The militiaman started to protest, but thought better of it when he saw the look on the marine's face. The guard inside the brig didn't try to stop him either, and he grabbed the cell's passkey from the lockbox and headed towards Kelassiter's cell.

Terrin was already at the bars, straining to find out what was going on. "Klein! Thank God! What's happening?"

"They've invaded, through the tunnels. We've got to get the militia together and make a stand."

"So why are you letting *me* out?"

Steve hesitated. He knew Vanessa had talked with his boss, and technically Terrin could have him executed for desertion if he wanted. "Because you've fought Hollings before, and I'd rather have you in charge of the defenses than Dr. Dumois." He wedged the passkey into its slot.

"But what if I'm a traitor?" Terrin pressed.

"Then you wouldn't have hired the Jaegers." Steve deactivated the lock and the door slid open.

Terrin shot him a wry smile, and stepped out into the dim corridor. "I'm still docking your pay," he said.

Once outside the brig, Terrin pointed to the barracks, "Round up whoever's left and bring them to the control room."

"Done, boss, but Dumois' already sent most of them out into the street," Klein yelled and disappeared down the dark hall.

Terrin streaked up to the control room and slugged the startled guard before he could try to stop him. The man toppled to the red carpet in a heap and Kelassiter mashed the button that opened the sliding doors.

Down on the street, Guibert had made a fighting retreat as the invaders pushed their way towards the corporate complex. Explosions rippled through the milling crowd as bodies tumbled and rolled from the force of the creature's explosive rounds. Those that weren't caught in the blasts were quickly caught by murderous creatures on the fringes whose slashing claws tore their tender flesh in bloody swaths.

Guy was running from corner to corner, using the crowd and the darkness to hide himself as he ran from the creatures to the corporate offices. He used the cover of a mob to dart into the next alleyway, and briefly saw Vanessa mingled in with the frightened faces. Suddenly, several rounds tore into the crowd and knocked them into a bloody pile.

"Get out of here, you stupid whore!" Guibert called.

Vanessa stood and wiped something gray off her cheek. "I'm not a whore," she whispered. There was a dead militiaman in the groaning pile of bodies, and Vanessa picked up his pistol. "Guy!" she shouted.

He ignored her and looked for some way to cover his retreat.

Vanessa raised the pistol and yelled again, but there was no reaction. She fired and the shot impacted on the wall just above Guibert's head. "Guy!" she screamed.

The startled marine looked at her briefly, but quickly returned his attention to the approaching carnage.

"Damn you! Look at me, you self-righteous bastard!"

Guibert thought Vanessa had really bad timing. The city was being invaded by something Humans had never seen before, and she picked that moment to throw a tantrum.

She fired again, this time catching Guibert in the lower leg. The flesh burst inside his boot and he fell to the ground, startled. He raised his weapon and pointed it at her, hoping to shock her out of whatever insanity had suddenly gripped her, but she only squeezed the trigger again. This blast caught him higher in the leg, and Guibert felt himself rapidly losing consciousness.

"*I am not a whore!*" she screamed in triumph. Another of the invader's rounds exploded nearby, raking her with fragments of bone and steel. She slumped to her knees and deliriously fired again.

Guibert flew back, clutching his ruptured throat and gurgling in his own blood.

Vanessa giggled deliriously and fired at the marine's convulsing body until it stopped moving. "I'm not a whore," she whispered. She was still chuckling when the warmaster ran her through.

Max connected his flamer to the napalm pack strapped to his full suit of red Brodie body armor. Oleg and the others pulled on whatever armor they could find, and armed themselves with an assortment of blasters, gatling lasers, and pulse cannons.

The Jaegers were standing in the entry-bay of their assault ship, and Max could see mobs of people boarding every other available vessel in the hangar. Freighter captains, retired shuttle crewmen, and anyone else that could fly a space ship had already been briefed and promised reimbursement by Kelassiter in case of emergency, but none were quite ready to handle the panicked crowd that pushed and fought their way onto their assorted craft.

The Jaegers finally lowered their gangplank and pushed away the confused individuals who tried to rush in. One of them was Lucretia D'Atalack, Jonn Stryker's former lover. "Max! Thank God! We've got to get out of here!" she cried and latched her arms about his massive shoulder.

"Go find another ship," he said and shrugged her off.

"WHAT?" she screamed. Her eyes shook and her lips trembled.

"I said go find another freaking ship, you leech!"

She was in shock, "B-b-but, you love me?! You-you slept with —"

"I was *paid* to sleep with you! Hollings wanted to hurt Stryker, and he paid me to get caught sleeping with you! Of course, I didn't expect the man to walk in right in the middle of the job, but I didn't expect you to be so *easy* either! Tip you a few trinkets and creds, and you fall in with anybody, don't you?"

Lucretia was silent. She *was* a leech. She attached herself to whomever could provide her with food and a roof over her head, and if something happened to that someone, she moved on to someone else. Lucretia supposed she had known it all along, but it was still a shock to hear someone else say it.

"Now get yourself out of here," Max barked and pointed to a filling transport.

Lucretia nodded dumbly, and walked silently away, vanishing into the bleating crowd.

Hunt turned back to his men and checked to see if they were ready for battle. "Klein? Where's Klein? He was with us a minute ago."

The others looked through their ranks, trying to decide who was who beneath the motley collection of armor, and shrugged their shoulders.

Hunt shook his head disgustedly and marched out into the street.

Two of the warmaster's pack were left on the warship, and watched as the *Raven* streaked into the landing bays of Tiko III. Anything that tried to leave was to be annihilated, but their tender, frail prey were certainly allowed to *add* more meat to the slaughter, and they let the ship pass unharmed.

CHAPTER THIRTY-FIVE

Tiko's End

Wriggle Street was dying below them in a flashing spectacle of explosions and screaming citizens, but Kelassiter had finally convinced Dumois that he wasn't the traitor. The scanners posted around the perimeter of the asteroid had finally picked up the enemy ship when it had fired and destroyed the power plant, but the automated defenses didn't seem to be responding.

Terrin went to the master controls and placed his eye over the access terminal. The computer recognized his retina pattern and he was instantly allowed into the complex programs that controlled the remote missile launchers. Of course he had no idea how to do this, but he only needed to bypass the security and Dumois would do the programming.

"I've already checked all this! There's nothing wrong that I can detect!"

Terrin answered him coolly, "I know, Thaddeus. Someone has obviously changed the program. But I want you to figure out a way to override it and fire those missiles. Got it?"

Dumois nodded embarrassedly. Before Kelassiter arrived, he had found himself in charge of an entire city, and, quite frankly, was a little overwhelmed, particularly since his new command was disintegrating under his feet. He crossed the bridge and sat at the terminal, beginning the sequence that would erase the launcher's programming and allow him to write another from scratch. He was relieved that someone else was in charge, and he could get back to what he did best.

Terrin turned back to the window and watched as his streets were torn apart. Mobs of citizens were fleeing into the hangar in an attempt to evacuate. It was going to be a bitch getting all of them back if he managed to save this place, he thought.

Hunt and the others entered Wriggle Street in the middle of the fighting. The first sight he saw was a large man wearing what Max thought was the ugliest body armor he'd ever seen. He was twisting some sort of bayonet in someone's chest, and some of the Jaegers were already prepared to fire.

"Hey, ugly!" Max yelled. The figure turned and Max had time to see that it definitely wasn't a human before his band drove it to the floor with a barrage of gunfire.

"What the hell was that?" one of them asked.

More fire erupted down the dim street and several more fleeing civilians darted past the mercenaries' position. "I don't know, but let's get down there and round up the rest of 'em," Max commanded. He leapt back to his feet and saw that the Jaeger's blast had put the creature down.

It had a long face by the size of its helmet, and huge, underset jaws that looked almost like the scoop of a bulldozer. The rest of its armor was covered in spikes and ridges that seemed to serve no purpose. Hunt stretched out his hand and reached for its weapon.

The thing shot out a spiked gauntlet and grabbed Hunt by the arm, jerking him down and slamming him into the rocky ground.

Max spun quickly, rolled up against a near wall, and whipped up his flamer, but the creature was already on its feet and kicked the nozzle out of Hunt's hands. It roared in defiance and Max saw that his band's weapons had indeed hurt it. The fact that their combined fire had failed to kill it was nothing short of amazing.

Thick plates of armor covering the creature's chest had been cracked and penetrated in several places and greenish fluid was leaking from its wounds. It went for its weapon and the mercenary scrambled for his knife. The thing was fast, but Max was faster and drove his long knife deep between the cracked armor plate.

The creature wailed and screamed and threw Max forward where he slammed into the blast doors of the corporate complex. The nozzle of his flamer still dangled from its cord, and the mercenary kicked it up into his hands with practiced ease. "Die, damn you! Die!" The napalm squirted out over the alien and covered it in flaming jelly.

Max watched in horror as it sizzled and popped under the intense heat, but still it wouldn't give in. It staggered forward, trapping him between it and the blast doors. It was dying, and it knew it, but it was going to take Max with it. He didn't have a chance.

The door he was leaning against suddenly opened and Max fell roughly into the hallway beyond. As soon as his body hit the ground, the door began to close again. Max was barely able to pull his feet inside before the heavy plate dropped into place and sealed him in.

Kelassiter and the others were still gawking when the Jaegers blasted the thing into a smoking heap. He saw the black man's surprise at the identity of his foe, and watched him reach for the thing's weapon. He screamed a warning and thumped his fist against the thick plexiglass window, but he knew the mercenary couldn't hear him.

It grabbed Max and threw him against the blast doors. One of the technicians reached for the button that would open them, but Kelassiter caught his wrist in an iron grip. It was too risky. They didn't know anything about this thing or how dangerous it was, but it had just taken a barrage of fire from the Jaegers and was somehow still alive.

The mercenary dazzled Kelassiter and his foe alike with the lightning draw of a large knife that he thrust deep into the beast's chest. It staggered back, and the mercenary flamed it with a quick blast of napalm. It burned and fell to its knees, but kept coming. Hunt was trapped against the door by his flaming foe, and Terrin was forced to take a risk.

Max was forever grateful for his decision.

Klein had just gotten the remaining miners armed and out of the barracks when Hunt fell through the blast doors. They shut immediately, barely giving the merc time to pull his legs through.

Hunt looked over his shoulder and saw gawking miners and his newest recruit. "Sweet mother, what the hell was that, Steve?"

Klein pointed toward the stairs and directed his men to the bridge. Then he grabbed Hunt's arm and helped him up. "I don't know, Max, but I've got a sneaking suspicion Hollings sent them." He couldn't read the mercenary's reaction to this beneath his red helmet. "Now let's get up to the bridge and see what Kelassiter wants us to do."

"Can't do that, Steve."

Klein squinted at Hunt. If he was going to betray them, this was it. "Why not?" he asked warily.

"My men are out there fighting these things — I gotta be with 'em."

"You go out those doors, I doubt Kelassiter'll let you back in."

"Chance I gotta take, Steve."

Klein hit the door button with his fist and Max darted out into the street.

Terrin saw the corresponding light come on and quickly punched in the override codes that turned off all the doors in the corporate building. Now only those in the control center would be able to open or close them.

There was a knock on the door and a concealed security camera showed that it was Klein. Terrin nodded and a technician allowed him in. "What the hell did you let him out for?"

Steve pointed down the street, "He's gotta protect his own. Besides, next to Jonn Stryker, I can't think of anyone I'd rather have out there fighting for us."

Max darted into the shadows and saw his men firing from behind cover. Oleg was inside the shattered aquarium of *Critters* with his trademark pulse cannon braced on one of the ceramic walls. Bright bursts of concentrated energy streaked from his gun and raced down the street. The bald mercenary's round glasses were fogged from the heat, and the black bandanna around his head was soaked with sweat. Max was turning his attention elsewhere when he noticed the black shadow that rose from behind his first mate.

"Oleg! Down!" he yelled, but there was no way he could get in a clear shot with the flamer. The first mate turned in surprise and was swatted like a fly onto the broken glass of the aquarium frame. The joints of his armor were padded with plasteel overlays, but the jagged glass slipped beneath and trapped him. The creature stood just behind the wiggling mercenary, using him as a shield and daring the others to fire past.

Max snarled and directed Tusagi, a man with a blaster rifle, to knock its head off. Tusagi was a good marksman, but the thing had ducked too close to Oleg's body to risk the shot. The creature raised its own weapon and fired. The air seemed to rip apart as a round sailed from the weapon and impacted on Tusagi's breastplate, blowing him backwards in a trail of thick white smoke. The body landed with a dull thud. When the smoke cleared, Tusagi's chest and innards were blown off the spine like an apple eaten to the core.

It sounded like the creature was laughing.

Oleg raised his head and looked into the black eyes of its helmet. With a snarl of disgust, he kicked it in the massive jaw and fell backwards. Fire immediately erupted from Max and the others, and turned the storefront into a charred and smoking ruin.

Oleg crawled out from under the barrage and readjusted his weapon's harness. A quick thumbs-up to Max said that he was okay and ready for action. The flaming creature that emerged from the burning store didn't agree.

Its gun spat screaming death, firing faster than any of them could believe possible, and three more of the Jaegers were shredded into bloody strips.

Hunt whipped a plasma grenade from his belt and slung it into the storefront. Immediately after the explosion, he ran to the ceramic wall and turned the flamer on the struggling creature within.

Hunt screamed a war cry as he coated the creature in napalm until there was no mistake that it was dead. When he was finished, he saw forty more of the creatures racing up the street.

It was a slaughter. Nine of his men were down and in cover, but only managed to squeeze off a few shots before the things were among them, firing their terrible weapons and stabbing through the motley armor of the Jaegers. Oleg fired pulser blasts into the melee, striking some who were already dead but didn't know it yet, and the hideous things besides. Hunt sprayed the flame across the street and managed to keep them at bay, but tears of frustration rolled down his black cheeks as the flaming liquid coated everyone in range.

Blasters erupted behind him and Hunt turned to see Klein and five militia men laying down suppressor fire from the open blast doors. "Get the hell in here! *Now!*"

One of the thing's rounds shot through the blast doors and impacted against the wall behind Klein and his men. Steve barely felt it in his thick Brodie suit but the flying shrapnel tore through the unprotected miners and they fell in a moaning pile of sprawling flesh.

Hunt's eyes widened with fear, "Mother Africa, Steve! Get those bodies out of the doorway — I'll try to hold them!"

Oleg backed through the portal, still firing the heavy pulser blasts, and somehow escaping the screaming death that rocketed around him. Steve started to pull in the dead and wounded and found Kelassiter by his side.

"You're going to be ripped apart!" Steve yelled.

"Shut up and pull!" said the boss.

The warmaster watched with approval as the pride slaughtered their prey. Two of his race were wounded by some sort of energy blast, but they pressed on and avenged themselves by gutting their opponents from crotch to chin.

More of the puny things emerged from the door to cover the retreat of the others. The warmaster fired his weapon into the portal and the unarmored ones fell in a heap. The big one with the flamer still blocked their advance, and another fired heavy energy bolts into their midst, but he knew they would soon be overwhelmed.

He stepped on the burning remains of a squirming

creature and crushed its helmet with his powerful foot. The rest of the pack darted under and around the jet of searing flame and rushed its wielder, but he barely managed to throw himself through the doorway just as a thick metal panel slid into place and severed one of the wounded men in half.

Klein stared in horror at what he had done. One last miner had been lying in the doorway when Max had leapt through the door. It had been a snap decision that had cost the militiaman his life, but the things would have breached the corporate complex otherwise. It was the right thing to do, but the still-kicking legs would remain in Klein's nightmares for years to come.

Terrin blinked unbelievingly and felt a warm gush rise in his throat, but he held it down. Now was the time for a leader, and he told himself a leader shouldn't vomit all over the wriggling remains of his men.

"Let's get upstairs and seal off the rest of this place," he muttered, "we'll make our stand in the bridge."

CHAPTER THIRTY-SIX

Reunited

Stryker, Tally, and Hendrickson exited the *Raven* into total chaos. Civilians were running toward them, and Stryker had to knock more than a few on their ass before they stopped trying to scramble into his stolen craft. Every vessel in the sinking city was loaded with the fleeing rats, and some were beginning to leave. Stryker shook his head, wondering if Todd would allow them to escape. Considering the illegality of what he was doing, he doubted it.

Jonn ran to a large freighter nearby and pushed through the milling throng to a captain frantically trying to count heads. "You launch and they'll blast you out of the sky!" he yelled.

The captain tried to look into the face-mask of Jonn's unfamiliar armor, "Who are you? Are you threatening us?"

Jonn realized his mistake and raised his visor.

"Sergeant Stryker? I thought you were gone!"

"Well, I'm back, and I'm tellin' you that Hollings ain't gonna let you leave."

"Sergeant, we're not being attacked by Mr. Hollings!"

the captain retorted. He pointed outside the hangar bay where Max and some of his men were being swarmed by lightning-quick creatures who stabbed and clawed their way through the Jaegers with savage fury. The creatures used guns that ripped the air, and had large jaws that Jonn had seen once before, in the smoke on New Akron.

This was the last part of the puzzle. This was how Todd planned on taking over Tiko. He had lured these things into attacking the city, and once they had over-run the defenseless place, he and his marines would finish them off and claim the iridium-rich sector for himself. But watching the ferocity and battle-lust of the hideous aliens, Jonn thought Todd had seriously underestimated his unwitting allies. Hollings had no doubt lured them here the same way he had done on New Akron, with a distress beacon.

In the dim red light of Wriggle Street, Jonn saw the aliens ripping Hunt's men apart. Silhouettes of torn limbs trailed black ropes of blood in savage arcs as the creatures raged through their prey. Someone with a flamer, probably Hunt, fended them off for a moment, and then he and another vanished from view. Jonn ran down the gangplank of the freighter and watched as Terrin and a Wolverine pulled the mercenaries through the closing door.

"Damn!" he shouted.

Those civilians that made it to the hangar had disappeared now and the various ships began to depart. The sudden activity drew the attention of the creatures outside, but Hendrickson was alert and slammed the large button that sealed the landing bay. A few shots ripped through before the massive steel door slammed into place, and Tally screamed as the rounds exploded near her. The fragments bounced off her stolen body armor, and she was shocked when Stryker started *removing* his.

"What the hell are you doing?" Hendrickson cried for her.

Jonn threw his helmet towards Tally and the Raven, "Load this stuff up, we might need it later."

Robbie nodded at Stryker with wide disbelieving eyes, "Are you nuts?"

"Look, rookie, Kelassiter is trapped inside the corp building with a traitorous mercenary on the inside and a screaming band of aliens outside. And I'm bettin' those things have a way of getting through those blast doors eventually."

"And?" Robbie continued in amazement, as Jonn flipped off his leggings.

"*And*, junior, I'm gonna crawl through the oxygen shafts and get 'em the hell out of there."

"Through the oxygen shafts?" Robbie asked. "You guys built a corporate headquarters with oxygen shafts that lead inside? I thought everybody but the videos stopped doing that a hundred years ago!"

"Yeah, well, that's why we did it, I guess."

Jonn ran for a ladder that led to the catwalks high above. He wore only the white undersuit. It offered no protection, but he never would have fit into the oxygen shafts in the powered armor.

Hendrickson continued to watch in amazement as the sergeant ripped off a large grill and disappeared into the airshaft beyond. "Come on, Tally," he finally said, "let's get the *Raven* ready. If those things can get through the blast doors of the control center, they can certainly get in here."

She watched the last few ships ascend into the launch tunnel where they vanished from view, "I hope they make it," she whispered.

The warship watched as their prey started to exit the asteroid. Almost casually, the pilot maneuvered in over the launch caves and the gunner trained his deadly cannons over the tightly packed swarm. Dense bullets the size of marbles were propelled along the length of the ship's gravitic guns and sprayed the massed vessels as they rocketed out of the asteroid. Several of them erupted in brilliant orange flame as the hyper-accelerated bullets slammed through their fusion reactors, and others spun feebly in place as they were shredded by the deadly spray.

When the survivors had thinned out, the warship quickly gutted them with more precise bursts. The gunners played carefully with their prey, making the helpless ships last as long as they could. Which, unfortunately, was not very long at all.

The warmaster brought up the breacher and pointed at the blast doors. The breacher took a strange net-like thing from his pack. The strands of the weapon ended in magnetic blocks filled with the same explosive used in their launchers, but were tamped with an unusually dense metal to concentrate the blast forward. The breacher tossed the net expertly against the door, and watched as it blew a neat hole through the heavy barrier. He then shambled back to his position in the rear of the alien party.

Kelassiter and the others heard the explosion downstairs and watched the aliens through the plexiglass window two stories above. It was dark, and the things hadn't seen the window yet, but as they rushed inside the building, Terrin saw one of them pause and stare at him through horrible black eye-slits.

Dumois stood and threw his hands into the air. "There's just not enough time. The missiles aren't responding. Perhaps they aren't even there. The diagnostics says they are, but the program's so mangled I don't know what's working and what's not."

Terrin was about to tell him to try again when one of the technician's shouted, "It's the *Constantine*, sir!

Shatterzone

She's approaching fast!"

"Damn it! I knew he was behind this, somehow."
Terrin flicked on the short-range transmitter but there
was nothing but static on the viewscreen.

The monitors hooked to the security cameras in the
building showed the creatures tearing through door
after door with their weird breaching device. Several
of the other stations were overrun, and the room
watched helplessly as their friends and co-workers
were murdered in a furious frenzy of bloodlust.

Finally, the camera in the hall outside the control
room showed the creatures gathering at the door. They
pounded it with the air-ripping rounds, but the door
only dented and charred. Finally, one of them brought
up the net.

Dumois almost had a heart attack when he saw Jonn
Stryker's head poke down through the ceiling.

CHAPTER THIRTY-SEVEN

Escape

The warship was still playing with the two Tiko fighters that had managed to get airborne when the *Constantine* drifted into view. The aliens didn't attack, but they were curious. This was the craft that had played with them for months now, but it had never approached a kill in progress.

The pilot continued to monitor their host, but didn't attack. Not yet.

The last technician vanished through the ceiling when the creatures finally breached the door to the control room. Jonn pulled him up into the oxygen duct with his cybernetic arm, and sent him scurrying down the shaft after the others. He quickly turned and followed, fire blasting apart the ceiling behind him as he crawled back towards the hangar.

Terrin reached the bottom of the ladder when the hangar door exploded inwards. He and Dumois quickly dropped the remaining distance and ran to the only ship left in the bay. One of the creatures stuck its massive head through the hole, and Terrin stopped to fire at it with his blaster, but it quickly ducked back out of sight.

Klein, Hunt, and a technician now dropped to the floor and followed in Terrin's footsteps. The last few men were caught on the ladder as one of the things leapt through the hole and fired at them. Gory spatters of blood covered the wall and twisted the ladder into a useless wreck, leaving Stryker stranded on the catwalk.

Suddenly, the *Raven* rose into the air, venting great clouds of swirling heat. Jonn was getting left behind — he was going to be alone. With the things.

No, you're not! Not again! his mind screamed. With a surge of all-natural adrenaline, Jonn leapt from the catwalk onto the *Raven's* back. The ship continued to rise and cleared the first level where it faced the mammoth door that would allow it to exit the asteroid. Jonn pounded on the *Raven's* black skin, desperate to get in before it left the pressurized hangar and flew into the airlock.

The bottom of the ship was rocking with the ripper's explosions when Tally heard a heavy thump on the roof. She activated the gunner's camera and it swiveled out of its exterior hatchway. The tiny viewscreen flickered to life, and she saw Stryker desperately trying to find a way in. "He's out there!" she shouted. "We've got to land and pull him in!"

Hendrickson scowled. "Not a chance. We might not even make it out of here now. Stryker's a goner, forget him."

Terrin had never seen the man piloting the ship before, but he couldn't help agreeing.

Tally had already lost one friend, and as frustration rose within her, she realized that Jonn Stryker might very well be the only one she had left. He had taught her a little about the ship's weaponry on the journey over. She still didn't really understand most of it, but she did know how to do one thing.

Tally flipped the switch that armed the ship-to-ship missiles and extended the launcher through a hatch in the *Raven's* roof.

"What are you doing?" Hendrickson yelled. He was aware of a sudden audience behind, men he knew only from slug clips.

"Wait a minute," she was watching her monitor intently, licking her lips like an anxious child, "he'll see it."

Stryker heard the hatch open, and watched the launcher pop up and swivel in place. He crawled up the side of the sloped ship and slithered into the launcher's housing, barely managing to pull himself in before it retracted.

Tally screamed with delight and flipped the switch that closed the exterior hatch, "I did it! I got him!" she yelled.

The mammoth airlock finally opened, and the *Raven* entered its protective maw. Minutes later, the opposite door opened and the ship shot out into the void.

The *Raven* stood out like the stars of their home-world against the black monitors of the alien warship. But it was the last survivor, and the pack had a policy about that. One was always left to run for help.

That way they brought back more.

Hendrickson punched in the navigational coordinates for Teraxiter and gulped when he finally noticed the message that flashed across the nav-screen. It read: ERROR: SYSTEM DOWN. The explosive rounds had done more damage than he thought. The Quantum drive was unharmed, but without the nav-computer the *Raven* was just as likely to appear inside a star or a planet as anything else.

"Great!" he cried. "Now what do we do?"

Stryker emerged in the bridge and placed his hand on Hendrickson's shoulder. He wiped a trail of blood from his nose with the back of his hand and looked out the viewport. "Now, we get some payback. Head for the *Constantine*."

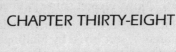

CHAPTER THIRTY-EIGHT

Confrontation

S tryker watched as Hendrickson whipped
the *Raven* around and headed back toward
the *Constantine*, then he turned to deal with
other business. He pushed his way back down the
short corridor that led to the bridge, squeezing past
Dumois and the others before finally cornering Max
Hunt at the dead end beside the cargo hold. He was
close enough to prevent the mercenary from using his
flamer, and Jonn kept a close eye on the man named
Oleg as he spoke. "Now, you wanna tell me what the
hell's goin' on?"

Hunt looked at him stupidly, "What are you talkin'
about now, psycho?"

"I'm talkin' about these things that blew up our
freakin' city. What the hell are they?"

"How should I know, you lunatic?"

"Because your *boss* brought 'em here!"

The bridge was silent as everyone stared at Hunt. "I
don't know what you're talkin' about," he said softly,
but his eyes betrayed him.

"Yeah," Stryker pressed, "tell 'em who hired you to

come to Tiko. And who paid you to sabotage our automated defenses and generally fu —"

"I didn't mess with your damn missile launchers!" the giant roared. "I *was* hired by Hollings to come out here and hang around for a couple of weeks, but he never said anything about an attack. Hell, he's screwed me as much as you. I got one man left and no ship to put him on."

"And that's *all* he wanted you to do?" Jonn shouted sarcastically.

"No. There was one other thing."

"Yeah?"

"I had to sleep with your girl."

Jonn's lip curled in hate. He stared at the man for a long time, and then finally spoke through grinding teeth, "You proud of yourself, little man?"

"No. But it was a job. Just like any other."

"Lousy mercenary."

"We're *all* mercenaries, Stryker. You just work for the same corp all the time."

Hendrickson shouted that they were near the *Constantine* and Jonn's more practical side took control at the threat of danger. He stuck his face into the mercenary's once more and growled a final question. "Last thing. Who you whoring for now?"

Max rose his head and tried to recapture some of his fleeting dignity. He nodded towards Kelassiter.

Jonn studied his eyes and tried to determine if Max was sincere. "Then you're mine now, Hunt. Got that?"

He nodded again.

Stryker suddenly turned away and dragged Terrin back to the bridge. "Okay," he grunted, "here's the plan ..."

Hollings sat on the bridge of the *Constantine* and watched his viewscreen with awestruck rapture. The alien warship had vanished, probably still chasing the few survivors, and the asteroid city was burning through its protective shell. Exterior cameras caught glimpses of the action as the dome that sealed Tiko III began to crack and splinter, and Todd almost wet himself with glee.

A communications technician interrupted his revelry, "Sir, we've got a transmission coming through."

"Hmm?" Todd beamed.

"A transmission, sir, from somewhere out there," he pointed towards the dying city.

"Yes, yes, patch it through! Maybe it's a few weary survivors, seeking refuge from the storm." He winked at Katanopolis — survivors would be perfect. Rescuing them would prove Hollings' good intentions and their accounts of the alien attack would clear him for good. They'd never be able to claim right of occupation, however; Todd knew how to manipulate Consortium law that far.

The viewscreen fizzled and Terrin Kelassiter's face filled the square.

Todd scowled. He had hoped Kelassiter was dead.

"This is Terrin Kelassiter of Tiko III. We have escaped our city and seek refuge on the *Constantine*. Will you comply with Consortium Code and provide us shelter?"

Todd studied Terrin's face for a moment, trying to read the intentions behind the cowboy's determined stare.

"Hello, Terrin. Why don't you just jump away? Are you planning some sort of Trojan Horse routine?"

Kelassiter grimaced and looked embarrassed. "Negative, *Constantine*." His hand stretched out on the viewscreen as Terrin twisted the tiny camera that projected his image back towards the cargo section. Todd saw Thaddeus Dumois vainly trying to reconnect frayed wires from a broken computer bank, and then the camera twisted back. "Our nav-computer's down.

We're not going anywhere unless you take us."

"Well, I think we might be able to arrange that. Under one condition."

"Yes?" Terrin asked impatiently.

"Will you sign over ownership of the sector?"

Kelassiter disappeared from the camera. Todd guessed that he was cursing up a storm and couldn't help but laugh. This was perfect! Terrin would sign over the sector and make everything neat and legal, or he would die out here where no one would ever find his lanky corpse, and Tiko would still be his! He couldn't lose, and, oh, how good it felt to make that bastard cowboy squirm.

Terrin returned, visibly trying to contain his frustration. "Those terms are acceptable, *Constantine*. Will you let us board?"

"Be my guest," Todd salivated.

"How'd I do?" Terrin winked at Jonn.

"Not bad. You looked pissed enough to kick a puppy."

"Think he'll fall for it?"

"Yeah, he's wantin' to see you sweat so bad he'd of let the *Fury* on board."

The deck crews looked with disbelief as the *Raven* glided into one of the *Constantine's* landing bays. They had never seen a ship quite like this before — not up close anyway. It was sleek, seemingly unarmed, and a dull black that seemed to absorb the very light around it.

Kelassiter was the first to exit. Stryker, Dumois, Klein, Hunt, Oleg, Hendrickson, and Tally were next, and the wounded technician was left behind to guard the *Raven*. All but Terrin and Thaddeus wore armor, and all except Stryker and Hendrickson had removed their headgear.

They were met by a marine squad, then were disarmed and escorted up the mammoth elevators to the "top" of the *Constantine*. There they walked through a series of passageways, and were eventually taken to the bridge, where Todd Hollings awaited.

Katanopolis left the bridge just before Kelassiter's message, and headed for the holding cells where a certain red-haired spy was about to satisfy his demented urges. There wasn't much time left — the plan had almost come to fruition and Katanopolis wanted to finish her while Todd was so distracted by other things. It wasn't that he would disapprove, but Katanopolis didn't want to show him his weakness.

Dreama was sleeping when the cadet unlocked her cell and allowed the grinning scientist in.

"Hello, Ms. Collaris. I trust you've been comfortable this last week?" Katanopolis pulled a scalpel from his coat pocket and held it up menacingly. Before she could react, he threw himself on her tiny cot and held the blade against her delicate throat.

Dreama prayed this wasn't the last sight she would ever see.

Hollings was gorging himself on some sort of green glop when Terrin and the others were led onto the bridge. Ten armed marines kept watch over the refugees/prisoners, and Todd felt completely protected.

"Ah, Terrin! Sooo …" he smacked his chops wetly and green goo stretched between his spotless teeth, "glad you could make it! Yours is the only ship they let escape for some *strange* reason."

It was the first Terrin and the others had heard of this, and a tense silence settled over the room.

Terrin was the first to speak, "You didn't try to save them?"

"Well, we would have, of course," he slurped up a stringy noodle from the glop, "but we got here too late."

"If you saw them, then you could've saved them, Todd."

"Now, now," he munched, "you shouldn't go insulting your host like that. Or I might just decide to throw you back out on your self-righteous little ass!"

Terrin's blood boiled at the thought of the screaming citizens dying at the hands of Todd's allies. He was tired of playing this coy game. "You think you're going to get away with this, you greasy piece of slime?"

Todd stopped chewing and a green glop fell from his lips and stuck to his yellow bib. His eyes began to widen and his face turned red as his shock turned into rage. "You *dare* to insult me in front of my own men?" he shouted.

Terrin smiled slightly as Hollings lost his cool. Todd became conscious of the others watching him, and tried to regain his composure. "I don't know what you're talking about. And even if I did, you can't prove anything." Beady eyes searched the room for Dr. Katanopolis, wishing that the tall scientist were here to support him.

"Oh, yeah? Well, what about him?" Terrin pointed to Max and the giant stepped forward.

Todd hadn't even noticed the others in his fixation on Terrin, but now attempted to ignore the mercenary and gobbled down another handful of green goop. "What about him?"

"Well, for one thing, you hired him to mess with my sergeant only weeks before we got invaded. That's going to make Fleet a little curious."

Todd licked a pudgy finger and stared at Hunt. "So, you sold out, eh, Max? I thought mercs were supposed to keep their contracts secret? Well, what good is his testimony anyway? He's just another type of whore. You could have paid him to say those things."

"Maybe so, Todd, but I know a few other things, too."

"Like what?" he feigned disinterest but heavy beads of sweat fell into his food and added salty seasoning.

"Like how you outfitted a band of Teraxian pirates with a stealth ship and had them blow up the *Fury* and an unarmed transport full of marines."

"Can you prove that, Terrin?"

"The ship's sitting in your hangar bay right now, you ignorant ass."

Todd had completely forgotten that Stryker had stolen the *Raven*. He shrugged his shoulders, "So? I'll jettison it somewhere and no one will believe you."

Terrin was looking at him like he was stupid and Todd felt his plans beginning to unravel. But there was one simple solution. "You're right, Kelassiter. You're just too smart. You could probably put enough of the pieces together to get Fleet looking in the right directions."

Todd pushed the tray connected to the arms of his chair away and leaned back. "So let me fill you in on the rest of the details." It was obvious that Kelassiter and everyone with him would have to die, and Todd couldn't help but gloat before he had Terrin killed. "Are you wondering how I managed to sabotage your little automated missile launchers?"

Terrin nodded and watched Dumois through the corner of his eye. That was exactly what he had been wondering since his friend had thrown him in jail a week ago.

"Point-six millimeters of armor," Todd said cryptically. "Katanopolis, being the genius that he is, devised a torpedo that could guide itself *into* a hull-cracked ship, and then disperse hundreds of tiny bomblets. These attach themselves to metallic armor and blow a shaped charge right through. We gave three of these to our pirates, and they used at least two to deadly effect. You see, Katanopolis carefully measured the charge each one carried, and made it just large enough to breach Mark IV Brodie suits, but not Mark Fives. As you well know, that particular model, worn by Jonn Stryker as well as most other corporate officers, is point-six millimeters thicker than the others."

He cackled and dug his pudgy fingers into the green goo once again. "We … *I* had to let him live, unfortunately, but not without some pain. Of course, I had no idea just *how* much he would suffer. Did you know that he hung upside down in a pool of his own blood for eleven hours?" Todd sighed with ecstasy. "You know, Terrin. Sometimes I don't know who I hate more, you or that lunatic Stryker. Anyway," he slobbered, "that cybernetic eye we stuck in his skull was no ordinary device. Katanopolis added some sort of gadget that could jolt the portion of Stryker's brain that responded to hypnosis. Then we programmed in what we wanted him to do, and … *voila*! It wasn't quite that easy," he frowned. "The device would only work when his natural defenses were down, like if he was drunk. I figured it wouldn't take long for that to happen naturally, but having Hunt boff his girlfriend was an effective catalyst."

Terrin was impressed by Todd's thoroughness. "But how did you get him into the security system?" he demanded.

"Oh, that! The eye has one other function as well. It has some sort of camera in it that took a picture of your eye and copied its retinal pattern. You're lucky, Terrin," Hollings cackled, "it's a one-of-a-kind device. We weren't even sure it would work! Thank you for providing us with a test subject!"

Suddenly, sirens blared and the lights of the ship grew dim. "We've got a launch, Mr. Hollings!"

The four senior technicians on the captain's level of the bridge had been in on the plot from the beginning, and were enraptured by Todd's recounting of such an elaborate scheme. They hadn't even noticed the alien warship moving in on their flank.

A single missile slammed into the hull of the *Constantine* and the technicians began to give instructions to the gunners and crewmen below.

"Looks like you underestimated your allies, Todd!" Terrin yelled over the blaring sirens.

He waved a pudgy hand nonchalantly. "Bah! My men will finish them. It's only one ship." Todd swiveled in his chair to make sure his men were doing their duties, and then spun back towards Kelassiter. "After we've thrown their worthless corpses to the Fleet dogs for investigation, we'll make sure to give you a decent funeral, Terrin!"

"And what about Stryker? What are you going to do about him? Do you even know where he is?"

Hollings paled and chewed a little slower. One pudgy hand slipped under his bib and inside the pocket of his impeccable blue sweater. "Of course I do. He's dead."

Terrin frowned a little, "What makes you think that?" It was hard to hear over the sirens, but he was sure Todd had almost choked before he pulled a small silver box from under his tray. It looked something like a remote control.

"Because I took precautions!" he screamed. "I had Katanopolis put a bomb in his freaking chest, and I pushed the button the second we got here! It sent a tight pulse beam out, triggering the explosive — I'm *terribly* sorry you didn't get to see your precious protector expl —"

Hollings' voice tailed off as one of the men in the powered armor reached up and unclamped his helmet. He lifted it slowly from his blonde, crewcut head, and Hollings' baggy eyes filled with panic.

CHAPTER THIRTY-NINE

Ghosts in the Machine

Katanopolis grabbed Dreama by her long red hair and jerked her towards him. The scalpel played gingerly along her throat and the tall scientist pressed his heavy body against hers. "Now, boy!" he yelled.

The cadet ran into the room and bound plastic cords around the girl's trapped hands, wrenching her broken arm painfully in the process. The two men dragged her from the bed and out into the hallway. It was the first time she had left her tiny prison in three weeks, and she would never enter it again.

As they pulled her down the passage, something slammed into the *Constantine* and shook it violently. The cadet managed to brace himself and Dreama, but the lanky scientist stumbled to his knees and smashed them on the grilled floor. He rose angrily and slapped Dreama for his own humiliation.

"What was that, Doctor?" the cadet asked timidly.

"Who cares, you idiot! Move!" Kat had expected the aliens to put up a little fight before the *Constantine* vaporized them, and the jolt reminded him that he didn't have much time. He had to do *it* before the fight was over.

They hauled Dreama past the security door that sealed the prison hallway and into the brig's control room. A series of podium-shaped computers lined the guard's chair, and Katanopolis bent Dreama over it.

She had thought he would rape her for several weeks now, but she didn't think he would do it in front of the cadet. She had tried to prepare herself for it by thinking that she would merely laugh at him or pretend to enjoy it while he violated her, but now that it was about to happen, all she could do was cry. *Why hasn't Terrin rescued me?* She felt so helpless and hated herself for it.

Katanopolis still had her by the hair and she felt him sawing at it with the scalpel. Was he going to maim her too?

He was fumbling behind her. Dreama thought he was taking off his belt and tears ran down her red cheeks. But instead, Katanopolis plugged a y-shaped cord into the console Dreama was bent over and stuck the other end into her damaged cyberjack.

"What are you doing, Doctor?" the cadet asked again.

"I'm interrogating her, you stupid fool! What does it look like I'm doing!" He stuck the other branch of the y-cord into a hidden jack at the base of his own skull, and plunged them both into virtual reality.

All the noise stopped, and the brig swirled away into a dreamy blue sea off the coast of Greece.

Dreama was disoriented and somehow paralyzed as he walked towards her across the choppy Aegean. White clouds floated by overhead and a brilliant computer generated sun shone down upon them. Katanopolis appeared as himself, only a little more handsome and slightly younger than she remembered. Then he shimmered and stepped *into* her. Dreama watched as his image penetrated hers and swallowed her whole. She felt his liquid form probing every crevice and cranny of her brain, and tried to run and escape, but it was no use.

This wasn't interrogation. It was mind-rape. It was even worse than the physical horror she'd dreaded.

The starboard pulse cannons of the *Constantine* fired at the warship, but impacted with nothing. One of the technicians nearest Hollings told him that the vessel was somehow confusing their scanners and targeting computers, but Todd didn't hear him. All he could see was the hard stare of Jonn Stryker.

"S-stay back! I don't know why this didn't work before, but it will now! Certainly at this range! I'll blow your heart out, Stryker!"

Terrin watched the marines who were still guarding them. Their faces weren't visible beneath the dark visors of their green armor, but the shifting of their feet and the way they held their blasters told him they were confused. The boss wasn't being threatened, yet he was screaming and shaking in his plush chair. One word from Todd could kill them all, yet he hadn't given it. Had he finally cracked after two months of playing with demons?

Jonn stepped towards Hollings, a blank expression on his face that was somehow more frightening than any other.

Todd leaned back further in his chair and pointed the device at Jonn's chest, but he was somehow reluctant to press the button. "I mean it! Stop!"

Jonn took another step.

Tears mixed with Todd's sweat and pooled in the fleshy rolls of his neck. "Stop!"

A final step and Jonn stood before him, calmly. Todd screamed and pushed the box up against Jonn's breastplate, but still wouldn't press the detonator.

"You're afraid, aren't you?" Stryker whispered. "Terrified that it won't work."

Todd looked at him through red, teary eyes and wailed in terror and humiliation, but still refused to press the button.

"Press it, little man. I've got nothing to lose." Jonn slowly placed his gloved hand over Todd's. He pushed slightly and Todd fought him, still terrified that his device would fail. Jonn pushed harder.

Click.

Dreama fought to free herself from the viscous scientist within the virtual reality of the ship's computer, but Katanopolis had prepared for this moment, and his envelopment of her was only a visual projection of a scramble program that paralyzed his struggling victim in cyberspace.

His voice reverberated through his liquid metal body, and Dreama felt it shake her eardrums violently. "Now, we shall be as one." A blue tendril of himself formed and wormed its way into Dreama's mind.

Every memory and thought and desire she ever had was open to the doctor as he tore through her mental filing cabinets and laughed at what he found. He took them out and toyed with them, switching emotions and sensations that blended into sickening associations. The innocent joy of bouncing on her father's knee mixed with the dirty feeling of her first awkward sexual experience, and the pain of her mother's death tangled with the mirth of long nights spent laughing with her girlfriends.

Pain and joy, love and hate, terror and peace; Katanopolis mixed conflicting emotions like mismatched socks pulled blindly from a drawer. Then he went after her desires.

Every sick and twisted thing her mind had ever considered was drawn to the surface of her conscious and displayed there like dirty laundry in front of the mad Katanopolis. Fleeting thoughts of murdering her parents and all-night orgies were dredged from the cesspools that normally collected her impure thoughts. The scientist examined them and laughed at her, imbuing the images with life and humiliating her further.

When Katanopolis bored of this, he reached inside her head again and pulled up the nightmare file. Dreama's fears were locked in a tight place, and she didn't normally allow them out, but the doctor tore her mental strongbox apart like paper. Ghastly images of a mutilated Terrin popped out like a jack-in-the-box. He bobbed and weaved on a coiled spring that looked like a meaty spine torn from its host. His upper torso was horribly maimed and his broken ribs stabbed jaggedly in every direction. Dead eyes drooped, pulling slimy stalks behind them, and Dreama screamed.

She screamed so loud the probe slipped out of her virtual ear and the blob that engulfed her recoiled for a second. She knew what had caused it: she had fought back.

Dreama screamed and punched and kicked and fought and bit and tore and scratched her way out of the encompassing form of Dr. Katanopolis. When she saw the glimmering Aegean again, she threw the shell free and scrambled to her feet. Confusing emotions and mismatched memories still spun around in her mind and the terrible guilt and shame made her want to vomit, but her virtual self had no reciprocal action. What he had done to her was worse than rape — was much more violating than anything physical. He had scrambled the very essence of her being. He had destroyed those sensations and experiences that had made her who she was, and she felt that the damage was permanent.

The silvery ooze started to coalesce and take shape once more, reforming into the tall figure of Dr.

Katanopolis. Dreama focused her pain into rage and struck again and again, mashing his head and brains into a pulpy pool. She wanted to laugh as her feet drove into his skull, but couldn't tell if it was a reaction she normally had to violence or one implanted by the nasty thing that squirmed between her virtual toes. In the end, she decided she didn't care and kept stomping Katanopolis into a chunky paste.

The computer interrupted her attack and sent electrical charges down the cord into Katanopolis' cerebellum. The doctor was caught off guard and had no defense programs ready to reduce the surge. In nanoseconds, he was knocked unconscious and his brilliant but twisted brain fried to an oozing crisp.

Finally, he stopped moving and began to fade from virtual reality.

Stryker still had his hand over Todd's and squeezed. The additional strength of the cybernetics and the power armor slowly crushed Todd's bloated fingers into the sharp edges of the remote, and blood trickled down his flabby forearm.

Jonn stood motionless and without pity, continuing to squeeze until the blood rushed down in rivulets and the fingers finally popped, mushing together into a wad of flesh and jagged bone.

The guards' view was partially obscured by Stryker's broad back, but any second now they would realize what was going on. Jonn reached down to the whimpering figure before him and grabbed a pistol from his belt. The guards finally reacted, but Terrin and the others jumped them before they could draw their weapons.

Hunt disarmed one and Oleg did the same. Terrin and Klein were wrestling with another, and Hendrickson was on his second. Hollings' blaster would do little to the armored suits, but the technicians made easy targets and Jonn splattered them against the plexiglass screen that shielded their position from the lower bridge.

Thanks to the cramped quarters of Todd's balcony, Kelassiter's escort was taken care of without casualty.

Stryker turned calmly in place and nodded at his companion's handiwork. The guards were stripped of their armor, and Stryker scolded them. "Next time don't bunch up."

Hollings' still whimpered in his chair, softly begging Stryker not to kill him. Jonn dropped the blaster in the green mound of goo that still sat on his tray. "I'm not gonna kill ya, but they are." He pointed to one of the viewscreens. A camera mounted outside the *Constantine* was focused on a large hole in her side. The aliens were leaping from their ship into the breach.

Terrin directed his group out of the bridge and Klein checked the hallway for any more guards. The passage was clear, and they quickly distributed the stolen blaster rifles and headed out the door. Thanks to the soundproofed booth, the gunners and crewmen below hadn't noticed that their command center had been ruined.

"You might wanna save a charge for yourself," Stryker muttered to Hollings as he walked out the door.

Dreama awoke in the real world and felt Katanopolis still leaning over her. The cadet was missing for some reason, and she tried to struggle out from under the convulsing scientist. Her broken arm betrayed her just as she was getting free, however, and she crumpled to the floor with Katanopolis still lying on top. She was twisted somehow and the doctor's face was next to hers. She was just about to throw him off her when she saw the cadet.

He was standing in the hallway that led to each of

the prison cells and had his weapon drawn. Smoke billowed from the far end where Dreama had thought the passage ended, but something scraped the grillwork far beyond her line of sight.

The lights had gone dim after the explosion, so she couldn't quite make out what it was that the cadet was looking at. He fired a shot, but then an explosion echoed through the metal hallway and he vanished in a cloud of smoke.

Terrin had come to rescue her after all! Someone was walking slowly up the hallway, and Dreama struggled to get free so that she could rush into Terrin's arms and forget everything that had happened with Katanopolis.

But what came out of the hallway wasn't Terrin. It wasn't even human.

Terrin and his band ran down the hallway that led to the elevators. Two unarmored crewmen went for their weapons but were mown down by a barrage of blaster fire before they had even touched them. Klein slammed the button that brought the elevator to this floor, but nothing happened. Stryker pushed his way to the front of the mob and slipped his fingers in between the doors and wedged them open. Wisps of smoke curled from the blackness and metal cables dangled loosely in the shaft. Jonn looked down the five story pit with his low-light eyes and saw the elevator lying in ruins at the bottom. Some of the things were trampling over it and running into a hole in the other side, heading into the ship. Others climbed up the wreckage and clawed through the sliding doors on the next level. They had made their breach in the bottom of the elevator shaft with pinpoint accuracy. Now they could go anywhere they pleased.

Dreama saw the thing raise a barbed bayonet and thrust it at Katanopolis' back, trying to spear them both to the grillwork. She heard it tearing horribly through the scientist and then felt it scrape against her collarbone.

She passed out and woke only seconds later, though it felt like much longer. It was ignoring her now, and she played dead, watching through half closed eyes. More of the hideous things passed by, but they continued to ignore her. Blood spilled out the dead scientist's mouth and dribbled thickly onto her cheek where it continued on to pool in the corner of her eye, forcing her to close it.

The darkness was terrible. Dreama heard heavy feet stomping by, and could make out some sort of racket at the other end of the hallway, like they were climbing on metal. She felt the cord still jacked into her head, and decided that if she couldn't escape physically, at least her mind could run away for a while.

She appeared inside the ship's computer again. She stood in front of several prison cells rather than Katanopolis' programmed Aegean, and ran through an open door into the main system. Security guards sat motionless against the wall with an odd assortment of gears and bolts scattered around them. It looked like Katanopolis was modifying their programming, but hadn't yet reactivated them. She could do whatever she wanted! Even the fierce Medusa program still sat frozen in stone at the central core.

Dreama decided to find out what was going on with the strange invaders and poked her head into the security room. Over a hundred tiny monitors showed scenes of the interior and exterior of the *Constantine*, and she sat back and watched as Hollings' marines and security police attempted to stop them.

One group looked different than the others, though. They were running down a stairwell and Dreama noticed a sign on the wall behind them that read LANDING BAYS. One of the figures suddenly faced into a camera and she gasped in shock. Terrin *was* on the ship!

Her surprise almost kept her from realizing the danger he was in. The monitor next to the one she had seen him in showed at least eight of the creatures gunning down the flight crews. One of them headed for a doorway marked STAIRS UP. Terrin was about to run into the things!

She zipped out of the security room and raced down the line that controlled the electronic locks to the ship's doors.

Terrin pushed on the handle but the door didn't budge. He pressed the electronic panel beside it, but nothing happened. Suddenly something beat on the other side and yelled in frustration. The malfunctioning door had saved their lives!

The Bag Lady staggered back into the security room and sorted through the monitors to find Terrin again. It had worked! She had managed to lock it electronically before he or the creatures could open it. Whether he knew it or not, Terrin and she had been together again. Now if she could only make it happen for real.

Hollings sniveled in front of his marines. It was humiliating. He was a *Hollings*, son of the founder himself, and this was no way for him to act.

He slowly sat up and wiped the tears and snot from his face with the sleeve of his blue coat. The four senior technicians were dead, and their brains still dripped from the plexiglass booth, but the monitors beneath them flickered with images of the aliens tearing through the ship and ripping the crewmen apart in their bloody path.

"You," Todd pointed quietly at one of the marines, "get me four new technicians. Then tell the communications officer to broadcast a message. I want every available marine to gather up here. We'll do better united than apart."

"Yes, Mr. Hollings," the marine answered quitely. Todd turned to the others and saw they were demoralized. "You may have lost your armor, but you haven't lost your honor. See if you can get below and reequip yourselves."

They brightened somewhat at this and walked out of the control center, purpose returning to their stride with every step as screams and explosions echoed over the monitors.

Terrin and the rest ran down a long hallway on the level above the hangar. They emerged at one end of an intersection just as several security guards came from another. Tally yelled "Look out!" and fired. Jonn didn't think she could lift the heavy rifle, much less fire it, but she did. And a man whirled in a gory dance of death to prove it.

They were in some sort of lounge, and all jumped nervously when a soda machine started dispensing drinks all on its own. Then a microwave lit up and a vid-player flickered to life. It was the commercial kind with thousands of vid-slugs that could be watched by pressing its corresponding number. A code was typed in by invisible hands, and everyone stood in amazement as a film called *Trapped* started to play.

Most ignored the electrical phenomenon, but Terrin seemed fascinated.

"Let's go, Terrin," Stryker growled. "It's just some kinda interference or somethin'."

"That's the movie Dreama and I saw before she left for the *Constantine*."

Stryker noticed that Terrin didn't seem to care anymore if his girlfriend's position remained a secret, and wondered if she could still be alive.

"Dreama!" Terrin shouted. "I completely forgot where we were. She's got to be on here somewhere. I've got to find her."

"If we don't get off here soon, we're all gonna get killed by these things."

Terrin reluctantly agreed and started to follow the others down the hall, but then he saw the camera mounted in the corner, and it hit him. "Jonn, wait! The door that wouldn't open, and all the junk in here acting up on its own. . ."

"Yeah?" he was getting impatient. It was time to fly.

"She's in the computer! She's in the ship's freaking computer!" He rushed excitedly to the camera and mouthed slowly, "Where are you?"

The vid-player stopped and another movie popped into place. It was a prison flick.

Dreama screamed in delight as Terrin nodded to her through the lounge camera. Then she scanned the other monitors and saw some of the creatures heading towards them. The lights were already dim throughout the ship, but Dreama rushed into the slaved system and turned them off in three of the four hallways Terrin and the others could take. Back in the security room, she saw that he had taken her clue and was running down the only lighted corridor.

Dreama stumbled into the core of the computer and called up the ship's blueprints. Terrin would have to head towards the rear to get to her, but they could then make their way to the escape pods on the level above.

The unarmored marines Hollings dispatched to retrieve new weapons entered a cargo elevator and punched the button that would send them to the barracks level below. The car shot downwards but stopped a floor short. The doors began to slide open, and the senior marine was going to tell whoever was trying to get on that they would have to wait for another car.

But the creature that stood in the doorway wasn't waiting for anyone. It leapt into the car and carved and howled a ballad of death. The men fought back, but they had no weapons and wore only the quilted Brodie undersuits. Bloody cotton fibers spun in the air and sank slowly to the floor as the creature gutted the men like deer.

Hollings was almost in control again. The new technicians were doing an excellent job of restoring order to the bridge, but they were gradually losing contact with the various sections of the ship that reported encounters with the aliens.

One of the replacements turned a sallow face to his boss. Todd looked at him expectantly and the young man whispered, "They're on the bridge, sir."

Immediately after he spoke, the door below the control center blew open and five of the things burst into the room.

There's only five of them, Todd thought, but when he actually saw the things with his own eyes, he knew he had underestimated them from the beginning.

The room below was better lit than the rest of the ship, but Todd now wished it wasn't. The creatures fired their deadly weapons into the cramped room and turned the bridge into a gory tangle of torn limbs and flesh.

Then one of them saw the control booth. Todd bolted from his chair and spilled the gooey green desert upon the once-clean floor. He dove into the hallway just as an explosive round shattered the plexiglass into deadly shards that killed the four men behind it.

There was noise from the hallway ahead and Todd crawled to the corner. A few of his armored marines had managed to kill one of the things! One man had lost an arm, but Hollings' new suit would pump the man full of drugs and keep him alive a while longer — long enough to protect his boss, at least. "Come on! We've got to get to the escape pods!" Todd shouted as he trundled down the hallway.

They found a stairwell that led down to the next

level and Terrin, Stryker and the others followed the blinking lights that were lead them to the brig. They were running up a long hallway filled with the mutilated bodies of dead security guards when the blinking stopped and the passage went dark. Everyone crouched in the corner and waited.

Dreama watched through the camera that overlooked the brig's control room. She could see her body lying motionless under the dead Katanopolis, and one of the things was poking at her with the barbed tip of its weapon. It knew she was alive.

The blinking in the hallway started again, flipping on and off so fast that it created a strobe effect that made Dumois sick.

"Something's wrong," Terrin whispered to Stryker. "I think she's in the next room, and maybe one of them's in there with her."

"Klein," Stryker grunted, "we're gonna rush the door and jump through. Hopefully, our ghost will open it as soon as we get there."

"Gotcha, Sarge."

Stryker looked the Irishman over one last time before finally deciding that he could be trusted. "Move!" he yelled.

The two marines ran headlong for the sliding panel at the end of the hallway. Seconds before they would have smashed into it with their thick skulls, the door slid open and Stryker and Klein stumbled over the kneeling alien.

It rose in fury and whipped its weapon up to fire, but Klein was quick on his feet and threw his armored body into the thing. The screaming rounds ripped down the hallway of the prison cells and tore long rifts in the gleaming metal.

"Don't let it fire that thing again or Dreama's gonna get skragged!" Jonn yelled.

Steve understood and rammed his finger into what

looked like the trigger. The alien roared a loud laugh and squeezed. The trigger crushed the armor and Klein felt his finger snap, but no rounds were fired.

Now Stryker stood and pushed the blaster rifle up under the thing's tusked jaws. He pulled the trigger and the alien flew backwards in pain. "Take her and run!" he yelled, and pointed at Dreama.

Steve grabbed her by the shoulder with one hand and kept the rifle in the other. Then he bolted down the hall towards the others and Kelassiter met him halfway.

"Is she okay?"

"She's pretty beat up, but I think she'll be fine, boss."

"What's Stryker doing?"

"He's finishing off one of those things. We caught it by surprise."

Terrin looked at him uncertainly.

"I think he can handle it," Steve assured him.

But Max wasn't so sure. He shoved Klein aside and rushed past, heading into the darkness where he heard the thunder of a blaster rifle firing in quick succession. "You gotta burn the suckers, Stryker!" he cried over the booming noise. When Max stumbled into the room, he saw that he was wrong. The thing lay dead on the floor, its head blasted into a thousand pieces.

Stryker was standing over it with his rifle, and saw that he had fired it fast enough to crack the barrel. "No, you don't," he said. "You just gotta shoot 'em. A lot."

Jonn and Hunt exited the room. Stryker was unarmed now, but as Dreama revived and hugged her lover, she told them that the entrance to the escape pods was directly overhead. They picked her up and backtracked up to the next level. Then they walked into a massacre.

CHAPTER FORTY

Shock Tactics

The last of Hollings' marines were making their stand in some kind of fancy atrium. Hollings was in the rear, guarded by two marines, one of which was missing an arm. Stryker, Kelassiter, and the others exited the stairway behind them.

Hollings was on the floor covering his head and saw them approach. He screamed and the marines guarding him turned to fire, but Hendrickson threw himself in front of the group and held up his hands. He still held the captured rifle in his hands but he held it by the stock, and his helmet was off so the others would hopefully recognize him.

"Don't shoot!" They paused and he continued, "We've gotta fight these things together or they're gonna wipe us out! Deal?"

The man standing over Hollings looked down at his boss and Todd nodded hesitantly. The marine instantly turned back around and started to fire back across the blackness of the atrium.

Tally couldn't figure out how everyone was able to

see in the dark and finally found the verbal command that activated the low-light system in her visor. What she saw across the flickering room made her switch it back off. She thought a few of the things were pinning everyone down, but now she saw that there were at least twenty.

"Stryker," Max yelled, "I think they're getting ready to rush us. Look."

Jonn looked through the rushing waterfalls with infra-red and saw that he was probably right. Some of the things were slinging their rifles across their backs and exchanging them for pistols and claw.

"Get ready, here they come!" he yelled.

They swarmed out of the waterfalls, crawled from behind the rocky sculptures, and leapt down from the balconies above. A few covered the advance with the rifles and several more of Hollings' marines exploded in a crack of thunder and lightning. Hendrickson didn't understand why they exposed themselves like this, but Hunt knew. He had seen them do the same thing to his men.

Terror was their weapon. They expected their prey to panic and fire wild or attempt to run, and then they could spear, slash, or stab them up close. Max decided that he wasn't going to fall for it twice.

"Charge!" Max yelled.

Jonn had never heard anyone yell "charge" in over twenty years of military service, but it worked.

The creatures were taken by surprise as Jonn, Max, Hendrickson, Oleg, Klein, and the unwounded marine guarding Hollings rushed out into the open to meet them. The rifles had to cease firing, and the things were momentarily put on the defensive.

Max parried a spear out of his face and cracked the creature in the head with the butt of his weapon. It staggered back into a fountain and the seven-foot-tall black rammed his rifle up under its chin. He pulled the trigger until so many particles had been stripped that the barrel cracked.

Hendrickson fired point blank into a charging alien and knocked it back — more out of surprise than the force of the weapon. He fired again and again and again until it staggered back into the shadows on the far side. He didn't think it was dead, but it was running with its tail between its legs for the moment.

Klein wasn't as lucky. He ran across with the others but fell on a slippery tile just as one of the things reached him. It roared and threw itself on him, slashing the joints of his armor with incredibly strong claws and ripping the tender flesh beneath.

Oleg couldn't believe how crazy it was, but he would have followed Max to the gates of Hell itself. He crossed the atrium and ran toward one of the things. Its bayonet ran deep into his shoulder, but his fall over a bench ripped it out of the creatures hands. Before he knew what happened, Stryker grabbed the rifle and ripped it out of him. Oleg crawled back and let the psycho finish his work for him.

Jonn had rushed out without a weapon, but Oleg painfully provided him with one. He stabbed its previous owner in the calf and it backed up slowly to survey its opponent more carefully. Jonn took the opportunity to whirl and raise the rifle high over his head. With a tremendous thrust he drove the heavy point through the shoulder blades of the one ripping Klein's guts out, and it arched backwards in agony. It staggered to its feet, and then limped painfully back to the others to regroup.

The other retreated also, but Jonn chased them into the darkness. Max and the others followed.

Tally and the one-armed marine were hovering over Hollings and fired at whatever target presented itself. Dumois was hidden just behind them and studied the aliens with interest.

Terrin dabbed Dreama's shoulder wound with his shirt tail and rubbed a finger across her lips when she tried to talk. "Shh!" he whispered. "Better save your strength; we've still got to get out of here."

"But, Terrin, I'm so afraid," she spoke like a four year old and started rubbing her hand up the inside of his leg.

Kelassiter looked at her strangely and pushed her away, "What's wrong with you? Is your head injured?" he ran his fingers through the matted hair over her neural jack and felt the sticky blood there. "Good God, what did they do to you?"

Dreama laughed loudly and tears rolled down her face, "I don't know, jerk. Why don't you figure it out?" She was so confused, she wanted to tell him something but every time she thought about it she'd get angry or cry or laugh, and she could never tell which until it happened. She wished she could have killed Katanopolis herself, and laughed.

Stryker and the screaming men behind him chased the things through a door which slid into place as they vanished behind it. They weren't foolish enough to think they had actually scared the aliens, but they had surprised them enough to make them reconsider their tactics.

They quickly took advantage of the situation and ran back across the atrium. Steve reached up a bloody hand as they bolted past and Oleg stopped to help. Klein was still alive thanks to the suit's bio-monitors and auto-injectors, but he wasn't going to be doing any more fighting with his intestines looping out of his ruptured gut. Oleg knelt and tore the shirt off a fallen security guard. He quickly made a makeshift bandage and laid it over the wound, then tied the ends off on the other side.

The others helped Oleg ready Klein for travel and they returned to Tally, Kelassiter, Dumois, and Dreama, but Hollings and the one-armed marine had vanished. Stryker flipped his eyesight back to infra-red and saw a large red blob disappear into a hallway that led off of the atrium and ran perpendicular to theirs.

"Damn it! Where does that tunnel lead?" he asked the remaining marine.

"To the escape pods!"

Stryker cursed again and the band followed him down the hallway. Terrin and Tally picked up Dreama and followed as fast as they could. They had just made it into the hallway when they heard a door somewhere off in the darkness slide open, and heavy footsteps plod through it.

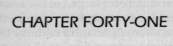

CHAPTER FORTY-ONE

Going-Away Gifts

T he one-armed marine stopped Stryker at the entrance to the escape bay. "I'm sorry — no one else goes."

His visor was up and Jonn could see the drugs that kept him going dilating his pupils madly. The suit had injected them into the marine's bloodstream when the bio-monitors inside detected shock, probably when he had lost some of his arm and the sphincter had cut off the rest to seal the suit. In dangerous environments, this would save a man's life, but on board the pressurized ship, the soldier should have disabled the system. It was a painful mistake.

"Get out of the way, marine," Stryker commanded. The other man made no move to help or hinder, and Jonn pushed the wounded man away.

He pushed back and syringes filled with adrenaline and Quickill once again shot the chemicals into his overtaxed veins. "I said, no one goes in!"

Jonn saw his twitching eyebrows and winking eyes. "You've overdosed. Disable the auto-injectors."

The marine started shaking violently and pulled

something from a belt pouch on his armor. It was an iridium grenade. A detonation in this hallway would probably crack Jonn's suit and certainly kill everyone not wearing armor, and he wasn't about to let that happen. One quick jab through the open visor and Jonn's fingers sunk into the man's eyes. The man raised his remaining hand in pain, and dropped the grenade, which Jonn caught casually. "Finish him," Jonn said to the other marine.

The man nodded and pushed his convulsing friend's head up. He stuck the barrel of the rifle into the slot and fired. "Forgive me," he whispered.

The door to the launch bay opened and Jonn looked into the chamber. Twenty rubber-rimmed holes led to the individual escape pods below. Ten people could crawl down the ladder and seat themselves in the circular "lifeboat," and then program the tiny Quantum drive in each to launch them wherever needed.

Stryker frowned grimly as he saw Todd scramble hastily down one of the chutes.

The marine guard stepped up beside him and spoke softly, "I'm afraid Mr. Hollings wouldn't allow anyone else in during the attack. He was afraid it would spark desertion."

"And?"

"And he jettisoned all but one of the pods before we started down here."

Stryker walked slowly across the chamber and saw the metal sphincter beginning to close on Todd's lifeboat. He knew why Hollings had jettisoned the other lifeboats. He couldn't let Jonn or Terrin or anyone who had heard his scheme survive. Hollings had sacrificed an entire crew so that he could get the damn sector and all its iridium.

The metal plates of the sphincter were sliding inwards, making the entrance hole smaller and smaller. There was no way any of them could make it into the pod before it sealed shut. Jonn had no weapon, and couldn't fire at the sniveling thing at the bottom of the hole to put him out of the world's misery.

Kelassiter cursed. *The greasy bastard is getting away.*

Dreama giggled. She realized there was no escape for them now, but her emotions were still scrambled.

The others felt hopeless and frustrated and tried to figure another way off the ship, but there was none.

The pod's entrance shrunk to the size of a melon.

Stryker was turned slightly sideways to those gathered at the door, and they saw that he was smiling.

Hollings stared up at him through tears and finally managed a hateful laugh, "We see who won, don't we, Stryker? And you can tell Kelassiter that I'll get rich off his iridium! And I'll take the money and destroy a hundred more pathetic cities like yours!" He had flipped, his laughter was maniacal and his flabby jowls shook with lunacy.

The hole was the size of a baseball.

Calmly, Jonn Stryker turned a dial on the iridium grenade from IMPACT to TIMED: TWENTY MINUTES. Then he smiled at Todd one last time, and pulled the activation pin. With reflexes trained over a lifetime of life and death struggles, he dropped it neatly through the closing hole just as the steel plates met and sealed tight.

"Here's your iridium," Jonn said.

CHAPTER FORTY-TWO

The Warmaster (Two)

Everyone stared in silence at the cold figure that returned from the escape pod. "Let's get out of here," Jonn said.

He walked out into the hallway and heard the things banging away at the door.

Tally couldn't take it anymore and cried what the others wanted to ask themselves, "How? The hangars have been overrun and all the lifeboats are gone! We're trapped!"

"Are you positive all the ships in the hangar were destroyed?" Terrin asked the marine that had accompanied Hollings.

The man shook himself out of his shock, "Yeah, it looked that way. They were chucking some sort of charge at the ships when the monitors went dead. I assume they finished what they started."

"There's only way to be sure," Terrin decided for them all. "What have we got to lose?"

Stryker and Klein nodded their approval, followed quickly by Hunt and Oleg. The others shrugged, there wasn't much choice.

Dreama pointed deliriously toward the far end of the hall they were in. "There's a big room that runs across the ship and puts you back out in front of the elevators," she giggled. "It's the only way unless we go back through the atrium."

The doors near them started to dent and tiny holes appeared.

"Let's move!" Terrin commanded.

They went through a barracks to cross back over the ship's midline. The things had already been here. The elevator doors were on the opposite side, and Jonn guessed this was one of the first places the creatures had attacked. Men and women had piled a barricade of beds and footlockers against the far door, but it hadn't done much good against the explosive rounds and powerful muscles of the aliens.

They walked through the silent morgue. Corpses were torn limb from limb and hung in grisly shapes impossible for living beings over the bedposts and locker tops. Huge pools of blood made the walk slippery and repulsive. When they had finally crossed the room, Hendrickson stuck his head out into the hallway. He motioned them on and they stood overlooking the dark elevator shaft.

Hendrickson was the first down. He hit bottom and jumped behind the corner of the wall. He signalled that it looked clear, and covered the rest as they descended.

Kelassiter and Oleg were next, manhandling Dreama as best they could down the jagged metal roof of the smashed elevator car. Dumois scrambled down, and then Hunt and the Hollings' marine eased Klein down the shaft.

Stryker was just about to join them when they heard the things thundering through the barracks behind them. "Go, I'll hold them!" Jonn shouted and jumped out into the elevator pit. "Throw me a rifle!" he called to the remaining marine. The man did so and Jonn caught it with his firing hand, keeping the other tight on the steel cable that swayed in the dark shaft. He braced his feet against the left wall and leaned out into the doorway.

They were coming in droves. At least twenty of the things rushed out of the barracks door and saw Jonn hanging in the elevator shaft. He fired the blaster into their midst and knocked several of them down, but with no real effect.

He looked up the shaft and a plan suddenly hit him. Unfortunately, it was going to piss the aliens off.

He saw several of the things raise their weapons and screamed through the amplified speaker of his Brodie suit. The aliens fired a salvo and the shaft exploded in a massive display of fire and smoke.

Kelassiter ran through the hangar holding Dreama's feet while Oleg held her head. The others were fast behind them.

The *Constantine's* drop ships and fighters had been ruined by well-aimed charges to the cockpit or power supplies, and nothing seemed to remain in the blackness of the hangar. But something strange stood out against the darkness. It was a sleek patch of black somehow darker than the rest of the hangar. It was the *Raven*. Terrin saw it and filled with hope, but then realized that its hull was probably breached like the others.

Hunt stepped up beside him and looked at the ship through low-light, and then infra-red vision. "Terrin, I know this seems crazy, but the only thing that's wrong with that ship is the thing standing beneath it."

Jonn dropped the rifle just before the creatures fired and hauled himself up the steel cable. His artificial limbs and the strength enhancers of the powered suit made the task easy.

Already the things peered in after him. One fired another round up the shaft and it whizzed past Jonn's arm before exploding on the roof above. Twisted steel debris and jagged metal showered him and bounced off the armor as he continued to climb desperately toward the top.

He heard another round ripping through the air and kicked at the wall, moving him out of its path so that it too struck the ceiling and exploded. He felt the cable he was climbing break, and he reached frantically for the other. The slight fall left him a sitting duck for the next round.

The warmaster saw the things approach. He had been waiting for some time now, and he wasn't known for his patience, but the red creature was a worthy opponent. It seemed to have spotted him, so he stepped out from under the black ship and bellowed the challenge of his forefathers.

Hunt saw the creature walk out of the *Raven's* shadows and casually stand before them. It had no missile weapon that Max could see, but that didn't stop Hendrickson and the others from firing their blaster rifles at it.

The thing disappeared into the shadows and the blasts pelted the landing gear of the *Raven*. When it re-emerged from the shadows, it pointed to the top of the ship where the breacher stood. It held the last of its nets above the black craft's hull, and threatened to drop it if the humans attacked.

The one on the ground waved the others away and pointed at Hunt. It roared a challenge that Max had to accept.

Jonn shouted into the suit's voice recognition system, "Quickill! Adrenaline!" He repeated the words four more times and the auto-injectors just above the thigh emptied their contents into his bloodstream.

In seconds, the heavy drugs worked themselves into his system. His arms now worked in a frenzy of motion to propel him up the elevator cables and another of the screaming rounds slammed into the roof, now only one floor above him. He continued on and suddenly felt the cables whipping out of his grasp. Looking down, he saw exactly what he had hoped for. The things were following him up the cable, he was drawing them away from the others.

The narcotics in his blood made the things look slow as they pulled themselves up the cables. Finally, he made it to the top level and swung out onto the floor.

Some of the pack slipped *down* the elevator shaft and ignored the individual scrambling for its life above them. They lurked in the shadows of the ruined pit and watched, holding their fire while the warmaster fought his personal duel.

Hunt looked at the others but no one had any fast solutions. He reluctantly stepped toward the thing and looked it over. It was bigger than the rest, and the spiked armor looked tougher and better fitted. Max raised his empty hands to show that he had no weapon.

The warmaster didn't care if Max was armed or not. He stepped forward, as if to sum up his opponent, but then struck fast and hard, catching Hunt off guard. The long spike jutting out of the thing's gauntlet penetrated the Brodie suit and scraped between two of the mercenary's ribs.

Max refused to scream and clubbed at the oblong head of his opponent, but it ignored his blows like it was dealing with an angry child. Then it reached up with one oversized gauntlet and removed its helmet.

Max could smell its fetid breath gush from its enormous lower jaw in a torrent of acrid death. Its eyes were black and lifeless and terrifying in its slender skull. Its jagged teeth gnashed slowly toward Max's throat, and he was still unable to move. *Why doesn't it just get it over with?* "Bite, damn you! Kill me if you're going to!"

But the warmaster loved the last few minutes of pain, and continued to slowly inch his silver fangs toward his struggling prey.

It was an old trick used in a hundred videos and even more real-life events, but Jonn didn't think the aliens would expect it. He scrambled to his feet and started running down the corridor he had traveled once before. A quick look back showed him that the things had already gained the landing behind him and were already in deadly pursuit. One of them fired its rifle and Jonn barely managed to dive around the corner of the hallway before the round tore apart the surrounding walls.

Terrin could make out a dim light in the cockpit of the *Raven*. The wounded technician they had left to guard the ship was somehow still alive! He was frantically signalling his boss, trying to get him to rush past Hunt and the warmaster so that he could lower the plank and let them on. He obviously didn't know about the breacher perched only a few feet above him.

Terrin pointed at the thing, hoping the technician could see his outstretched hand in the darkness, but it was a futile effort. Hendrickson was nearby, and Terrin suddenly got an idea. He was just about to say something when the things that had been watching from the elevator shaft started to advance again, finally sensing that their leader's personal challenge was quickly coming to a close.

But Max wasn't done yet. He slammed his forehead into the chin of the warmaster and rammed its jagged teeth into its snout. The warmaster staggered backwards in pain, and Hunt fell to the floor.

Terrin whispered something in Dream~ the tattered cord that still hung from he plugged it into one of the many monitor the hangar floor.

She appeared in the ship's computer once again and issued one final order. Before the command had been processed, Dreama had jacked out and waited with continually mixed emotions to see the results of Terrin's plan.

A second after the warmaster screamed, the lights of the hangar bay sparked brilliantly to life. Terrin closed his eyes, and everyone in power armor was protected by their polarized visors. Only Dumois and Oleg were blinded along with the aliens.

"Shoot it!" Terrin yelled to Hendrickson and pointed at the thing that stood blinking painfully on the roof.

Robbie aimed and fired three times, each burst knocking the creature back another quick step before it finally toppled to the hangar floor. Robbie smiled when he noticed it was tangled in its breaching net.

The other things covered their eyes from the light but fired blindly anyway. The rounds exploded haphazardly through the group, miraculously only singing Kelassiter, Dumois, and Dreama as they picked themselves up and ran towards the lowering gangplank of the *Raven*. Oleg and the other marine charged the warmaster. He had been hit by one of the rounds and was reeling from the blow, and they shoved their rifles up under the joints of his breastplate and helmet. They each fired over twenty times before their barrels finally cracked.

Jonn finally reached Hollings' control booth and rifled through the pockets of the four dead technicians he had killed earlier. As he suspected, each man had a single metal key secreted away. A quick glance at the instrument panel told him that he would need only ee of these, and he deftly rammed each one home. He knew that they would have to be turned simultaneously or the system would lock him out for the second attempt. This was a problem, but the four things that leapt through the door after him were even worse.

Stryker grabbed one of them by the serrated tubes that led from its mask to its chestplate and used its momentum to hurl it out of the control booth. It landed on the sparking panels and dead computer banks below without taking any real damage, but it was out of the fight, at least.

The other three rended and ripped with oversized claws that tore easily through the joints of Jonn's armor. He was backed up against the far window, his back plates grinding against the jagged plexiglass that still hung in the frame. He was trapped and these things were going to kill him if didn't think of something fast.

One hand snaked down to the creature's thigh and tore loose the massive pistol it carried there. Jonn rammed it into the thing's jaws and pulled the trigger, shattering its skull with the same kind of round used by their rifle. The next shot went into the second thing's breastplate where it ripped through and exploded powerfully enough to burst its chest open. The third creature caught the next round in its groin, and screamed as the explosion blew out whatever organs it had there.

Immediately, Jonn turned his attention back to the keys. He only had one chance to get this right. He tore off his helmet and placed his left and right hands on the two farthest, and then bit solidly on the one in the middle. He heard more of the things lumbering up the hallway, and twisted his head and wrists.

The keys turned in their socket smoothly and a black panel lit before him. A female voice announced

softly, "Self-Destruct system activated. Ten ⌐
terminal drive overload."

Now he just had to get back out the hallway, ⌐
the elevator shaft, and run the final gauntlet to the
others, who had hopefully found a way onto the *Raven*.
He had heard everything that his friends below had
said, thanks to the communications system in the
armor, and now he used it to send them a reply.
"Everyone on board yet?"

"Almost!" It was Hendrickson.

"Be there in about one minute," Stryker grumbled.

He ran back through the door and smashed into
three more of the things. Somehow, his momentum
carried him through and he rumbled on down the
hallway. He felt several long claws dig into back but
kept running, dragging the things with him. Like a
mule pulling a plow, Jonn stamped down the hallway
with the things in tow. At the elevator shaft, two more
leapt out and ripped into his suit with slashing claws
built into their huge gauntlets. Jonn felt his flesh tear,
and dove into the black pit.

Hendrickson and the wounded Klein were the last
up the gangplank. Robbie turned and fired to cover
them, and saw a writhing clump of creatures and
something else fall roughly to the bottom of the elevator shaft. Whatever was in the middle then tore
loose of the stunned tangle and ran with all his might
across the hangar floor. It was Stryker!

Air splitting rounds followed him and impacted
near enough to crack the battered remnants of his
armor, but still Jonn kept running. The *Raven* started to
rise with its door still open, and Hendrickson slid off as
the plank shook beneath him. He straddled one of the
gangplank's struts and fired at the mob that followed
Jonn.

The battered marine finally got close enough to leap
for the door and Robbie grabbed him by his bleeding

mbs. With one last burst of strength, Stryker pulled himself over the lip of the gangplank and scrambled up into the ship with Robbie right behind him.

Hunt was at the controls. Tally watched him wheezing and trying to remain conscious as he piloted the craft up to the launch bay.

"Make it quick," Jonn whispered to Robbie who panted beside him, "she's gonna blow."

Hendrickson finally realized what Stryker meant, and jumped to his weary feet. "Move it! She's goin' up!"

Hunt understood, but the launch doors were opening slowly. He focused every last bit of his concentration and repositioned the ship, lowering it dangerously close to the frame that bordered the rising portal. Finally, he slammed the throttle forward and the *Raven* burst through the narrow opening and sailed off into space.

Epilogue

Todd Hollings held the egg-shaped device in his hand and watched as the timer clicked to seventeen minutes. He was months away from the nearest planet, but minutes away from death.

He cried and laughed and screamed and ranted, and finally tried to hold the dial in place with his pudgy fingers, but it was no use. He managed to break off the timing switch, tearing his nails bloodily in the process, but the timer inside continued to slowly tick away the last few minutes of his life.

Madness had been his since birth, but now he bathed in utter lunacy, and images of Stryker making that impossible shot spun deliriously about his skull.

He looked at the grenade again, watching his life click away in the dispassionate device. Suddenly, he threw it against the small light panel that was the only illumination in the pod. It shattered, leaving him in total darkness. He could no longer see the numbers on the grenade.

But within seconds, Todd Hollings scrambled in the darkness to find the grenade that would end his life.

With bloody fingers he tried to read the numbers as they ticked away. But it was no use. He'd ruined that, and now he'd have to live with it.

For a few minutes more.

The warmaster was still alive. The puny white things had torn his chest and skull apart with repeated blasts of their weapons, but he would live. He was the warmaster, after all.

But now the others were standing over him, looking angrily at his bleeding remains. They had destroyed an entire ship, but their losses were incredible. Several of the pack had died at the hands of these puny things. It was shameful, and it was the warmaster's fault.

They descended on him slowly, gnashing their silver teeth and scooping out his innards with their huge claws. The warmaster protested, screaming through his slime-filled throat that he was their leader! They agreed, and ate him with respect.

They were still feeding when the nuclear reactors of the *Constantine* exploded.

The *Raven* sped away as fast as her conventional engines could carry her, but was still scorched by the fiery blast that washed over it.

But it survived.

A week later, Dumois had just about finished work on the nav-computer and Stryker had finally come out of a deep coma. He was terribly mutilated, but he was alive. The things had ripped out half his side and he hadn't even known it, thanks to the drugs he had overdosed himself with.

Dreama, Klein, and Hunt had also recovered, thanks to Oleg's expert care, but Kelassiter still despaired at his love's scrambled emotions. Maybe with time and a little care she would be herself again. Dumois thought so, and Thaddeus tended to know about these things.

"Are we ready to give it a try?" Thaddeus asked Terrin as he slammed the panel of the navigational computer back into place.

Kelassiter nodded with a smile and looked about the motley crew. "Sure."

Thad screwed in the locking bolts and flipped the power switch on. The machine whirred to life and everyone present sighed with relief. "Where to?" Dumois asked. "Tiko corporate headquarters? Fleet base?"

Terrin thought about it a second and looked at the expectant faces around him. Then he stuck his hands in his back pockets and looked out the tinted eyes of the *Raven*. "Neither. How about we just hang together for a while? Maybe rest up a couple of weeks and then form our own merc group or something. I don't know about the rest of you, but I'm a little tired of corporations right now."

"Then who you gonna work for?" one of the men asked.

"Ourselves."

There was a grunt of approval and Dreama placed her head against her lover's shoulder. It was the right emotion for once.

Hunt nodded at Oleg, and the mercenary returned his approval. "But what the hell will we call ourselves? The Tiko-Hollings-Wolverines-Jaegers? " he laughed.

Terrin turned and smiled back at the black giant, "How about just … the *Survivors*. That's what we are."

Tally dabbed at the scabs around Jonn's neck with a burning disinfectant and the burly marine jerked with aggravation. She looked up at him, afraid of his reaction but still determined to treat his wounds. His grimace softened and he noticed her big brown eyes for the first time since Teraxiter.

The Survivors, he laughed. It was a lot better than *the* survivor.

And at least he wouldn't have to be alone anymore.

Novels

The River of God
by Greg Farshtey

Five adventurers journey into space and brave the terrors of the "river of God," to find that madness, murder and riches beyond imagining await within.

Sole Survivor
by Shane Lacy Hensley

The shatterzone. Huge, deadly, filled with mineral wealth. Two MegaCorporations clash on the fringe of the shatterzone, locked in a struggle for the rich mining of the sector. Fighting for profit first and survival second, they encounter unexpected danger from a third party ...

Beyond the 'Zone
by Ed Stark

Written by one of the creators of *Shatterzone*, this novel takes the reader, for the first time, *through* the amazing and lethal shatterzone. What lies beyond the edge of the universe ... besides death?

THE POSSIBILITY WARS

Novels and Anthologies

Storm Knights
by Bill Slavicsek and C. J. Tramontana

What were the first few weeks of the invasion of Earth like? Who were the heroes who stepped forward to stop the Gaunt Man and his Possibility Raiders? Find out in Book One of the Possibility Wars, as Earth is held hostage by invading realities.

The Dark Realm
by Douglas Kaufman

Book Two of the Possibility Wars Trilogy, as a brave team of Storm Knights travels to Orrorsh to confront the unspeakably evil High Lord known as The Gaunt Man.

The Nightmare Dream
by Jonatha Ariadne Caspian

The conclusion of the Possibility Wars Trilogy! The Storm Knights are Earth's only hope in a race to prevent its annihilation!

Out of Nippon
by Nigel Findley

This full-length novel takes you from the intrigue and manipulation of the realm of Nippon Tech, to the horror-haunted jungles of Orrorsh. There, corporate greed and scientific experimentation clash with the occult and the ancient terrors of the land.

Strange Tales of the Nile Empire
edited by Greg Farshtey, Greg Gorden and Ed Stark

A short story anthology of evil villains, pulp heroes and daring adventure in the Empire of the Nile — a realm of two-fisted, guns-blazing, non-stop action!

Dragons Over England
edited by Douglas Kaufman and Ed Stark

A new queen shares the throne of the British Empire. Elves, dwarves, and fairies roam the Scottish countryside. Join the quest to rid the fantasy realm of Aysle of evil and darkness in this short-story anthology.

Mysterious Cairo
edited by Ed Stark

Last of the "free cities" of the Nile Empire, Cairo is the heart of the pulp-fiction realm. Weird scientists outfit pulp heroes with strange weapons, hardbitten detectives track gangsters through the underworld, and new Storm Knights are created in the war against evil. Short stories in the pulp magazine tradition.

Novels

Extreme Paranoia:
Nobody Knows the Trouble I've Shot!
by Ken Rolston

In the year of The Computer 194, A.B.O. (After the Big Oops), Troubleshooters find it almost impossible to complete their missions. Our Hero finds it no different. Is it because this time his mission is to assassinate the High Programmer Whatta-U-SAY? Read this mindlessly deranged and fun-filled book and find out.

Title Deleted for Security Reasons
by Ed Bolme

Yes, the novel that is so classified, we can't even tell you the title. Follow the adventures of James B-OND-1 as he [DELETED] and then [DELETED] while performing [DELETED DELETED] with that great-looking femclone! It'd be treason not to read this one, folks!

WEST END GAMES®

RR 3 Box 2345 • Honesdale, PA 18431

Please send me the items I have checked.

SHATTERZONE™
- ❏ 21101 **The River of God** $4.95
- ❏ 21102 **Sole Survivor** $4.95
- ❏ 21103 **Beyond the 'Zone** $4.95

TORG™
- ❏ 20601 **Storm Knights** $4.95
- ❏ 20602 **The Dark Realm** $4.95
- ❏ 20603 **The Nightmare Dream** $4.95
- ❏ 20607 **Out of Nippon** $4.95
- ❏ 20604 **Strange Tales From the Nile Empire** $4.95
- ❏ 20608 **Mysterious Cairo** $4.95
- ❏ 20605 **Dragons Over England** $4.95

PARANOIA®
- ❏ 12302 **Extreme Paranoia** $4.95
- ❏ 12303 **Title Deleted for Security Reasons** $4.95

I am enclosing $_____ (please add $3.00* to cover postage and handling for the first item and $1.25 for each additional item).

Send check or money order — no cash or C.O.D.s, please.

❏ Please send me your catalog of games and books.

Name: _____

Address: _____

City: _____

State: _____ Zip: _____ Tel: (____) _____

*For deliveries to Canada, add US $5.00 for the first item ordered and US $2.50 for each additional item.

Allow 4-6 weeks for delivery.